"CAN YOU GIVE US A CAUSE OF DEATH, DOCTOR?"

It seemed so obvious. There was no bloody ripped-out throat as in Farmer Morgan's death last month, and Reg Brown was a habitual drunk; but given what had been going on in Brytewood the past few weeks, one couldn't help wondering. Alice bent over the body and looked at his staring eyes, his pale skin, and his shrunken, narrow wrists. There hadn't been a frost last night, but it had rained, and his clothes were still damp. He'd no doubt have caught pneumonia if he'd lived. He was thin. Wasted from alcohol. Pity they didn't ration that!

She was about to stand and tell Sergeant Jones to go ahead and call for an ambulance to collect the body when she noticed a bruise on Reg's neck: A faint mark, like a large insect bite.

BOOK YOUR PLACE ON OUR WEBSITE
AND MAKE THE
READING CONNECTION!

We've created a customized website just for our very special readers, where you can get the inside scoop on everything that's going on with Zebra, Pinnacle and Kensington books.

When you come online, you'll have the exciting opportunity to:

- View covers of upcoming books

- Read sample chapters

- Learn about our future publishing schedule (listed by publication month *and author*)

- Find out when your favorite authors will be visiting a city near you

- Search for and order backlist books from our online catalog

- Check out author bios and background information

- Send e-mail to your favorite authors

- Meet the Kensington staff online

- Join us in weekly chats with authors, readers and other guests

- Get writing guidelines

- AND MUCH MORE!

Visit our website at
http://www.kensingtonbooks.com

BLOODY AWFUL

GEORGIA EVANS

KENSINGTON BOOKS
Kensington Publishing Corp.
http://www.kensingtonbooks.com

KENSINGTON BOOKS are published by

Kensington Publishing Corp.
119 West 40th Street
New York, NY 10018

All Kensington titles, imprints, and distributed lines are available at special quantity discounts for bulk purchases for sales promotion, premiums, fund-raising, educational, or institutional use.

Special book excerpts or customized printings can also be created to fit specific needs. For details, write or phone the office of the Kensington Special Sales Manager: Attn. Special Sales Department. Kensington Publishing Corp., 119 West 40th Street, New York, NY 10018. Phone: 1-800-221-2647.

Kensington and the K logo Reg. U.S. Pat. & TM Off.

ISBN-13: 978-0-7582-3482-7
ISBN-10: 0-7582-3842-1

First Printing: July 2009
10 9 8 7 6 5 4 3 2 1

Printed in the United States of America

Chapter One

Gloria Prewitt, district nurse and werefox, all but wobbled off her bicycle seeing the doctor's car parked in front of Mother Longhurst's cottage. Given the longstanding coolness between Alice Doyle and old Mother Longhurst, the reputed village witch, Gloria was agog with curiosity and tempted to park her bicycle and toddle up to the front door on some pretext. The war gave so many excuses: checking on blackout, it was so easy, after all, to a miss a chink where light could escape, reminding about first aid training or evenings knitting comforts for the troops.

But Gloria was running late already, and she'd see Alice later. Right now she had to get up to Cherry Hill Farm. Old Mrs. Longhurst had scalded her arm with boiling jam a week earlier and the dressing needed changing.

Gloria saw nothing odd about the common surname. Brytewood was full of Longhursts and plenty of other old, established families. Old and odd, Gloria often thought. Not that she could talk. The good residents of Brytewood would crack their false teeth if they ever discovered the district nurse went furry at intervals and roamed the woods and downs as a bushy-tailed fox.

One person suspected she was more than she appeared and

Gloria was making darn sure he never, ever, got a glimmer of her other nature.

As she rode across the village green and up toward Cherry Hill Farm, Gloria wondered what on earth Alice was doing. Had old Mother Longhurst really called her in professionally?

"It worked, I see."

Alice stared. Mother Longhurst *was* a witch but, "How did you know that?" Did the knife of petrified wood give off a magical aura?

"You're alive, aren't you? If it hadn't worked, you'd be dead."

So much for a magical aura. Alice wasn't that sure she believed in them anyway, whatever her grandmother claimed. "Yes, it worked." Killing a vampire wasn't normally part of a county doctor's day, but needs must as the saying went. It was 1940 after all and with Britain under daily threat of invasion, everyone had to do their part.

That her part entailed disposing of an antisocially and destructively bent vampire spy was just her unfortunate luck.

"What happened?" Mother Longhurst asked, taking the knife from Alice and wrapping it in a tattered cloth. "When you got him, I mean?"

Just what Alice did not want to relive but she was alive because of the witch's help. "The vampire disintegrated." After bleeding all over her. "Just crumbled into a pile of dust and muck." It took ages to clean the mess off the gravel drive.

"Always wondered what would happen, or even if it would."

"You weren't sure?" Dear heaven! She'd put her faith in an apparently untested magical implement. Oh, well. It had worked and that was what really mattered.

"Dear me, no! I've never had cause to use it, nor did my mother. Although my old grandmother used to talk about a vampire in these parts, back in the time of the fourth George. She was the one who passed the knife on to me. Glad to know she was right and it did what it was made for."

So was Alice.

Very.

"Did your grandmother make it?" She couldn't tamp down her curiosity. Much as the knife revolted her, not the least for the way it seemed to absorb the vampire's blood, she couldn't help her rather morbid fascination.

Mother Longhurst had a really nasty cackle. Showed her missing teeth too. "Her? Never! Alice, you might be a doctor with letters after your name and all, but you know nothing about these things." That, Alice was more than ready to concede. "This knife," Mother Longhurst indicated the bundle on the table, "was made long before my grandmother was born, long before any of the trees in Surrey were acorns or conkers. Long before recorded history. They say it came down from the Druids."

A few days earlier, Alice would have politely scoffed at that anointment. Now, she just nodded. "That accounts for the strange runes and hieroglyphics on the handle?"

"Maybe." The old woman seemed to clam up, pulling the bundle toward her. "But it's served its purpose."

"I might need it again. I think there's another vampire in the area." Think? She was pretty darn certain. She'd taken him into her surgery and called an ambulance for him. Before he disappeared.

Mother Longhurst shook her head. "You'll have to find another way. This knife is spent. Will be decades, maybe a century or more, before it has power again."

Smashing! "It won't work again?"

"Not for you, doctor. Not for you. Maybe not for anyone alive now. You had it when you needed it. Now it awaits the next time."

"Back hidden in the apple tree?" Despite her disappointment, Alice was curious.

"Maybe it's time to pass it on." Alice was not going to ask how or where. Knowing one witch was quite enough, finding there were half a dozen in the village would really ruin her day. Or week. "There's a witch over in Bringham, I might just hand it to him for safekeeping," Mother Longhurst mused. "Better see if he's to be trusted first. There's strong magic in that knife."

A point Alice would never dispute. "Thank you for lending it," she said, as she stood. "You're right I wouldn't be standing here without it." And hoped to high heaven the other one was long gone. Bombs and air raids were quite enough.

"You did well, young Alice. You and that young man of yours. When's the happy day?"

She'd been asked that question at least ten times a day since the news of her engagement rippled across the village. "Soon. We just had banns posted, in case Peter gets posted somewhere else, and we hope his family can get up from Devon."

Old Mother Longhurst shook her head. "They won't. Best go ahead and marry him while you can. Things are too uncertain these days to wait."

Since she'd actually been thinking along those lines herself, Alice just smiled.

"They won't be up this side of Christmas, you go ahead and marry him. Once you have a little one in the cradle, then they'll come. You mark my words."

She didn't want to. For Peter's sake, she wanted his family there, but his mother had been awfully lukewarm about it on the phone. "We'll see. Thank you again for the loan of the knife."

"The village should be thanking you and that young man of yours."

"The village had best not know. There'd be flat panic if the news got out that vampires were rampaging across the North Downs."

Mother Longhurst let out another loud cackle. "Would liven up the place a bit!"

Between bombs dropping, falling in love and dispatching vampires to wherever vampires went when they disintegrated, Alice had quite enough excitement to keep her going for a long, long time.

"Bye."

Alice had the door open when Mother Longhurst added,

"If you and your intended need any potions, you know where to come."

Alice restrained the smirk. So far she and Peter had done very nicely without.

Starting the old shooting brake that her father before her had driven across the countryside, Alice headed toward a row of cottages on the outskirts of Brytewood village. Seems two members of the Boyle family were coming down with mumps. Just what the village needed with a new batch of evacuees expected.

Mrs. Longhurst's scalded arm was healing nicely but just as Gloria was leaving, Julia, one of the land girls, came in with a bloody hand from too close contact with a scythe. After cleaning the wound, telling Julia she was darn lucky to still have hand and fingers attached and dispatching her with Tom Longhurst to the hospital to get it stitched, Gloria was on her way home.

Until she was flagged down by a young woman in one of the farm cottages.

"Nurse, I hate to bother you but two of my evacuees have this awful cough. I was thinking of calling the doctor in but then I saw you leave the farm and I thought I'd ask you to have a look at them."

"Of course. It's Mrs. Grayson isn't it?" She'd been one of the host houses when the evacuees first arrived. She'd taken two children and their mother, if Gloria remembered rightly.

"That's right, nurse! Fancy remembering!" Mrs. Grayson's smile welcomed but did little to ease the weariness in her face. "If you'd have a look at them. I'd be so obliged."

"Of course!" Gloria propped her cycle against the house and went into the open door. The kitchen was warm and cozy, a pot simmered on the old-fashioned black stove, a kitten slept on the hearth rug and a baby napped in the pram in the corner. The scent of baking added to the feeling of well-being.

"That's my one," Mrs. Grayson said, nodding toward

the pram. "I hope he doesn't get it too. The other two are proper poorly."

Gloria followed her up the narrow stairs. The back bedroom looked out on fields and the downs beyond, but was chilly compared to the warmth downstairs. The two little boys snuggled together under ample covers. They would be better for the warmth of a fire but the fireplace was blocked. No doubt to keep out the drafts and chill from the chimney. Both boys wore clean pajamas, the sheets were crumpled but ironed and the room was neat and tidy. Mrs. Grayson did right by her evacuees.

"Here we are, boys, Nurse Prewitt was passing and said she'd have a look at you."

"Hello," piped up the younger one who'd been lying down while his brother read from a tattered copy of *Dandy*.

"Wotcher, nurse," the elder said, "I'm Jim and this 'ere is me bruvver Wilf," he went on, clearly identifying his East End origins.

"How are those coughs, then?" Gloria asked, perching on the edge of the bed. "Bothering you?"

"Not all the time," Jim replied, "but when it comes it's awful bad. Hurts my chest, it does. Don't it, Wilf?" Gloria popped a thermometer in Jim's mouth and turned to his brother for corroboration.

Wilf nodded and pulled himself to sitting. "Gets on me wick it does," he said, as great hard, dry rasps shook his little chest. "Sorry," he got out between coughs before he bent almost double with a fierce burst of paroxysm of coughing and he upchucked all over the bedclothes, the floor and the thin rug on the floor.

"Oh gawd! I'm sorry!" he said with a weak wail.

"Never mind, Wilf," Mrs. Grayson said, "I'll get you cleaned up."

Gloria hadn't the heart to leave her to it, not after Jim bit the thermometer in shock and the baby downstairs decided he was missing the fun, and started crying.

By the time the two boys were washed and changed, their

bed made up with fresh sheets and the baby settled, to say nothing of making sure Jim hadn't swallowed the end of the thermometer, Gloria was only too ready for home. She even declined the offer of a cup of tea.

"I'll definitely ask Dr. Doyle to call," she told Mrs. Grayson.

"Whooping cough, is it? I remember my younger brother having it."

"Can't say for sure, the doctor will make a diagnosis, but keep them warm, and if it gets any colder, you might want to think about moving them down into the parlor and lighting a fire there. If you can spare the coal."

"I thought of that. I'd bring them down here but I'm scared my baby will catch it."

It was probably inevitable. A worry too. The baby wasn't more than eight or nine months. "What about the boys' mother?" Wilf was nowhere near school age. Surely she'd come down with him?

"She's up in London. Her own mother got bombed out last week. I told her to bring her back down here if she liked, we'd squeeze in somehow. I'm waiting to hear from her but I don't have the phone so she has to call Madge White next door but one. The boys got sick just after she left. I didn't tell her. Thought she had more than enough on her plate but now I'm not sure. If they're really ill . . ."

"Why not wait until the doctor sees them tomorrow?" The boys were in a clean house and well cared for. Many were far worse off. "Just keep them warm and give them children's aspirin to bring their temperatures down. Do you have any?"

"Only the adult, but I cut them in half and mash them up with a spoonful of jam. It works. Or will as long as I have jam. Couldn't make as much as usual on account of the sugar. I should have gone down to Whorleigh's in Brytewood. He seemed to have plenty."

For a price beyond Mrs. Grayson's pocket. What went on under the counter in the village store was really a scandal.

"Let's hope they're well before your store of jam runs out. And now, I really must be off."

"Thanks for stopping, nurse. Don't know how I'd have coped with all that on my own."

Perfectly well, if a bit more slowly, Gloria guessed. "The boys are lucky to have you."

"They're not much trouble. Not like some of the evacuees I've heard of. Mrs. Smith down the lane had two girls who were crawling with lice and stitched into their clothes. Would you believe it?"

Gloria would. She'd seen plenty of it when the first wave of evacuees arrived.

She'd been longer at the Graysons' than she'd realized. Now the days were drawing in, it was almost dark and she hated cycling the lanes with the miserable shaded light that the blackout required. As if an enemy plane up how many hundred feet would see the flicker of light from a bicycle.

But she wasn't about to break the law.

Keeping as close to the edge as she dared, without risking landing in a ditch, Gloria followed the lane as best she could. A long gap in the hedge showed she'd reached the heath, and when she sensed the trees ended, she guessed she was somewhere near the munitions camp. They were keeping a very tight blackout after the trouble a few weeks back.

Soon the road pitched downhill sharply and Gloria readied for the first bend. She wobbled a little in the dark, even considered getting off and pushing her cycle but the sooner she got home the happier she'd be.

The second bend undid her. If she hadn't been so engrossed in avoiding the hedges, she'd have heard the car engine coming behind her. As it was, by the time the narrow beam of shaded lights caught her, it was too close. The driver steered sharply to avoid her, but clipped her back wheel.

She went over the handlebars and ended up in the damn ditch after all.

The car stopped, narrow slits of headlight angled in her direction.

"I'm frightfully sorry," a voice called in the darkness.

So was she.

And damp and muddy into the bargain. She was going to have to wash her uniform when she got home and dry it in front of the stove. "Can you help me out?"

"Absolutely! I've a torch in the car. Hang on a tic."

He was back in moments, the unshaded beam of light wavering in his hand, in complete contravention of blackout regulations. As the light glanced over her face, the man gasped. "Stone the crows! It's Nurse Prewitt!"

Her rescuer (and attacker come to that) had the advantage there but his voice was familiar. "Yes, it is. Could you give me a hand?" The ditch was deeper than she'd expected.

"Righto! Let's get this off you first."

A weight was lifted off her shoulder and she realized her bicycle had landed on top of her. "That feels better."

"You'll feel a whole lot better still when we get you out of there." She grabbed a pair of strong hands and scrambled up the side of the ditch on her knees but when she tried to stand, her right leg buckled under her and she cried out in pain.

"Damn!" She forgave herself swearing. "I think I've done in my ankle."

Before she barely finished speaking, he'd scooped her up in his arms. Nice strong arms at that. Rubbing her face against the twill of his mac wasn't part of the plan, but she did it anyway, leaning into him as his arms held her close. He smelled of hard-working male and fresh air. Her heart gave a little flip and another.

Come off it! This feeling helpless had to be affecting her nerves. She was used, quite literally, to standing on her own two feet and was most definitely not going whoosy over the first strong man who picked her up. Ridiculous!

She gave a little giggle, which he probably took for impending hysterics. He stiffened and held her very carefully. "Better get you on dry land."

Good point, her legs were cold and wet and she was probably dripping all over him. Whoever he was.

He sat her on the bonnet of his car and in the weak light from the torch still somehow in his hand, she looked down at her ankle. Her foot hung crooked.

"It's broken." Just what she did not need with new evacuees due any day now. And she'd torn her stockings. Where was she going to get another pair? She couldn't cycle into Dorking with her leg in a cast.

"You look bad. Is the pain awful?"

She looked up at his face. Small wonder his voice sounded familiar! It was the supervisor from the plant. The absolutely dishy man that half the single women in the village (and a few of the married ones) were constantly mooning over. And he'd had his arms around her! "Mr. Barron!"

"Guilty as charged." In the beam of light he smiled. It was a very nice smile. Sexy even. No, it was not! Sexy was not what she needed right now. Helpful, strong, responsible, thoughtful. Not sexy.

"Mr. Barron, I hate to bother you, but would you mind driving me to the hospital?"

He hesitated. For all of three seconds. "That bad is it?"

"Afraid so." She lifted her leg a little. "Look."

"Crikey! I'll get you there. And I'm sorry! Let's put you in the car then. Back seat might be best, you can prop that leg up."

It wasn't the most luxurious back seat in the world. The stuffing was coming out of the cracked leather in a couple of places, but with a rolled up blanket behind her and what was left of her nurse's cape over her legs, she was as comfortable as she could hope to be.

With her battered bicycle on the roof, they headed down the hill. "Won't take us long, I hope," he said. "I feel terrible about this. I should have seen you."

She knew just how limited human eyes were in the dark. "Don't worry about it. I'm not dead yet." Crippled and disabled maybe.

"I should hope not! I'd never be able to show my face in Brytewood again if I'd dispatched the nurse to the hereafter."

"I'm not heading there any time soon, I hope. Assuming you make it down this hill safely."

"I'll get you there, don't worry."

It sounded very much like a promise.

Balderdash! More like an earnest hope on his part.

Or hers.

Sitting in the dark, she had a serious talk with herself. She was in shock. That was it. She'd seen the symptoms in patients. Confusion went along with it. Her chest was tight because she was suffering from shock. She'd had a nasty tumble and broken her ankle. That was why her heart was racing and she was feeling like jelly inside.

It had absolutely nothing to do with Andrew Barron up in the driver's seat. She was out of her mind. The man hauls her out of a ditch (after putting her there in the first place) and she goes all wobbly. Ridiculous! The utter last thing she needed was involvement with a human male. It was bad enough Sergeant Pendragon suspected she was a bit more than she appeared.

But she'd brushed him off and everything was fine.

She'd be fine,

Just as long as she never, ever, felt Andrew Barron's arms around her again.

Chapter Two

"We are facing a difficulty." Hans Weiss glanced at the other two vampires in his landlady's unheated parlor. He wasn't entirely convinced they weren't involved somehow. How else could a vampire disappear without a trace, except at the hand of another stronger, older vampire?

"Difficulty?" Schmidt said, his voice sharp with worry. "You, my friend, are sounding too much like these damn island monkeys. It is a disaster!"

Bloch appeared to agree. "What I want to know is how Eiche was exterminated. Assuming he really is destroyed and not just gone to earth somewhere."

That amounted to an accusation of desertion, but Weiss let it pass. For now. Who wasn't concerned at the apparent destruction of a fellow vampire? And a loyal, committed German to boot.

"Can we really rely on this fairy?" Schmidt asked. "What if she's lying?"

"Our masters believe her," Weiss pointed out. "Seems taking her blood forged a connection that they are using to track us."

"They might have warned us," Schmidt muttered.

Bloch just scowled.

"That would have defeated their purpose. We all enjoyed

her blood and her struggles. Too late for regrets." Weiss said. "We have to accept reality and go forward. They want results and we need to provide them."

"Or they'll do what?" Bloch asked. "Report us to Churchill and his cabinet?"

"Some of us have bloodkin being slowly starved," Schmidt reminded him. "We can not risk them."

"Before I risk my existence, I want to know what, on this accursed island, can destroy one of us?"

Weiss held back the smile. Bloch had handed him the perfect opening. "I agree, my friend. And that is your assignment. Find out what or who has this power and we will destroy them." Bloch's barely concealed temper was a delight to behold. He could not refuse without admitting the task was beyond him. They also needed him for another task. But that could wait.

Bloch recovered fast. "And no doubt you have a good cover set up for me?"

Sarcastic bastard! Weiss smiled. "That we will tailor for you."

"Indeed."

"Pity our agent was arrested," Schmidt said. "She would have been useful."

"She still will be."

"Indeed?" Bloch smiled. "Is she sending messages from the Tower of London?"

"No, I go to her."

"In prison?" Schmidt sounded totally amazed.

"In hospital. Remember she had that fall?" Not any sort of accident, Weiss was convinced. "She was arrested, yes, and repeatedly questioned, but she's still in traction. Can't be moved. She's in a private ward in hospital. Most convenient." He couldn't resist the smile. "We have another two weeks, I believe, before she leaves for prison and subsequent trial. Plenty of time to pick her brains. We will see her tonight."

* * *

In different circumstances, Bl*och would have enjoyed the run. Nothing like racing across open country in the dead of night, leaping railway lines and rivers, and outrunning a blacked-out train to remind one of the invincibility of vampires. Eiche he discounted. The arrogant fool had no doubt been ridiculously careless. Present company was another thing entirely. He resented and despised Weiss: smug, opinionated and acting as if he were running the war for his own entertainment.

But his means of access to the hospital where Miss Waite was imprisoned was nothing short of ingenious. Of course the bombing raid that had the hospital staff running around at sixes and sevens to cope with the injured made it even easier. If the Luftwaffe had arranged it for their convenience it couldn't have been better. A climb up a dark corner of the building and short dash across the roof, with all the delicious human pain and suffering under their feet, followed by a short swing down to a darkened window.

"I thought you might be dropping in," Miss Waite said, as they climbed in through the window and Weiss eased the sash down. "How are things?"

"We need your help," Weiss said, as he crossed the room.

"Fair enough," she replied. "Tell me though, is my erstwhile nephew safe?"

Weiss hesitated all of three seconds. "Eiche? That's partly what we came about."

"Thought so. Snooty police and a chap from London were down here this afternoon. Going on they were all about how he's disappeared from Brytewood and did I know where he was." She gave a chuckle. "I told the truth, said I had no idea. Got away alright then, did he?"

"He can't go back to Brytewood." Clever that. Weiss always did have a way with words. "We need your help to get another agent into the village."

She looked from Weiss to Bloch. "What the blazes can I do, flat on my back, handcuffed to the bed?"

She had a very good point but Weiss brushed her concerns aside. "Quite a lot, my dear fraulein." That was risking it a bit. Damn! Had Wiess no sense of survival? He'd be jabbering on in German next. "You know that village in a way we do not. What do they need? If we can send Willi in as a vital addition to the community, he will be welcomed and pass with less scrutiny. What does that village lack?"

She laughed. "What isn't it short of!" She shook her head, adding a few more creases to her wrinkled forehead. "Let me think."

They waited in the silent room, as she plied her mortal mind to their problem. Bloch hoped she didn't suggest he arrive as a traveling acrobat or fortune teller.

"Ever baked bread?" she asked, with a sly twist to her mouth.

"Not in the past hundred years or so." That took the edge off her smirk. His father has been the baker in his village. "Bread's just flour, yeast and heavy work." Which would be a snap with vampire strength. No more straining of muscles to heave sacks of flour or knead mountains of dough. "What do you have in mind?"

For a mortal flat on her back, she was downright gloating. "Our village baker was one of the first casualties of the war: run over during the blackout. The shop sits empty and there's a small flat above it. You lot work out the logistics of getting some sort of authorization and identity card, and taking over the lease, or perhaps requisitioning it and you'll be in business. The village will welcome you with open arms. Their only other choices now are a bus into Leatherhead to buy bread or to make do with the dreadful stale stuff Sam Whorleigh has shipped in from Dorking."

Not quite the cover Bloch would have chosen but worth the sacrifice for the cause. "I'll be Block the Baker." Sounded like a character from a children's card game.

Weiss was thoughtful a minute or so. "The papers will have to be faked and sooner or later the cover will get blown but should stand for a month or so. We can do a lot of damage in a month."

"Good show!" The old biddy smiled as if she'd single-handedly defeated the army and air force together. "Pity I won't be there to see it."

"Yes," Weiss replied very quietly, with a meaningful glance at Bloch. "You won't be."

Her smug expression lasted just as long as it took Weiss to grab her wrist and put his hand over her mouth. "Take her femoral," he hissed, as he bared his fangs and bit into her wrist.

Sucking on an old lady's thigh wasn't exactly a thrill. But it was blood and Weiss was in charge so Bloch pulled off the covers. Amazing how much she still struggled but he held her unplastered leg to the mattress and, leaning over the bed, bit. Funny how wrinkled old crones still had warm, rich blood and plenty of it. They both fed until her struggles ceased and Bloch felt her heartbeat slow to a standstill. He lifted his mouth, cleaned the wound with his tongue and rearranged the covers over her lifeless legs.

Weiss did the same, smoothing the sheet under her chin.

"We'll have to get busy with your papers," he said. "We've no time to waste, and there's no one there now to expose you."

Other than the vampire killer. Unless that ridiculous fairy had it all confused and Eiche had skived off on his own.

Weiss was out of the window. Bloch followed, up to the roof, and down the dark corner, just as several ambulances came speeding up the drive, sirens going. How wonderful. The bombs they'd heard earlier must have landed well.

Chapter Three

Gloria wanted to crawl away and hide. As if falling in a ditch wasn't bad enough, Andrew Barron insisted on driving right through an air raid before parking in a space reserved for ambulances and carrying her into Casualty, refusing all offers of wheelchairs or trollies, striding across the place as if he owned it, and putting her on the first free bed before drawing the curtains around her. "I'll make sure someone sees you right away," he said, and disappeared, with a rattle of curtain rings.

Didn't he realize patients were seen in strict order according to the severity of their injuries? If he knew, he obviously didn't care. Darn him! She was absolutely in no condition to get up and run after him and to top it off, the bright lights overhead let her see just how muddy and disheveled she was. He hadn't even stopped to take her shoes off before covering her with a blanket. Yes, the warmth was welcome but honestly!

"Let's have a look at her," a voice said as the curtains were pulled back. "You have a seat over there, sir. We'll let you know how she is in a jiffy." A doctor she didn't recognize crossed to her bed. "What happened to you, then?"

"I fell off my bicycle in the blackout." She'd leave off the little detail about Andrew cutting too close. "I landed in a ditch. Luckily Mr. Barron found me and brought me in. I think my ankle's broken."

He was about to make some comment about patient diagnoses—she could sense that from the look on his face—when he noticed her crumpled and muddy uniform. "District nurse?"

"Yes. I'm Gloria Prewitt from over in Brytewood. I was on my way home from making a visit when this happened."

"Let's have a look at the damage." Didn't take much more than a look, and a few winces on her part, as he took off her shoe, for him to concur. "We'll have you off to X-ray and get it set for you. You won't be riding that bicycle for a few weeks, nurse."

They had wheeled her down the hall, Andrew, ignoring the orderly's disapproving glare, following close behind, when the first ambulances arrived.

Gloria understood. A mere broken ankle ranked a long, long way behind air raid casualties. Andrew wasn't too impressed at her being shunted into a corner. She calmed him down by telling him she was better off forgotten. If someone remembered her, they might take the bed from under her. Her ankle was beginning to ache and she was only too glad to have it propped up and supported.

Andrew chafed at the delay. "Surely I can get someone to take you up to X-ray. For two pins, I'd wheel you up there myself."

"They will. Once things calm down." Assuming there wasn't another raid. "Andrew, would you be really kind and see if you can scrounge a cup of tea?"

He nipped off and returned bearing a tray, two brimming enamel mugs of tea, two bowls of soup and slabs of bread and dripping. "I told the woman in the canteen I was on my way to take my girlfriend out to dinner when she fell and broke her ankle. She took pity on us."

"So I see." Gloria wasn't too sure about the "girlfriend" bit but . . . "Thanks." She took a long swig of tea before balancing the bowl of soup on her lap. "I'm famished and if the casualties are bad, we could wait all night." The soup was cooled and too salty but full of onions and potatoes and even chunks of meat. It would keep her going, but surely he needed more than bread and soup for dinner. "Mr. Barron, do you want to go on home?"

"And leave you here? Good lord, no!"

"We could be hanging about all night."

"Won't bother me." He gave her a grin. "Of course, I'd much rather you called me Andrew. After all we are sharing a bed."

She almost spluttered her soup over the aforementioned bed. It was on the tip of her tongue to make some sharp comment until she met his eyes. Seemed after all, she was very glad he was keeping her company sitting on the end of her bed. They could be here ages and waiting with him was better than being alone. Far, far better.

Andrew wasn't too sure what to make of it all. The second his cheeky comment was out of his mouth, he regretted it. Until she smiled. A lovely, wonderful accepting invitation of a smile.

Yes, dammit, he was very happy to be sitting on her bed. Even if it was only a sterile, iron hospital bedstead. What sort of bed did she sleep on at home? A romantic four-poster with curtains? Unlikely in her little cottage. A lush divan with silken cushions? Perhaps a classic mahogany one, with a high curved head.

"Soup's not bad is it?"

"Eh?" Fast switch called for here. She wanted to discuss vegetable soup and he'd much rather picture her in a bed with silken hangings and linen sheets. Or no hangings at all. No sheets even. Dammit, dispense with the bed. "Yes, pretty good."

"Yes, thanks for getting it. I enjoy a good bowl of soup."

Self-possessed, confident Nurse Prewitt was fumbling for conversation. Could be the shock and pain but maybe she was feeling what he was. "It's good but the company makes it smashing." She blushed. Not much of a blush, just a little pink across her cheeks, but he found it totally wonderful.

He was nuts: he'd half-killed her and now he was making passes.

"Mr. Barron. Andrew," she said, her voice severe but a little smile quirking her mouth. "You're flirting."

"Would you rather talk about hospital soup?"

She chuckled. A deep, sexy earthy chuckle as her green eyes glinted. "We could talk about bread and dripping." She barely finished the sentence before she laughed again.

"I can think of far more fascinating subjects."

"Really? What would they be?"

"You."

"Me? That would be a pretty short conversation."

"But an interesting one."

She looked downright wary. "Hardly. I'm the district nurse and I ride around on my bicycle checking for head lice."

"There's a lot more to you than that, Nurse Prewitt, and we both know it." For a minute, she looked scared. Was he being too forward? Maybe. There was an artificial intimacy about sitting on a bed. Better back up a bit. "Where did you train?"

"Westminster."

"And you didn't want to stay there?"

"Lord no! I hated London. Too many buildings and hard streets under your feet. Brytewood suits me so much better." Her eyes lit up as she smiled. "Besides, I grew up not far from here. Near Reigate. I like this part of the country."

"Your parents are still there?"

She put her spoon down and shook her head. "No. They're both dead." It was said in a way that didn't invite further questions. "I like the air here. And the open countryside."

"I like it too." Particularly when she was around. "Never thought I'd end up here, but that's the way it is. Hasn't exactly been peaceful though."

"We're not exactly in the middle of a peace."

As if to underscore her words, a voice called. "Excuse me, excuse me. We need to get through." Andrew pulled his legs up to sit cross-legged as a team of orderlies rushed past, pushing two trollies with injured occupants, covered with bloodstained blankets.

"Poor devils," Andrew said. "Did you see one was just a child?"

She nodded. "Makes me think I should be out there helping, not lolling about."

"Since, my dear Nurse Prewitt, you can't even stand, you can hardly be ministering to the wounded."

"Doesn't stop me wanting to."

It wouldn't. He half expected her to hobble off and start helping out. They could certainly use her. Amid the noise and clamor no one could miss the urgency and barely controlled panic. A stark awareness of the uncertainty of life nowadays that had him blurting out, "Nurse Prewitt, once we get you patched up, would you come and have dinner with me one evening? Maybe go to the pictures? Er . . . Gloria?" Might as well go the whole hog while he was at it.

She stared. Eyes wide and lips parted. Damn! He should have waited. Chosen a better time. He'd only just run her over and now . . .

"You mean go out together?"

"Yes." He couldn't read her face. Creased eyebrows suggested she was thinking about refusing. He was willing her to agree, praying she'd say "yes" and didn't quite understand his panic at the possibility of refusal. "Fancy the idea?" Damn! Why the hell did it matter so much? He'd asked umpteen girls out. Some accepted, some refused, but this time it truly mattered.

"Alright," she said, sounding surprised. "Best wait until I get a cast and crutches."

"I dunno. The rate they're going, we'll be here all week. We could nip out and come back. No one would be any the wiser."

"We would!"

A lot wiser no doubt.

"Alice!" Gloria said.

Andrew looked over his shoulder and almost baptized himself with soup. "Er . . . Dr. Doyle," he managed, as he dabbed vegetable soup off his pullover.

"Good evening to you both," Dr. Doyle said, with a tired smile. "Planning on absconding with a patient were you, Mr. Barron?"

"I'd bring her back. Promise. Never thought we'd be missed with all this going on." He nodded toward the still bustling activity down the corridor.

The doctor sighed. "It's terrible. I thought the vicarage bombing was awful, but this is a hundred times worse. They got a boarding school and a restaurant at the top end of the town and several houses." She shuddered. "Still . . . better keep busy."

"Did they call you in to help?" Gloria asked.

"No. I was here checking on poor Mrs. Roundhill. They're moving her to a nursing home. They need the bed." She gave a wry smile. "They could use this one too."

"Get me X-rayed and plastered up and they can have it. Gladly. My ankle's already swelling." She shook her head. "Sorry, Alice, here I'm whining and you have people horribly injured."

"I don't call that whining. Besides," she sent a speculative look his way. "You've got company."

"I should hope so," Andrew said. "I ran her over."

"Well I never." Dr. Doyle grinned. "That'll be a story to tell your grandchildren."

"Alice!" The flush earlier was nothing to the scarlet that flooded Gloria's face now.

Andrew stayed quiet. Wasn't a bad idea but . . .

"Dear Gloria, I'm not suggesting joint children, although

you do have the most eligible man in the village sitting on your bed, and feeling guilty. Take the opportunity."

"You'd better take yourself to the wounded!"

"Yes, dear, I will." She looked at Andrew. "Now's your chance. She can't run away."

After Dr. Doyle left they stared at each other. Gloria spoke first.

"Alice does go on."

"Don't worry. We agreed on dinner and the pictures. I'm not asking you to bear my children." Not yet at any rate. Wasn't a bad idea but that could wait. At least until after they had dinner.

"That's nice to know," she replied. "Since it might be a while before I can even get to the pictures. Come to that, it might be as long before I get this seen to."

Not quite that long. Twenty minutes or so later a pair of orderlies turfed him off the end of the bed and wheeled her away.

Leaving him bereft.

The idea of Nurse Prewitt— alright Gloria—bearing his children was rather delightful. And he was stark raving crackers to even think about it in the middle of a war.

Chapter Four

"All I can say, Gloria, is I think you're nuts. He's handsome, intelligent, bedworthy and a gentleman to boot. I don't understand your hesitation."

Gloria was tempted to tell Alice that if you turned furry at intervals, you didn't get involved with men. Better not. "It's such a cliché: he runs me over, I break an ankle and then he takes me out to dinner to make up." The whole scenario belonged in a Mills & Boon. Reading them was a smashing way to escape the stresses of war, actually living one was another thing entirely.

Alice didn't give quarter. "Bully for clichés. You can't turn him down after you said 'yes.'"

"I was suffering from shock."

"You will be, if you keep on this way."

"Look, Alice. I'm injured. Sick people don't go out to dinner." That sounded so wet.

"You're not sick. They didn't even keep you overnight."

"Only because they needed the bed."

Gloria had never seen Alice this stubborn. Still, two could play that game. "Just because you're getting hitched, you're out to play matchmaker."

"Of course. Love is wonderful, Gloria. Even a little bit of it and no, I'm not saying you should marry him, fall into bed or take lifelong vows on the strength of dinner. For heaven's sake go, have fun and enjoy yourself. Darn it, we could all be dead any day."

No denying that. Although Gloria put her chances of survival a bit higher than your average human.

"He's got it all set up and doing things in style. He's booked a table at The White Horse. You can't let him down."

"It's not just that, Alice . . ."

"It's not anything, Gloria. You're going if I have to manhandle, or rather womanhandle, you into that car tomorrow night. If you say any more about standing Andrew Barron up, I'll get Gran to talk to you. She'll make you see reason."

No idle threat that. While Mrs. Burrows had always treated Gloria with friendliness and kindness, you didn't have to be Other to see the strength of the woman. "I'm going, but I'm not exactly comfortable about it." Complete truth that. She was on tenterhooks inside. She'd fancied Andrew since the day he got off the train and walked into the village. She'd just had the good sense to keep at a distance. Until now.

"Gloria, you'll have a wonderful time. I'll come in and help you wash your hair and bring my electric hair dryer. What are you going to wear?"

A dress! "Something I can haul myself in and out of a car in and keep my dignity, and, Alice, I don't need help deciding. I can get myself upstairs using my arms." Moving far more easily than any human could. Much as she loved Alice, she could just imagine the look on her face if she ever suspected her friend and coworker turned furry and ran over the heath when all respectable villagers were tucked up safe in bed.

Gloria got to her feet using her crutches, hugged Alice good-bye and closed the door behind her.

Driving home, Alice tried to ignore the needles of guilt. What if Gloria really didn't want to go out with Andrew

Barron and had only been bulldozed into agreeing? No! Gloria might have reservations; after all she, Alice, had plenty about Peter once upon a time, but Gloria was not one to be pushed where she had no intention of going. Was she?

Alice was so wound up agonizing over the rights and wrongs of it all, she almost hit the dark figure running across the road. A swerve and a screech of brakes had Alice avoiding a collision. Thank heaven! They'd had quite enough road accidents for one week thank you very much. The car came to a halt at the side of the road, narrowly avoiding the ditch.

Heart pounding, Alice yanked on the brake and looked around. The waxing moon was hidden behind the clouds leaving the night dark enough to keep the pickiest air raid warden happy. "Anyone there? Are you alright?" Alice called as she opened her door.

The silence of the night was the only reply.

Damn! She had seen someone or something. She got out of the car and listened. Gran had made her practice and now Alice used all her Pixie hearing to cast around her. A small animal, a mouse or stoat, moved through the ditch, another several scurried in the hedge opposite and somewhere in the cluster of trees by the allotments, a larger creature, a badger perhaps, snuffled in the earth.

Other than an owl overhead, there was no sign or sound of life.

Didn't mean there wasn't something out there. A few weeks ago she'd learned the hard way not being alive didn't stop some creatures.

She waited for several minutes, every Pixie sense alert, but nothing stirred other than the four-footed creatures looking for dinner.

And Gran was expecting her back for hers.

Alice got back into the car and headed for The Gallop, the house she'd grown up in and shared with her grandmother and her brothers when they were home. Not that Simon, now a POW in Germany, was likely to get home any time soon, and she worried daily about Alan, as they didn't even know where his ship was most of the time.

As she pulled into the drive, Alice noticed a chink of light in the kitchen curtains. Gran must have missed that. Better take care of that right away.

The aroma of fresh baked bread greeted Alice the minute she opened the door. Closing it carefully, she parted the blackout curtain and stepped into the warmth of the kitchen.

"Gran, that's smells wonderful!"

"Thought you might fancy some, my love," Helen Burrows replied, looking up from her knitting. Air Force blue this time. Probably made a nice change from khaki. "I made extra. Thought you could take one to Gloria in the morning. How's she doing?"

"Irritated at being cooped up, feeling guilty that Mrs. Jenkins has organized the villagers to bring her meals, and a little uncertain about whether or not she wants to go out with Andrew Barron tomorrow night."

Gran smiled. "She'll go. You mark my words. Here, take your coat off. There's a mushroom pie in the oven." She rolled up her knitting as she stood. "I'll get it out while you wash your hands."

They split the pie. Amazing really what Gran could make out of very little. She'd no doubt found the mushrooms in one of the fields and although Alice was getting tired of carrots, they did liven up the look of food on the plate.

The fresh bread, the honey Gran produced from the pantry, and a nice cup of tea rounded off the meal nicely.

"Delicious, Gran," Alice said, licking the last trail of honey off her finger. "Nothing like fresh baked bread. It really is a treat."

"You didn't hear the news then?"

"What news? About the mother of Mrs. Grayson's evacuees disappearing?"

"Hadn't heard that."

"She went up to London to help out her mother, who'd lost her house in the Blitz. She spent the night in an emergency shelter with her mother, then they went out to buy her mother new clothes and nobody has seen them since. Mrs. Grayson is getting more than worried. Those boys are pretty sick."

"No one's checking?"

"Of course. Mrs. Willows is in contact with the WVS in Shoreditch but so far, not a sign. After several nights of heavy bombing everyone's inclined to think the worst."

"Those poor little boys."

"They don't know anything yet. Mrs. Grayson thought it best to wait until they get well. Sometimes people do turn up in hospital." They also disappeared off the face of the earth. At least Jim and Wilf had a good billet and Mrs. Grayson was willing to keep them.

Gran refilled Alice's cup. "After that, we need my good news. There's a new baker moving into Stone's."

"Where did you hear that?"

"From Doris." Their charlady carried news all the time. "Seems Roger Hudson got a call asking him to make sure the shop was cleaned up and the flat over it in order and he asked her to take care of it. She said he was also told to get ready for a bulk shipment of flour."

Good news. "That will put Whorleigh's nose out of joint. He won't have much market for his day-old bread any more. Wonder who he is. Or she." Wasn't impossible these days. It was downright interesting the jobs women managed quite comfortably when there weren't men blocking the way.

"Time will tell, my love. Maybe it's a CO sent here for war work."

Would Gran never stop poking over her one-time prejudice? "If it is, someone else can have him. I've got mine." Her love, her Peter. Her own.

"Anything else?"

Better see what Gran made of it. Alice mentioned the fast-moving shape that supposedly disappeared or . . .

"Humm," Gran sipped her tea. "No sign of anything?"

"No, I listened as you've been teaching me." Developing her Pixie powers after years of pretending they didn't exist had been interesting and tiring. "The only creatures alive were animals."

"If you saw something, my love. There was something. I'm going to talk to Howell Pendragon in the morning, and you'd better have Peter sharpening stakes."

"Surely Gran, we won't have another vampire!" One had been more than enough to last a lifetime.

"We know there were two. Maybe more. The wrong sort seem to travel in packs."

Lovely! "And is there a right sort of vampire, Gran?"

She ignored that. "I'm going to talk to Howell and we'll see." After last time, Alice wasn't the least sure she wanted to "see" anything. Not that she'd had much choice then. "Oh, by the way, dear, there was a phone call for you. A Doctor Pettigrew from Dorking. He wanted to talk to you about Miss Waite's cause of death."

Chapter Five

"All correct, I trust?"

Bloch shrugged. It was bound to be but how in Hades Weiss had all this prepared in a couple of days was beyond him. He opened the identity card. So, he was now William Arthur Benjamin Block, 28 years old and declared physically unfit for military service because of flat feet and asthma, but apparently possessed the stamina to work long hours in a bakery.

"Finding Eiche's killer is our priority," Weiss said, "but we need results for our benefactors in Adlerroost. Flattening that munitions factory would be an appropriate gesture."

"I'll need supplies: plastic explosives, detonators." And better luck than Eiche.

"You'll have what you need." Bloch hoped so. He fully intended to succeed, come what may.

"And I go, when?"

"Tomorrow. Wednesday. Time to ready things and open for business on Friday."

Bloch shrugged. "Pity we can't change it to Block's Bakery, but I don't plan on staying long."

"You'll stay until you succeed and start by finding Eiche's killer."

If there was one. But that he'd keep to himself. "He shall die. Slowly."

"No!" Weiss frowned. "I have orders. When we find the killer, we capture him. Incapacitate if need be. They want him in Adlerroost."

Of course. They'd played power games with vampires and fairies, why not a powerful human? All the more reason to see this one dead. He did not want to see the Nazis breeding a race of vampire killers. "I will be there Wednesday."

Doris Brewer put her hand on her hip and looked the new baker in the eye. "Like that, is it?" She didn't need the money this badly. Cleaning up Stone's Bakery and the flat over it took the better part of three days. She'd expected that. It had been a sorry sight after sitting empty all that time but after generous application of ammonia and washing soda, the place was clean and no longer smelled of mice. They no doubt still lurked in the walls, but after the way the man was acting, he could get his own traps and use his own ration coupons for cheese.

"I expected more than this," his high and mightiness announced, striding around the shop and narrowly missing her bucket of soapy water. "Are the machinery and ovens in working order?"

"Don't ask me," Doris replied, pushing her sleeves up. "I clean. I don't take care of no ovens or machinery."

"So, you're my servant?"

He had to be off his rocker. "Oh, no, I'm not. Just came in to clean as a favor for Mr. Hudson."

She might not have spoken. "I will need you every day. You will clean after the shop closes. Do not forget."

Every evening? And who was going to take care of Joey if she wanted that many hours? Which she didn't. But she found herself agreeing.

"Very good. You may call me 'Sir,'" he told her as he

turned and went upstairs. To find something else to go on about no doubt.

Sir, indeed! The only person in the village Doris had ever called "Sir" was Sir James Gregory over at Wharton Lacey and if this Block person thought he was Sir James's equal, she was the Duchess of Devonshire.

Fueled with righteous indignation, Doris picked up her bucket, almost spilling the lot as he hissed into her ear. "Where are my sheets and furnishings?" Who did he think he was, creeping up on her like that?

"It's not my job to provide them." The cheek of some people! Mrs. Chivers and Miss Dake had spent the morning hanging blackout curtains for him and now he expected sheets and blankets.

"Who will get them for me?"

At least he hadn't asked her. "Best talk to Mr. Hudson about that. Time for me to go." She tipped the bucket down the outside drain. Loaded it and her mop and broom onto Joey's push chair, grabbed her coat and left before he could make any more demands.

Honest, the cheek of some people!

Bill Block watched the servant Doris march up the lane in high dudgeon. If all the locals were as easy as that to compel, he'd have the entire village as his personal fief in a fortnight.

It was a thought.

Meanwhile he had a delivery of flour to chase up, and someone somewhere had to produce bedding and a nice warm neck. He should have made use of the stupid servant whilst she was within grabbing distance but no matter. He'd stroll down to the pub once it got dark and help himself.

"You look lovely, Gloria," Alice said, as she combed out Gloria's hair. "This color suits you so much better than it ever did me." The dark blue dress, with a flared skirt and neckline

Alice had tugged as low as possible, did a lot more for Gloria's appearance than her nurse's uniform. "Andrew is going to drop his jaw when he sees you."

"Just as long as he closes it again. If I have to start the evening looking down at his tonsils, I'll make him say 'Ah!'"

"Ah! You're beautiful!"

"Alice, you do go on."

"Only when I have to. I've got your handbag. Your coat and gloves are downstairs. He'll be here soon, and you really don't want him to see you bumping down stairs on your bottom, do you?"

"Couldn't be worse than pulling me out of a ditch." But starting off upright was definitely more dignified.

She made it downstairs, hauled herself to standing, courtesy of the banisters and newel post, and Alice helped her on with her coat.

"Darn it, Gloria. We should have waited and let Andrew put your coat on."

"I told him I'd be ready when he got here and ready I will be. Just taking my coat off and balancing crutches is going to be bad enough." This being incapacitated was for the birds. She'd be much more sympathetic with patients from now on. It was amazing the simple things that needed two hands. She had to sit down to put on her gloves, and trying to button up her coat whilst balancing on crutches was close to an acrobatic feat.

But she was ready, more nervous than when taking her nursing finals, and convinced this was a loony idea. What was she thinking, even agreeing to go out with him? Taking the risk of getting close to a mortal man. Particularly a mortal man she really fancied. She should pick up the phone right now and say she'd changed her mind, couldn't go out, was in too much pain and that . . .

There was a sharp rap on her front door. "I'll get it," Alice said.

"'Evening, doctor," a warm, friendly voice said. Alright, a

warm, sexy voice, and Andrew Barron stepped into her kitchen and her heart did a flip. And a triple back somersault.

He was lovely. Handsome, gorgeous. Gloria's mouth went dry, her heart raced and her hands sweated inside her knitted gloves. "Hello," she said.

Andrew said nothing for a minute. Just smiled. Infinitely better than the dropped jaw Alice prophesied. "All set?" he said. "Let me help you out to the car."

One step outside the door and Gloria thanked the heavens she had a nice, firm brick path, not the picturesque gravel so many villagers preferred. She made it to the car, and got into the passenger seat under her own steam, much, she suspected, to Andrew's disappointment. And her relief. She wasn't sure she trusted herself in his arms when she didn't have pain to distract her.

After spending an unnecessary amount of time propping her cast on a box and pillows and wrapping a rug around her, Andrew walked around the car and got into the driver's seat.

The drive across country, in the dark, could best be described as sedate with awkward conversation. Somehow the ride brought back Gloria's memories of the pain and discomfort of her previous ride with Andrew. She tried hard to blot that out. She was here to have dinner and enjoy an evening with a distinctly good-looking man.

Andrew pulled up in front of the hotel and Gloria faced several stone steps up to the entrance.

Didn't slow down Andrew Barron. "Hang on to those crutches," he said, as he swept her up in his arms and strode up the half dozen steps. The door was held open for them by a young officer in uniform, and she was inside, Andrew setting her on her feet by a roaring fire.

"You really did yourself in, didn't you?" the officer, a captain she noticed now they were in the light, said as he shut the door and rejoined his pals standing by the bar.

"Not too badly," Gloria replied and that was all she was saying. If Andrew as much as mentioned a ditch . . .

Bless him, he didn't. Just walked beside her as they crossed into the dining room and a stooped, gray-haired waiter showed them to their table.

"What would you like, Gloria?" Andrew asked over his menu.

"To go straight home" was downright churlish, and somehow not quite the truth. Sitting across from Andrew, comfortable with a cushion at her back and her leg propped up, she was . . . content. She seldom went out. Never had dinner with a man who as good as made her mouth water, and darn it, she was going to enjoy herself.

The selection wasn't that brilliant, but more than she'd have picked from her pantry at home or the kindhearted offerings of the good women of Brytewood. She couldn't help wondering where they found duck but decided to try it anyway. Some pond was no doubt lacking its usual quackers.

It was the bottle of wine Andrew ordered that distracted her from weighing merits of tomato soup or potato fritters.

"Wine, Andrew?" Wartime prices were prohibitive.

"Of course," he replied, grinning. "It's a celebration."

"Then, sir," the stooped waiter said, "may I suggest the claret. A very nice one, we've had it since before the war."

It was lovely of Andrew to go to the expense and it did add to her sense of comfort and coziness. Nothing quite like being indoors, curtains drawn against the night and sipping French wine with a handsome man.

"A penny for your thoughts," Andrew said.

"Alright." Maybe not all of them. "I was just thinking how really nice this is. Beats reheated toad in the hole at home."

"I've always liked toad in the hole. Especially when the sausages are all brown and the Yorkshire pudding crispy."

"You've obviously never eaten Miss Millard's then." Gloria paused to take another taste of wine. "Her Yorkshire is soggy."

"Then, Nurse Prewitt, dine with me every night and you'll never have to eat soggy toad in the hole again."

"If we came here every night we'd soon be skint and happy to get anything."

"I'd like to be here every night with you, Gloria."

Somehow lighthearted suddenly became serious. Thank heaven for the arrival of soup.

"Where did you work before you came to Brytewood?" Better ask questions before he started.

Andrew looked up from his soup and smiled. A nice smile. A very sexy smile. It really wasn't fair. Why was she so attracted to him when it was a downright risky idea? "You're not going to believe this."

"Try me." He couldn't have a past stranger than hers.

"Only if you promise never, ever, to say a word of this outside this room."

"Alright." What was this deep, dark secret?

"I was in France, in Lyon, training to be a chef. Came back in August of '39 when things looked really dodgy. I was searching for something to do. I knew the Army wouldn't have me because I have a heart murmur left over from rheumatic fever as a child. An uncle in the War Office suggested I apply for a job in munitions. I nearly fell over when I found out it was setting up and running an entire plant. I actually told them I wasn't qualified.

"The old duffers on the interview board didn't bat an eyelid. Said I'd been a prefect and head of my house at school, so I knew how to organize and get on with people. Since most of the workers would be women, they needed someone who could handle women. I have five older sisters and that presumably gave me that qualification." He shook his head. "Not that I ever 'managed' them. They all bossed me around mercilessly from the time I was in nappies."

The way he said it showed he loved them, bossy or not.

Gave her a little pang for what she'd never had. Or had there been others? Sisters? Brothers? She'd never know.

"So, on strength of those very flimsy qualifications and, I suspect, a whole lot of favors owed to my illustrious uncle, I got the job. And I'm nowhere near as incompetent as I feared. I have munition engineers and designers who handle all the technical stuff. I just keep it going smoothly, as best I can. My biggest headache—and this is between us, you have to swear."

She nodded. "I promise. Cross my heart and hope to die." She made the old playground gesture.

"Is my Deputy: Williams. Ninety-five percent of worker problems are because of his hamhandedness. I swear he lives to stir up trouble. I know he resents me being younger and makes snippy comments about public schools. He can't stand that I went to Winchester and he went to some high school in the Midlands. As if it mattered in the middle of a war, but it does to him."

"I know him. He's been sick a lot recently." Peter had mentioned it in one of their meetings.

Andrew nodded. "Yes. Lost weight, even fainted a couple of times on the job. You'd feel sorry for him if he weren't such a nasty piece of work. Still, I didn't bring you here to talk about Jeff Williams."

Nor her. The man gave her the willies. He had nasty leering eyes and the way he'd paired up with Miss Waite's creepy nephew didn't add anything to Williams's allure. "You've led an interesting life. Did you really want to be a chef?"

"Very much, upset my parents no end. They wanted me to be a barrister, but my marks in my Upper Certificate were pathetic. I'd never get into one of the Inns of Court. So they sent me to Oxford, to Dad's old college: Exeter. I so distinguished myself at cricket and rugby, I failed to get my degree. That did upset them. Should have really. I'd wasted their money and three years of my life. They had this big family confab—my sisters came home for it—on 'what do we do about Andrew?'

You wouldn't believe some of the lunatic proposals. Well, I thought they were lunatic." Again that lovely smile.

She was not getting seduced by a smile.

"Seems the only thing I'd done that met with unanimous approval was getting really good marks in French on my Higher. So they decided to make a linguist out of me. I insisted on the chef bit. I'd been over there five years. Worked in two hotels and a restaurant and clawed my way up from vegetable chopper and general dogsbody to trainee sous chef. The war really scuppered my plans, but I thank old Uncle Stephen for getting me this job. If not they'd probably have me parachuting into France because I can speak the lingo and between us, Gloria, I'm terrified of heights."

"I'm glad you're here and not behind lines." Or worse, in a prison camp like Alice's brother.

"I'm glad I'm here too, Gloria. Very, very glad."

His gladness gave her a dry throat. Soup helped. So did a few gulps of wine.

"You've had my none too illustrious life history, how about yours?" She'd been dreading this. "You grew up in Reigate, your parents died and you became a nurse." Not quite in that order. "What happened in between?"

She took another gulp of wine. Not that it would help—the reverse probably— but to buy her time to decide how abbreviated a version she could get away with.

As she set her glass back down, the air raid siren let out a long, piercing wail.

The stooped waiter paused to speak to a couple at another table, before making his way to Gloria and Andrew. "I'm sorry, sir and madam, but it appears we are under attack. We have made provision for our guests down in the cellar if you would please bring your gas masks and follow me."

Gloria hadn't waited for that obvious information. She was already standing on one foot and struggling with her coat.

Andrew was around the table helping her and handing her her crutches. Her gas mask was at home. Too bad at this point.

The cellar entrance was through the kitchen. The young officers were already down there for the bar evacuated first.

Gloria gave one look at the steps, called out "Watch out, I'm throwing my crutches down," sat on the top step and bumped down. So much for dignity and Alice's borrowed silk stockings. She'd have to replace them somehow.

At the bottom, one of the young officers helped her to her feet and another handed her her crutches.

Andrew was right on her heels. She was glad he was there. Just being close to him make her feel safe. Or as safe as one could with the prospect of Heinkels and Messerschmidts overhead.

As the last people descended, Andrew bagged a corner with an old sofa. Not exactly luxury and comfort but it was better than her Anderson shelter in the garden. She didn't have Andrew's arm around her out there on her own either. War brought a few small pleasures.

Chapter Six

The Pig and Whistle might be a ridiculous name, but Bloch could forgive it, given the reception he received.

"So you're Mr. Block," the fat landlord said with a smile. "Welcome to Brytewood, and what may I get you?"

For this he'd been well briefed. "A pint of bitter, please."

The landlord held a heavy glass mug under the tap and slowly filled it with rich amber liquid, easing the pressure to form a head, before dabbing the bottom of the mug on a towel and handing the beer to Block. "Here you are, sir. Tonight it's on the house. Tell you what, you and Mr. Whorleigh here need to have a chat. Seeing as how you'll be working together like."

What was the fat landlord talking about? He was calling to a slender, tall man, at the other end of the bar. "Mr. Whorleigh, you'd best be meeting your new competition. Mr. Block here is reopening Stone's bakery." Competition? Another baker? "Mr. Whorleigh is the village grocer," the landlord explained.

Whorleigh turned to look at Block and gave a halfway friendly nod. "Baker, eh?" he said taking a drink from a three-quarters empty tankard.

"Yes, I'm Bill Block." He took a couple of steps toward the man and held out his hand.

For a second, it seemed he would be refused but then

Whorleigh extended his hand and grasped Block's firmly. Too firmly for friendliness. Far too firmly for comfort if Block had been mortal.

Block met pressure with pressure.

Whorleigh smiled as realization hit Block.

This was no human. Whorleigh, the village grocer, was Other.

If he was the vampire-killing Other remained to be discovered.

Fast.

Block released his hand. "So, you and I are fellow traders."

The idea did not appear to thrill. "Good luck, the last one got himself run over. If I didn't have bread sent in from Dorking, we'd not have any."

"I plan to alter that."

Whorleigh gave a noncommittal nod. "Experienced in the trade are you? Or are you one of those Ministry of Food conscripts?"

"My father was a baker. I grew up learning the trade."

"I see," Whorleigh paused to drink from his beer. "Local was he?"

"Not at all. I don't know this part of the country in the least. I'm looking forward to looking around. I've heard there're some good walks." Nice touch that. Set up his desire to wander and look around.

Whorleigh shrugged. "Used to get groups of ramblers on weekends before the war. Not many these days." He drained his beer and set the empty tankard on the bar.

Bloch took the hint. "Let me buy you another."

"Don't mind if I do." Taking the refilled glass with a nod of thanks, Whorleigh went on, "Let's get ourselves a seat over in the corner and talk this out."

Talk what out? That, he would no doubt discover.

"This is how I see it," Whorleigh began once they'd sat down at a table tucked in a far corner. "This village is big enough for both of us. We just need to come to an agreement." Bloch listened, an amused smile tweaking one corner of his mouth. "You do all the baking, bread, rolls, cakes if you want and can get the fat and sugar. I'll stop selling any bread. That way they'll have to come to you or get on the bus for it. They'll come to you. Buses aren't as reliable as they were before the war." Bloch nodded. So far this was clear enough. "I take care of customers who're registered with me and . . . the rest."

At the pause, Bloch gave Whorleigh all his attention. "I take care of any extras. That's my bailiwick. Silk stockings, makeup, off-the-ration things that are hard to find. Understand?"

Bloch understood the black market was alive and thriving. "Of course." There had to be some way to use this to his advantage. And if this Whorleigh was the killer, soon the peasants of Brytewood would be without their supplier.

How unfortunate for them.

Bloch was sorely tempted to dispose of Whorleigh this very evening and report his success to Weiss, but if Whorleigh wasn't the killer, it might just pay to let him live. He could be handy and Weiss was always carping on about unnecessary deaths bringing unwarranted attention.

"I believe," Bloch said, eyeing Whorleigh over the rim of his glass, "we can work together. How about we drink up and take a stroll and cover detail better not discussed here?"

After a brief hesitation, Whorleigh agreed, downed his beer and crossed to the door, giving a nod to the knot of men clustered around the dart board.

Sergeant Howell Pendragon of the Home Guard, Red Welsh Dragon and long-time resident of Brytewood, watched as the door closed and the heavy curtain dropped into place behind the two men. "Another newcomer?" he asked the landlord, Fred Wise. "Place is full of them these days."

"He's the new baker. Surprised you haven't met him," Wise replied.

"Not so far. Will soon no doubt. Where's he come from?"

"Dunno. Didn't catch that, but mind you, will be nice to get fresh bread in the village." Wise paused to pull a pint for a customer down the bar. "Still," he went on, "can't but wonder why we got a new baker, you'd think he'd have gone to one of the big cities. Not complaining, you see, but it does make one ask."

"It does indeed," Pendragon agreed.

"You'll be losing your young lodger soon, won't you?" Constable Parlett, now off duty, said from down the bar.

Pendragon nodded. "Yes, will miss him. Nothing quite like young company."

"He isn't moving that far!" Wise said, with a bit of a chuckle. "It's nice to see the doctor and him together. Make a nice pair they do, and this way he'll be staying in the village."

"Unless he gets posted somewhere else," Parlett said. "I'd hate to see it but with a war on, who's to say?"

"I bet they leave him here, especially with the nurse laid up now and all the extra evacuees arriving," Pendragon said, voicing his own hopes. "Due tomorrow are they? Or is it Friday?"

"It was yesterday," Parlett said. "The WVS ladies got the tea urns and all set up and then got a message: Trains were cut because of bomb damage on the lines."

"They'll get here soon enough," Pendragon said. He downed the last of his beer. "I'll be off home. See you gentlemen tomorrow."

As he walked toward his cottage, he frowned to himself. Something about that baker chap seemed wrong. Other was Howell's guess. He really wanted to hear what Helen Burrows had to say about him. He valued the Pixie's opinion. She'd been right about that Oak chap and he wanted to know her impression of Mr. Block, the new baker.

* * *

The darkness of the blackout was no impediment to Bloch's vampire sight and it gave him the edge over mortals. Seemed Whorleigh had no trouble negotiating the narrow path between the hedges and the lane either. Another indication he was Other. Why not just rip his throat out and take his blood? The temptation was very strong and the chance he might execute the wrong person wouldn't weigh heavy on his mind.

"You and me, Block, we work together, see?" Whorleigh said. "You trust Sam Whorleigh to see you right. Just let me do my bit on the side and you set up your own."

How, precisely, he would manage that when Whorleigh had the black market cornered was a puzzle, but not one he was likely to waste his brains on. With Whorleigh dead, the pickings would be up for grabs but for that, he needed his contacts. Better stay the execution.

But a nice deep draught of Whorleigh's blood would sustain for several days, and help bind the creature to Block. That couldn't be anything but useful.

They were a hundred yards or so away from Whorleigh's store, on a deserted stretch of country lane, the Pig and Whistle behind them beyond the bend.

Block put his arm around Whorleigh's shoulders. "Old pal, we will deal well together."

Whorleigh stiffened. Interesting. "We'll work together alright. You and I. You just stay your side of the street and I'll keep to mine," he replied. "That clear?"

The friendly tone didn't conceal a thing. The man dared to utter a warning to Wilhelm Bloch? He was in need of a little judicious humbling and binding. "Perfectly clear, old chap. We understand each other, don't we?" The church wasn't far ahead. Would be no trouble to drag the grocer over the stone wall and feed.

Bloch's gums tingled at the prospect.

Keeping a tight hold on Whorleigh's shoulders, Bloch steered him across the road. Whorleigh resisted a moment, before accepting Bloch's direction. "You're an interesting man, Block," he said.

The creature had no idea exactly how interesting.

The dark shape of the lychgate loomed ahead. Bloch drew him closer, ready to swing him into the shadows. A quick glance ahead and behind showed the lane still deserted.

Perfect.

As his fangs descended, Bloch tightened his hold on Whorleigh, counting to himself the paces to the lychgate ahead.

Whorleigh slipped out of his grasp and disappeared.

Impossible!

Bloch was the only person in the lane.

How in the name of all the damned and cursed had that happened? Bloch snarled to the heavens in the frustration of rising hunger. His now descended fangs brushed his lips. He wanted blood and his victim was gone. Not just gone, he'd disappeared into the night.

If nothing else, Bloch had the satisfaction of suspicions confirmed. Whorleigh was Other.

Whether or not he was Eiche's slayer was immaterial. The creature was now prey.

Bloch ran at vampire speed, all pretense of mortal gone. At Whorleigh's shop he halted. He needed an invitation to enter the creature's abode. Such an invitation was unlikely to be forthcoming.

Bloch could bide his time and consider the question that nagged him. What was Whorleigh and how had he disappeared? Those thoughts took precedence over the question on his possible guilt.

Samuel Whorleigh watched from his perch on the lychgate. This was a crimp he'd not anticipated and didn't quite understand. He'd sensed menace in Block from the first, but not enough to cause concern, until they left the pub and Bill Block put his arm around his shoulders and exuded a burgeoning sense of menace. More than Whorleigh had encountered in decades.

If he'd been mortal, harm would have befallen him. No doubt about it. As it was, he slipped out of the hold and wrapped himself in invisibility. Perched atop the lychgate, he had the satisfaction of watching Block's confusion.

Satisfaction was soon replaced with worry. Block represented trouble. Danger.

Whorleigh had suspected as much from a handshake that revealed no pulse.

Only one sort of creature walked the earth without a pulse or heartbeat and Whorleigh had never heard good of vampires. What to do now? He knew of one Other in these parts: the white witch, old Mother Longhurst. He had to talk to her and keep his eyes peeled for Bill Block's next and unwelcome approach.

"A penny for them," Peter Watson said to his love, his intended, his fiancée (he loved that word): Alice.

"My thoughts?" She smiled, looking up from her knitting. They were sitting either side of the kitchen stove while Mrs. Burrows presided over the knitting circle in the lounge. "I was wondering if Gran will take pity on me and turn the heel. I'm worried about Miss Waite's odd and unexpected death, and hoping Gloria and Andrew are getting on well."

"Matchmaker."

She grinned, only too happy, Peter guessed, to neglect the sock. Alice had many strengths, knitting socks apparently wasn't among them. "And why not? They're both single. They're attracted to each other, a blind person could see that, and all they needed was a little nudge."

"What if they're not meant for each other? Ever thought about that?"

"Then it won't work out. We did."

He couldn't argue with that. Wasn't about to. "What about Miss Waite? Gossip in the village says it was suicide. Don't spies carry cyanide pills in their teeth?"

Alice hesitated. This was likely some official secret but . . . "It wasn't cyanide, Peter. That's unmistakable, skin goes pink even after death. She was pale as could be and shriveled." She paused. "Not unlike the state we found Farmer Morgan in."

Peter went cold. No prizes for guessing that implication. Morgan had been killed by Oak, the vampire spy Alice had destroyed. "Have you told your grandmother?"

"No, why worry her until I'm sure that's what it is? But how can I be sure? I can hardly say to the medical officer, 'Maybe a vampire killed her.' They'd have me committed and strike me off the medical register as insane. And I could be wrong. I just wish there'd been a local inquest. She was whisked off somewhere and no one knows or won't tell. But we do know there is another vampire somewhere. The one who walked out of my surgery, and if he's come back . . ."

"The one who disappeared on you the day we met? We owe him a big 'thank you.'"

That brought a smile to her lips, and a naughty twinkle to her eyes. "We'd have met anyway, Peter. Somehow. I don't think we'd have missed each other. We were meant to be together."

"Meant to elope?" They'd had this conversation before and he always lost but didn't stop trying.

"Now that we've had the banns called? No way, Peter Watson. You are making an honest woman of me in Brytewood parish church. No havey cavey off to a registry office for us."

And since it was the price of winning her, he'd put up with all the folderols and fuss.

"Want a warm drink before you go?"

"Kicking me out?" he asked.

She gave him a playful swat. "Twit. Best for everyone if the good women of the village see you leave before they do. Gran doesn't mind you staying, you know that, but she would mind gossip. So, it's Horlicks and an Osbourne biscuit for you, my love, and then off down the lane. At least for tonight."

Fair enough. Village gossips could shred a reputation faster than unhooking their corsets. He stood and crossed the kitchen to stand close, wrapping his arms around her waist and pulling her against him. He was hard and he wanted to make darn sure she knew it.

"Peter," she said, her voice tight, "are you trying to distract me?"

"Of course." He kissed the back of her neck. "Just a little."

"If you really want to prove your devotion, get the biscuit tin off the dresser."

"Kiss me first."

She turned in his embrace, leaning into him so her breasts pressed against his pullover. Damn, they both had far too many clothes. He wanted her naked, skin to skin, warm and loving under the covers, but he'd settle for what he could get, and what he could get right now was her kiss.

Her mouth found his. His hand slipped under her cardigan and fumbled for buttons and she pressed her lips against his.

He was drunk. Intoxicated with the sheer heady sensation of her mouth on his and her tongue searching, reaching for his. They touched, she gave a little sexy whimper and deepened the kiss until they were locked in a wild embrace of glorious sensual need. Her hands came around his waist to clutch his bottom and pull him closer.

What had he ever done to deserve this? A warm and loving woman who desired him. Heat built between them, fueled by repressed need and scorching want. He deepened the kiss even more, turning so Alice had her back to the sink. He pressed her against the cool china and rubbed his body against hers. He had to break it off soon or they'd never stop, and he'd end up having her against the draining board.

Not a romantic prospect.

Not the way to endear himself to the most fabulous woman in creation.

Screwing up his resolve, he broke the kiss and pulled back. A few inches.

"Peter!" Her stifled cry showed her frustration and need. "Why stop?"

"Because two minutes more and we'd end up naked on the kitchen table and cause untold scandal when some good woman of the parish walks in with the tray of used teacups."

"True." Her sigh seemed to hang overhead, looming up near the clothes airer suspended from the ceiling. "Better get on with that Horlicks you wanted." She put the kettle on the gas and reached for two mugs off the dresser. "I bet Gloria and Andrew are having something more exciting than Horlicks."

Chapter Seven

Andrew had the best spot in the house, or rather the cellar: a battered sofa tucked in one corner. He pretty much preempted it, saying she needed to keep her leg propped up, air raid or not. It wasn't a lie but Gloria stifled a twinge of guilt as she reclined on the dusty cushions and everyone else sat on upturned tea chests, rickety old chairs or the floor.

The light from the low wattage bulbs was no use for reading, as one customer realized as he gave up on his newspaper and folded it to sit on. There was nothing to do but wait. For whatever was or was not going to happen. The group of young officers who'd been propping up the bar now hunkered down to one side and started a game of cards. Seemed Gloria's best course of action was to lean back against Andrew and hope it was all a false alarm and they'd be upstairs again in no time, and she could finish her soup.

It wasn't a false alarm.

After the seemingly endless drone of planes overhead and ack ack fire, there was comparative silence. The only immediate sounds were whispered conversations among the hotel staff clustered and the odd exclamation from the card players.

"Think that's it?" Gloria asked Andrew.

"Could be. Who knows? Best wait for the all clear."

Seemed it was going to be some wait. No one moved. Nothing happened. Apart from the arrival of an air raid warden checking gas masks.

"You know I could fine you both for not having them," he said.

"Sorry," Gloria said, before Andrew could reply. "I know we should have brought them, but I left mine at home. I always keep it with my nurse's uniform . . ." Better drop that in. " . . . and forgot it tonight. My mind was taken up with crutches and how I was getting around."

"Nurse are you then?"

"I'm the district nurse based in Brytewood." That should be worth something, darn it. Most people had more to do than make a fuss about gas masks. Although she'd nagged her share of school children for leaving theirs in the playground.

"Well, nurse, you know better, but . . . let's hope you don't need it tonight."

Didn't everyone share that hope? Gloria smiled at him. "Let's hope they're just flying over." Although that meant London would be getting it.

"Time will tell. They came over a couple of nights ago. Dropped half a dozen bombs, that was all, but they caused a bit of trouble." He moved on to chat with the soldiers.

"He didn't even ask about yours," Gloria said to Andrew. "Just picked on me," she added with a little dig in his ribs.

"Good thing too. He wouldn't fine a nurse but I mightn't have been let off so lightly."

"Your work is important."

"But since I can't tell anyone what it is, not much of an alibi."

"Everyone in the village knows, or has guessed. Especially after the trouble back in September." When she'd raised the alarm. Not exactly easy since she'd been in her fox skin at the time.

His chest moved, as if he held in a laugh. "That's still an official secret."

"I won't tell. I promise."

"I know," he whispered it, his lips almost touching her ear, his breath warm against her skin. "Wouldn't be here with you otherwise, Gloria."

"We wouldn't be down here at all if it weren't for the damn Luftwaffe."

As if on cue, another flight passed overhead. More this time. Suddenly feeling hideously vulnerable, Gloria clutched Andrew's arm, now handily wrapped across her chest. His free hand stroked the back of her neck. "Hang on, old girl," he whispered "This building's lasted centuries, you don't think it's going to crumble for the Jerries, do you?"

She hoped to heaven not. She tamped down the fox stirring inside. Stifled the instinct to run from danger. It was ten days to full moon, she didn't need to change, couldn't anyway with her leg in a cast but wanted to. She longed to shuck her human face and run free, away from this hotel and the town for the safety of the woods.

Which weren't safe in the least. Nowhere was.

Andrew's lips brushed the back of her neck.

She hoped no one else heard her sigh. They were in a public place after all. She ought to move. Get up and go somewhere else.

But where else did she want to be right now but caught in his arms?

She leaned closer, resting her head against his chest. In the uneasy quiet, she could hear his steady, human heart beat. She was utterly loony. Accepting his invitation was stupid, snuggling up to him like this, insane. But who had time for sanity as another flight of bombers approached?

"Andrew," she whispered, kissing his wrist. It was his closest bit of skin.

"Scared?" he asked.

"Scared witless," she replied, the sound of antiaircraft guns all but drowning her words.

"Nah!" His arm held her a little tighter. "You'll always have your wits about you, Nurse Prewitt. It's not the first time either of us has sat through this, won't be the last."

She was beginning to wonder. Planes droned overhead in waves. "Poor London is going to get it bad." If it wasn't already. How long did it take to fly from here to London? It had been a good thirty minutes since the first wave passed overhead. "Maybe we're going to be lucky tonight." Unfortunately "lucky" here meant someone else was disastrously unlucky.

"I'm lucky just being here with you," he said.

She smiled. Couldn't help it. It shouldn't feel this fantastic just sitting close to him, feeling his warmth and solid strength. That wasn't all she was feeling. He was unmistakably aroused. Blush burned her face. She'd done this. It wasn't exactly her fault, she told herself, but she was having a definite effect on Andrew Barron.

"Doing alright?" he asked quietly.

"If I have to be stuck in a hotel cellar, waiting for bombs to drop, I'm glad I'm here with you."

His laugh, a peal of sheer delight, got them quite a bit of attention. Just as well the light was so poor they couldn't see how red her face was. "Sorry," Andrew said, to the world at large. "I just realized, I think I'm in love."

Talk about dropping clangors. What was she supposed to say to that?

Not much it seemed.

"Good luck!" someone called and one of the card playing officers let out a wolf whistle.

"You do pick your moment, don't you, young man?" a woman said.

The general hilarity went right over Gloria's head. She was too busy worrying what she was going to do about it. If he was falling in love, having the brief fling Alice advocated seemed a downright rotten thing to do. But now was hardly the time to break up with him. Break up? They'd barely started.

Her stomach rumbled, a reminder of their interrupted dinner and the first bomb dropped. As if pulled by a string, everyone looked up to the rafters.

"He's a long way off," a male voice said, only to be drowned out by one much closer and louder.

Gloria clung to Andrew. Damn her conflicted feelings. Right now he was what she needed, his closeness, his strength, his presence.

"Can't last all night," he said. A third one fell. Much closer. Then a series of explosions that shook the building. A woman screamed. A voice calmed her. Andrew's arm tightened around Gloria.

"Sorry I got you into this," he said,

"Don't be silly. This could just as easily be happening in Brytewood." Most likely was happening in Brytewood. "I hope everyone there's alright." Gloria shut her eyes. It was impossible not to think back to the awful night the vicarage was hit. Mind you, that had worked out very well for Alice and Peter. Maybe she and Andrew . . .

No! She was not even entertaining the idea. Alice didn't turn furry on moonlit nights. Alice's life was simple and straightforward. She didn't have a deep earthy secret she hid from the world. She and . . .

Andrew kissed her!

In front of all these people he kissed her. Not a wild, passionate kiss. Maybe no one else even noticed. It was a "don't worry, I'm here" sort of kiss. Just a brush of his lips on hers.

Then why did she feel it deep inside? Why was her body softening against his while her nipples went hard? "Andrew," she said, for want of anything more intelligent or thoughtful.

"We'll be out of here soon," he promised. "They can't keep this up forever."

Only all night if they felt like it.

"Wish old Jerry would just drop the lot and go home!" a voice called across the cellar.

As if on cue, there was another explosion, two of them, close enough to shake the building. Amid the crashes and noise overhead, Gloria wasn't sure if she grabbed Andrew or Andrew grabbed her. Hardly mattered as she shut her eyes and clung to him as they both waited for another explosion.

Which never came. Just aircraft noise overhead until that too faded or was drowned out by sirens and shouts outside. Seemed an age before they gave the all clear. Alice waited as the others stood and left. She was safe, alive and had no wish to be carried upstairs, or give everyone one a demonstration of how to haul yourself upstairs using your arms.

By the time Andrew and she emerged, most of the others had dispersed. No one seemed to want to finish dinner. At least no one apart from Gloria. She was suddenly and ravenously hungry but they probably should go out and look at the damage.

The smells of cordite and brick dust filled the air. Glass panes, still with the brown tape attached, lay shattered on the pavement. Strange how bright the night was, almost as if . . .

"Stone the crows!" a voice said. "Someone won't be driving home tonight."

"Stand back, stand back!" another voice called. "Got to get the hose through."

"Andrew, was something hit?" Gloria asked.

"Let's have a look-see." He helped her though the door and to the top of the steps. A few yards down the street, Andrew's car was burning like a 5th of November bonfire, right next to a vast pile of rubble that, if Gloria remembered rightly, had been an ironmonger.

"Oh, my God!" Andrew said, looking from Gloria to his burning car and back again. He was obviously dying to run to check.

"Go and look, Andrew. See what they can do. I'll wait here." Not much point, it was obvious his car was done for.

Fifteen firemen—watching minutes later, he agreed.

"We're stuck here until the buses start up in the morning,"

Andrew said, as he came back and sat beside her. "If only I'd parked it the other side of the street." He put his arm around her shoulders and held her tight. Was it to give or get comfort? Didn't matter. She put her head on his shoulder.

"We can 'if only' all night." Gloria replied. "Shouldn't we see about finding an aid post or somewhere? We can't stay here."

"I don't see why not. It's a hotel isn't it? And the only damage is a few broken windows and some cracked plaster. I'm going to see what I can do." He stood up and she instantly missed his touch.

She sighed and wondered where the nearest wardens' post or rescue center was. Surely the hotel would close for the night?

Seemed not. In a few minutes, Andrew was back, brandishing a room key. "They gave us a room in the back," he said. "Should be quieter than out front and . . ." he broke off. "Christ! Gloria, I never thought, I'd better get another room, I didn't mean . . ."

He might not have been thinking, she certainly wasn't. Just having him back within touching distance was all she wanted right now. She reached for the key, closing her hand over his, "Andrew, one room will do me fine, as long as I have towels and soap to wash with." After the past few hours, she understood what Alice meant about seizing the moment. If it had been the White Horse and not that ironmonger, they'd be gone. They weren't and she did not want to sleep alone.

"Sure?"

"Absolutely. There is the little matter of getting up those stairs." They were wide, yes, but tall and had two bends. Her arms ached just looking at them.

"I'll take care of that. That's a doddle," he replied.

Not quite. He had to pause at each turn and set her on her feet for a few moments to catch his breath, but he got her up there, the waiter pressed into service to carry her crutches and open the door.

It was a beautiful room—or once had been—with a four-poster bed and heavy curtains, vestiges of prewar splendor. The frigid cold and the barren fireplace were harsh reminders of wartime.

"No chance of a fire, I suppose?" Andrew asked. He was being optimistic.

"Sorry, sir. Takes all we've got to heat the downstairs. I can bring extra blankets if you want."

They did want. "What about hot water bottles?" Gloria asked.

"I'll send one of the girls up with them," he promised and nipped out the door. Before they could ask for anything else, Gloria guessed.

"While we're waiting, I'm going to investigate the toilet," Alice said, "and hope it's not up or down a flight of stairs."

"I'll go downstairs and chivvy everyone along. I don't want them forgetting we're here."

The toilet was just a couple of doors down the hall, right next door to a vast tiled bathroom of glacial splendor. Guessing hot water was in short supply, and the logistics of a bath sheer impossibility with her cast, Gloria settled for a quick (and cold) wash in the basin in the room, sat down in a chintz-covered armchair and asked herself what she really thought she was doing.

Quite simply, she was going to spend the night in the same bed as Andrew Barron and hoped to high heaven they didn't spend the night sleeping.

She wanted him plain and simple. Wanted more than his arms around her, much more than his kisses. Wanted him in every way a woman needed a man and she didn't intend to wait.

A cold wash and an unheated room did nothing to cool the heat inside.

She was a floozy.

A loose woman.

She was being bold.

Far too forward.

And didn't give a damn.

Death and injury had bypassed her, she was going to grasp hold of life.

Before she lost her nerve, she crutched it over to the side of the bed, took off her clothes, folding them as best she could, on one leg. Left on her petticoat so as not to seem too fast, and nipped between the covers, pulling them up to her chin.

She'd done it.

So far.

All she had to do now was wait for Andrew.

Chapter Eight

She was not getting cold feet over this. Alright, she did have cold feet but of the physical sort. It was cold as a tomb in here and she suspected the sheets were damp into the bargain, but it was nine hundred percent better than trying to find a shelter.

Gloria was debating getting out of bed and putting on her cardigan, when the door opened.

Andrew came in, and she felt warm all over as he met her eyes. He wasn't the least unhappy to see her in bed. Good. His eyes widened as his rather lovely mouth curled up in a very slow smile. Her goosebumps weren't just because of the cold. She grinned back, only half noticing the ancient waiter carrying a load of blankets and a chambermaid bearing a pair of stone hot water bottles.

Gloria did her best to look calm and unconcerned as if she habitually stayed in hotels without luggage and the presence of hotel staff in the room was a matter of course.

If the burning in her face was anything to go by, she failed utterly.

"Where do you want the blankets, sir?" the waiter asked.

"Er . . . Put them on the chair." Andrew replied. "We'll get them when we need them. Many thanks."

"No trouble, sir. We only wish we had coal for the fire but with all the shortages, heating is kept for the ground floor."

"That's alright." Andrew seemed as eager for them to scoot off as she was.

"Hot water bottles, madam?" the chambermaid asked.

"In the bed, please." Where else? Gloria took one and held it close, while the maid slipped the other down near her feet.

"Will that be all, sir?" the old waiter asked.

"Yes, rather. Thank you."

"Morning tea, sir?"

Would they never leave?

"Yes, I suppose so." He looked at Gloria. "Eight sound alright?"

"How about seven thirty? We should try to get back to Brytewood by nine." Andrew nodded. "What about buses?" she asked.

"We've a timetable in reception," the maid replied, "but often they run late after a raid. Detours you know."

She could imagine.

"Right then. Tea at seven-thirty, please," Andrew said and as good as bundled them out of the door. Closing it behind them, he smiled at Gloria.

Now, she wasn't cold one little bit. Heat flushed right down to her toes. Well, not quite to her toes. It pooled a good bit higher as a thrill fluttered between her legs.

"Fancy a drink?" Andrew asked, holding up their unfinished bottle of wine.

She bit back, "Not really. I fancy you!" and nodded. "Thanks."

"I rescued it from the dining room," he went on. "It was sitting undisturbed on the table right where we left it. Not a drop spilled."

"I was thinking earlier, I wished we'd brought it down to the shelter, but now's even better."

He handed her a glass of the deep red wine and poured one for himself before raising his glass. "Here's to us."

She wasn't about to wonder what that meant. Now was all that mattered. Blame it on hormones, shock or unbridled lust, she wanted Andrew Barron in the worst, and most likely best, possible way. "To us." She raised her glass and sipped, not breaking contact with his gorgeous blue eyes.

"Look," he said. "I've got to nip down the hallway. Be back in a jiffy, I promise."

"I'm not going anywhere."

Except perhaps into her dreams, as he closed the door and left her alone in the now decidedly chilly room. Who gave a fig? Just as long as he didn't get lost on the way back, she'd be happy. This was outrageous, definitely scandalous and without a doubt, truly wonderful.

Funny how a deluge of doubts evaporated with a few bombs. Alright, not funny for the poor people who get it and not funny over Andrew's car, but they were both alive, young, attracted to each other, and delighted to be together.

He was back in minutes, his jacket over his arm and his shirt hanging out.

"I hope you didn't meet anyone on the way back."

He blushed. Just a wee bit but it somehow reassured that he didn't do this every weekend. "I think we're the only ones up here. The boozy lot from the bar all left, probably late for some curfew. And the other couple in the restaurant had hied off home. We have the place to ourselves," he paused, "Gloria."

She swallowed. It helped ease her tight throat. Sort of. "Aren't you cold?"

"Yes. It's like the Arctic here and the bathroom . . ."

"I know. Freezing. Made my lean-to bathroom seem positively cozy by comparison." Damn it! She did not come here to talk about deficiencies in comfort of her cottage. "It's warmer in bed and I put one of the hot water bottles on your side."

Hardly seductive but it didn't seem to put him off. "You're a brick, Gloria."

He unbuttoned his shirt and she, shameless Gloria that she was, watched, all but mesmerized as he slipped each button from its buttonhole. As if aware of her scrutiny, he turned his back and draped his shirt over the chair, giving her a lovely view of his broad shoulders. A view much enhanced as he pulled his vest over his head and she got an eyeful of his naked back.

She clenched her fists to restrain the sudden urge to run her hands over that beautiful skin and trace the muscles in his arms.

As he sat down to take off his shoes, she unclenched her fists. Darn it, very soon she had every intention of touching him, of feeling him skin to skin and running her hands all over his luscious body. Just watching his arms as he untied his shoelaces and eased his shoes off sent her pulse racing.

He pulled his sock off, set his bare foot on the faded red carpet, crossed the other foot over his thigh and started all over again.

She was beginning to understand the appeal of striptease acts and she had her own personal solo performance.

He stood. There was a soft metallic sound as he unbuckled his belt.

Gloria knew it was rude to stare but really, how could anyone not? She'd never realized just how long it took a man to unbutton his flies. Was he taking his time to tease, or was he . . . shy?

That she didn't think. A shy man would have insisted on separate rooms.

Ooh! He bent to take off his trousers and gave her a lovely view of his nice firm posterior. Good thing he couldn't see her lick her lips. Or maybe he'd be flattered. The look on his face as he crossed the room toward her wasn't that of a self-conscious man.

"Andrew," she said. It came out a bit like a squeak but she didn't try to hold back the grin. She could just imagine him without the white cotton interlock drawers.

He had the bottle in his hand. "Want to top off your glass?"

"Not really, I'd rather you got in and kept me warm." Forward, yes, but darn it, hot water bottles only warmed so much.

"I can do both."

He could indeed. Sitting beside him in bed, sipping wine wasn't a bad way to spend an evening. But she could think of better. "What are you going to do about the car?" Why in heaven's name did she ask that?"

"I'll worry about it in the morning. It isn't going anywhere. Ever. Apart from the junkyard. Maybe they can use the metal to build a Spitfire."

She did not want to talk about planes or bombs or war. Not now. She swigged down the entire glass. It would go right to her head very, very soon, so . . . "Kiss me, Andrew, please."

She must have put the glass down somewhere. He probably tossed his across the room, wine and all. His hands came to her shoulders, she caught the scent of wine on his breath and his lips met hers. She kissed back, excitement rippling through her at his touch. He was warm and male and heady as the wine on his lips and she almost swore when he broke the kiss.

"Sure you want this, Gloria? I can sleep in the armchair if you want."

There were times a man should be a perfect gentleman. This was not one of them. "No, you won't!" Just in case he didn't quite get the message, she wrapped her arms around his neck and this time, *she* kissed *him*. Pressing her lips on his as she opened her mouth. He hesitated, maybe one sixteenth of a second, before he warmed to her kiss, taking her mouth as his tongue found hers and she let out a little sigh of utter pleasure as he pulled her close.

When they came up for air, she took a deep breath and grinned at him. "Oh, Andrew!"

"You are utterly wonderful," he replied, stroking the hair off her face. "Wonderful."

She kissed his chin, his lower lip and his mouth, needing, wanting more. Much more.

Seemed Andrew was of the same mind. He kissed back, deepening it, caressing her tongue with his, holding her close. His hands, stroking her back and shoulders, were cold but she felt warmth anyway. Heat, need and lust poured through her in a wild spate of desire. His hands slipped the straps of her petticoat off her shoulders. He paused a moment or two as he looked at her breasts. Then, with a smile curling his mouth, he stroked his hands over her breasts. She couldn't hold back the groan as her nipples went hard.

His touch ignited something wild inside her—a rush of wanting that sent her mind into a spin. Her petticoat, bunched around her waist, was in the way. She wanted him skin to skin. She wanted him inside her. She wanted him as close as man and woman could be. She wriggled her hips, taking her hands off him to ease down the crumpled silk and kick it away.

He helped her.

Burrowing under the covers, he stroked her belly and thighs and the cluster of now-damp curls between her legs. Gloria rolled on her side, pressing herself against him, running her foot up and down his leg, feeling his erection against her.

That damn underwear had to go.

"Take these off!" Her hands tugged at the elastic and he obliged with a bit of shifting and wiggling of his own. Tossing the underwear across the room was a bit flamboyant but who'd complain? It just added to the moment.

The real moment came when she stroked the side of his impressively hard cock. Dear heaven, he was so erect. She slipped under the bedclothes, glad he'd left the light on. What she would have missed if they were in the dark!

As she caressed him, he stroked her breasts, then found his way back between her legs, arousing her until she moaned and rocked her hips.

This was wild and wonderful but . . . "Andrew, I want you!"

"Love, we should make this last."

"Why? Next time can be slow! Not now!"

She didn't understand the urgency, the raging need, but wasn't about to fight it. She wanted him. "Now."

"Hang on a tick, Gloria. Better get a French letter."

He'd brought them with him? He planned this? So what? Darn good thing he had as she hadn't. The bed cooled fast without him but he was back in seconds, the paper envelope already open.

"Won't be long."

She pulled back the blankets to watch as he rolled the pale rubber over his erection. She was tempted to offer help. Next time.

He was ready.

So was she.

She put her leg over his thigh and rubbed her body against his. His hands cupped her breasts, holding them steady. He bent his head and kissed her left breast. She thought she'd leave the bed. Her hips and chest did as she arched her back to bring her breast closer to him. When he lifted his mouth her peaked nipple hardened even more in the chill air. As she caught her breath, or at least tried to, he went for her right breast, stroking with his tongue as his hand played the other one.

Her hands went wild, stroking his back, his hips, his bottom. She ran kisses over his chest and shoulders as she grasped his hips to pull him closer.

He rolled her on her back, settling between her legs. There was no longer any chill in the room. Just wild heat stirred by sexual need. His erection stroked between her vulva as he rocked his hips against her.

Stroking was nowhere near enough. Not now. She spread her legs wide, moving the wretched cast to one side and bending her good leg so her foot was flat on the bed to angle her hips toward him.

He understood her need completely. Pausing only to open

her gently and ease inside her. "You are so wet," he said, "wet for me."

And he was making her wetter by the second. As he stroked her nub, her hips rocked instinctively, her body responding to his need. He shifted so his cock was right between her lower lips. He rocked, and she felt sweet pressure against her opening. She arched toward him and he was inside.

She cried out. It was too much. It was wonderful. It was perfect. He filled her. Stretched her. Mounted her. She was gasping, panting, her body arching to bring him deeper, her hips rocking in her need.

"Ready, love?" he asked.

Ready? She was so far beyond ready, she didn't think there was a word for it. "Please, Andrew. Please!"

He began to move, back and forth in a certain, steady rhythm as passion built between them. She kissed his shoulder and tasted sweat. She nipped his skin, holding on with lips and teeth as he increased the pace, until he was driving her hard and wonderfully. Wild sensations burgeoned, possessing her brain, filling her spirit. Need and pleasure roared in her mind. She was letting out cries, gasps and whimpers as her climax grew, peaked and burst in a wild cascade of pleasure and a great cry of happiness. He continued, driving her higher until he came with a wild whoop of satisfaction and collapsed on her.

He made to move. But she grabbed hard and held him close. Not wanting him to leave her, wanting to feel his cock between her legs forever, until dawn and beyond.

"I'm too heavy," he said. "I'll squash you."

She laughed. "I want to feel you inside. I like being squashed."

He lay on her, taking some of his weight on his arms, but they were skin to skin. Hot and sweaty. What better way to spend a cold October night? She couldn't help the groan of disappointment as he softened inside her and withdrew.

"You are utterly and totally wonderful, Gloria," he said and kissed her.

"Wonderful yourself, Andrew. My love."

She was vaguely aware of him shifting and sitting up. He must have disposed of the French letter. Didn't take him long. He was back, his arms around her. She snuggled close, and shut her eyes.

Whatever tumult and trouble awaited outside this haven of a room, for this moment in time, they were both at utter peace.

Chapter Nine

"The phone's for you, dear," Gran said, popping her head around the bathroom door.

Alice turned off the tap and looked up, toothbrush in hand. "That's early. Emergency? Where is it?"

"Not an emergency. It's Gloria."

If she were calling this early, it had to be an emergency. "I'll be down. Tell her I'm on my way." Stopping only to rinse and spit, Alice ran downstairs. "Gloria," she said, picking up the receiver. "What's happened?"

"Better sit down first."

"What on earth, Gloria? Just tell me. My bath water is getting cold."

Gloria told her.

She'd been right. Sitting down would have been a good idea. "For heaven's sakes, Gloria, are you both alright?"

"Oh, yes. We're about to have breakfast, once Andrew finishes with the police. They want his license and so forth and proof it was his car. His log book's at home and everything else is charred to a cinder."

"Anyone hurt?"

"I haven't heard. A shop down the High Street got a direct hit. They think that's when the car ignited, but the flat over it was empty. Thank heaven! There was other damage, mostly on the outskirts of the town."

Could have been so much worse. "What did you do last night? Spend it in a shelter?"

"We were in a hotel, Alice. An almost empty one at that." There was a pause. "We got a room."

Oh! Four little words told almost all. "And Andrew behaved like a perfect gentleman?"

"Thank heaven, no!" The earthy chuckle told the rest of it. "Look, I must run, Alice. We'll be back once we finish here and can get a bus. I called because of the evacuees. I doubt I'll be there to help."

"Yes, I know. I'll phone Lady Gregory and have her call in some extra help. The WVS were running it after all."

"Don't you dare tell anyone what I just told you!"

"Don't worry. I'll give the expurgated version. Mind you, if these Sheffield evacuees are as late arriving as the London lot were, you'll be back before they get here."

"We'll see."

"I'm glad everything went well."

"'Bye Alice."

Well, well, well. Nothing like a big surprise before breakfast. From not being sure she even wanted to go out with Andrew, Gloria had moved fast.

"Everything alright, dear?" Gran called.

"Yes, Gran." Sounded very alright, actually. "Gloria will be late getting up to the village hall today. I'll tell you the whole story once I have clothes on." Would give her time to decide exactly how much to tell Gran. Although, knowing Gran, she'd most likely put two and two together.

Once Alice was back downstairs, Gran had a cup of tea waiting and an egg and fried bread ready in the pan. "Eat up love, you've got a long day ahead."

"Gran, this is the second egg we've had this week. You're not getting them under the counter are you?" She hated to ask.

"Good God, no, Alice. I've bought the odd packet of biscuits from Whorleigh but why would I pay his ridiculous prices for eggs when Mother Longhurst is willing to swap for vegetables? I promised her a sack of parsnips to make wine. We have more than we will ever eat."

True. Some of their attempts at vegetable growing hadn't been that successful but the parsnips had pretty much taken over. Gran had already made parsnip soup and parsnip pie. Mother Longhurst would be saving them from parsnip cake and parsnip jam. "Want me to drop it off?"

"If you would, please, dear. She asked if I could get them to her this morning. She says the moon is right for starting yeast."

Once upon a time, Alice would have scoffed at the witch's pronouncements. Not any longer. Not since she destroyed a vampire thanks to Mother Longhurst's help. Alice would never again laugh at the witch's dictums. "I'll drop it off first thing."

"Thank you, dear. Another cup?" Gran held up the teapot.

"No thanks, Gran. I need to get going."

Sack of parsnips in the back, Alice headed down the hill into the village center and toward Mother Longhurst's cottage at the far end, near the river. This morning, Alice wasn't the only person seeking the witch. As she parked, Sam Whorleigh was hammering on the front door.

"Morning, Mr. Whorleigh." She might despise him but she'd be polite.

"Good morning, doctor. Seen Mother Longhurst?"

Hardly likely, since he arrived before she did. "No, I haven't. I stopped to bring her something from Gran."

He eyed the sack in her hand. "Going into business are you, doctor?"

Smarmy twit! What did he think running a medical practice single-handed was? "Not in the greengrocery line. I assure you."

"Darn." He shook his head. "I've got to see her. Left Peggy running the store. I have to speak to Mrs. Longhurst."

He was sweating. From nervousness? Worry? What could be that urgent? Dire need for a calming potion perhaps? She was about to leave the sack on the front step, guessing old Mother Longhurst had gone out early to gather berries or something vital to her kitchen.

"I came earlier," Whorleigh went on. "Hoped to see her before I opened the shop but she wasn't here."

That had Alice a trifle worried. She was an old woman. Seventy if she was a day, more like eighty. "I'll look inside."

The door, as Alice expected, was unlocked. She shut it firmly behind her. If the old woman had collapsed or fallen, there was no point in letting Sam Whorleigh get an eyeful. The main room was as cluttered as usual. And cold. The fire had been out some time. Odd that. Mother Longhurst kept the fire going in all but the warmest days of summer. She was known for poaching firewood and hadn't let wartime circumstances stop her.

In the lean-to kitchen, a half empty bottle of milk sat on the table alongside a pot of honey and the crust end of a loaf of bread.

Upstairs, the attic bedroom was empty, the bed either made or unslept in.

Alice came back down, gave the cottage another look-over. Nothing was disturbed. Her coat was missing from the hook by the door. She must have gone out walking and gathering and absentmindedly forgotten to bank up the fire.

"She's gone out," Alice announced to Sam Whorleigh. "Maybe she'll be back in a while."

"I'm not so sure about that," he replied, sounding a bit like the voice of doom.

"Doctor?" Alice turned. Doris Brewer stood there, obviously on her way to work, her pinafore under her coat. "Has something happened to Mrs. Longhurst?"

"I don't think so, Doris. She seems to have gone out."

"Yes, she did, doctor. Yesterday real early it was. She borrowed my bicycle, said she was riding over to Bringham and would I feed the cats at lunchtime as she wouldn't be back until later. I fed them, let them out and never thought any more about it. I was cleaning the bakery until late."

"Was there no light in her cottage last night?" Silly question that. If there were, who'd notice in the blackout? "Forget I said that, Doris. I wasn't thinking." But she was now. Something was definitely wrong. "Doris, you go on. I know you have to get to work. Mr. Whorleigh, you might as well get back to your shop. I'll go and speak to Sergeant Jones."

Doris went off, expressing hopes that "nothing nasty" had happened. Sam Whorleigh didn't budge. "But I have to talk to her. It's important." Whatever it was, he was in a stew. "You don't understand, doctor, there's something she needs to know."

"I'm sure there is, Mr. Whorleigh, but she isn't here." She was reluctant to leave him. Maybe it was her bias, but she didn't trust him not to go poking and prying. "Look, I'll give you a lift back to your shop. I'm sure you'll hear the minute she gets back." She wouldn't, not yet at any rate, think "If she gets back."

Once she spoke to Sergeant Jones, she'd call the local hospitals. Just in case.

The senior arm of the local law was gathering the outside leaves off his cabbages. Crime was obviously not heavy this morning. "Sorry to bother you, Sergeant, but I need to report a missing person."

"Oh, doctor!" He shook his head with a half smile. "Half a dozen people already have. "It's Nurse Prewitt right? I know. I've had two phone calls and four people knock on my door to tell me she hasn't taken her milk in and never came home last night."

Heaven help them! It was only a matter of time before

Andrew's landlady hit the village with the news he never came home last night either. "Gloria's not missing. She phoned me. She got caught in Dorking during that raid and stayed the night. This is about Mother Longhurst. She went out on Doris's bicycle early yesterday and hasn't been seen since."

"Now that does sound bad. Any idea where she might have gone?"

"Doris Brewer, who lives across the road, said she mentioned something about riding over to Bringham, but expected to be back midafternoon."

"Any idea why she went there?"

"None." Something rattled around Alice's memory. "She mentioned Bringham to me a week ago, but I can't remember what it was about."

"If you remember, doctor, let me know. I'll go talk to Doris. Level-headed girl that. Know where she's working today?"

"Not sure. She comes to us tomorrow. Maybe Mrs. Helson? She mentioned cleaning up the bakery for the new baker. She could be there."

"I'll get on it. I need to pop by and see the new chap anyway."

"I'll call the hospitals. Just in case."

"Let me know if you hear anything, doctor."

"I will."

As she pulled away, Alice remembered. The stone knife! Mother Longhurst mentioned passing it on to a witch in Bringham. That had to be it. She'd ridden over and something happened on the way back. Definitely check the hospitals.

She stopped by the phone box in front of the post office and called Gran.

"Will you call around, Gran? Say you're phoning for me?"

"Of course I will, dear. You think something's happened to her?"

"Sounds like it. Of course if she's unconscious they might not have her name." Come to that. "What is her Christian name? Better check her records."

"It's Margaret, Alice. I know that. Leave it to me. I'll call around and call old Jones if I hear anything." She paused. "Her going to Bringham has me a bit worried. But we'll talk at lunch. Don't worry about it now."

Which of course meant she would. How could she not? Telling her grandmother good-bye, Alice hung up.

What a day. And it was barely past breakfast. Everyone would have plenty to talk about over their morning coffee. She was beginning to be really worried about the old witch. Good thing she only had three calls to make this morning.

Chapter Ten

"Here you are, nurse. Back home safe and sound."

Gloria eased herself down from the lorry and took a firm grip on her crutches. "Thank you so much, Mr. Wallace. We'd still be waiting for a bus if it weren't for you."

"Glad I came by when I did. Not much chance of getting a bus when Jerry just bombed the bus station, is there?"

None at all as it worked out. "Thank you again."

"Want a cup of tea?" she asked Andrew, who'd helped her get out.

"No thanks. Must get up to the plant somehow." To underscore his point, he climbed back into the lorry. "If you'd drop me by the Post Office, Mr. Wallace, I can walk down to my billet from there."

Wouldn't have killed him to walk from here but he'd made his point.

"Good-bye, Mr. Wallace. Mr. Barron." She made a point of smiling at the farmer before hobbling up the garden path.

Smashing!

And that's about what she felt like doing. Starting with her head. She was an utter and total fool and Andrew Barron was a pig. She had to chuckle at that, having ridden back with Farmer Wallace and a load of shoats.

She shut the door behind her, and with certain acrobatics she'd mastered in the past week, took off her coat and filled the kettle. Amazing really what you could do with one hand.

As the kettle boiled, she sat down at the kitchen table and considered the events of the past twelve hours.

Yes, Andrew was a pig. He'd barely spoken to her all morning. Yes, he had been occupied with air raid wardens and the police over his car, but how much time would, "Gloria, I had a wonderful time last night. You are the most fantastic woman in the world" have taken?

He'd been taciturn at breakfast, curt when she tried to make conversation during the interminable wait for a bus, and barely spoken ten words on the ride back. In fact, she'd suspected he'd been on the verge of turning down Farmer Wallace's more than welcome offer of a lift.

But he'd been glad to get back all the same. Just couldn't spare the time to have a cup of tea with her. Damn!

Maybe it was part her fault. She had rather thrown herself at him, but he'd been more than willing and heck, he'd had a packet of sheaths in his pocket, so he'd obviously considered the possibility of ending the evening in bed.

Damn and double damn him! Maybe that was what it was all about, buy her dinner—when all she got was soup and lumpy porridge and toast for breakfast—and sweet talk her into bed. And hadn't the Luftwaffe cooperated nicely?

Nothing like adrenaline flowing to ease inhibitions and roil up physical need.

Not any more! She hobbled over to the stove, risked scalding and scarring to pour the water into the teapot with one hand, while standing on one leg. Then put the lid on and waited for it to brew.

She should have listened to her instinct and never gone out with him. Humans—human men, she amended—were nothing but trouble for a Were.

But she had enjoyed the best sex she'd ever had. Not that

her experience was that extensive. Pity Andrew turned out to be a pig. She'd just drown her sorrows by lining her stomach with tannin.

She was halfway though her second cup and thinking she should call someone and ask for a lift down to the village hall, when the phone rang.

It was Alice. "Gloria, everything alright?"

She'd keep the truth to herself. "I'm unhurt, so's Mr. Barron. His car is a charred heap." And part of her wished he were. No, not really.

"Mr. Barron? It's like that is it?" It most definitely was. "Yes, Alice."

"That must explain why he just had a set-to with the new baker."

Really? "What happened?" Not that she was interested.

"Not much really. Seems Mr. Block—the new baker who just opened up shop this morning—stopped him on the street and asked if he wanted bread deliveries up at the plant. Seemed he didn't and was quite explicit about it. I doubt old Mrs. Poley will ever quite recover."

Gloria had to smile. Mrs. Poley was so "nice" she asked for poitrine of lamb instead of breast. "Was blood spilled?"

"Fortunately, no. But I don't think either will be buying the other a pint at the Pig and Whistle any time soon."

Too damn bad. Didn't seem as if he'd be buying her one either. "Are the evacuees arriving today?"

"That's why I called—not really to quiz you about last night. We got a call from the stationmaster in Leatherhead that they are on their way. If you'd just man the tea urns and hand out sandwiches it would be a help."

"Come and get me."

"I'm on my way."

At least she'd be busy all afternoon. Nothing like a village hall milling with tired and fractious children to take care of ruffled sensibilities and a bruised heart.

* * *

"Tell me," Gloria asked Alice, once she was settled in the passenger seat. "Did anyone notice we were gone last night?"

Understandable worry. Better set her mind at rest. Then find out what had or had not happened last night. "Six people reported your milk not taken in to Sergeant Jones. Not sure if Andrew was missed, but don't worry." Better reassure her there. "Mother Longhurst disappearing has completely taken over village gossip and knocked out any speculation about your whereabouts or activity last night."

Gloria turned a rather shocked face in Alice's direction. "What happened?"

Alice told her.

"So, she left yesterday, to ride her bicycle over to Bringham and hasn't been seen since?"

"That's pretty much it. Gran called all the hospitals. No one meeting the description has been brought in since yesterday. Sergeant Jones asked the police over in Bringham to check on things but seems she just disappeared."

"She must have had a heart attack or collapsed on the way. She wasn't young after all. Far too old to be riding a bicycle especially over the hills between here and Bringham."

Alice didn't seem convinced. "I don't know, I really don't. She's old, yes, but I saw her last week and she was as hale and crotchety as ever."

"She called you in?" She sounded rather disbelieving. Understandable.

"Not professionally. She'd rather die first." And maybe had. "I stopped by about something else." And no way was she telling Gloria why. "I went by this morning with a sack of parsnips Gran promised her." Make it sound utterly mundane. Gloria would not understand about stone knives and slaying vampires. "I can't but worry, thinking she might be lying in a ditch or by the side of a lane somewhere."

"If she is, she has my sympathies."

That would have been a great opener to ask about Andrew and what appeared to have gone wrong, but they were at the village hall. Alice's curiosity would have to wait to be satisfied.

Andrew Barron knew himself to be a fool. A total, unmitigated ass. No two ways about it. If Pete Willows hadn't rolled up in a jeep just in time, he, Andrew Barron, responsible government employee, in a top secret project (well, supposedly top secret, seemed the whole village knew about it) would have ended up brawling with the baker on the village green.

Brilliant move on his part.

"Something wrong, sir?" Willows asked. "I hear you had a rough time of it last night."

The lad didn't know the half! But rough was the wrong adjective. He wasn't thinking about it. Not right now. Sooner or later he'd have to sort out why he'd acted with such abandon. He could blame it on the stress of the evening, anxiety, the proximity of the sexiest woman he'd ever met, or tell the truth and say he had the self-control of a rat. "Got caught in a raid. No one hurt. At least not in our part of town. One shop got it, and they think the force shattered my petrol tank and caused the fire."

"Good thing you weren't in it."

"Yes. When we get up there, can you see what we have that we can spare for a vehicle? I don't fancy cycling all this way and am not going to ask you to make this trip twice a day."

"Wouldn't mind, sir, but I'll ask. Bet we have something, but it might be one of the big lorries."

"I bet they eat petrol."

"They do. We'll see what we can manage."

At least it was his own car that burned up. He'd have had a hard time explaining if he'd been using government property to take Gloria out to dinner.

Gloria! What was he going to do?

Apologize? Crawl into a hole? Spend the rest of his waking hours up at the plant?

That was impossible. He had to see her again, even if she clobbered him one.

Gloria poured out her *n*th cup of tea. Nothing like being swamped with evacuees to forget her own frayed sensibilities. They'd been expecting twenty-five and thirty had arrived. Instead of two teachers, one was sent. Gloria liked her on sight. Mary Prioux was obviously dead on her feet. Who wouldn't be after eighteen hours' travel with that many children? But after a cup of tea, "As strong as you can make it, I need the caffeine," she was taking charge, calming anxious children and chewing out a group of boisterous boys who'd been caught looking at the girls under the toilet door.

"Thank you for putting all this on," she said, as she came back for another stack of sandwiches. "I don't think any of us have seen real ham since we left Guernsey."

"One of the farmers donated it and Mrs. Gibson cooked it," Gloria said. "Enjoy it, as you might not see any more for a while." She actually nicked a couple for herself.

"Are things short here? They were up in Sheffield."

"Not too bad. Most people grow a lot of their own vegetables and keep chickens. There's a lot of bartering going on. I've heard things are scarce at times in London."

Mary nodded. "Have to be. Sheffield was no picnic. It was a mistake that sent us there. The children were pretty much miserable. Most are country children. I think they'll be happier here. And safer," she added.

"We get our share of bombs." It was only fair to point that out. "The vicarage got hit last month and there was damage to a couple of houses. Dorking and Leatherhead have had some nasty raids." She was not about to offer any more specifics about Dorking raids, not with several curious ears about to flap.

"But round here it's been mostly fields that ended up as craters and a pig sty. We've been lucky I suppose."

"I hope your luck holds," Mary said. "I'd hate for the children to be bombed out a second time." She shrugged. "Oh well. Enough of that. Better get on with feeding the masses. How long are we going to be waiting do you think?"

Gloria looked over at the children. Poor little blighters worn out after a long, slow train ride, and no doubt wondering where they were ending up next. "Once the word gets out that you've arrived, people will start coming in. Must be rotten having to wait and see if anyone wants you."

Mary nodded. "And there's always someone suffering the humiliation of being the last to be picked. Like choosing teams at games."

That had never been a worry for Gloria. Once everyone realized how fast she could run, she was always picked first. Never stopped her being aware of how different she was though.

Alice came over. "How are they holding up?" she asked Mary.

"Some are worried, some are scared. I've a few bent on showing just how badly they can behave but most are so weary they're past caring."

"What about you? You've got to be dead on your feet."

"Pretty much," Mary admitted. "But just getting here was a relief. Three times we got shunted into sidings or stopped on the tracks as there was bombing in a town ahead. Daylight doesn't stop that it seems. Between us," she lowered her voice, "some days I wonder if sending them all away was the best after all."

"They'd be under the Germans, if they hadn't!" Gloria said. Just thinking of being invaded gave her icicles under the skin.

"I know but they'd be with their families and in their own beds. My sister stayed, she's married with two little children. I get those Red Cross letters from her once in a while. I know she watches what she says but so far seems the worst the Germans have done is make everyone drive on the right-hand side and forbid taking boats out. No one can fish so food's a problem but so it is here." She shrugged. "I'd better stop or someone will accuse me of defeatism."

"Not us," Alice and Gloria spoke in unison.

"I think you're brave," Gloria said, "coping with other people's children while you're worried about things at home."

"Some days, I wonder if we'll ever see home again," Mary said, with a sigh, "but I mustn't grumble. I've just had the best ham sandwich I've eaten in months and enough cups of tea to need a stroll down to the ladies'."

"I like her," Gloria said, as Mary crossed the village hall. "Certainly more agreeable than those two old sticks who came down with the Shoreditch children."

"About thirty years younger too," Alice added. "It's got to be hellish worrying about what's happening at home. I wonder if I'd have gone or stayed."

"Let's hope we never have to make that choice."

"Let's hope someone turns up soon for these children. The committee ladies are all in a tizz wazz over not having food for another meal."

"They'll come." Gloria hoped, for the sake of the poor little blighters, three of whom were now asleep on the floor.

"I hope. Mrs. Chivers was dropping heavy hints that Gran and I should take half a dozen as we have such a big house. I told her Gran was already doing her share of war work, and my hours were so erratic it just wouldn't work out."

Made sense, Gloria supposed, although there was lots of space up at The Gallop. It had come in handy after the vicarage bombing. "Better keep your house free for emergencies, like last month."

"Tell her that, please, if she starts up again within earshot."

"Promise." Gloria had wondered why Alice had never taken in evacuees. Mind you, she hadn't either. She had housed June Groves for a week after the vicarage was bombed but that had been it. The last thing Gloria needed was a couple of inquisitive children in the house when she needed to shift.

And now three inquisitive little girls walked across the hall.

"Excuse me, nurse," one said, "but is anybody going to come for us?"

Gloria's heart clenched for them. "Yes, someone will. I promise."

Providence was on her side. Not five minutes later, Tom Longhurst walked in and headed straight for Mrs. Chivers and her stack of forms and papers.

"Mr. Longhurst," Mrs. Chivers's voice boomed. It all but echoed off the rafters. "What can we do for you?"

"Mother sent me," he said. "Told me we have room for three children."

In an instant every child in the room sat or stood upright and thirty pairs of eyes begged to be chosen.

"What age?" Mrs. Chivers asked, determined to keep perfect records.

"Old enough to help peel potatoes and make their own beds. And they have to know how to ride a bicycle."

A couple of giggles broke the very pregnant silence. It was on the tip of Gloria's tongue to ask him to please take all of them and save twenty-seven the pain of not being chosen.

"I can make my own bed," a girl called from halfway down the line and blushed crimson as everyone looked at her. "And I can peel potatoes. I have to. My brothers eat so much."

Two boys, the brothers Gloria guessed, rolled their eyes. One muttered, "Shut up, Sara."

"Sara, are you?" Tom Longhurst asked.

"Yes, sir." She stepped forward.

"Well, Sara, I have a farm. Do you know what end of a cow the milk comes out?"

"Of course!"

"You pull the tail hard, right?"

"Only if you want to get kicked in the belly."

Just then Mary Prioux reappeared, puzzled at the giggles and sudden silence. "What's happened?" she asked Gloria and Alice.

"First claimant arrived," Alice replied. "Tom Longhurst. He and his mother have a farm about three miles away."

"I see, and Sara?"

"I think it's called stacking the cards in her favor. She overheard him say he would take three and she's offering herself and two brothers as a special deal."

Mary smiled. "I'd best see what's going on between them."

As she approached, Tom Longhurst smiled, and yes he did have a *smile*, no one was immune. Mary smiled back. Gloria could have sworn a spark flashed between them. They talked quietly, Sara took a step closer, Mary called to the boys, who picked up their battered suitcases and walked over to the table.

Five minutes later they were gone, the sound of Tom Longhurst's damaged silencer fading into the distance.

"Who exactly is he?" Mary asked, as disappointed quiet settled on the clusters of children.

"Tom?" Alice asked. "His family have worked the farm on Cherry Hill for generations. His father died a couple of years back so he got an exemption and works the farm with help from the Land Army."

"He's got a charming smile."

Even schoolteachers weren't immune, it seemed. "He's utterly charming," Alice replied. "I think he's charmed every female under thirty for a fifteen-mile radius. He was born with the knack."

"Alice?" Gloria asked, the single word loaded with questions.

Alice grinned. "I fell for him one summer when I was home from school. I was sixteen and susceptible. Yes, he's pleasant and charming and all that, but changes girlfriends as often as most men change their shirts."

"Oh!" Mary looked crestfallen for all of thirty seconds.

"Still the Marriot boys will be happy up on a farm. They live on a dairy farm in Forest."

"They'll be in their element," Alice agreed.

Other villagers arrived soon after. At one point there was a queue waiting for the WVS ladies to complete forms. The village had come through again. There would be some cramped cottages but every child had a roof over his head, and the gift of a day's holiday and a long weekend to settle in before they started school on Monday.

Mary looked as if she could use a break too. Once she got her billet.

"Have another cup of tea," Gloria offered. "If we don't drink it, it'll go to waste."

She was filling the cup when Mrs. Chivers came over. "Miss Prioux, we don't have anywhere for you yet."

"No," Mary agreed, sounding too tired to care too much. "I'm sure I'll find somewhere."

"Of course, what was I thinking? Nurse Prewitt, can you give Miss Prioux a place? You have a spare room don't you?

She couldn't refuse. Not when Mary was looking right at her, a glint of hope in her weary eyes. It was the last thing Gloria needed. She couldn't have another person in her cottage. Impossible. She liked Mary, felt a seldom experienced connection to her but how could she change and run with someone else in the house?

"What about it, nurse?" Mrs. Chivers was like a terrier with a rat.

What about it? It wasn't as if she was likely to change any time soon. "Of course. I'll be glad to have you, Mary. Grab your suitcase and we'll cadge a lift from Alice."

"A lift home? On one condition. You come and have dinner with Gran first."

Mary stopped midstep. "Are you sure? I hate to intrude."

Alice shook her head. "She's expecting Gloria, not that Gloria knows that and let me tell you, Mary, if I didn't bring you back with Gloria, my grandmother would have a thing or two to say about it."

"She would too," Gloria added. "You might as well know from the start, you don't argue with Mrs. Burrows."

"She sounds like my grandmother." Mary replied. "Thank you, it will be wonderful to eat with just grown-ups. The children have been good, all things considered, but the thought of an entire evening and night without them is wonderful."

"Come on then, Mary. Grab your crutches, Gloria, and let's see what Gran has in the oven."

Chapter Eleven

A very satisfactory first day of trading, Wilhelm Bloch decided. Aside from the rather irritating incident with that impudent mortal who ran the munitions plant. Really! The foolishness of the man! He had the cheek to take a vampire by the shoulder and shove. Bloch almost wished the man had punched. Would have been interesting to watch his reaction when his phlanges shattered but that would have garnered the attention Weiss was so eager to avoid.

The bell on the door pealed out. Bloch brushed his hands on his apron, a gesture so like his father's he almost smiled, and went forth to greet his umpteenth customer of the day.

"Good afternoon, madam." It was an old woman, upright, energetic. A bit stringy for nourishment, unless he got desperate. "What can I get you?"

"Good afternoon. Mr. Block, isn't it? A brown loaf, please." As he reached one off the shelf, she asked. "You don't happen to have Hovis, do you?"

Whatever the hell it was, no! "No, madam just bread."

Her gray eyebrows shot up. "Oh, I see."

Maybe he had been too sharp. No point in pissing off the old biddies. "Try Mr. Whorleigh, he might have some."

"Oh, yes." She took the loaf, put it in the basket over her arm and handed him a small silver coin.

Sixpence. Those boring lectures on currency were coming in handy here. "Here you are, madam, tuppence change." He felt quite pleased with himself remembering the strange vernacular. "Anything else I can get you?"

"Not today, thank you but would there be any chance of getting two dozen bridge rolls next Wednesday? For the church whist drive."

"By all means, madam." Once he found out what the hell bridge rolls were. So far today he'd been asked for Chelsea buns, crumpets and a Sally Lunn. Demanding peasants! He'd been tempted to ask them if they wanted a nice strudel or Bauembrot. Once the invasion came, he would and delight in their discomfort. Meanwhile . . . "Bridge rolls, madam. I'll see what I can do. No promises."

"I understand. If you can, it would be lovely. Good afternoon," she said and walked out.

Odd woman. Something strange about her. But then weren't all mortals a bit odd? Including the grocer Bloch was convinced was Other.

Bloch turned the sign to Closed a few minutes later and spent a satisfactory half hour counting the day's take and contemplating even better sales tomorrow. His bread was good. He hadn't forgotten how his father had beaten the process of baking into his none too obedient son. Strange after all these centuries to be following his long dead father's footsteps but if it served his purpose, which it did very nicely, he would not complain.

He'd soon discovered the advantage of leaving the register drawer open too. Just in case Weiss was monitoring sales. No reason why this trading effort shouldn't provide a little personal income. Who knew what lay ahead?

Whatever the others might say, Wilhelm Bloch had no intention of serving the Third Reich for eternity.

He scooped up the money and locked it in a small strongbox. He'd bank some in the account Weiss had set up. But not all.

All he needed now was the impudent servant to arrive and clean, and then he'd take a stroll back to the Pig and Whistle and look for an accommodating neck.

"Mary's a nice girl," Gran said with a tired nod of approval. "She'll be good company for Gloria. If it doesn't bother Gloria too much having someone else in her house."

Odd comment, but Alice knew Gran never spoke meaningless words. "Right now, having someone in the house is just what she needs. She must have a heck of a time coping with her leg in a cast. I'd considered asking her up here until the cast is off, but . . ."

"Lots of 'buts' aren't there, my love?"

Alice wouldn't argue. The world seemed full of them right now. Not much point in dwelling on them. "Want a warm drink before we turn in?"

"Yes. Be a dear and put the milk on and tell me, did you hear any more about Mother Longhurst?"

"Not a thing. Odd isn't it?"

"More than odd, dear. I'd go over to Bringham myself and see what I could find out, but there's something here in Brytewood that's worrying me."

Alice took two mugs off the dresser. Milk warmed and sweetened, she handed a mug to her grandmother and sat down opposite her on the other side of the fireplace. "What's bothering you, Gran?"

"The new baker."

Alice took a sip of the sweet milk and waited. Gran would tell in her own time.

"What would you think of a baker who had no idea what Hovis was?"

"I'd say he was suspect or been living under a rock for the

better part of his life. How could anyone not know what
Hovis is? Even now, there are ads plastered everywhere."

"I suspect he's Other."

Alice was lucky she didn't get warm milk down her nose.
She'd swallowed just in time. As it was she just gasped and
stared. "Other? Another vampire, you mean? What shall we
do? Start sharpening stakes?" Pity she'd returned the magic
knife, but if Mother Longhurst was right and it wouldn't work
again for years . . .

"Don't be so hasty, dear."

"Gran, if he is a vampire—as you suggest—shouldn't we
take care of him?"

"I said he was Other, my love, and suspect. Don't jump ahead
of me. We should first be sure that this one had evil intent."

Alice wasn't too sure "innocent until proven guilty" ap-
plied to possible vampires. "Aren't they all of evil intent?
Why wait until something bad happens?"

Gran was silent a moment or two as she put her mug down.
"We wait, Alice. Not until something bad happens, I hope, but
until we know for sure this one means harm."

"Don't they all mean harm?"

"Most, yes, but once I met one who did not." Alice was dying
to ask more, but Gran shook her head as if forestalling all
questions. "I want to talk to Howell about this"—consulting
Sergeant Pendragon made sense—"and I want you to go down
tomorrow and see what you think of him."

She was not sure about this one iota. "Doesn't it seem more
than coincidence that he arrives just a day or so after Miss
Waite was found dead in hospital?"

"Maybe, but who's to say they're connected?"

"Beats me, but her so-called 'nephew' proved to be a vampire, she was arrested as a spy and then conveniently dies
before she's well enough to get interrogated."

"You never did say what she died of, dear."

"They never found out. No one is supposed to know this,

but I heard her body was whisked off by a contingent of hush hush army people, and even the local police were told it was out of their jurisdiction."

"I don't suppose we'll ever know, dear." Gran drained her mug and stood. "Is Peter coming over this evening?"

"No, he said he was going down to the Pig with Sergeant Pendragon."

"I'm off to bed then."

She might as well follow.

Peter Watson wished to heaven he could down hold his beer like Howell Pendragon. Had to be something about a Dragon's metabolism, or the man had hollow legs. By Peter's count, the sergeant had downed five pints, at least. He'd switched his empty glass for Peter's full one twice. If he hadn't, Peter would need to be carried home. Instead, he was feeling comfortably mellow, but beginning to wonder why Howell was determined to sit tight until closing time. Peter had a job to get up for in the morning.

"Ah!" Howell said, with distinct sounds of satisfaction. "Time for another I think." He stood and picked up Peter's empty glass.

"I think it's my turn to buy."

"Let me get this one, lad," he said as he headed for the bar. "You can buy another time. When we're here for relaxation."

So, if they weren't here for entertainment, what were they doing here? It would be nice to know what was going on. Peter felt a bit out of his depth a good bit these days. Maybe he should spend more time with humans. Mind you, he was marrying a Pixie in four weeks, so he'd better get used to the way Others carried on.

Howell Pendragon reached the bar with his two empty tankards almost at the same minute as Wilhelm Bloch arrived to order a pint of bitter.

"Put that on my tab, Fred," Howell said. "You'll join me, Mr. Block, won't you?"

Bloch hesitated but nodded. "Thank you. Most hospitable of you."

"How's the first day of business been then, Mr. Block?" Fred Wise asked.

"Good." He smiled. "Very good."

"Let's celebrate then. It's not every day a new baker opens up shop. Come and sit with us."

Block didn't seem entirely thrilled with the invitation, but no doubt aware several pairs of eyes were watching him, he gave a smile and joined them.

"This is Peter Watson," Pendragon said, with a nod in Peter's direction. "Came to help out for the war effort and ends up marrying our doctor."

"Indeed." Block inclined his head. None too impressed by Peter's fantastic good fortune, it seemed. "Good to meet you, and good health." He raised his mug.

"Cheers," Peter said. So, this was why they'd sat here all evening. The sergeant wanted a close look at the new baker.

Howell raised his glass. "Welcome to Brytewood. Here's to fresh bread for the duration,"

They all drank to that.

"Had a good first day?" Pendragon asked. "Survived the scrutiny of the good women and old biddies of the village?"

Block gave a halfhearted smile. "Business was good. I hope it continues."

"Oh, it will, don't you worry. Staff of life, bread."

Howell was rather overdoing the jolly good fellow act, or was he trying to appear as if he'd downed five pints and about to start on his sixth?

"You were working late this evening," Peter said. Might as well add his share to the conversation. "Long hours, eh? Up early in the morning too."

"Up early, yes," Block replied. "But tonight I waited in vain for the woman expected to clean up the shop. She did not return. I had to sweep the floor." He sounded downright disgruntled as he downed his beer.

Snickering would be rude, but honestly, who did he think he was? "Would that have been Doris Brewer?" Peter asked.

"Perhaps. I didn't catch her name."

"I bet it was. She obliges for a lot of people in the village, including my fiancée." Had to get that in. "You must have misunderstood. She only came in to clean as a favor. She mentioned it to Alice, as Doris skipped most of her regulars for a couple of days. She's booked solid. I don't think you'll get her back."

Not good news to Baker Block. "That's impossible. She must."

"Go easy, young fellow," Pendragon said. "Steal Doris and you'll upset your best customers."

"But I must have a cleaner!"

Someone should point out that even Sam Whorleigh had been known to push a mop and broom around when necessary. Peter picked up his beer and drank to hide his smile. Where had this idiot come from?

"Not local are you?" Pendragon asked.

"No. Although I like the area. I may stay once this war is over."

"It grows on you," Pendragon went on. "Nice people. Accepting of outsiders which is more than you can say for some places. Been here twenty years myself. Came when my son was a lad. He's gone now though. He's off doing his bit for King and Country."

Block smiled. "As are so many young men." He raised an eyebrow at Peter.

Peter swallowed. The inevitable question he never quite knew how to handle. Might as well meet it head on. "I'm a CO. They sent me here as an ambulance driver, then decided I was needed to check for head lice and scabies."

"A CO?" Block repeated. Sounding downright perplexed.

Was he playing stupid? Had to be. Well he, Peter Watson, was not about to offer any more personal details.

"Where did you move from, then? Come far?" Pendragon asked.

"A distance," Block replied. "Yorkshire."

"You lost your accent fast, lad!" Pendragon laughed.

Block appeared to not share the joke. The man glowered at them both as he tipped his mug.

Fred Wise called for last orders.

Peter felt a nudge. "Time we left, lad. We've got to get up for work tomorrow. Goodnight, Mr. Block."

"Goodnight and thank you for the beer."

"My pleasure."

Block drained his glass and put it on the table. If it went on like this he might never have to spend money in the Pig and Whistle (ridiculous name for a hostelry) as long as he stayed. Was free beer worth the inquisition? He'd been instructed that a village pub was a good place to gather gossip. Mortals tended to get indiscreet when intoxicated, but so far he'd been the one providing information. Good thing he'd been prepared for it.

And he had a name for that servant. He needed her to return. He could coerce her, but was it worth alienating the village? Was that a warning the old man had given? How amusing. But worth considering.

Finding sustenance was his first concern. He needed a lone mortal.

He found one.

A visibly intoxicated individual, asleep, sitting with his back to the churchyard wall. In the light and shadows of the waxing moon, the creature appeared pathetic. Did they permit vagrants to sully the village? That would change very soon, but for now, he'd serve a useful purpose.

Aware that there were still patrons from the Pig and Whistle strolling home, Bloch picked up the sleeping man, muffling any waking cries with his hand, and leapt the wall.

A quick run and he was on the other side of the church and well sheltered from the eyes of curious peasants. It was a matter of a few minutes to rip open the man's shabby coat and tear his collar, exposing his scraggy neck.

There was a mutter of protest as Bloch dug his fangs into the pale skin, then came the heady rush of power as he drew on the life-giving mortal blood. It was always and ever a temptation to drain his donor dry, to savor the thrill and sweetness of the last few heartbeats, but Bloch was not making Eiche's mistakes. He would not leave corpses and risk discovery. He took just enough to last him a day or two and then left the old sot sleeping.

He might look around in bewilderment when he awoke inside the churchyard instead of on the grass verge, but no doubt the fool was too drunk to know where he'd collapsed.

Satisfied, replenished and energized with the warm blood racing through his veins, Bloch ran: leaping headstones, vaulting the wall, he raced down the lane toward the bakery. Passing a few last stragglers from the Pig, leaving them aware of nothing but a passing gust of wind.

What if he stopped and told them he was a vampire and out to take over the village for the victorious German Army?

No doubt the ignorant fools would shake their heads in disbelief at the mere mention of "vampire."

They would soon learn.

Chapter Twelve

Adlerroost, Bavaria

Bela Mestan eased back into her cell from the open window. It was not a dream or an illusion. Against all the laws of nature, three times now, she had passed the barrier of forged iron that ringed her window. She was no longer a prisoner of these foul humans.

With that knowledge came decisions. She had to clear her head of the giddiness of triumph. She was perhaps the only living Fairy able to pass forged iron. The power and strength she'd absorbed at the vampire Eiche's destruction, strength that increased each time one of those hideous vampires fed, gave her a chance of freedom. Indeed at one point, as she clung to the stone walls of the schloss and felt the autumn wind on her skin, she felt she could truly fly, like the Fairies of legend.

She'd satisfy herself with running. Far, far away.

She had to think and plan carefully. She could not risk capture. When she fled, it had to be for life. To never again be forced into servitude by these liars and deceivers. She would never forget or forgive the ignominy and shame of the pain of their fangs in her flesh. But the hateful bond that was forged had been twisted by chance to her advantage.

Eiche, the second to feed off her, had died and she had absorbed his strength.

What if another vampire perished?

Small chance. One being destroyed was beyond likelihood. A second would venture into impossibility.

Unless the English possessed magic unknown to Fairies.

The door opened. She'd been so lost in her thoughts, she'd failed to hear her captors approach. She must not make that mistake twice.

Zuerst and Zweiten, her gaolors and interrogators, closed the door behind.

"Fraulein," Zuerst said. "You look flushed. Are you not well?"

As if her health, or lack of it, was of any great concern. As long as she still linked with the vampires, she could be lying inert for all they cared. "I'm well. Just a little tired. There has been movement. Bloch has been active and angry."

"You sense Bloch's anger?" Zweiten asked.

"Yes. He is often angry."

"Why?"

"I don't know why. I can not keep the link all the time." Couldn't stand to.

"The others are angry?"

"No." Thank all the woodland gods! "Just Bloch. You told me to focus on him."

"We know what we ordered, fraulein," Zuerst snapped. "Tell us about Bloch."

"He is moving but not far. He is around heat at times." That got them mildly interested. She had to be confirming what they expected. "He recently fed."

"Did he kill?" Zweiten asked.

"Not that I could sense." She had sensed every time Eiche had killed. The connection worried her. Kept alive the horror of them feeding off her, but . . .

"Fraulein, pay attention! You know the price of failing us?" She nodded. "Disappoint us and your family dies."

She schooled her face to passivity. They were liars. Only her sister Gela lived, and she clung to existence by faltering hopes. "I have answered all your questions. Told you all I sense and feel from the vampires. I link to them whenever you order me to. What more do you want of me?"

"Do not try us! You are one of the woodland degenerates. Fail us and you die with your family."

She was more than weary of their threats, lies and bullying. Bela shut her eyes a moment, to connect with the air outside. "Do you want me to continue to link with Bloch? What about the others?"

"Are they gathering?" Zweiten asked.

"Weiss and Schmidt have once. Schmidt is feeding every day off his host." Maybe that was a mistake. She did not want them to ever suspect what the vampires' feeding did to her.

"Forget Schmidt!" Zuerst said. "Concentrate all your efforts on Bloch."

She nodded. "I will."

"You are serving us well, fraulein. We will not forget," Zweiten said. As if she'd forget either. "Is there something you wish?"

She stared with surprise. "Wish?" To run free in the woods. To find her sister. To avenge her parents' slaughter.

"For your comfort."

She might never have the offer again. "Some more blankets perhaps?" They might be useful when she fled. "The nights are getting chill."

"You will have them, fraulein. The Reich is not ungrateful for your cooperation."

They were gone. Leaving her worried. Why this concern over her comfort? To relax and disarm her before the next horror? Were there more vampires waiting? That thought had her shuddering.

She must escape and soon. Leave while she still had the strength to pass the barrier that surrounded her window.

But where? Her home in the Sudetenland was overrun. What did she need? Sweet earth under her feet and woods to run in. It was all she longed for now. Once in her foolish youth she'd tried living in a human city. Never again.

Beyond her window, woods and mountains stretched in all directions. What else did she need?

Only Gela, her sister.

And revenge.

Chapter Thirteen

Pain prevents sleep. Gloria's leg ached like nobody's business. Worries keep you awake. Gloria was worrying. If she had two good legs, she'd give in, get up and clean the house or wash the windows. No, that would be a bad idea. She'd take off all the glued tape she'd put up so painstakingly to protect against glass breaking, a year or more ago.

Darn. Her options appeared to be to lie in bed awake, or sit up in bed awake. She did the latter, reaching for the torch under her pillow and pondering if it was worth the effort to get up and turn on a light so she could see well enough to read.

She'd no doubt bump into something on the way, make a frightful din, fall over or drop her wretched crutches and wake Mary.

That was another problem. She had nothing against Mary. Liked her on sight in fact. But how was she going to manage shifting with another person in the house?

One more worry to keep her awake. A couple of codeine tablets would take care of the bone deep ache in her leg but do nothing for the cramping of her heart. Better take care of the leg. Moving as quietly as she could, she bumped downstairs into the kitchen, got herself a glass of water and swallowed two codeine.

It helped the leg pain.

The clock on the mantel struck one. This was verging on the ridiculous. Here she was, losing sleep over Andrew Barron while he, no doubt, was snoring his head off.

Damn him! She grabbed her crutches, clumped over to the phone and scowled at the list of phone numbers written on her pad. Yes, she had Andrew's right there.

She picked up the receiver.

"Number please?" an impossibly cheery voice asked. Gloria gave the number and the telephonist paused. "Nurse Prewitt, not an emergency, I hope."

Darn. It was going to be all over the village by morning. Let it be! "Just something came up." Very convincing that, ha! She hoped the darn exchange was too busy tonight to listen in.

Come to that, what in creation was she going to say to him?

The phone rang its familiar burr burr on the other end. After seven ringing tones, the receiver was picked up. "Hello?"

She couldn't, for the life of her, remember what she meant to say.

"Hello?" He sounded sleepy and irritated, not a good beginning for a serious talk about their future together. Assuming they had one, of course.

"Andrew?" Silly that. Who else would it be?

"Yes, Andrew Barron speaking."

"It's Gloria."

He was silent a good several seconds. Shocked, stunned and flabbergasted no doubt. "Gloria?" he repeated, sounding confused. "What's the matter?" His voice was worried now.

"Nothing."

"Gloria," he spoke slowly, "you called me in the middle of the night to tell me nothing is wrong?"

Did sound a bit ludicrous put that way. "Not exactly. I called because I wanted to talk to you."

"I see." That was most likely as truthful as her "nothing." "Something on your mind?"

Yes, but now it came to the point . . . Oh dash it, she'd gone this far. In for a penny, in for a pound. "Andrew, when we got back this morning, why were you so cool towards me?"

It was out. She'd done it, asked it, and no doubt the silence on the line pretty much said she'd blown it utterly.

"Gloria," he said, after what seemed an eternity. Was he tired? Cross? Just plain fed up? "You want to talk about that? Now?"

"Yes." This was totally lunatic.

"Alright." That she doubted but wasn't about to contradict. "What did you expect this morning, Gloria? You wanted me to kiss you good-bye with Fred Wallace watching?"

Yes, she had. "What's so unpleasant about that?"

"Nothing!" Now he sounded peeved. "I was trying to be discreet, Gloria. You want the whole village talking about us?"

Sounded like a pretty nice idea. "Why not?"

"Christ almighty, Gloria! Here I am trying to do the right thing and avoid village gossip and you . . ." Words obviously failed him.

She still had plenty. "I was just a bit confused, Andrew. Last night we . . ." Made love like a pair of demented rabbits. ". . . were intimate. You said you loved me." But men did all the time didn't they? "In the morning you were more concerned about your damn car than me." Unfair that but she was just getting going, "and when we got back, I barely merited a handshake."

Exasperated sigh wasn't the word. Fair enough, let him explain things.

"Gloria."

"Yes?"

"I meant every damn word I said last night. In case you didn't get it the first time: I love you. It wasn't a string of meaningless words nor was it a ruse to get you in bed. I love you. Got that?"

"Yes." So far anyway. "Why the polar ice cap act?"

It was more like a tsk of exasperation this time. "My mistake, Gloria. I thought you might regret what happened."

"Why the hell would I?"

"Well, dear, women have been known to regret afterwards, especially if . . ."

"Andrew Barron! Women you customarily associate with might. I don't!"

"Alright."

"No it's not! Do you think for one stupid, asinine minute, I would have gone to bed with you and made love like we did if it wasn't what I wanted?" Let him put that in his pipe and smoke it!

He did. For several seconds. "I've upset you."

Very perceptive of him! "Yes, you have."

"Gloria, this might be better to wait until morning."

"Why?"

"I'm not at my best at 2 a.m."

Who was? "Look, Andrew. I'm sorry I woke you but I've been lying awake wondering how things are between us and if you ever wanted to see me again." Silly that. They were bound to see each other.

He understood. "Have you been listening to me? I want to see you but I don't want it broadcast all over the village."

"Why not?" She was pushing the issue. She did understand, but didn't need his misplaced chivalry.

"For crying out loud, Gloria. Do you want the old biddies talking about you over their knitting?"

Sounded like fun. "I like you, Andrew, I think I'm beginning to love you, but don't quite get all this havey cavey business."

"What do you want? Me to kiss you in the middle of the High Street?"

"Yes, Andrew. Twelve o'clock on Saturday. You're off work this weekend, right?"

Splutter was the word for the noise echoing in her ear. "You can't possibly be serious!"

"Perfectly. If you want to take me out Saturday night, kiss

me at noon in the middle of the High Street. Right in front of the Post Office. See you then!"

It wasn't nice to bang the receiver down but if felt very satisfying.

She leaned against the banisters and sighed. Her head was spinning.

"Gloria, are you feeling ill?"

Heaven help her! She'd as good as forgotten she had a visitor. Mary stood at the top of the stairs, her coat over her long flannel nightgown.

"I am feeling . . . cold."

Mary came down the stairs. "Is something the matter?"

"Not exactly. I just . . ." Mary sat beside her on the stairs. Gloria shook her head and shared the gist of her recent conversation and an expurgated version of the night before.

"You know what I think?" Mary said. "You're upset and this had best wait until morning. Are you feeling alright?"

"A bit lightheaded and sleepy."

"Are you on pain medicine?"

Gloria nodded. "I took a couple of codeines a while back."

"Let's get you to bed and we can talk about this in the morning."

She was wobbly and weary but made it back to her bed. "Thanks, Mary."

"Good night, Gloria. Sleep well."

She did. Until hours later, when the door opened and a soft voice called, "Gloria?"

Chapter Fourteen

Gloria opened her eyes. Someone in the house? Of course! "Mary?"

"I didn't want to wake you earlier but would you like a cup of tea?"

Might help the fog in her brain. "Thank you." She pulled herself to sitting and took the proffered cup. "You're an angel. Did you get one yourself?"

"Yes, have had two actually. Hope you didn't mind me poking around your kitchen."

Gloria took a sip of tea. It was warm, wet and reviving. "For bringing me this, Mary, poke all you want. There isn't much, but I think there's some bread left for toast."

"I found it but its best use might be as a murder weapon."

Damn. Was it that stale? "Sorry." Somewhere there was a packet of porridge oats but she'd last had porridge with Andrew and memories of that little fiasco stirred a vague flicker in her brain. "Holy smoke!" She was wide awake, her heart pounding in the morning quiet. "Mary, did I call Andrew last night and wake you up?"

Mary nodded. "You told me about your challenge to him."

"What challenge?"

Mary told her.

Gloria barely missed dousing herself with hot tea. Heavens! What was she going to do? Pack up and run away? Join the Army Nursing Corps and hope to get posted thousands of miles away? Shift for good and live in the woods for the rest of her life? "I was insane."

"I don't think so. Just upset and full of codeine."

"It's never done that to me before."

"Maybe you've never had that worry before."

Maybe she should never leave the house again. "What the heck am I going to do?"

"Start by getting dressed. I'll scrounge up something for breakfast. Maybe bread and milk? Then we hash things over," Mary said. "If you want, that is. I don't want to intrude."

"Since I intruded on your sleep with my dilemma and insanity, I think you're being the soul of understanding."

"Who hasn't had men problems?"

Good question and one Gloria pondered as she washed and dressed. Seemed Mary was going to be an absolute brick. Maybe having her in the house would be super.

Until full moon.

Once dressed, Gloria went into the kitchen. A bowl of warm bread and milk sat on the table.

"Did you find the honey?" Gloria asked. "On the right-hand side in the pantry."

Mary fetched it and put a fresh pot of tea on the table. For some minutes, conversation lagged.

As she pushed her empty bowl aside, Gloria asked. "Alright, Mary, let me get this straight. I called Andrew, in the small hours, and told him to kiss me at midday in front of the Post Office."

"That was the gist of it, and who's Andrew?"

Someone I really fancy. The man who knocked me off my bicycle and got me this cast. The gorgeous human I had superhuman sex with the night before last. "He's this chap. He runs the place up on the heath we can't talk about and he took me out to dinner on Wednesday."

"You've just been out with him once?"

Actually they'd been very much in, but that she was not discussing. "Yes."

"You've fallen for him in a hard way, haven't you?"

"You could say that."

Mary smiled. "Put it this way, do you regularly call up men in the small hours and demand they kiss you in the middle of the village at high noon?"

"Not regularly. Not ever actually. I had to be out of my mind."

"Or maybe lost your inhibitions."

"Lost my marbles more like! What the blazes am I going to do?" Hardly fair to dump this on an almost stranger just hours after she'd arrived in Brytewood.

"Either meet him in the High Street on Saturday or stay in your house all day until Sunday. If this is how it is here, I don't think I'm ever going out to dinner with anyone."

Gloria laughed. A bit of a tight, strangled one but it was a laugh.

And then the phone rang.

It was Alice. "Gloria, want to do any shopping? I'll pick you up. Gran wants us to see what we think about the new baker."

One man was more than she could cope with right now. "Why?"

"Long, convoluted story. Can I explain when I get there?"

Explain what? "I suppose so." That sounded ungracious. And did she need to go shopping? If the pantry was anything to go by, yes. And she was safe today. Andrew would be up at the munitions camp. Better go today than risk tomorrow.

"I won't be long. Get your shopping list."

"Alright."

As she replaced the receiver and clumped back into the kitchen, she saw Mary was washing up. "We need to work out a fair division here," Gloria said. "You made breakfast. I can wash up."

"It's not that much and I'm glad to help, honest. I'm going out soon. Thought I'd best go down to the school and see what I can do to get ready for Monday."

"Alice is coming down to take me shopping. Do you have your ration book handy? Is it alright with you if I register your name at Whorleigh's?"

"That's the grocer?"

"The one and only. There's more choice in Leatherhead, but it means a bus ride. I pretty much manage with what we have here. We've a butcher and the Post Office sells a few things. Some of the farmers come around from time to time with fruit and vegetables. And the bakery just reopened." She'd have a few questions for Alice when she arrived. "I'll get what I can for the weekend. And if you want to hang on a few minutes Alice can give you a lift to the school."

Mary shook her head. "I should get used to the walk, but a lift would be nice, this time, since I've no idea where I'm going."

"It's hard to get lost here. The village isn't that big and if you do, everyone else knows their way around.

"Sounds a bit like home."

Alice dropped Mary at the school, and headed back toward the village center.

"What's going on?" Gloria asked.

A very good question. Alice could hardly tell sensible, practical Gloria that Gran thought the new baker might be a hostile vampire. Better pick her words very carefully. She pulled the car to the side of the road by the church and turned off the engine. "This is going to sound really vague." If not totally ridiculous. "But Gran thinks there's something odd about the new baker. She wants me to get an eyeful and let her know what I think.

She was insistent I ask you to come. She said you had a good sense for people." Whatever Gran meant by that.

Gloria gave her such a worried look that Alice wished she'd never agreed to this farcical idea.

"She thinks I can sense things about people? How?" Gloria asked.

"I think she means you have a knack for knowing if people are malingering or trying things on. She believes the new baker is up to something."

"And I'm supposed to intuit this?"

"No, Gloria. You're supposed to go in, buy a loaf of bread and let Gran know if you 'feel' anything odd about the man."

"Right now, I think there's something odd about most men!"

"Difficulties with Andrew?"

Gloria let out a long sigh. Difficulties? If this was what happened when you let your heart lead your head, she was reining in her heart. For good. "More like a tangle of Gordian proportions!" She retold the whole fiasco. Only this being Alice, she got the unexpurgated version.

"Oh, my giddy aunt! You'd not been drinking before you took the codeine, had you?"

"Drinking, Alice? While I'm clumping about on crutches? Give me a break!" Perhaps not the best expression to use in the circumstances. "I'd had a cup of cocoa with Mary Prioux and that was that."

"Definitely an odd reaction. What are you doing tomorrow? Standing by the bus stop and pretending it's a bus you want, not Andrew?"

Very funny! "I'm thinking of getting the dawn train up to London and staying there all day."

Alice let out a little snigger. "Is that journey really necessary? Sorry Gloria, I know it's not funny but seriously, what are you going to do?"

"Right now, I'm going shopping for the weekend. I'll

decide later what to do about Andrew." Going up to Town for the day sounded better by the minute.

Alice reached across the car and hugged Gloria. "For want of better or more brilliant advice, follow your heart."

"I did that on Wednesday night and look where it got me."

"Cheer up. Look at it this way. If you're in a tizz wazz over this, think what it's doing to him."

That was a thought. Although he, presumably, knew how he felt. She was the one lost at sea here. "You know this is all your fault, Alice." Might as well get her back for the "necessary journey" crack.

"Me? How is it my fault?"

"You were the one suggested I go out with him. Told me a fling would do me good."

That silenced her for a good ten seconds or so. "The fling did you good. It's the aftermath that threw you off kelter."

Was that what it was called? Gloria leaned back in her seat and looked out across the churchyard. Odd. "I wonder what Sergeant Jones is doing by the church."

"Eh?" Alice looked too. "Constable Parlett is there as well and Reverend Roundhill." She shrugged. "Maybe the Germans dropped more of those pamphlets overnight."

As they both watched and wondered, Constable Parlett walked up to the car. "Good thing you're here, doctor. Would you mind coming and have a look? Seems as though old Reg Brown had a couple too many last night."

Chapter Fifteen

"You go on ahead," Gloria said. "I'll come along at my own speed."

Alice hesitated but she was needed. "Be careful on the gravel."

"I'll walk with the nurse, doctor. See nothing happens to her," Constable Parlett said.

Alice grabbed her bag from the back seat and went ahead. A glance at the recumbent Reg Brown and Alice knew she wasn't really needed. Reg Brown might have downed a few too many last night but he was now permanently sober.

"He's gone," Alice said as she stood up and brushed grass and mud off her skirt. She looked at the sergeant. "Odd that he should be over here, isn't it?"

Sergeant Jones nodded. "Must have wanted a change of venue."

Alice turned to Reverend Roundhill. The poor man looked more haggard and worried every time she saw him. His wife had never gained consciousness after the bombing, at this point wasn't expected to and it was only a matter of time before their vicar was a widower. "What do you think, Reverend Roundhill?"

"I don't understand it, doctor. Old Reg used to sit by the

wall to drink. His wife wouldn't let him have alcohol in the house, and I think he'd made himself unwelcome in the Pig. He'd often pass out and I'd rouse him to get home, or call for the law to help, but he was always in the same spot." He pointed across the churchyard. "Down there by the corner of the wall. There's a grassy patch he used to pick. I don't think he ever came into the churchyard."

Alice tamped down the irreverent levity that suggested he'd been struck down for sacrilege. "We'd better call to have him picked up and I'll go and tell his widow."

"Let me do it," Reverend Roundhill said. "She was a church-goer even if Sam wasn't."

Alice wouldn't argue. She hated breaking death news to a family and doubted it would ever get easy.

"Can you give us a cause of death, doctor?" Sergeant Jones asked.

It seemed so obvious. There was no bloody ripped-out throat as in Farmer Morgan's death last month, and Reg Brown was a habitual drunk; but given what had been going on in Bryte-wood the past few weeks, one couldn't help wondering. Alice bent over the body and looked at his staring eyes, his pale skin, and his shrunken, narrow wrists. There hadn't been a frost last night, but it had rained, and his clothes were still damp. He'd no doubt have caught pneumonia if he'd lived. He was thin. Wasted from alcohol. Pity they didn't ration that!

She was about to stand and tell Sergeant Jones to go ahead and call for an ambulance to collect the body when she noticed a bruise on Reg's neck: A faint mark, like a large insect bite.

"Something wrong, doctor?" Sergeant Jones asked.

What wild instinct took over her tongue and made her act against all professional ethics, she'd never know. "No. Nothing wrong." Other than that a man was dead. If she voiced her sus-picions aloud, they'd think she'd been drinking. Human law could do nothing anyway. Alice stood and snapped her bag closed.

And caught a very odd look from Gloria standing to one side, doing her best to balance crutches on the damp gravel.

"Something was wrong, wasn't it?" Gloria asked, as she got in the car.

"What do you mean?"

"About the body."

Gloria knew her too well, that was all. "He's been drinking himself to death for years and finally succeeded. Sad really but . . ." She shook her head as she put the key in the ignition. "Too many people are dying these days and it isn't going to get any better."

"Most likely worse." Gloria let out a very long sigh. "I was talking to Mary last night. She's worried sick about her family left on Guernsey and what's happening with the Germans there. Seems only a matter of time before they cross the rest of the Channel. Do you really think a few concrete barriers and some barbed wire will hold them back?"

"It's more than just those dragon's teeth across the fields. I've heard the beaches are blocked with barbed wire and mines and heaven knows what."

"I hope it works." She sighed. "Where are we stopping first?"

"We can go anywhere you like. I'll park close. The law is too occupied to worry about parking where I shouldn't."

"Let's start at Whorleigh's." Get it over with. If there was anywhere else to buy things, she'd go there. She despised the way Sam Whorleigh shamelessly gouged prices, kept things below the counter and got away with it. She didn't like to think of either of the policemen taking bribes or choice cuts of bacon on the side but how else was Whorleigh carrying on his little black market sideline with impunity?

Funny how when she actually spoke to him, her animosity eased. Most likely because she needed food. She did have the strength of will to turn down his offer to save her a couple of tins of baked beans when they came in next week. At the butcher's she'd been prepared to splurge her coupons on a couple of pork chops but gladly took his offer of a nice slice of liver. Two slices, when she mentioned she had the evacuated schoolteacher in her house. Nice to get something off-ration and save her coupons. Alice took the lot back to the car while Gloria just hoped Mary liked liver. Pity she had no bacon, but she was not going back to ask a favor of Whorleigh and heck, she had onions. Masses of them, in fact. Onions and nice gravy would be fine.

"You should be in the middle of the street, but I'm not fussy."

Before Gloria had time to register that Andrew stood right in front of her, he had her in his arms, lifting her off her feet. Her crutches clattered to the ground as he plastered his mouth on hers.

She was about to say something but it was impossible with her lips as good as glued to his and what was there to say? Her brain zapped out and nothing mattered. Except Andrew, his arms around her, and the sheer and utter bliss of his kiss. A kiss that went on seemingly forever. She opened her mouth and their tongues touched. She was vaguely aware she should say or do something but she had no idea what. And it didn't matter anyway.

They kissed on, his arms holding her tightly as his tongue caressed hers and she let out a little moan and wrapped her leg around his.

"Whoa, darling," he said, easing his mouth off hers, his eyes bright with an excitement that she fancied mirrored her own. "We can finish this later." Carefully he set her on her good foot. Keeping a hand on her waist as she grasped his shoulder. "Here," he handed her one crutch, then the other.

"Why did you do that?"

"You asked me to. Delivered it as an ultimatum unless I'm very much mistaken."

Yes, she had. Or rather codeine in her brain had.

"I said tomorrow." At least she thought she had.

He grinned, no other word for it. "I couldn't wait. I can come back tomorrow if you like. I don't mind."

"Oh, Andrew!" There were no doubt umpteen perfectly intelligent things she should say but why bother?

Especially since every word was being monitored by some very interested villagers.

As Gloria looked around, the flush burned her cheeks. Heavens help her! Mrs. Chivers was watching from Worleigh's doorway with her gossip accomplice, Miss Brown. A fascinated postman stood with the pillar box wide open and grinned at her and Andrew.

"Congratulations," he said, with a smirk. "Never a dull moment around here is there?"

Andrew was lapping it all up. "Thank you," he replied. "Lovely day isn't it?"

"Well, I never," Mrs. Chivers bustled up, eyes all but wobbling out of their sockets with curiosity. "And should we be congratulating you, Mr. Barron?"

Gloria stood upright—or as upright as was possible given her current condition—and smiled at Mrs. Chivers. Nosy old bizom! "Good morning, Mrs. Chivers. Nice morning, isn't it?"

It was actually a glorious, fantastic and brilliant morning and somehow she had to extricate herself from this. She cast a desperate glance at Alice. "Shouldn't we be getting back?"

"After we stop by the baker. Remember?"

"I'll come with you. I need a nice fresh bloomer loaf myself," Andrew said.

The man was taking every advantage. Serve him right if she did wear bloomers the next time they went out.

Which meant . . .

"Nurse Prewitt," Miss Brown said, coming into the conversation. "Well I never did . . ."

Quite possibly. "Didn't mean to bother anyone," Gloria said with a smile."

"I did," Andrew whispered. She was tempted to slug him

with her crutch but she'd caused enough gossip for one day. She'd be lucky to live it down before Christmas.

"Let me carry your basket, doctor," Andrew said.

And darn Alice, she relinquished it with a grin. "Maybe I should drop you both at Gloria's after we finish shopping."

Andrew shook his head. "Would be lovely but I've got to get back to work. I'll just nip to the baker's and then I must be off."

Seemed Mrs. Chivers and Miss Brown were just on their way to the baker's too.

This wasn't funny, not when she hopped up the steps into the baker's—with Andrew chivalrously holding the door open, of course.

"Brought the village in with you, did you, madam?" Block asked.

It felt like it. "I just need a small brown loaf."

Once she'd paid for it, and taken her tuppence change from her sixpence, Gloria was ready to scarper as fast as possible. Alice lingered. First she went on about an order for bridge rolls her grandmother needed for the whist drive next week and what time they should be picked up, given it was early closing day. Then she took forever deciding between bath buns or a round of buns—which it turned out he didn't have. After all that, she almost forgot the loaf of bread she'd come in for.

Not like Alice at all.

Once that was taken care of, Alice suggested Gloria and Andrew wait in front of the shop while she nipped down and brought the car up. "To save Gloria walking."

Gloria was about to point out her leg was broken, not amputated, when Andrew said. "You haven't killed me or battered me with the blunt end of a crutch so . . ."

So what? So she was fast losing her reason and sanity and resolve and Alice was down the pavement at a run.

"I've someone in the house now. An evacuee. One of the schoolteachers."

"So, you don't want me there?"

No! "I do." God, she really did. She was already yearning for a repeat performance of ten minutes ago. Her reputation was shot so why worry? "Please come. Come for dinner." She could surely spin the liver out with extra gravy and potatoes.

"How about I come for a cup of tea after dinner? I'll grab something to eat in the plant canteen. I need to stay later since I stole away in the middle of the day."

For her. "See you later then."

"Oh! Yes!"

Alice picked that moment to pull up beside them. Andrew gave Gloria a chaste peck on the cheek, hideous disappointment that, and helped her and her crutches into the car.

"Tonight," he said as he closed the passenger door.

It was a promise.

"So," Alice said as she pulled away from the curb. "Things are set right between you and Andrew?"

"I think so." And hoped so.

"You think! Gloria, you massage each other's tonsils in the middle of the village street and you just 'think' things are alright. You might as well face facts. The village gossips will have you pregnant by teatime."

That was what Gloria was afraid of.

Chapter Sixteen

Interesting, these Inselaffen. Wilhelm Bloch shook his head as he closed the door on the sudden crowd. So much for cold and undemonstrative. He really had to find out where those two lived. Mortals as unrestrained as that could surely be bent to his purpose. The woman was the village nurse and he had a name for the man. "Mr. Barron" shouldn't be too hard to find.

A little eavesdropping at the nurse's house (once he found out where it was) would do the trick. He'd see to it in the next few days.

The door opened again. One of the multitude of badly dressed, gray-haired village females walked in and asked for a small Hovis. He was ready now. Wasn't making that slip again. "Sorry, madam. I've been trying to get Hovis flour with no luck. Maybe in a week or two." He palmed her off with a small brown loaf. Not the same as a good pumpernickel but it kept these peasants happy.

"By the way," he said as he handed the old crone her change. "You don't happen to know the village nurse's address do you? I promised to deliver her order and I've mislaid her address."

Pause while the old bizom gave him a curious look. "You mean Nurse Prewitt? Our district nurse? She broke her leg."

That was the one. Couldn't be two nurses on crutches. "Yes, that's her name."

"She lives the other side of the green. The opposite direction from the church. Up on the left, there's the old almshouses, and a row of nasty new houses Mr. Lynch put up just before the war, and just where the road bends and that's her house. Number 16. There's a big horse chestnut just across the road a bit further along. If you get there, you've gone too far."

If he'd been hampered with a mortal brain he'd have lost half of her rambling explanation. He wasn't so he hadn't missed a word. "Thank you. I'd have been mortified if I'd failed to get her order to her."

"You deliver?" The old hag's face cracked into a wrinkly smile. "How wonderful!"

"Not as a general rule. Wish I could but with the petrol restrictions, you know." She nodded. Probably couldn't drive to visit her cronies as much as she wished. "I told the nurse I'd deliver. On account of her having difficulty getting around."

Well damn, he thought, as he closed the door on her. He'd be getting a reputation as a Good Samaritan if he wasn't careful.

But he knew where to find the nurse. It was only a matter of time before he could bend her to his use. It was so easy to impose on a woman's mind.

"Well dear, what do you think?" Gran asked, as Alice walked in for a quick cup before surgery hours.

"I think we might end up having a double wedding."

"What!" The teacup in Gran's hand hit the stone floor.

"Gran! I'm sorry!" Alice leapt up and grabbed a cloth.

"Alice, child you gave me a start. Who else is getting married?"

Alice looked up from the floor. "I'll get the dustpan and brush."

"Wait a minute!" Gran was aerated indeed. "You can't say

things like that then nip to the broom cupboard for a dustpan and brush. Who is getting married?"

"Unless I'm very much mistaken, Gloria and Andrew."

"Well I never. Give me another cup and you tell me everything."

"First thing, Gran," she said, as she sat back down. "This is between us, not for public broadcast, promise?"

"Of course, dear. You know that."

She did but she also knew Gran was a demon for a tasty snippet of gossip. "Well . . ." She related the interesting events of the morning.

"He kissed in the middle of the village street?"

"At high noon!"

"Well I never! Gloria has always seemed such a nice, quiet girl."

"She still is. When not on codeine. Obviously pain and the stress of the air raid," she'd omit the details about their overnight stay, "was preying on her mind."

Gran shook her head. "And a man who can't make up his own mind doesn't help. I'd not have thought it of that Mr. Barron, he seemed a very straightforward young man but you never know do you? I suppose they stayed together that night in Dorking and he was hit with an attack of nerves, or conscience or a haywire sense of honor or whatever they call it nowadays."

Now it was Alice's turn to spill tea. Only hers went down her nose.

When she finally got her breath back and fished out her hankie to wipe her face, she said, "Honestly, Gran!"

"Am I mistaken, dear? I don't doubt Gloria said more to you than you've just told me."

She'd never been able to lie to Gran. "She was a bit torn up."

"What woman wouldn't be? Here she'd given her all, and he goes all strong and silent on her. At least she had the sense to sort things out."

"With a bit of help from her pain medicine."

Gran brushed that away with a flick of her hand. "A couple of codeine pills wouldn't make her do anything she didn't want to do. Not Gloria. Now, dear that is interesting and very good to hear but what about my original question? What did you think of the new baker?"

What did she think? Alice paused and considered. She no doubt missed half a dozen key facts because the immediately preceding incident had rather occupied her mind. "He struck me as . . . odd. Very pleasant. He remembered your order for bridge rolls by the way and promised faithfully to have them for you. But . . ." How in heaven's name was she going to put this into sane meaningful sentences? "There was something odd about him." Very scientific and solid that was!

Gran grinned from ear to ear. "Odd indeed, Alice my love. But it's wonderful, you sensed something about him."

Had she? "I'm not sure I did, Gran, maybe I saw him as a bit odd because you'd mentioned your suspicions."

"I don't think so, my love. You're tapping into your skills. They've been dormant so long it takes time but you're right he's Other and there's something not right about him. We must keep an eye on him."

Easier said than done. "You're worried, aren't you, Gran?"

"Let's say I am very, very concerned. We knew there were at least two vampires, now it seems there are more. We have to be on our guard. While you're busy with your patients, I think I'll walk down to the village and talk to Howell."

"Let me give you a lift."

"Not to bother, Alice. Save your petrol for your patients. The walk will do me good."

Gloria had just settled down to peel potatoes when there was a knock on the door.

"Who is it?"

"Me, Peter," a voice said. "Alright to come in?"

"Of course, as long as you don't expect anyone to open the door for you." She was not getting up again until she had the lot peeled and cut up.

"Thought I'd pop in on my way home," he said, as he closed the door behind him. "I have something I want to suggest and . . ." He held an enamel plate covered with a greaseproof paper. "Mrs. Chivers stopped me in the lane and asked me to bring this up to you."

It was two baked apples, still warm and smelling of cloves. "Lovely. We can have one each for pudding. I'll get Mary to make custard. I'm not even trying to stand at the stove and stir." He put the dish on the draining board. "Would you like a cup of tea?"

"Only if you let me make it."

"It's a deal."

He was a nice man, but not a patch on Andrew. She wondered if quiet, thoughtful Peter had ever kissed Alice in the middle of the village street. Of course not! She'd have heard about it long ago. And on that score, every darn tongue in the village was no doubt wagging. Peter had no doubt heard about it half a dozen times.

As he filled the kettle and put it on the stove, he said, "I was thinking about you and Andrew."

She knew it! "Yes?" Neutral and composed was the way to act. Even if her heart skipped a couple of beats every time she heard Andrew's name.

"I haven't said anything to Andrew yet. I wanted to see what you thought first."

She thought Andrew was gorgeous but . . . "Yes?"

"Where's the tea?"

Did she care? "On the shelf, next to the sugar. But why not reuse the leaves in the pot?" She hadn't picked up Mary's ration and they were running low.

"Good idea. I heard they were talking about cutting the tea ration."

"They might have an uprising if they do." Why were they jabbering on about tea and food rationing? "You wanted to say something about Andrew?"

"Yeah. Cups and saucers?"

Heaven give her strength! "On the dresser." Was the man blind?

"Oh, yes. Of course. Right in front of my nose." He finally got them, found spoons and the milk and as the kettle boiled, topped up the pot. "We'd best let it sit awhile."

She wouldn't argue with that. "About Andrew?"

"Yes, right. It's like this . . ." Why the hell did he have to pause? "I've been covering the clinic up at the camp and seeing as many as I can in the village. They've increased the number of workers at the camp. They need someone there every day. If I do that, I'll never get to anyone down here, and Alice needs back-up. So . . ." Another pause although it seemed this wasn't about Andrew and her. "I know you're still very much laid up but how would it work if you covered the camp clinic each day? You can pretty much do the job sitting down. Insist everyone comes to you, and I cover your job, since I can ride a bike. We're probably breaking some law or other but . . ."

"I imagine everyone is far too busy to notice what we're doing in Brytewood."

"Think it would work then?"

"My being at the camp is no problem." Quite the reverse in fact. "We can say you're working under Alice's supervision. It should work." Only had to last until she got her cast off.

"Splendid! I'll mention it to Andrew. Doubt he'll complain." He gave a little grin.

Not in a million years. Assuming he really meant what he'd said and done a few hours earlier.

And that brought its own set of complications. Which she had to face. She couldn't pretend much longer they were just any old human courting couple. "Think the tea's ready yet?"

Peter lifted the lid and gave the pot a stir. "Looks like it."

He handed her a cup and poured one for himself. "There is another thing I want to ask. For Alice this time."

"Alright. What is it?"

"She's got her heart set on having a white wedding dress and had dug out Mother's dress but moths had had a heyday on the silk. So could you ask around? Maybe someone has an old wedding dress? Or there's a length of white fabric tucked in an attic?"

"I'll do what I can."

"Bless you, Gloria. You're a pal." He drank down his tea in one gulp. "Best be off. I'll let you know what Andrew says. Bye!"

As if Andrew was likely to complain!

Would she? Oh! Drat! This was supposed to be a fling. A little bit of self indulgence and look where it was ending up. She ached for him. Needed him. Yearned for him. Although it might be that was just her body's awareness of the full moon tomorrow. Who was she deluding?

And the coming full moon was another set of questions. She couldn't fight the change but how in the name of all sanity was she going to shift and run? Maybe once she changed, she could ease her injured leg out of the cast and manage on three legs. Maimed animals did.

And maimed animals ended up killed by stronger and healthier ones.

Her life was spinning out of control. She had to get a grip. She was going to have to shift and darn well hope for the best.

"Hello!" It was Mary. Nice normal, predictable school-teacher Mary, opening the door. She didn't have to worry about full moons or shapeshifting or what to do about falling like a ton for bricks for a human.

"Hello. Survived Friday?"

"What's a day in school after the trip down here? The building's full to the seams. How they are going to absorb another thirty I don't know. They're debating doing it in shifts. Reception in the morning, second year infants in the afternoon, first year juniors in the morning, second after lunch but beats me how that will work."

"And will drive the mothers barmy. Particularly the ones who are working in Leatherhead or Dorking."

"To say nothing of the teachers who'll end up working ten-hour days."

"Worry about it when it happens, is my advice," Gloria said. "Mind you, your children aren't going back home after a few weeks like some of the Londoners."

Gloria shook her head. "Not a hope." She caught sight of the pan of potatoes and the heap of peelings. "Want some help? I need to do something to keep my end up and besides, I'm ravenous. It's been a long time since breakfast."

"You didn't get lunch at school? They bring it out from the kitchen in Leatherhead."

Mary's laugh was definitely weary. "Let's put it this way. Mrs. Banting, the head, is apparently a real stickler about clean plates. She took one look at the dark gelatinous substance in the shepherd's pie and told the staff no child was compelled to finish it. Just as long as they ate all the vegetables."

Gloria knew Mrs. Banting well. "That awful?"

"Yes, but everyone went to great pains to assure me that it wasn't always that bad. The local pigs will be feasting this weekend."

"Lucky pigs. I've supper half ready. I hope you like liver."

"Love it as it happens but if I didn't I think it would still sound marvelous. Here," she said, as she went over to the sink to wash, "let me give you a hand."

"Don't you have stuff to do for school?"

"Masses but I'll take care of that when your handsome visitor arrives."

Darn Andrew! Yes, he'd promised, threatened, whatever to come by this evening.

"Handsome is he?"

"Can't say myself, not having met him, but the village thinks so. Although there is one group who think he's a bit old for you, but that's counterbalanced by those who think he's just the right age to settle down. By the way, is it true he kissed you in the middle of the village street?"

Her face burned. "Yes."

Mary's chuckle went from tired to downright naughty. "He follows directions well."

"Except he got the wrong day!"

"You're moaning about that?"

"No, but I am wondering what the heck comes next."

"You've plenty of company on that score. The mums outside the gate were positively buzzing with speculation."

Inevitable but . . . "Sure it wasn't about changes in the cheese ration?"

"No, nothing about cheese." Mary pulled out a chair. "The big topic was you. There was a little sly debate about whether or not you'd done the deed so to speak, but on the whole, the big question was when the wedding was going to be." Who, in their right mind, lived in a village? "Do you have another knife?" Mary asked. "I'll help chop the onions."

She did more than that, pretty much cooking the meal while Gloria clumped around and laid the table while trying to decide which of her worries to fixate on first: Andrew or the need to shift in twenty-four hours. Both prospects seemed likely to cause permanent brain trauma. To say nothing of heartache.

Chapter Seventeen

"I can't stay long, Howell," Helen Burrows said, as she stepped into his warm kitchen. "I just wanted a word with you."

"You'll stay long enough for a cup of tea, won't you? I just made a fresh pot." He had indeed. It sat on the kitchen table, under a rather unexpected pink and yellow crinoline lady tea cozy. "Say you'll have a cup," he urged. "It never tastes the same by myself"

"Thank you, Howell, I will. Don't want to put you to any bother."

"Nothing for you, Helen, would be a bother." She smiled. Men never changed. Just as well, really.

"Here," he said, as he took her coat and hat. "You have a seat by the fire and I'll make us some toast. Young Peter picked up a fresh loaf for me this morning. Makes a nice change to have our own baker once again." He reached for the bread knife and board and took the loaf from the bread bin.

"It's that new baker I came about. I want to have a word about him."

He looked up from slicing. "You do, do you? I wondered how long it would take you to cotton on to him. Don't miss much do you, Helen?"

"That's how I've stayed alive this long."

"I could say the same," he said, as he put four slices under the grill. "Fancy honey on the toast or Marmite? No dripping I'm afraid. Peter polished off the lot at breakfast."

"Honey would be lovely but don't you dare use any of your butter ration!"

"All out my dear, but I've the best honey in the village if not the county."

"From Mother Longhurst?"

"Of course! That's another puzzle. It's not like her to leave the village, much less walk off and never come back."

"She didn't walk off. She borrowed Doris Brewer's bicycle and that never came back either."

He checked the toast, turning it before sliding the pan back under the grill. "Bad, very bad. Are the police taking it seriously enough?"

"They're doing what they can. Alice had me call all the hospitals. She's not in any of them."

"She wouldn't be. Not Mother Longhurst." Odd comment that. "Peter told me she went off to Bringham with that knife of hers. Risky."

"From what Alice said, she was passing it on. To another witch."

"Do you know of another witch around here?"

Good point. "No, but then I've lived here twenty-five years and never knew there was a Dragon living down the road." He had a naughty, rather sexy chuckle. "See my point, we Others keep things to ourselves. What worries me is Mother Longhurst riding around the countryside with such a powerful magic tool on her person. If she handed it over to a responsible person, that's one thing, but if she was attacked or died and it fell into the wrong hands . . ."

"Would the wrong hands know what to do with it?"

"Since we don't know that, best we concentrate on our immediate problem."

Howell nodded. "You think we have another one of those to deal with?"

"Vampire?" Might as well say it aloud. "I'm afraid so."

"The so-called baker?"

Dragons never missed anything. "Who doesn't even know what Hovis is."

"Ah!" He gave a little twisted smile. "Shoddy training wouldn't you say?" He turned fast at the smell of burning, and grabbed the toast from under the heat. "Just in time!" He spread each slice with honey and cut them into quarters. "Here you are." He put half on a plate and passed it to her. "Eat up and let's put our thinking caps on."

They both chewed in silence for a few minutes, Helen thinking hard. By the crease between Howell Pendragon's eyes, he was doing the same.

"Well," she said, after making a sizable inroad into the toast. "We agree the baker is another one of them."

"You're sure?"

"That he's a vampire? No. But he's Other."

"Agreed. First time I met him, he struck me as Other, and then Samuel Whorleigh . . ."

"What about him?" Was he up to something aside from cornering the black market?

"Seems our jovial baker gave Sam Whorleigh a bit of a scare a few nights back."

"What happened?"

"Sam the grocery man eluded Bill the Baker, one evening, by leaping up onto the roof of the lychgate."

"So Samuel Whorleigh is Other? What sort of Other?" Might explain how he got away with flouting the law. An Other who went off the rails meant no good for anyone.

"That I don't know. Goblin or Brownie, I suppose. Maybe even a Leprechaun. Doesn't matter does it?"

"Might if we need him on our side."

"Samuel Whorleigh is on no one's side but his own,

but there's no love lost between him and the baker, that's for sure."

Helen took a sip of tea. Howell certainly knew how to make a nice cuppa. Nice man too. "We're no nearer knowing what to do are we?"

He shrugged. "You know they found Reg Brown dead in the churchyard?"

"Alice mentioned it. You think there's a connection?"

"Most likely his heart gave out. He had more beer than blood in him I wouldn't doubt. Alice say anything?"

She shook her head. "No. I feel as though we're waiting for a disaster to happen."

"If only we had that knife back. Why did she take it away?"

"Apparently it won't work again for a hundred years."

"Oh. Want another cup?"

"Please."

"You're right, we're all at sea," he said, as he topped up her cup. "What we need is a vampire expert." Unfortunately, the only other vampire she knew of was in France. "By the way, Helen, there's something I want to ask you."

"Yes?"

"If you're not busy, how about we go to the pictures tomorrow night?"

Of all the questions in creation he might have asked, this was not one she'd expected. The man put all the charm of the Welsh in his smile. "You're asking me out?"

"Yes. Want to come?" Howell Pendragon, the ever confident, ever sure of himself, looked, and sounded, anxious.

How could she hesitate? "Of course."

His big face almost split in two as he grinned. "Smashing! We'll have to get the bus, unless I cycle and you ride on the carrier."

"Chance be a fine thing, Howell Pendragon! You come and pick me up like a nicely raised young man would, and we'll get the bus together."

"You're assuming I was nicely raised. Maybe I was dragged up."

He was getting above himself. In a nice way. "If you were dragged up, Howell, then you've done a good job of fooling everyone here the past twenty-odd years." Just so she wouldn't appear too eager, she drained her tea and put the cup back in the saucer. "I must be off. See you tomorrow."

"Six alright? We can get the bus that comes at a quarter past."

"I'll be ready."

As he helped her into her coat, she couldn't help wondering what Alice would have to say about this. Hopefully nothing. And if she did? Helen Burrows smiled. Too bad.

"I'll do the washing up," Mary said, jumping up as Gloria pushed her plate away.

"Another day, I'd argue with you," Gloria replied, "But tonight, I feel worn out."

She looked it too: dark circles under her eyes and an odd flush on her face. "Feeling under the weather?"

"I've got a few things on my mind."

Not the least being Andrew Barron. They'd chewed him over thoroughly during dinner. Seemed poor Gloria was wondering if getting what she'd demanded was really what she wanted.

"You know what I think? You worry too much. Just have fun and enjoy his company and see what happens."

"That's what Alice says, but I know what happens when we get together. Our libidos go haywire."

Or went together in the right direction. Mary scraped the plates and stacked them in the sink. Talk about going haywire. She was on the verge of that. She'd better get this sorted out as it was full moon tomorrow, the perfect time to feel water on her skin again. Real water. Not the nasty chlorinated stuff she'd made do with in the swimming baths in Sheffield. There was a large pond near Cherry Hill Farm. "I thought I might go out tomorrow night. Not sure what time I'll be back."

Gloria gasped. Shock? Why was it really so odd to go out of a Saturday night? "Fine, have fun. Not much to do around here."

"I'll help get supper before I leave."

"Don't bother. I'll get toast or bread and cheese. You're not here to cook for me, Mary."

The tension eased in her neck and shoulders. She'd agonized over how to broach the subject and it had been that easy. "I don't mind. I lived in a hostel in Sheffield and missed having a kitchen." She rinsed the plates and put them in the rack to drain. There was a knock on the door, and a rather dishy man poked his head around the door.

Time to make herself scarce.

She hung around just long enough for a polite introduction, grabbed a cup of tea, and excused herself on the grounds of having school records to go over. Not entirely a lie but instead of paperwork, she wanted to study the map she'd borrowed from school.

She had to find the easiest and, more to the point, most discreet way to get up to that Hammer Pond on the downs.

"Hope I didn't scare her off," Andrew said.

"More likely she didn't fancy acting as chaperone."

"Think we need one?"

"Not as long as you're sitting that far away."

He took care of that in a flash, picking Gloria up, carrying her over to the sofa by the fireplace and sitting next to her. Very next to her. They were touching waist to knee and she could feel every inch of his skin through his trouser leg.

She really wanted him naked.

He put his hand on her thigh.

"Andrew," she said.

"Yes, love," he replied. As he turned to face her, she grabbed his head with both hands and kissed him. Long, hard and very, very thoroughly.

He responded with nothing short of enthusiasm and for several minutes they had far, far better things to do than waste breath on conversation.

They had to stop for air eventually. Andrew's eyes gleamed as he smiled. "You haven't changed your mind then?"

This was insanity and this time she couldn't blame it on any drug. Just him and what proximity did to her reason. "No." Heaven help her. This was insanity but a wondrous insanity. "I think I love you, Andrew."

"Only think? You insist I make a public declaration in front of half the village and you 'think' you love me." He was still grinning and his arm curled around her shoulders felt really, really nice. "You're not playing fast and loose with me, are you, my girl? Toying with an honest man's affections? Taking advantage of my . . ."

She shut him up with another kiss. A kiss that ended up with her bra unhooked and her heart racing. His hand on her breast was magic, stirring wild need and a hundred images of him naked and over her, under her and all around her. She whimpered as he broke the kiss.

He didn't move his hand though.

"Gloria," he said, his voice husky. "I want you so much it hurts." Going by the bulge in his trousers she could well believe that. "What I really want is to strip you naked and carry you upstairs and make slow love to you all night."

"I bet Mary will be tactful and keep her door closed."

"Dammit it's not that, Gloria. Well it is sort of, but I can't stay. I need to get back to work and finish up a couple of things as I'm off tomorrow. How about we could go out? Have dinner. Go to the flicks. I won't suggest the dance hall in Leatherhead but anything else you fancy?"

Damn and double damn. She had to think fast here. "Are you off all day?"

"Yes."

"How about we go out in the afternoon and see the matinee? Sounds silly but I feel safer if I'm home before dark. I don't like being gone in the evenings. After . . ." she paused, feeling the lie burn her tongue.

But it worked. "Don't blame you. Let's make it lunch then. Lunch and the matinee and I promise to have you back home before dark. Fair enough?"

Perfect. She'd be alone in the house. Mary was going out. Gloria hugged the satisfaction inside. How she was going to change with a plaster cast on her leg, she'd work out later.

Chapter Eighteen

It had worked. After a nice lunch and a Saturday afternoon matinee, Andrew was off home and it was barely dark. Wasn't easy to give him that last kiss and shut the door behind him, but Gloria managed it.

She had to.

Her breast still tingling from his caress and her lips aching with his kisses, she made herself send him home with lame excuses of a headache, her cast aching and fatigue.

She hated lying but how in creation could she tell him the truth? "Andrew, it's full moon and I need to turn furry" might put him off a bit. A bit! He'd go running off into the sunset. Which, come to think of it, was pretty close to what she was about to do.

With a bit of luck.

She sat down on one of the kitchen chairs and stared at her clunker of a cast. How in heaven's name was she going to manage? She did not fancy getting stuck in the woods, naked with a broken leg and her crutches back in her cottage.

At least Mary was out. And after tonight this wouldn't be a worry for another month. Gloria leaned back and shut her eyes. She needed this, her animal was close to the surface.

Very close. Outside was dark, she felt the pull of the moon as it rose slowly. The woods called.

What was she hesitating for?

Because she was scared. She'd been shifting every full moon and sometimes in between since she hit puberty, but never before with . . . She scowled at the heavy plaster cast than seemed to anchor her to the floor. This was risky, tricky and probably a big mistake, but the fox inside called out with need and she knew only too well how her human self suffered if she kept her fox at bay too long.

She stood, balancing herself on her crutches. Decided against a coat—just one more thing to take off—and made for the kitchen door. Closing it behind her, she hobbled and hopped over to her toolshed. Once inside, she left the door ajar, and stripped. She had no idea what was going to happen but at worst, she'd run lopsided through the fringe of woods that backed onto her garden. Just taking on her fox skin would sate the rising need.

It was a cold night to be wearing nothing more than a plaster cast but it wouldn't be for long. Her spine rippled, she went on all fours, watched the fur rise on her hands, her fingers shorten and her nails elongate until she had claws. Her face shifted with the expected twinge of pain. In an instant, she sniffed with her fox's nose: smelled the ripened apples on the tree, the newly turned earth where she'd taken up the last of the carrots, the smoky scent of a distant bonfire. Doused, she hoped; or Sid Black and his cohorts would be banging on someone's door.

A few more ripples down her back and the shift was complete. She shook herself to awaken every inch of her fox and peered back at her right rear leg. The cast was still on, but loose and far too big for a fox's limb and rubbing her flank. Now was the time to test and hope to heaven she didn't do some permanent injury. She stepped forward and wiggled and lifted her back leg. The cast slipped off. How she'd get it back on was a problem for later.

Gingerly, she set her back foot down and put weight on it, expecting pain, hurt or at least a twinge.

Nothing.

Her leg was firm and steady. Maybe all those old vixens' tales of healing with shifting held true. Who knew? Who cared? Not her fox, who yearned to run. Casting a last look at her clothes folded behind the lawnmower, she nosed the door open and slipped out.

The moon was rising over the hedge. Stealthy as any fox, she walked soundlessly across the paved area between the shed and the house, avoided the dustbins and paused a minute.

She smelled human nearby and slunk into the shadows. As the gate onto the lane opened, she fled, darting through the carefully cultivated gap in the hedge and racing across the narrow strip of woods. She was through them and facing the expanse of the common when she realized she was running without pain or difficulty.

Incredible.

Thrilled at moving with an uninjured body, she sped out into the night, across the village green and toward the common. She ran low and fast, the moon rising above.

Hanging his coat up, Andrew noticed he still had Gloria's gloves in his pocket. He pulled them out, remembering how he'd taken them off in the cinema, telling her he'd keep her hands warm. She'd taken him up on it too. He looked down at the gray knitted gloves, with three rows of cable across the back. Had she knitted them? A friend? An aunt? Her parents were dead, but surely she had cousins, aunts and uncles. He had a whole army of them.

He held the gloves to his face, rubbing the wool against his cheek as he caught her scent and a whiff of floral perfume.

Lavender? Violet? He wasn't sure, just something sweet and woodsy. If she was going to church in the morning, she'd need her gloves.

He pulled his coat back on and walked the couple of hundred yards or so back to her cottage.

It was pitch dark. She kept a good blackout. Damn, everything about his Gloria was marvelous. He walked up the path, saw a sudden movement, probably a cat on the prowl, and knocked on her door. Not a sound. He opened it and put his head round the heavy curtain.

Lights were on in the kitchen, curtains drawn and no one there.

"Gloria," he called. "Gloria?"

He went in and closed the door behind him. She wasn't in sight but her coat was hanging on the hook by the door.

Mary, he remembered, was out for the evening.

Was Gloria in the bath? That thought was downright enticing. "Gloria," he called again, a little louder. "It's Andrew. I brought your gloves back."

No reply. Had she gone to sleep that quickly? Seemed so. Better not wake her.

But he really wanted to.

He put her gloves in the middle of the kitchen table, where she couldn't miss them, and looked around for paper. He found a pad beside the phone with a well-sharpened pencil attached by a string. She was nothing if not precise. And lovely and sexy and his. And right now upstairs in bed. Alone.

Terrible for a woman like Gloria to sleep alone.

Alone and not feeling well. He didn't blame her being rattled by the night in Dorking. He'd been shaken. He'd also felt like one of the gods of creation.

He wouldn't wake her, just peek in on his sleeping love and give her a secret kiss.

* * *

Seemed to Mary it was a darn long walk, but the map had been right: the path from the churchyard skirted the common before climbing up the ridge of the downs toward the Hammer Pond and now she was there. She stood in the shadow of the trees and looked out across the dark expanse of water. The surface was still as the dark sky above, only a few tiny ripples breaking the reflection of the full moon overhead. Her grandmother would have called this a magical night. Her grandmother hadn't ever been evacuated to the mainland miles from the sound and scent of the sea, with only a patch of fresh water to ease her aches and needs.

Her mother and grandmother and all her aunts and cousins were still on Guernsey within sight and sound of the sea they loved, but if what she'd heard was to believed, forbidden near the beaches.

Mary smiled. It would take more than the Luftwaffe, the Kriegsmarine and the entire German armed forces to keep an Island Nymph from her birthright. Gran and everybody were out tonight. Mary sensed it. Bathing in the sweetness of salt water, while she shivered in the woods and looked around nervously.

Damn! She hadn't walked all this way to dither. She took off her coat and folded it carefully, then her cardigan, blouse, skirt, shoes and stockings.

She shivered in the chill air. October was no time to be standing around in the altogether. But as water called for the first time in months, Mary ran. Her feet barely touched the ground until she leaped into the pond, staying below the surface until she had to come up gasping for air to dive under, curl and twist in the glory of the water.

She was no longer cold, her entire soul, body and spirit renewed as the water caressed her body and eased away the stresses, worries and fears of the past months. For a few glorious minutes, she forgot war and exile and danger and reveled in the joy of her natural element. Why would she ever leave?

Because she had to live in the human world. The days of Nymphs living permanently in ponds and underwater caves were long gone. They had to adapt, to pass as mere mortal. But for now, she could sate her spirit with the glory of the night and the sheer bliss of losing herself in a body of water larger than a swimming bath.

She'd walk this far, and ten times longer, to feel this peace. This rightness.

Laughing to herself, she went under again, toward the center of the pond and the deepest water. She was in no hurry to go back to the cottage.

Young Jim Clegg slipped out of bed. Mrs. Grayson said there was a full moon tonight, and he was going to turn his money—what there was of it—the way his grandmother used to. Grannie said turning your money and bowing to the moon meant good luck. He and Wilf needed some luck. They were sick of being ill. Mrs. Grayson was nice enough but she wasn't the same as Mum, and it really wasn't like being home in London.

Quietly he closed the door to the landing. Mrs. Grayson always left a light on there for them, and Jim was not going to let a light show and help some German plane find a target. He lifted the lid of the Wills tobacco tin where he kept his money and took it all out—a shilling he'd earned helping Mr. Longhurst turn hay, a threepenny bit and a handful of coppers—and put it in the pocket of his pajama jacket. At the window, he pulled open the heavy blackout curtains.

Silvery moonlight and dark shadows crisscrossed all the way across the back garden and the fields beyond. Jim opened the window, shivering a little in the chill air, but he wanted to look at the moon, high over the woods. Jim squeezed his money tight in his fist. Grannie used to mutter something when she turned her money—silver, she used to say. He had silver and coppers. Not knowing what Grannie's magic words were, Jim said the Lord's prayer to himself and turned his coins.

Nothing happened, but good luck was what his grandmother promised, and he'd done his best and was getting cold. As he pulled the window closed, he caught movement to his right. He'd seen a fox one night but this was a person standing by the edge of the field of cabbages. A poacher? No one poached cabbages, did they? This person who looked around, then swift as you like, leapt into the air and flew! Arms outstretched, he was in the air and whizzed over the cabbages and up into the big oak tree in the middle of the cornfield.

Jim blinked and looked again. He hadn't dreamt it. There, sure as eggs, was a dark shape perched in a low branch of the tree. Then, a few moments later, it took off again and flew across the fields until it was out of sight in the dark. Who, what was it. A witch? No, they used broomsticks. Magic? What sort of magic? And why here?

"Jim?" It was Wilf awake. "Wotcher doing?"

"Just looking at the moon and . . ." He broke off. What had he seen? "I'm coming back." He shut the window, drew the blackout back and climbed into bed.

"You're cold, Jim," Wilf complained. "Keep yer feet to yer side of the bed."

Jim reached for his hot water bottle, it had cooled but was warmer than his feet. Still he'd worked magic with the full moon and . . . Oh! Had he conjured up the flying man? A nice thought but Jim had too strong a streak of practicality to really believe that. Still, he had seen that man fly. Maybe he was an angel. He'd ask Reverend Roundtree next time he went to Sunday School.

If he ever got out of quarantine.

Maybe he'd ask Mrs. Grayson in the morning.

Chapter Nineteen

Once through the fringe of trees and across the allotments, Gloria paused. Her leg not only supported her, she could run as well as ever. She set off like a streak in the moonlight, away from the village, and in a wild fit of excitement, headed for Box Hill, zigzagging between the barriers of concrete dragon's teeth that traversed the fields, splashing through the river, and climbing the chalk escarpment, until she paused halfway and looked back at the dark valley in the moonlight.

She sat on her hind legs, raised her head to the moon and called in the night. A great contentment washed over her. She was alive, whole and alone under the night sky. She wouldn't think about having to change back and once again being stuck on crutches. For now, she'd revel in the night. She stood, swung her tail and raced back down the steep incline, and followed the bank of the river almost to the outskirts of Dorking, then crossed the river and raced back. By the time she ran a wide loop across country and approached Brytewood from Fletcher's Woods, her energy was lagging. She paused in the shadow of a hedge and rested. Wild runs were heaven but she needed to be cautious this close to the village. There were still plenty of farmers and villagers willing to shoot a fox to protect their henhouses.

Something moved in her peripheral vision. She turned, keeping low to the ground, and watched. There was a creature, with the silhouette of a man, but it wasn't a man. Couldn't be. No human ran that fast and no human could possibly leap into the air and fly over the trees and out of sight.

Holy smoke! The fur rose on her neck and down her back. It was the same creature she'd seen weeks back near the munitions plant. Andrew's plant. That time, before she'd raised the alarm, she'd watched while he laid what proved to be explosives.

It, he, whatever was back. Nowhere near Andrew this time, but if it meant harm last time, it intended harm now.

How to warn Andrew? "While I was running furry over the fields . . ." was not a good opener by any measure. Worrying, she set off home.

Back through the gap in the hedge and into the shed, door still ajar, she sagged onto the concrete floor weary, spent and worried. And she'd better get a move on, and get back in the house before Mary returned.

Shifting back always took less energy, but left her shivering. As she reached for her clothes, she realized she was putting weight on her broken ankle. And it felt fine. Darn. Must be a vestige from shifting. She pulled on clothes and sat on the bench to don her cast.

Some hope! Try as she would to point her foot and ease it back into the cast, she could only get it so far, but her anxious gymnastics confirmed her ankle was no longer broken.

Good news really. But terrible. How on earth was she going to explain this? A miracle didn't sound convincing.

Oh well, she picked up her shoes and her cast and walked barefoot over the gravel path to her back door. She'd just go to bed. Maybe treat herself to a bath first as she'd dearly missed having a good soak. Maybe between now and the morning inspiration would hit. Her foot would shrink, or something would happen to explain things.

As she closed the back door and pulled aside the blackout

curtain, she noticed the kitchen light was on. Drat! Mary had to be back home. With a bit of luck she'd gone to bed and had left the light on.

Gloria stepped around the heavy curtains, and saw Andrew sitting by the fireplace.

Their eyes met and she gasped. "You're here!"

He gave her an odd look. "I came back as I still had your gloves. I saw you'd gone out. Seemed odd, given that you told me you were tired and wanted to go to bed early. I thought you'd perhaps nipped out for ten minutes, but you've been gone . . ." He glanced at the clock on the mantelpiece. "Three hours."

"Counted the time did you?"

"Yes, while I worried myself sick over what had happened to you." He came toward her, stopping almost midstride. "Gloria, what the hell? Your leg? It's . . . you had an accident?"

She'd be blind to miss the stark worry and anguish in his eyes. He was scared, worried and hurt for her and she had no idea where, in all creation, to go from here.

The exhilaration from her run evaporated and all she felt was fatigue.

"What happened, Gloria?" He took the cast from her hands. "This didn't fall off, did it? What were you doing?"

She might as well tell the damn truth. If he did the sane thing and ran screaming from her, so be it. "I think, Andrew, we both need to sit down."

"You need shoes or slippers. Darn it, Gloria, you were walking about barefoot."

Bare pawed actually. "Let me sit down. I'm alright, honest I am." But perhaps facing the worst challenge of her life: telling the truth about herself to the man she loved.

That realization had her all but reeling. Good thing the fireside easy chair was handy. She sat down and tucked her legs under her, so Andrew wouldn't see the cuts and dirt on her feet, and looked up at him. "Please sit down. This won't take long."

"What won't? And hadn't you better do something about those cuts first?"

No point in asking what cuts. No point in doing anything but getting on with this before she lost her nerve. "Andrew, if you love me, sit down and listen." He sat, sort of reluctantly but he was sitting. "And please don't interrupt. No matter how odd this sounds."

"Odd" wasn't the word. But she had his attention. She might lose everything but . . .

"I bet you noticed the full moon."

He nodded. "Yes, but what does . . ."

She waved her hand to stop him. "Let me finish, please." Hesitate and she'd flub this. "This is going to sound preposterous but bear with me. Every time there's a full moon something happens. I turn furry and go running in the woods." Crikey! He was thunderstruck. It was going to get worse. "I change my skin into a fox."

There. She'd done it. Told a mundane mortal her secret. She looked up at his horrified face and knew she'd lost him.

She blinked back the tears and swallowed, forcing the tight muscles of her throat to move.

"Blimey, Gloria. Why?"

A question she'd asked herself repeatedly over the years. "It's the way I am. The way my parents were. Most of the time I'm Nurse Prewitt but when the moon calls, I answer."

He hadn't run screaming. Not yet at any rate.

He ran both hands through his hair and let out a gasp that sounded as if it came from deep in his gut. "If any other human being had said what you just said, I'd say they were drunk or insane."

"I'm neither and I suppose technically, I'm not really human."

"If you're not human, Gloria, then neither am I nor anyone else in this village."

As the full meaning of his words hit her, she was out of her seat and wrapping her arms around his neck. She pressed her head against his chest and inhaled the scent of male. Worried male. Dear heaven! He sat here three hours wondering where the heck she was.

"Andrew?" He wasn't running away screaming. Yet.

"Any more secrets, my love?"

"That's the big one."

She pulled back a little and looked up at him. He was still worried. Hardly surprising. He brushed the hair off her forehead and kissed her. Gently. It was hardly more than a brush of his warm lips on her chilled skin, but they were together, his arm around her as his heart beat against her shoulder.

"Andrew?" She had no idea what to say next. "Don't leave me." "Please understand." "Don't repudiate me." All lingered on the tip of her tongue as her heart all but froze with anxiety and the hideous prospect of losing him.

He'd kissed her, hadn't he? Not a real *kiss* but a sweet kiss, a friendly kiss, a farewell kiss.

Please no!

"Gloria, it's alright," he whispered. "Stop shaking. I have you. It's alright." He whispered it again and again, until his words registered in her racing brain. "Come on, love," he said. "You sit here. I'm going to make you a cup of tea, and then you can explain things to me."

She was clinging to him. She made herself let go of his sweater. "Andrew. I need more than a cup of tea." He nodded. He probably needed something stronger than tea too. "If you look in the dresser, at the back of the bottom shelf, there's a bottle of brandy." She'd brought it back from France, smuggled in her dirty laundry the summer before the war. A lifetime ago. Long, long before Andrew.

"Got it!" He stood up from rummaging in the dresser. "How's your milk supply?"

"I beg your pardon?" She was strung out and that slowed her brain but how did those two questions connect?

"Milk, Gloria. You have enough for tea. Do you have enough for two mugs of warm milk?" He held up the bottle. "Would go down a treat with this."

It was close to sacrilege to pour aged Armagnac into a mug of milk, but she could live with it. "Look in the pantry."

Andrew, bless the man, warmed milk, found mugs, even put the saucepan in to soak and handed her a mug. "This'll warm you up." And sat beside her.

Warm her? He'd been ultragenerous with the brandy, but who'd complain? "I suppose," she said, after a couple of sips, "you have some questions."

He nodded. "First, what in Hades happened to your ankle?"

This one was relatively easy. She told him. As best she could. "I'm not really sure how it happened but I don't think it's broken any more."

"Gloria, I saw it broken, remember? Your foot hung loose."

No wonder words failed him. "I can't explain it."

"We're going to have to. Somehow."

He said "we." "Doesn't it give you the willies knowing I go furry in the full moon?"

He let out a dry laugh. "Gloria, my love. It gives me the screaming abdabs, but seems I've going to have to get used to the idea."

"You really mean that?"

"Darling, to be honest I'm not sure what I mean. I feel as though you slugged me between the eyes with a mallet but I look at you and you're still you."

"I'm sorry."

"What for?"

"For not being what you thought I was."

"You're more than I thought you were."

You could say that in trumps! But he wasn't fleeing. He was sitting beside her and acting as if it didn't matter . . . Much.

They both went quiet.

"Gloria," he said after a few moments. "Tell me one thing."

"Alright."

"When you're a . . . I mean when you change and become a fox, do you kill?"

"Not usually. I used to when I first changed. I'd kill a rabbit, or a small animal but I gave it up. I don't like raw meat and it seemed unfair to take prey from the real animals who do need it for survival."

He nodded. "What about humans, do you go near them?"

"Not usually. No need. I run to be alone. I sometimes go near human places, and last month . . ." He looked at her. "Up at the camp, remember?"

"When the guards heard umpteen foxes crying at the same time?" She nodded. "That was you?"

"The first one was. I saw someone lurking around, planting bombs."

"Fuses and explosives."

"Alright, explosives. He was obviously up to no good. I wanted to raise the alarm, but I could hardly run up to the guards as a fox, and I wasn't about to shift and race across the heath naked, so I cried. The wild foxes joined in. I never understood it but it worked. They must have heard me and added their cries."

Now he was utterly struck dumb.

"Christ almighty, Gloria! You saved all our bacons. To say nothing of what it would have done to the war effort!"

She had to smile. "That was rather the point of it all."

He went very quiet, leaning back on the sofa and closing his eyes, but he kept his arm around her shoulders. And he didn't move.

"Gloria," he said after what seemed an age. "I still don't know what to say." He had company there. She'd no doubt said far, far too much. "You feel the same, sound the same, your skin tastes the same on my lips, but you've just asked me to believe the preposterous."

Another silent pause. She was getting fed up with them.

Although, in all fairness, she could hardly expect him to jump up and down with glee.

"Gloria, my love," he said eventually, tightening his hold on her shoulders. "Remember how Alice fell down the rabbit hole and after that nothing really made sense?"

She did. "The thing is, that all turned out to be a dream. This isn't, Andrew." Sometimes it had seemed like a nightmare, but no point in going into that now.

"You're right there."

How did he sound? Accepting? Worried? Dubious? Horrified beyond measure? No, not that one. Confused perhaps, but through it all he kept his arm tight around her shoulders. To make sure she didn't turn furry on him, perhaps?

She looked up at his dark eyes, and he smiled. "My love," he said, "I've not the foggiest notion where all this is leading us, but we'll damn well go there together."

It was all she needed, all she'd hoped and dreamed for. It was too good to be true, but nothing less than she should have expected from Andrew Barron. "Thank you," she whispered, "I love you so much. Thank you for still loving me." How, after only a few days had they reached the point of loving? Not that it mattered one iota.

"Thought I'd walk away?" He kissed her. "Have others?"

"I never, ever, told anyone else. Only you." Would she have ever told him if circumstances hadn't precipitated things? She had no idea. Why waste brains pondering the unfathomable? Far better to kiss him again.

But this one wasn't a sweet, reassuring kiss. As their lips met, a fire flared within her and the same need seemed to hit him with a wild surge. It was no mere kiss. It was a wild meeting of need, passion and desire. His mouth took hers. As his warm lips pressed hers, she opened to him. And took over, finding his tongue, seeking the warmth and sweetness of his mouth and meeting him, lip to lip and tongue to tongue as her hand stroked his back and he held her against him and they sprawled in a tangle of arms and legs in the big armchair.

"Gloria," he whispered as they both paused for breath. "Is Mary out all night?"

"I think she went into Leatherhead with some of the teachers."

"If she did, she's missed the last bus."

Gloria was not in the mood to worry about Mary. "They'll probably get a taxi back."

"Best take advantage while the coast is clear." He stood and somehow gathered her up in his arms at the same time. "Upstairs?"

Yes, please! "Seems like a smashing idea to me."

"I won't stay all night, no point in getting tongues wagging."

"I think they are already!" She laughed from the sheer joy of being in Andrew Barron's arms.

"Best not give opportunities to confirm their suspicions." He was right, but at this point, she didn't give a twist for village gossip.

"Let's get upstairs."

He took the stairs two at a time. "Which room's yours?"

"The front one. But hang on. Put me down. Got to close the curtains."

"Excuse, excuses," he muttered, as he put her on her feet after sliding her down the front of his body. Just to let her know how interested he was perhaps?

She chuckled. "That would get the tongues flapping if you walked in there, window uncovered and the light behind us making nice, clear silhouettes."

He grinned. "Damn Hitler, spoiling my fun."

"Not for long." She slipped around the edge of the door, crossed the dark room and pulled the curtains closed, flicked on the light and called out. "You can come in now."

By the time he had the door open, her jumper was on the floor and her skirt zipper halfway down.

"Here, let me help with that."

What woman in her right mind would argue? "Alright, if you insist." Didn't take him long to have her skirt in a ring by her feet and his hands under her Liberty bodice. Damn, she'd have worn something a lot sexier if she'd expected this.

His kiss on her neck had her forgetting her inadequately seductive underwear. He didn't seem the least put off by it, not that she had it on for long.

Besides, he had on far too many clothes. She went for his pullover, yanking it off as he eased the straps of her petticoat off her shoulders. They ended up in a lovely tangle of arms and clothes, on her bed. Then she went wild, unbuckling, yanking and unbuttoning as she pulled off her clothes and helped with his.

They were naked.

He was ready.

Definitely and decidedly ready.

And she was just about panting for it.

"Oh, Andrew," she said, as he stroked his hand over her breasts and down her chest to her waist and along her thighs.

"Magnificent, Gloria," he whispered as he caressed her waist and ran kisses down her arms. "You are just the same as ever, so perfect so beautiful. Nothing's different."

"Apart from my ankle," she reminded him, "and that, right now, is a distinct improvement."

"Yes," he agreed. "We'll worry about those ramifications later."

Much later. "Dear Andrew." She grinned as she eyed his erection. Ready and willing wasn't in it. "You are so magnificent." She stroked the side of his cock with her fingers and throwing caution to the winds, let instinct lead as she kissed the head of his cock and circled it with her lips.

"My God! Gloria!" he said and went completely silent. He hadn't fainted, not if the movement of his hands in her hair was anything to go by. She swallowed him deep, forgetting the night, her run, and the sticky problem of her now mended ankle. Nothing mattered but him and her and her narrow bed and this little room up in the eaves.

"Hold on," he said, at last as he pulled her head away. "Much more of that, darling, and I'll go full throttle."

"Let's go full throttle together," she replied and grinned at him. Talk about unromantic images.

"Sure?"

"Yes!"

"Just a jiffy."

Didn't take him long to reach for his trousers and grab the necessary little white paper envelope. In no time at all, he was sheathed and ready. Together they pulled back the bedclothes. Need overcame them both in a fast, wild coupling. He was deep in her and she decided to put her mended ankle to the test, wrapping her legs around his waist and locking her ankles to hold him close.

Just as well Mary was out of the house! They lost themselves in each other, both groaning and sighing and giving wild cries of love until Gloria came in a wild leap of passion and he followed with wild jerks of his hips and a loud, "Oh God! Gloria," before he sagged onto her.

She relaxed her legs, and rolled on her side, wrapping her right leg over his hip as they lay together in a lovely sweaty tangle of legs and arms and sated passion.

She must have dozed off. She woke as he kissed her and whispered her name.

"You're dressed."

"Yes, It's a bit nippy to stroll home in just a string vest."

"Now that would get the tongues wagging." If anyone was around to see.

"I hate to leave you."

"Don't then." She was feeling reckless.

"Don't tempt me, love."

She shouldn't and he was right but damn! "I wish I could."

"Look, love. I have an idea. In the morning I'll go up to see Dr. Doyle. Tell her your cast came off and it looks as if your ankle is healed and could she have a look. After all, it could have been just a sprain all along. That night was busy. They could have muddled up the X-rays."

If was flimsy and unlikely to convince Alice, who was nobody's fool, but right now, sated and light-headed from wild sex. Lovely wild sex, she amended to herself—Gloria couldn't manage any better. "Come back early."

"I will."

It wasn't until he was gone and she was drifting off to sleep, that she remembered the creature she'd seen on her prowl. She sat up. She had to tell Andrew, but not at . . . She looked at her alarm clock . . . three-thirty in the morning. She'd tell him at breakfast. And where was Mary? She was a grown woman. Gloria wasn't her nanny.

Chapter Twenty

Bela clung to the stone wall of Adlerroost, basking in the moonlight. She was free of her prison and intended to stay that way. Letting the power of the night seep into her bones, she reached out her mind to her sister. "Gela, Gela!"

The reply was faint, but it was there. "Bela?"

"I am free, sister. I'm coming to you."

"Bela, how can you get here without them catching you?"

She had no idea. Just knew, in the depths of her soul, she would free Gela, or they would both perish. She would not serve her vile human masters again. Ever. "I'm coming, just keep your mind open to mine. If it's light before I reach you, I'll find somewhere to hide and come for you tomorrow night. But I will come."

"Wait." Bela waited, heart pounding. What had happened? "Are you there, Bela?"

"Of course. What happened?"

"I moved. There is a patch of floor that the moonlight reaches. I'm sitting there now, waiting. Oh, Bela if you can get me free of this horror."

"I will."

With that thought driving her, Bela eased her way along the outside walls, clinging to window ledges and gaps in the stonework, until she returned to just above her window. She wanted to view the entire compound and assess her best way out. It was quite amazing. From her cell, she'd only seen a narrow strip of the front courtyard and the gated drive leading off into the woods. Now, she realized Adlerroost was a veritable fortress, with many outbuildings and everything surrounded by high wire fences, and patrolled by guards with dogs.

The dogs weren't the worry. She could calm any animal but the guards were less likely to respond to a Fairy's will. Not that she was about to let a few armed guards stop her. Nor was she planning on clinging to the stone walls until dawn. She eased her way around the building until she was above a number of low, metal outbuildings that abutted the schloss walls. Climbing down, she let herself fall onto the roof below. Lying flat, she waited and listened to the guards walk by. She had maybe ten minutes. She looked around, judged the edge of the roof was perhaps eight or ten meters from the three-meter high wire fence. It was a great leap, but she had the strength of vampires. Now was the time to use it. She balanced herself on the roof ridge.

Swift as if she were running on dew-dappled grass, she raced along the ridge. As she approached the edge, she summoned her strength and leapt, skimming the fence and its circles of barbed wire to land on the soft grass outside. Not hesitating even a Fairy heartbeat, she raced toward the safety of the distant trees.

Once in their shelter, she climbed the closest one and perched on a branch, leaning against the trunk. She was free. To stay that way, she had to put as much distance between her and Adlerroost as possible. Her captors had never before come to her in the small hours, but who knew if tonight was the one time they decided their wishes superseded her need for rest?

"Gela?"

"Bela?"

"I am free of my prison and am coming to you. Keep your mind open and lead me."

"Yes!" Bela could picture her sister's smile and sense her budding hope. She would not fail her.

Staying high in the trees, just in case a dog could follow a Fairy's scent, she crossed from branch to branch, swinging and jumping until she reached the edge of the trees. Open fields and a small town lay ahead. Keeping her connection to Gela as her compass, Bela ran, barely touching the ground, avoiding the town, but pausing at a small farm to refresh herself with milk from a sleeping cow in the barn. Then she was off again, delayed as she detoured another village and two more towns. She was nearing Gela but dawn was coming.

"I can not get there tonight, sister. Tomorrow."

"I'll be waiting but, Bela, take care. You do not know the evil these creatures are capable of."

Now was not the time to argue. "I will stay safe, Gela. Who knows better how to hide than a Fairy?"

A few kilometers away, she found the perfect roost in a copse of trees. Scaling the tallest, she settled to rest, just as dawn streaked across the horizon.

Only a few more hours and the Mestan sisters, the last survivors of their family, would be free.

Chapter Twenty-One

Mary had been so engrossed in the sheer pleasure of the water, she lost track of time. The moon was low in the sky by the time she stepped out of the pond and realized she hadn't remembered to bring a towel.

Too late now. She pulled her clothes on over wet skin, tried very hard not to shiver and pretty much failed utterly. There wasn't much she could do about her hair dripping down her neck, except hope she didn't meet anyone on the way back. She headed for the woods and the footpath down to the village, but ended up skirting the woods for a good hundred yards before conceding she was lost.

It was a world easier to find your way along cliff paths than among the Surrey woods.

What now? She could hardly wander around until dawn. She looked at the moon reflected in the dark water. The moon had been behind her when she emerged from the woods. A bit of quick thinking about the current position and its path in the sky and she set off at a brisk walk in what she hoped was the right direction. She didn't find the footpath but she did notice a lane in the distance and headed for it. Reasoning the village was in the valley, she set off downhill and soon the road emerged into farmland.

The village was still a long way off. She decided to stay on the road, rather than try cutting across fields. She walked on, nipping over a hedge when she heard an engine approaching. She might well have been offered a lift, but didn't fancy explaining why she was strolling the countryside, with dripping wet hair.

She waited until the vehicle passed—a lorry, she thought, and then followed the hedge to find a gate. Climbing over hawthorne hedges wasn't an experience to repeat if avoidable. She found a stile and she was halfway across when she glanced over her shoulder. In the distance was a dark shape. Some instinct had her off the stile and behind the hedge. She peered over, curious as to who else was wandering the countryside in the middle of the night. In the far distance was a silhouette of a man. Leaping. No, flying! He leaped in the air and soared over the trees until he was out of sight.

Incredible, but no more incredible than Mary Prioux being a Water Sprite. So, she wasn't the only Other in the neighborhood. Interesting, but best forgotten. She did not want any encounter with a creature who could fly. She stifled the suspicion that anyone out at this hour had to be up to no good. She was, wasn't she? It was part and parcel of hiding one's nature in an alien land.

The last wasn't entirely fair. Yes, she did feel like an outsider, but she and her pupils had been welcomed and offered a home. It was her job to fit in. Somehow. It was being landlocked that felt so confining.

After that she walked faster, until the village came into view. Taking her bearings from the church tower, she set off at a run in the waning moonlight, cutting across fields and allotments and finally finding herself in the lane leading to Gloria's cottage.

She nipped into a cottage doorway as Gloria's gate opened. And Andrew Barron walked out.

Good for Gloria! He'd seemed a nice man, the one time

Mary had met him. Now she really had to be inconspicuous. She was pretty much hidden in the middle doorway of a row of cottages that fronted onto the lane, unless he looked her way.

He obviously had far more interesting things on his mind than a shadow in a doorway.

She waited until his footsteps faded and ran the last few yards to Gloria's gate and the back door.

Making her way in the dark wasn't as hard as it would be for a human. Mary took off her shoes and tiptoed upstairs. Not a sound from Gloria's bedroom. Good.

Undressing in the dark, she paused only to dry her hair with a towel as best she could, before falling into bed.

What a night! But she'd found water deep enough to sustain her soul and that was what really mattered.

Alice smoothed the creased and yellowed fabric. Trying to turn the confirmation dress she'd worn when she was fifteen into a wedding dress was no doubt an exercise in futility, but darn it. She wanted a white wedding with as many of the frills as could be managed in wartime. Selfish perhaps. Self-indulgent definitely but after all, one only had one wedding day and she wanted a long white dress and veil.

Only this dress was cut for a flat-chested teenager and the skirt stopped at her knees.

"Alice, dear, I thought I heard you." Gran, in dressing gown and nightie, stood in the doorway.

"Yes, I woke early and had an idea." She held up the yellowed dress. "I thought this might be adapted to a wedding dress."

Gran rubbed the fabric between her fingers.

"It's still good. Maybe if we can get more cloth, we can make the bodice and sleeves out of this and use something else for the skirt. It's a start. Isn't the veil in there somewhere? That was real Brussels lace."

Yes, it was, and it had been a terrible embarrassment at the

time as everyone else had plain net veils, but Alice had worn
it so as not to disappoint her great-aunt Lily, who'd given it to
her. "Let's see if we can find it."

It was still in the box with the name of a shop in Brussels.

"We've half a dress and a veil," Gran said. "All we have to
get is something new, something borrowed and something
blue. I already have a silver sixpence put away safely. How
about we go downstairs and get warm? It's cold up here."

That, Alice would not argue with.

The old dress and veil looked worn in the brightness of the
kitchen, but Gran's insistence that a good soak in a blue bag
would freshen it up was convincing. Now all she needed was
another three or four yards of silk. Right, might as well wish
for oranges or bananas.

"How about you put the toast on dear? I'll get the kettle
going."

Alice reached for the loaf and remembered Gran's reservations about the new baker. Gloria and Andrew's encounter pretty
much overshadowed concerns about national security. Still the
man—or whatever he was—made a nice loaf of bread. Alice cut
four good slices and was reaching for the matches to light the
grill when the doorbell rang.

"You get it, dear. It's bound to be for you. I'll see to the toast."

It was Andrew Barron himself. "I'm sorry to bother you
this early but something came up."

"Not an injury at the plant?" Of course not, he'd have
phoned for that. "Come in."

"It's about Gloria."

"Something wrong?"

"Not exactly. It's her leg."

"It's bothering her?"

"You could say that but not really." He ran his hand through his hair. "I'm making a hash of this. Really she's fine. Better than fine but we need your help. Will you come see her?"

What was going on? Something, but nothing urgent it seemed. "I need more specifics than that. Gran's making breakfast, how about you come and have a cup of tea and a piece of toast and tell me all about it?"

That offer didn't ease his anxiety one iota. "Look, this will sound utterly bizarre, but I don't think her ankle's broken after all."

Really? "You feel qualified to make that decision?" A bit snippy yes, but for a man who ran a vital cog in the war machine he was definitely a ditherer.

"Right now, yes! I do. Please come. Give her a call if you like. I'm not making sense, am I?"

Seemed frightfully rude to agree. "Gloria knows you're here?"

"Yes!"

And Gloria was no one's fool, even if the love of her life was a spectacularly poor communicator. "I'll come. Let me get my coat."

Alice put her head around the kitchen door to warn Gran she'd be late for breakfast and nipped into her office and grabbed her bag. "How did you get up here?" she asked him. "Drive?"

"Er . . . no, I cycled up here."

Of course his rather spiffy car was a charred hulk. "Put your cycle in the back and I'll drive us down."

He was singularly uncommunicative on the drive into the village. Which left Alice wondering what in the name of sanity was going on. She kept telling herself that Gloria wouldn't have sent him to call her out without a very good reason.

It still didn't make much sense.

* * *

Gloria was dressed, sitting on the side of the bed. She looked at Andrew as they both walked in. "You told her?"

"Not everything."

She had never seen Gloria look so flustered, but that pretty much passed Alice by, her attention being riveted on Gloria's legs dangling off the side of the bed.

"Gloria, what's going on and how in hell did you get that cast off?" Alice was not normally given to swearing but in the circumstances felt justified. "It's been barely a week since you broke it."

"It came off," Gloria replied, "and then I noticed my ankle was alright. It wasn't broken after all. Had to be some sort of confusion in Casualty."

One look at Alice's disbelieving eyes and Gloria knew that line wasn't working. Yet. "Bizarre, isn't it? I bet things like that happen all the time. Misdiagnoses, X-rays jumbled up, records muddled."

"Gloria, I saw your X-rays. Your tibia was fractured."

"Had to be the wrong X-ray."

"For crying out loud, Gloria! Talk some sense!"

"Tell her the truth, love," Andrew said.

"No!" How could he? "Andrew!"

"Sounds like a good plan to me," Alice said, perching on the side of the bed. "What happened? It didn't just drop off."

"Trust her, Gloria," Andrew sat on the opposite side of the bed, holding both her hands. "Trust her. She's your friend and she's a doctor. She's bound by patient confidence. Professional ethics and all that."

Did the Hippocratic oath extend to this? Probably not. And even if it did, Alice would flip her wig. She was so practical, guided by science and reason. Not shapeshifting and animal magic.

"I'm your friend, Gloria," Alice said, "not just a doctor. Tell me."

What a temptation, but it could mean the end of her career. Who'd want a nurse who turned furry?

"Tell me, Gloria," Alice repeated. "It didn't just fall off!"

Oh dammit! "Actually, it did!"

Alice started. "Come off it, Gloria. Make sense."

"Listen to her, doctor," Andrew said, squeezing Gloria's hands. "It will."

She might regret this the rest of her life, but Andrew accepted her and what else really mattered? Even losing Alice's friendship and her job paled in significance beside Andrew's acceptance.

"Alice, this sounds far-fetched, but it did just drop off, and hold onto your hat. The next bit skirts the perimeters of reason." Deep breath time. She was taking a blind leap of trust for the second time in only a few hours. "It came off, Alice, because I'm a shifter. When the moon is full, I change my skin and become a fox. The cast no longer fit my leg and just dropped off. I wasn't sure what to do, so I tried a couple of steps and found I could run as well as ever. So I did. When I shifted back to me, my leg was still alright." It was done. If Alice called for the men with straitjackets, Andrew would send them away.

"Goodness gracious!" Alice looked, and sounded, astonished. Not shocked, horrified, or repulsed. Just really surprised. "You become a fox at the full moon?"

"Yes."

Alice smiled. No, she grinned. "You mean you can run around as a fox and no one knows it's you?"

"Yes."

Alice looked at Andrew. "And this, I presume, is not news to you?"

"Not this minute. It was late last night."

"Alright, Gloria. Your secret is safe with me. Seems I will have to perjure my professional honor to sort this out, but you're not alone, you know. There's another shape changer in the village."

Andrew tensed. He wasn't the only one surprised but . . . "Not possible, Alice. I know another Werefox if I meet one."

"He doesn't change into a fox, Gloria."

"Who is it?" Andrew asked.

"Not my secret to share. But I think he might," she paused and gave Gloria a big hug. "The other shifter aside, you're not the only Other in the village. There's a few of us and I think we might need you. Are you willing to do what you can for the war effort and use your extraordinary skills to fight the enemy?"

Now she was the one bewildered. "How?"

"Come up to The Gallop and talk to Gran."

"Mrs. Burrows?"

"Yes. I've a secret too. I'm Pixie. So is Gran and there is the other shifter and Mother Longhurst, until she disappeared. We had a problem last month that we took care of but there's another now. And you might be just what we need."

"Look here, doctor, this doesn't make much sense to me," Andrew said.

"If you can accept Gloria for what she is, a couple of Devon Pixies shouldn't be too hard to swallow. The shifter we'll see about later. I think for now, you'd best come home with me and talk to Gran. She's sort of in charge."

That, Gloria could understand. Mrs. Burrows was one formidable old lady.

"Are you willing, Gloria?" Andrew asked.

What did she have to lose? Better not answer that! "Yes. I'll leave a note for Mary. She's still asleep. She was out late last night."

"Good, I'll drive you. No one will hear this from me. I promise."

How could she not believe her? And what the heck was a Pixie? Seemed they were more than little creatures who sat around under toadstools in picture books.

* * *

Mrs. Burrows was the biggest surprise of all. "You're Other too, Gloria? Wonderful! And a Werefox, eh? Pity there aren't more of you but one must count one's blessings and you're willing to join us? Splendid! Now let me think." Gloria would have welcomed that opportunity too. Things were racing ahead and it took all she had to keep up and Andrew looked totally at sea. "Tell you what, Alice. We need Howell up here." She turned to Andrew. "Mr. Barron, can we trust you?"

Wrong thing to say. Andrew's brows all but met. "Mrs. Burrows, I would protect Gloria with my life."

"I know that!" she replied, a trifle testily Gloria thought. "You're in love with her. The whole village knows that. What I'm asking is are you to be trusted with the secrets of other Others?"

"If it doesn't harm Gloria or my country. I will keep your secrets."

"Good lad, I'd hoped so! You rode your bicycle up here, didn't you? Be a good lad and ride down to the village and tell Howard Pendragon I need him up here. While you're at it, might as well tell Peter too. Invite them to stay for lunch. Tell them I have important news. Get going, then."

"You'll be alright, Gloria?" he asked, not moving an inch.

"Yes."

"Fine then. I'll be off."

"And tell Howell to bring some Brussels sprouts. I'm almost out."

Andrew left.

Mrs. Burrows bustled off into the pantry.

Alice gave a little smile. "Let's go into my office. I need to X-ray that leg. Just to be sure. Then we concoct your story."

"You give her a cup of tea first," Mrs. Burrows said, coming back with an apron full of potatoes. "She looks all done in."

No point in arguing that. Gloria felt all done in and it seemed things were just starting.

Chapter Twenty-Two

Wilhelm Bloch approached the summons with confidence. Whatever Weiss might or might not decree, Bloch could respond. He'd used his week in the village well. The cover was flourishing. The female servant had failed him, unlike the lad he'd impressed to clean for him and was a handy source of sustenance too. He'd easily last for the week or two, more if needed. And after a night reconnoitering the countryside, Bloch knew the lie of the land, the position of the munitions plant and perfect places to site explosives. There would be no bungling on his watch.

But Eiche's disappearance was still a mystery. To the villagers Gabriel Oak was just an old woman's nephew who left in a hurry after his aunt was arrested as a spy. Overcome with righteous shame, seemed to be the consensus. With the Waite woman dead, no one could ever trace Eiche's origins. Their unit was safe and anticipating the coming victory.

But until then, he had to endure the incessant meetings in Weiss's billet. Bloch often wondered about the invisible landlady. Had Weiss killed her? Did he keep her confined to feed off? Or was she an active who worked for the cause like the now dead Miss Waite?

As if the disposition of a mortal mattered.

"Well," Weiss began, "soon we must consider the days after the invasion. But for now, we follow our directives."

The "for now" was impossible to miss. Weiss had plans, did he? Understandable. They all did. Perhaps they should compare. No! It was best to keep one's schemes to oneself.

"Well, Schmidt?" Weiss began and Bloch was forced to listen to Schmidt's activities as an ambulance driver, and his success in gathering a list of disaffected Britons: a number of his host's fellow black shirts, gone to ground after Mosley's imprisonment, and interestingly a good few were Communist confederates of his host's parents.

"The Communists are a tightly organized cell," he said. "They could be useful."

"Indeed?" Weiss echoed Bloch's own curiosity. "How?" They would be some of the first in the camps, when the invasion came.

"As a sop to our so-called masters, to win us a little space to act on our own perhaps, or, the reverse. I can bind them to my will and use them for our purpose."

It was a good plan. Bloch wished he'd come up with it. He couldn't object to Schmidt binding these humans to him; he'd done the same with the youth who cleaned for him and would have used the woman Doris the same, if she hadn't eluded him.

"And now, Bloch?" Weiss asked.

He permitted himself the indulgence of a satisfied smile. "I have become an indispensable member of the community. Incredible how gullible these Inselaffen are. Fill their guts with bread and they respond with adulation. The fools accept and trust me. I could put anything in their bread and they would gorge on it. Later perhaps? For now, I have scouted the area around and observed that munitions plant. It still functions around the clock. It must be put out of action and soon. There are several places I can conceal explosives until we receive the signal."

"It is to be destroyed but not by explosives. After Eiche's failure, our masters have another plan."

"Indeed?"

"Indeed. Seems we are no longer trusted with dangerous toys like explosives. We are to set flares a specific distance from the camp and they will send bombers."

"To the site we designate," Schmidt said.

"And we will indicate the correct one," Weiss said. "Leaving that plant intact will not serve us, and destroying it will earn a little respect for our abilities and trust in our loyalty."

"What is the plan?" Might as well know.

"Flares will be delivered to you tomorrow, in a shipment of flour. Be ready to plant and light them at a signal."

"And when will I get this signal?"

"The afternoon before the attack. You will receive a postcard giving the exact time. Place the flares in position an hour in advance." He handed Bloch a sealed envelope. "That shows where you are to position the flares. Memorize it and destroy it. And be sure you place them exactly as shown. Eiche failed. You can not."

"I won't."

So, Bloch thought to himself as he ran back across country, an attack was imminent. Good. Nothing like a nice mass of carnage to crack the confidence and complacency of those pathetic villagers.

The coming week would be interesting.

But one thought nagged at him. Had the others not noticed? Or were they playing their own dark games? He'd been tempted to raise the point, but some instinct held his tongue. Maybe they hadn't noticed. Impossible. That Fairy creature always invaded their thoughts when they met and often when they didn't. But not this time. Had she lost her skills? Or was there another reason for her absence?

* * *

"Now, Gloria, tell me about your Otherness." Mrs. Burrows passed her a cup of tea and then took a seat opposite at the kitchen table.

Gloria took a deep breath. She wanted Andrew close but he hadn't returned. She'd trusted Alice, and Mrs. Burrows seemed totally unperturbed at the announcement of Gloria's furry alter ego.

"Alright, but first, Alice said you were a Pixie?"

"I am. Full-blooded and proud of it. As was Alice's mother. Her father was a plain garden human or so we thought but now Alice is harnessing her skills—she's so powerful—I think he had to have Other blood in him."

Ask a question, get confusion. "Forgive me, but I never imagined there were others in the village with a second nature."

"*Others*," the old woman replied with a smile, giving the word emphasis. "I had not suspected you, but another did."

"Sergeant Pendragon?" Mrs. Burrows nodded. "What is he?" He had to be the other shifter Alice mentioned.

"That is not my secret to tell, but you sensed he was Other?"

Gloria nodded. "Yes, I suppose I did. I didn't think about that but last month I'd been out on the heath, as my fox self, and saw an intruder laying mines or something around the perimeter of Andrew's plant. I didn't know what to do, so I raised the alarm as best I could. Afterwards I knew I had to tell someone. So I told him," she paused. "At the time he said something that I now realize implied he sensed my Otherness." Funny how right the term sounded.

"That Howell doesn't miss a trick. But he would never intrude. Can you share your Other self with him? With us? Brytewood and England need you. There are enemies among us."

That last sentence sent a chill down her back. "Yes, but they arrested Miss Waite."

"My dear, the sadly departed Jane Waite was just a minor pawn in this game. There are far more deadly creatures lurking about than a retired schoolteacher with Nazi sympathies."

The chill curdled in her gut. She looked at Alice, who'd just come into the kitchen. "What is going on?"

Mrs. Burrows glanced up at the clock. "Best wait until the men get here and we can pool all we know. Make a plan of attack."

Mrs. Burrows wasn't loony or senile. That Gloria was certain of, but only about twenty-five percent of this made sense.

Alice coming into the room switched the conversation but rather complicated things. Seemed Gloria's X-rays, far from showing a healed or healing break, showed no signs of any fracture. At all.

"Seems healing is one of your strengths, Gloria," Mrs. Burrows said with one of her smiles. "Interesting."

"Downright confusing, if you ask me."

"Will make your fiction about jumbled X-rays more believable," Alice pointed out.

With all this talk of Otherness and enemies and England needing her, Gloria had almost forgotten about that little wrinkle. "What should we do? You call the hospital?"

"I think we'd better go with the fiction of a sprain. I'll fix you up with a totally unnecessary crepe bandage and have you take it easy for a week or so and by then something much more interesting is bound to happen and no one will notice you're not injured any more."

"I think you're right there, my love," Mrs. Burrows said, with a funny sort of smile.

Alice shook her head.

Gloria decided to give up trying to follow all this. "I wonder why Andrew's taking so long?"

Andrew was almost at the crossroads in the center of the village when the plane flew overhead. It was so low, the German markings were unmistakable as were the concentric circles of the fighter plane on its tail. Andrew stopped in the road and watched as the German plane looped and doubled back, climbing higher as it tried to evade pursuit. He didn't succeed. The RAF pilot matched him twist for turn, firing nonstop. The strange ballet circled overhead, until the Luftwaffe pilot surged ahead and looked as if he'd be off home with a tale to tell, when the gunner scored a hit, the sound clear in the crisp autumn air. The German plane went into a dive with a tail of billowing black smoke. A dark dot fell from the plane, its descent slowed as the mushroom canopy of his parachute opened.

After a triumphant dip of its wings, the RAF plane straightened and turned north, heading for home.

And Andrew shook his head. Damn! He'd better alert someone. He pedaled like mad the rest of the way, arriving at Sergeant Pendragon's gate about the same time as a panting red-faced ARP volunteer.

"Got to see the sergeant!" The man must have run all the way from the ARP post in the parish hall.

Seemed the meeting with Mrs. Burrows and the doctor would take second place to this. "Did you see where the pilot landed?"

"Over near the Longhurst farm, seemed like. They sent me to get the police and the Home Guard out. The damn field phone's on the blink." He bent over to catch his breath again. "I need to get up to tell Sergeant Jones too."

"Pendragon has a phone. Come in and use his." He was making free in the circumstances . . .

"What transport do we have?" Andrew asked, once inside the Pendragon kitchen. "I could call the plant and ask for someone to bring a lorry down."

"Sir James has the Home Guard jeep," Sergeant Pendragon volunteered. "We could call him."

"Alice is closer than Wharton Lacey," Peter said.

Pendragon took charge. Calling the police house, and finding Sergeant Jones was off for the day but Constable Parlett

was already cycling up to Cherry Hill Farm after Tom
Longhurst called in the news.

Peter phoned Alice, then grabbed his first aid kit while
Pendragon called up to the Longhursts.

"Well, I never," he said, as he hung up. "Don't think we
need to call out the Home Guard. Seems the pilot landed in the
middle of Tom's mother's cabbages and is bleeding in their
kitchen."

"Badly injured?" Peter asked.

"Who knows? Can't be too bad if he can still walk but it'll
be good to have the doctor look at him. Not that you wouldn't
do a fine job, lad," he added.

"You won't be needing me," Andrew said. He'd take the
chance to talk to Gloria and find out a little of what really was
going on. "Oh," he added, "almost forgot. The doctor and
Mrs. Burrows sent me to down to ask you, Sergeant Pendragon, and Mr. Watson if you'd come up to The Gallop for
lunch. Something's come up." He was not about to go into details. "Maybe later?"

"Urgent?" Peter asked.

"Moderately, but it can wait a couple of hours."

"I'll talk to her on the way," Watson said.

Alice was unlikely to expand on the subject with P.C. Parlett in the car. "I'll see you." It was quite a relief to cycle away.
Andrew met Alice coming down ten minutes later. She pulled
up. "Going back?" she asked.

"Yes. You'll have a car full and I want to see Gloria."

"Don't pepper her with questions, promise? Coming into
the open to you took a lot, and now she's had to face us. It's
not easy."

"Does she think I won't love her?" What a thought!

"Wouldn't hurt to reassure her. I've no idea how long this
will take. We might need to send the pilot to hospital. I'll let
you know."

"Righto."

Alice continued into the village and Andrew started the hard uphill pull to his love. He was darn well going to reassure Gloria he loved her. With Mrs. Burrows around he wasn't going to be able to reassure her as completely as he'd like to but it was a lovely day for October. While they were waiting for everyone to get back, they could go for a stroll. Or something.

He was rather partial to the idea of a "something" with Gloria.

Alice picked up Peter and Sergeant Pendragon. Passed Constable Parlett pedaling and stopped long enough to put his cycle in the back before driving on up toward the Longhurst farm. She was tempted to ask how he'd planned on arresting a prisoner of war on a bicycle but bit it back. Would have been interesting though.

Of course if he was injured badly . . . "Did Tom Longhurst give any specifics about injuries?"

"Just the man was bleeding. Can't be too hurt if he could walk into the house, can he?" Pendragon replied.

Given she remembered her father telling tales of a man who'd walked hundreds of yards with an arm shot off, she wouldn't take an oath on that. "Hopefully. Do you have your bag, Peter?"

"Yes, I grabbed it."

"And I have my handcuffs," Constable Parlett added. "We can take care of one German." He sounded downright chirpy at the prospect. No doubt it would give him something to crow about at the next policeman's get-together.

As she turned into the narrow road that led up to the Longhurst farmhouse, she couldn't miss the balloon of white silk billowing in the field. "Good heavens! It's yards and yards of silk!"

"Peter," she said.

"Yes?" he replied.

"I'll go in and check on the injuries. How about you see what you can do about the parachute."

"If you like." He sounded confused.

"Nice bit of silk there," the constable said. "I know my wife . . ."

"I'll give her what's left over," Alice told him. "I need a wedding dress."

"Oh! Right! Yes!" At last Peter cottoned on. "I'll get it, my dear."

He was as good as his word, setting off across the fields the minute she parked the car. Gathering up all that silk would be quite a task but she fancied Peter was up to it.

Tom Longhurst met her at the door. "Glad you got here, Alice. He seems alright but pale as a sheet and I think he needs stitches."

She paused at the threshold. Half of her wanted to turn on her heel and leave him to bleed to death. He and his lot had bombed the vicarage, dropped countless bombs, killed hundreds of people and had no plans to ease off any time soon. It was because of his lot that Simon was now sitting in a POW camp in Germany and she was supposed to take care of this creature. Why? He was best dead!

She was a doctor, had taken an oath to heal the sick and care for the injured. She took a deep breath and stepped into the Longhurst kitchen.

"I'm so happy to see you, Alice," Mrs. Longhurst said. "I did what I could but he's going to need stitches."

"I'll take care of him."

"I'd best do the official bit first," Constable Parlett said, and strode into the kitchen toward the pair of uniformed legs stretched out from a wingback chair by the fireplace. "I'm Constable Parlett of the Surrey Constabulary and I arrest you as a prisoner of war."

A tired voice replied. "*Ja. Ja.*"

"I need you to surrender all guns and weapons," he went on. Seemingly oblivious to the fact the man probably didn't understand a word of English."

"They're on the table, constable," Tom said. "I took them off him." Parlett looked quite let down. He'd obviously fancied disarming a dangerous enemy combatant. "Unloaded it too. Bullets are in my pocket. Seemed the safest place." He handed them to the constable, who seemed at sea about how to proceed next.

Fair enough. He'd not had much practice.

"How about I have a look at him? I speak a little German too."

She crossed the room. "*Guten Tag. Ich bin Artzin.*"

The man opened his eyes and turned to look at her. He stared. "*Alice! Mien Gott!*"

Her jaw just about hit her knees in shock. Of all the impossible coincidences. "Hans? Hans Falkenau?"

"Oberleutnant Hans Falkenau," he replied, with a nod.

It was beyond reason. Here she was in the farm of her first lover. And first heartbreak, come to that. Her second big love bleeding in front of her while his discarded parachute was being commandeered by her fiance to make her wedding dress.

Strange things happened in wartime.

"You know him, doctor?" the constable asked.

"As it so happens, yes. Years back, we were both students in Dresden."

Tom gave a dirty chuckle. She'd slug him one when she had the chance and no witnesses.

Chapter Twenty-Three

Talk about heart stopping! Hans looked older. Hardly surprising. It had been seven or eight years. He was disheveled too. Rather to be expected after jumping from a burning airplane and narrowly missing death. His left sleeve was ripped and the deep gash on his chin had almost stopped bleeding.

This was not the sort of old lover's meeting that anything could prepare you for.

"So," Hans said, "you are now a doctor. That was always your dream."

"Took some work but I managed it." Career was a safe enough subject. As long as they avoided his. Or Simon's. Or Alan's.

"You assist your father?"

"He died. I took over the practice."

"Ah!" He gave a nod of sympathy. Obviously not wanting to ask how.

"Excuse me, doctor, but maybe you should talk in English so's we all know what's going on," Constable Parlett said.

She was about to stitch up Hans, not reveal state secrets. Not that she knew any. "He doesn't speak much, if any, English and I think it's in all our best interests to get him stitched up and out of here as fast as possible, don't you, constable? If he understands what's going on I think it will move things along."

He gave a grudging nod. "Will it take long?"

"I'll know after I have a better look." She reached for her bag. "Could I have some warm water please, Mrs. Longhurst?"

"Course you can, doctor, and I'll get you a towel and a flannel. Anything else you need? Might as well get everyone a cup of tea, while we're waiting."

God bless old Mrs. Longhurst. She'd keep everyone out of her hair while she saw to Hans.

"Hurt anywhere else beside the chin and your arm?"

"I don't think so. I'll have a few bruises but . . ." He winced as she palpated his arm around the ripped sleeve.

"Tender?"

"A bit."

"Look, Hans, I'll stitch you up, use antiseptic and give you a couple of painkillers. They'll do a thorough check later."

"Where, Alice? Where are they taking me?" He sounded scared witless. Had Simon been wounded when he was taken prisoner? Had some doctor stitched him up? They must have, right? Geneva Conventions and all that. "Alice," he asked, again his voice low and urgent. "For pity's sake, tell me"

"Honest, Hans. I don't know." She wasn't sure anyone else did either. "Most likely they'll take you into Leatherhead or Dorking. To the nearest police station. Someone there will know what to do. We're a bit off the beaten track here." Or were they? Not too remote to get visited by vampires.

Hans winced as she stuck the hypodermic needle in his cheek. "Sorry, this'll sting a bit."

"So," he said, as she waited for the numbing to take effect. "I finally make the visit I promised years ago."

"Well, life intervened."

"Indeed it did. How are your brothers?"

She couldn't avoid this after all. "Alan is in the navy. Hardly an official secret that. "And Simon," she paused to pick up a needle and suture thread, "he was taken prisoner at Dunkirk."

"Ah!" He let out his breath as she gently manipulated the edges of his cut. "If they ever do an exchange, I will ask to be traded for him."

Nice thought but . . . "Something tells me you're both going to be stuck where you are for a good long time." She closed the last stitch and covered them with a sticking plaster. "Now let's have a look at your arm. Didn't you have a flight jacket on?" She had no idea what German pilots wore but she doubted they flew in shirt sleeves.

"I took it off. The old woman insisted."

"Let's have a look and hope it's not broken." She was feeling decidedly iffy about broken bones today. He had a full range of motion and the cut was more of a bad graze than anything else. A generous application of aquaflavine and he was set. Or as set as he was likely to be for a while. "What about your sister?"

"Gerda is married. She has two children now. Clara and Claudia."

"When you get to write tell her I say 'Hello'." That wasn't breaking any law. Was it?

"I will tell her fate brought me down in your village and you rescued me from a mob of angry peasants with pitchforks."

"That might get inked out by the censor."

"I could ask her to visit Simon, or at least write if you know where he is."

"When I find out where they take you, I'll write." This was ludicrous, trading promises of letters and visits as if they were still students. "We'd best get going. I know Constable Parlett is itching to carry you off."

"Finished at last, doctor?" the aforementioned constable asked, as she started tidying up.

"He's all yours, constable."

"He can have a cup of tea first," Mrs. Longhurst said.

"Everyone else has had one. You'll have one, doctor, won't you?"

"Would be lovely."

"Here we are then." Alice took hers and Mrs. Longhurst handed another to Hans. "You let the other get cold, drink this one up. Make you feel better."

Hans gave the mug of milky tea a dubious look. He was going to have to get used to English-style tea. "Drink it," she said, taking a sip of hers. "It's a gesture of hospitality. Don't refuse."

"For you, Alice, I will." Bravely he sipped the warm tea. "Different," he said and he smiled at Mrs. Longhurst. "Zank you!"

"There! I knew he could speak English!" Parlett said, sounding irate.

"And you," Hans said, smiling at him, "have a hat like a piss pot."

Alice was very proud of herself for not smiling. "Behave yourself," she told Hans.

"I will, Alice. I promise."

Just then Sir James arrived, spruce in his Home Guard uniform, and took over. It gave Alice's heart a bit of a lurch to see Hans driven off to some prison camp, somewhere in the wilds of who knew where. Would she try to find out where he was?

"Hadn't we better get back?" Peter asked. "Your grandmother is expecting us."

Yes, Gran was waiting and the man she loved had just filled the back of her shooting brake with white silk. Murky and muddy white silk, but she had her wedding dress, courtesy of Hans Falkenau. She would write and thank him.

She squeezed Peter's hand. "Let's get going."

"You know, it's funny," she said, half to herself as they drove home. "I've tried so hard not to think about the friends I had in Dresden and one, literally, drops out of the sky into Brytewood." Now, she couldn't help thinking about the others: Hans's sister, Gerda. Had she married Rudi, the young lawyer she'd been engaged to? Paul Tannenbaum, who was training to be a priest. Dieter Wolf, who owned a boat and took them for rides down the Elbe. It was a lifetime, several lifetimes, ago.

"I'm afraid Parlett is going to view you as suspect ever after this," Peter said.

"I imagine that's the least of our worries right now. You don't know all that's been going on."

"That's right. Helen was summoning us all up to The Gallop." Pendragon said. "Trouble?"

"More of a problem that Gran believes is a great advantage." Better be more specific. "We've discovered a new Other in the village."

"Just the one?" Pendragon asked.

"One on our side."

Andrew made it back to Alice's house, panting and huffing after pedaling up the hill like a man possessed, to find Gloria and Mrs. Burrows peeling potatoes and chatting as if they hadn't a care in the world.

"Everything alright?" Mrs. Burrows asked, as she scooped up a handful of peelings and dumped then on a folded newspaper.

Hardly. He felt a bit of a twerp coming back here when Alice and the others were off to apprehend an enemy combatant.

"Don't you worry, young man," Mrs. Burrows said. "I doubt a lone pilot, one most likely in shock, disoriented and probably injured to boot, can cause much harm but they'll be busy awhile I imagine and then they have the drive back. We've got lunch on the way, I don't suppose with all the excitement you remembered the Brussels sprouts."

"Sorry."

"Never mind. We'll make do with carrots and cabbage, we've baked eggs and onions. Oh, the days when we used to have a nice piece of sirloin or a leg of lamb for Sunday lunch."

"I think we're going to have a feast," Gloria said.

"It's as good as ready. Once we finish these potatoes, I think you need to try that ankle out, Gloria. See how it really is. Why don't you and Mr. Barron take a stroll up to the orchard? Take a basket with you. Right at the far end, by the gate that leads onto the lane, are three Christmas Pearmains. See if you can find any ripe ones." She crossed to the pantry and produced a stout basket. "Here you are. See what you can find and do take your time. It's going to be ages before they get back."

"Do you get the feeling we've been thrown out of the house?" Andrew asked, as the door closed behind them.

Gloria grinned. "Definitely. She pretty much warned me she would. Told me I had to tell you all I knew about my . . ." she paused, "Otherness."

What the blazes did one say to that? "Oh."

"Do you want to hear?" Her voice went flat. Scared?

"Hell, yes, Gloria." He took her by the shoulders and turned her to face him. "Christ Almighty, I love you, Gloria. I have no idea what life will be like with a wife who turns furry, but I'm not backing off."

"I didn't actually say I'd marry you. Don't actually remember you asking me."

"I'm asking you now. Are you going to tell me 'no'?"

"I'm going to tell you about being furry."

He took a deep breath. "Do you really want to go and pick apples?"

"It'll get us away from the house. In case they come back sooner than expected."

Highly unlikely, given the distance up to Cherry Hill Farm and back. "Let's go then."

The orchard was twenty or so trees, beyond the vegetable garden. No doubt intended to serve a Victorian-sized family.

Most of the trees had been picked, but Gloria seemed to know her way around and led the way to a trio of trees at the far end.

"How's your leg?" he asked. She didn't appear to have any trouble walking on it.

"Feels just as it should. I'd never know it was broken." Forget picking fruit! She took his hand and tugged. "Let's go sit on the gate, you fire questions at me and I'll answer."

All he had to do was decide where to start.

Perched on the gate, they looked across cornfields waiting to be plowed under after harvesting, and on the left, the rising ground to the heath.

They weren't here to admire the Surrey Hills.

"Tell me," he said, reaching over to hold her hand. "When did you first know about being," he made himself say it, "a Werefox." Hadn't been that hard. Not really. Just sent his mind in a twist, that was all.

She squeezed his hand. And kept hold of it. "I never knew my parents. I was led to believe they were dead. I was raised by an aunt: Auntie Ethel. Whether she was my real aunt, I don't know but she knew my parents and talked about them, had photos. I went to the local girl's school, joined the Brownies and the Girl Guides, played hockey and was the champion runner in the school and pretty much did what all the other girls at school did. Most had parents, some of the boarders didn't, so I sort of felt like everyone else.

"Auntie Ethel gave me the usual talk girls get about periods and said once I started, she had a lot to explain to me. In the arrogance of youth, I assumed she meant about babies and that I'd already picked up from the girls at school and a friend whose mother bred Pekingese. But that was not what Auntie Ethel had to tell me. She told me I was a shifter, a shape changer, and soon I would have to heed the call of the full moon.

"I only half believed her, but she'd never lied to me and I didn't think she was about to start. She warned me to keep the secret to myself." She looked at him. "You're the first person I ever told."

For that, he kissed her. "I love you," he said, holding her face in his hands. "Your secret will always be safe with me. It's our secret now."

She blinked, her eyes shiny, and kissed him back. "There's much more."

"Go on." Holy smoke! She had to have been terrified. "Weren't you upset?"

"Not then, it was all rather over my head. But the full moon came ten days later. Auntie Ethel told me she couldn't help me change but an old friend of my mother's was coming for me. Since I'd never before had much mention of anyone connected to either of my parents, I was dubious and curious at the same time.

"Thursday came. It was May so the days were drawing out and not long after I'd finished my homework and was settling down to listen to the Archers on the radio, an old man—or so he seemed to me at thirteen—drove up in a rather swish black car and rang the doorbell.

"My aunt introduced him as Mr. John Barrett and said he and his wife would help me. Then I got scared. The thought of going off with a total stranger, armed with nothing but the newly discovered knowledge that I was a Werefox, just about gave me the willies. I refused to go. Said I had homework to do. I remember John (he told me to call him John—stunned me no end as I'd never been allowed to call an adult by their Christian name) said he understood, he'd been terrified the first time he turned, that Auntie Ethel was a wonderful woman and had taken good care of me for my parents' sake but this was something she couldn't teach me."

"So you went?"

"Yes. I drove away in that fantastic car. I later learned it was a Lancia, and sat in the back seat with his wife, whom I called Evie, and she talked about being a Were. The drive took a while. They lived down in Sussex near Cuckfield on acres of woods and open country. To make a long story short, I changed with them and ran in the woods and fields all night. I slept most of the next day—I assume Auntie Ethel phoned the school and said I was ill, and then they took me home after lunch.

"It became a routine, they'd pick me up and let me run with them. When the full moon fell on a weekend, or school holidays, I'd stay several days. I learned to separate my selves. They taught me that. In Reigate I was a pupil at Madisson Mead School. In Cuckfield I was a fox running free. I never met another shifter, and they both died not long after I went up to Westminster to start nursing. Then my aunt died. When I finished training, I came back this way." She looked his way, her face taut and worried. "That's pretty much it."

One hell of a lot, he thought. "How the heck did you manage in London?"

"It wasn't easy. Some months, especially if I was on nights, I'd have to skip changing. Didn't feel good, but I learned how to hold it in. When my aunt died, she left me a little money and I bought my cottage here. I used to get the train down and change and run. I got to know the people here. Met Alice— she was in med school then. When the old district nurse retired, her father backed me for the job."

There had to be more, a whole lot more. It could wait. He needed time to digest all this. She seemed to be mulling it over too. She'd gone silent. Pondering her odd adolescence? Scared of his reaction? He let go of her hand and put his arm around her shoulders. He'd pull her close if they wouldn't be in risk of falling off. "Gloria. Marry me."

Now she went really silent. He'd swear she wasn't even breathing until she let out a gasp. "You mean it?"

"Hell, yes. I want you, Gloria."

"Furry nights and all?"

"You bet. You can keep my feet warm."

Her shove did unbalance him, the grass was damp but as

she tumbled on top, he really didn't care. "It could be difficult," she said.

"Being married often is but I don't think that's any reason not to. Do you?"

She looked at him as if he were demented. Perhaps he was. Then she smiled, "Yes, please," she replied, wrapping her arms around his neck, and kissed him.

Now he really was demented. Crazed, wild and thrilled. Her mouth was sheer magic, the touch of her tongue, a miracle. As he fumbled with her coat buttons, she let out little whimpers of joy that suggested she was equally demented. Her hands were under his sweater, yanking at his shirt and caressing his vest. He wanted her naked. He needed to be naked. Ached to feel her skin to skin once again. "Will you come home with me?" he whispered into her hair as they paused for breath. "I want you."

She hesitated. She was a public figure with a reputation to preserve. Damn! He was a selfish cad just asking her.

"Yes! I want you too. Let's hope this confab of Mrs. Burrows doesn't take too long."

He'd clean forgotten their reason for being up here.

Chapter Twenty-Four

"What's the matter, Alice?" Gloria asked. She'd never seen her friend so on edge.

"Are you alright, my love?" Mrs. Burrows asked almost simultaneously.

Alice thought about it a minute. "Yes, I'm alright but the pilot that bailed out was someone I knew. A friend from the year I spent in Dresden. Rather gave me a bit of a turn."

There were times that the English tendency for understatement amounted to ludicrous. "A turn! Honestly Alice! I'd say it was a bash with a crowbar between the eyes!"

"Nasty shock, I would think, my love," Mrs. Burrows said.

"It was."

"A nice lunch will pick you up. Come on, everyone. I lit the dining room fire since there's so many of us." She organized everyone into carrying warmed plates and dishes and for the next half hour or so they ate their fill. And talked about village politics, the new evacuees, the situation in the Channel islands, and Alice's delight in having a wedding dress—or at least the beginnings of one.

No one mentioned Gloria's little idiosyncrasy.

That was to come.

After they cleared away the dishes, Mrs. Burrows produced

an apple crumble and a jug of custard. "I think it's time to get down to business," she said, passing around plates of steaming crumble and custard. "Gloria, you know Alice and I are Pixies, you don't know about Howell."

Sergeant Pendragon's face creased in a tight smile. "Want me to tell them, Helen?"

"Indeed I do."

He nodded, a bit of a twinkle in his eyes. "I'm a Dragon." That was certainly a conversation stopper. But seemed it was only news to her and Andrew.

"I beg your pardon," Andrew said. "A Dragon? As in St. George and the Dragon?"

Howell Pendragon let out a great laugh, but a laugh with a bit of a roar in it. "No, Mr. Barron, not like that, as in a Welsh Dragon. I come from the rock of the mountains."

"So you shift?" Gloria asked. "You change? You have wings?" Now that was a thought. Her Earthbound existence seemed pretty mundane by comparison. No wonder she'd felt he was someone to confide in. It made sense now.

Not to Andrew. "Wait a minute here. You mean Dragons as in fly across the sky and breathe fire?"

Pendragon nodded. "When needed. Don't do the fire-breathing bit much these days. Trouble with the blackout."

"Incredible," Andrew muttered.

"More incredible than me turning furry?" Gloria asked.

"Well, yes. I've seen foxes. I've never seen a Dragon."

"Actually you have," Peter said. "You're sitting opposite one."

"No disrespect or anything, but the wings and the fire-breathing are a bit out of the ordinary."

"I've seen both," Peter replied. "Didn't recognize it for what it was at the time but the sergeant saved my skin. Later, I saw him half change, right here in this house."

"I see."

Gloria wondered if Andrew really did. "Can you change any time?" she asked. "Is there a time you have to change?"

"No, little fox. I change when I choose. No call of the moon for me. Just as well really. I'm rather large when I shift and, as Andrew pointed out, a fox might pass unremarked, but a Dragon would never blend into the Surrey hedgerows."

"When do you change then?" It was wonderful to meet another shifter. Not that she could see them running through the woods together.

"When needed, Gloria, when needed."

"Just a minute here," Andrew said, panic in his voice. "I'm trying to keep up with all this. Finding Gloria is more than I thought bowled me over. Then I find Dr. Doyle and Mrs. Burrows are Pixies, and to top that off Sergeant Pendragon breathes fire and grows Dragon wings. I keep thinking what else I've missed." He looked at Peter. "What about you?"

"Nothing Other about me," Peter replied. "I'm just a CO but I do understand your confusion. Took me back a bit at first."

"Anyone else in the village who's more than they appear?"

An odd silence followed Andrew's question.

"Yes," Mrs. Burrows replied, "but it is not our place to reveal them, unless they mean us ill. Those of us who are Other prefer to keep our natures hidden. I'm sure you see why."

Andrew nodded slowly. "Yes. Quite understandable. You mentioned some . . . Others who might mean ill. Who might they be?"

Pendragon broke the silence this time. "Vampires."

Andrew Barron managed not to laugh. Dragons, Gloria and Pixies he could swallow—at a big stretch—but . . . "Vampires? They don't exist."

"Some might say the same about Pixies and Dragons," Alice said. "To say nothing of a district nurse who changes into a fox."

She had a point.

"So," he said, after a deep breath and a few seconds' hesitation. "Would I be right in saying you think there are vampires in Brytewood?" He scarcely believed he'd actually said it.

"Not think," Peter replied. "Know. Alice and I encountered

one a few weeks back and she did him in. Repelled him with magic and then staked him. He ended up a heap of slimy ash on the drive out there." He angled his head toward the door. "Quite a woman I've got here."

Either they were all infected with some sort of lunacy or he was stark raving bonkers, but he believed Gloria. Had seen the impossible with his own eyes. "Will you give me a chance to catch up here?" Not that he really had any expectation of doing so any time in the immediate future. Or his lifetime come to that.

"Best not bother to try," Peter advised. "Just run along beside them and try to keep up. That's what I do."

"And you're not anything special? A Goblin? Boggle? A centaur on moonlit nights?"

He smiled. "Nothing special, apart from being Alice's pick for a husband. All this Other stuff is mind boggling, no two ways about it, but these people are what they say they are, and we do have a bit of a problem in the village."

If there were vampires flitting about at night, he was right. "So, Alice killed a vampire and you think there're more?"

"That's the long and short of it," Mrs. Burrows said. "Anyone like some more crumble?"

Everyone declined. Proved at least they had normal human limits to their appetites.

"What happened with this vampire Alice killed?" The words echoed in his skull. Was he as loony as the lot of them?

"It's a long story," Alice replied. "But you need to know to get the hang of things. Gloria too, although she knows more than you do."

The look on Gloria's face rather belied that statement.

"There were two and now a third. The first one, I'd no idea what he was. I found him injured up in Fletcher's Woods, brought him back here, called an ambulance and in the meantime he walked out on me. Killing my dog in the process. The other was Miss Waite's nephew. After she got arrested as a spy, seems he went a little berserk, first attacked Peter and Joe Arckle—the father of those two boys trapped in the vicarage after the bombing—and then us. The sergeant," she smiled in his direction, "fought it off the first time, then, and I really don't quite know how, I finished him off. With a bit of help from Mother Longhurst."

"Old Mother Longhurst, who lives down by the river, or did until she disappeared," Gloria explained.

"I'm worried about her," Alice replied. "She went off to meet someone and hasn't been seen since. If by some off chance the vampire found out what she was . . ." She shook her head. "Anyway now we strongly suspect there's another one in the village."

Peter spoke up here. "We don't yet know for sure that he means ill, but have a pretty strong suspicion and the snag is, last time we had this ancient Druid knife of petrified wood, courtesy of Mother Longhurst."

"Can't you use it again?"

Alice shook her head. "Unfortunately, no. First, because we gave it back, never dreaming we'd have another vampire to deal with and second, even if we hadn't, Mother Longhurst claims it won't be fully effective again for a century or more. Plus, she's disappeared and so has the knife."

"I've never met the old lady in question," Andrew said.

"No reason why you should have," Gloria said. "She's reputed to be a Witch."

Why not? What was a Witch after Dragons, Pixies and the woman he loved growing a great brush of a tail once a month? "You think harm came to her? The vampire?" Crikey, he was joining in now.

"We don't know," Mrs. Burrows said. "People do disappear in wartime, but she was riding a bicycle cross county, not through one of the towns, and there was bombing in Bookham Thursday night but it hit a field. And besides, she was already missing by then."

"We've checked every hospital from Epsom to Guildford, no one fitting her description was brought in, and so far," Alice paused, "no body that could be hers has been found. She just disappeared."

"I think Mother Longhurst's disappearance is a red herring," Mrs. Burrows said. "Sad and a worry. Lots of people in the village depended on her but we need to keep our minds on our troublesome newcomer."

"The baker!" Gloria said, speaking for the first time in a while. No once contradicted her. Interesting.

"Really?" Andrew asked, feeling two jumps behind everyone else here. "Any particular reason?"

Alice grinned. "Our first inkling that he might not be what he claimed was when he didn't know what Hovis was."

"Odd, true, but a bit of leap to assume he's a bloodsucker. "Anything else?"

"He's Other," Sergeant Pendragon said. "I sensed it the first time I met him. I think he recognized I was too. He tried to enter my mind. I blocked him but he's been leery of me ever since."

It sounded odd, out there in the realm of the fantastic. But any more fantastic than the rest of the revelations in the past 12 hours? He needed a week to sort all this out and knew he wouldn't have anywhere near that. "You said the first was linked to Miss Waite. You think the vampires are spies too?"

"Not an unreasonable assumption, given the circumstances," Pendragon replied.

No, it wasn't. "What about this pilot landing? Any connection?"

Pendragon and Mrs. Burrows looked at Alice. She shrugged. "Who's to say? It looked as if he was shot down. His injuries weren't inconsistent with bailing out of an airplane that was falling apart. Not that I've seen many," she added. "Besides, I knew him from my year in Dresden. Hans is definitely not Other. I'm not saying it's impossible he's involved. He's undoubtedly as committed to his side as we are to ours, but to all appearances he was just a pilot who was shot down." And there were plenty of those on both sides.

"I think," Gloria said quietly. "I may have seen this vampire creature last night."

Andrew jerked around to face her. "Why didn't you tell me?" Damn! She could have been in hideous danger.

"Because things have been a bit busy since I got back and at the time I wasn't thinking, 'Oh, that must be a vampire!' I just thought it was odd."

"What was odd, my love?" Mrs. Burrows asked.

Gloria told her.

"You think anyone else saw this?" Pendragon asked.

"Who's to say? It was late. People around here tend to go to bed early, especially now with the blackout, but there's always someone awake, watching with sick relatives. Checking on henhouses. I've no idea what they'd make of it if they did."

"Which direction was he going?" Andrew asked. Was his plant a target once again? What else about here could be?

"Towards the village and he was roughly coming from the direction of the Longhurst farm."

Gloria had everyone's complete attention.

"You're certain?" Alice asked.

"I'm certain I saw a human-looking creature fly. As for direction, I'm pretty certain. He could have been up at the farm cottages, or even from Wharton Lacey, it's in the same direction."

"Coupled with the sudden arrival of a German pilot the next day," Peter pointed out.

"Yes," Alice said, "but if that was all connected, it's rather up a gum tree right now. Hans is under arrest and either on his way to a POW camp as we sit here, or will be by morning."

"I don't think it has anything to do with it," Mrs. Burrows said. "From what we can piece together, the vampires arrive surreptitiously. Not in the middle of the morning in broad daylight. And if this pilot came here to contact them, it's a pretty unreliable way to do it. We need to ignore distractions and concentrate on what we know and how best to take care of the intruder in our midst."

"Hadn't we best make sure he means harm?" Gloria said.

"He's a vampire, isn't it a given?" Peter asked.

Nods and agreement went around the table.

"Not necessarily," Mrs. Burrows said. "There are others, not vicious, but these invaders can not mean us well."

Interesting. "You mean to say . . ." Andrew began.

She brushed him off with a wave of her hand. "Later. We've more immediate worries. The first one killed. We have no proof that will stand up in court but we know." Nods and agreement came from Alice, Peter and Pendragon. Gloria looked as perplexed as Andrew felt.

"Has this one killed?" Peter asked.

"Maybe," Alice said. All eyes turned to her. "Reg Brown was found dead in the churchyard on Friday."

"Maybe he drank himself to death," Pendragon said.

"Maybe," Alice conceded, "but he never before drank himself to a stupor behind the church tower. He usually collapsed on the grass verge by the wall where his wife or someone would find him and take him home. And . . ." she paused. "He had a bruise on his neck."

"A bruise, not teeth marks?" Pendragon asked.

She nodded. "A large, discolored bruise. No visible bite marks and no ripped out throat like poor Farmer Wilson but unusual nonetheless."

"He's shown his hand. It's war." Pendragon said.

"We have to be sure it is the new baker," Gloria said. "What if we get the wrong person? There are plenty of newcomers in Brytewood. Several arrived last week."

"We're not talking about schoolchildren," Pendragon replied.

"You're thinking of Mary?" Alice asked. "No, she might be Other, but there's nothing evil about her. The earlier one oozed malevolence. And we know the baker isn't quite as au fait with modern baking as he makes out."

"The new baker is the obvious one," Pendragon said. "We must see to him."

"We need to be sure," Alice said. "We can't destroy some innocent Other just because he's not one of us."

"What more proof do you want?" Peter asked. "Pendragon recognizes he's Other and we already have a body."

"I'm game to do what I can to help," Andrew said, "but we need to be 100 percent certain we have the right blighter."

"Fair enough," Pendragon replied. "You, Peter and me, we'll get together and smoke him out. Set a trap."

"Just boys?" Alice asked in an uncharacteristically quiet voice. "No girls allowed?"

"It's going to be dangerous," Andrew said. "Once we . . ."

"Put a sock in it," Gloria said, giving him a jab with her elbow. "How many hundred women do you employ at your plant doing dangerous work every day of the week?"

"That's different."

"Really? There's a war on, Andrew Barron, and seems it's just arrived on our doorsteps. We all work on this."

"Better listen to her, my love," Mrs. Burrows said. "Might as well start the way it's going to be the rest of your life. I think you'll do very well together. Now, Howell, how about you and the young men take care of the dishes. We'll look at that silk Alice brought back. Can't let vampires intrude on what's really important, can we?"

As the three women closed the back door behind them, Pendragon handed Andrew a folded tea towel. "Here you are, lad. You'd best wipe, Peter can put away, he knows his way around this kitchen."

Pendragon filled the sink with water and swished the metal soapsaver until he had enough suds to satisfy him. "We don't have too long," he said scrubbing a plate before handing it to Andrew. "They could be back any minute. So we'd best get things agreed fast. We need to strike this blighter out and do it fast. No time to waste."

"You mean the er . . . vampire, sir?" Andrew asked, handing the dried plate to Peter.

"Yes. The women are right, up to a point, but we need to act fast and eliminate him before he causes the trouble that Oak creature did."

"So, we work on our own, sir?" Peter asked.

"We prepare the way, or rather you do." He stacked a couple more plates on the draining board. "Gloria and Alice are right, it would be a travesty of justice if we disposed of an innocent creature, so we need to smoke him out. You two have an advantage there."

"Come again, sir," Peter said. "We do?"

"Yes, you two." He turned and gave a sly grin over his shoulder. "I'm thinking you'd be more than a little committed to protecting those young women outside busy with a parachute."

"You know that, sir," Peter replied. "I'd do anything for Alice, but she killed a vampire. I watched her do it. You can shift, so can Gloria, and as for Mrs. Burrows, I doubt there's much limit to what she can do."

"And I suppose you're going to round off your objections by saying you and Barron are just a pair of puny mortals."

"We've our limits," Andrew said. "I'll do anything I can to protect Gloria, and the rest of the village come to that, but what can we do?"

"Smoke him out. He knows I'm Other but you two are just as you appear: two nice young men. Chat him up in the Pig, pal around a bit, and once he shows his hand we have him."

Seemed awfully flimsy and Andrew didn't like to ask what happened when he showed his hand.

Peter had no such constraints. "I'm game but shouldn't we arm ourselves for when he gets nasty? Oak stakes and mistletoe, along with Alice's magic, worked last time. Assuming this is the same sort of vampire."

"They come in different varieties?" Andrew asked.

"So Helen informed me," Pendragon said. "It's to do with blood lines and who made them vampire, she claims."

Amazing the things one never learned at university.

"So," Peter said, "we buy him a beer and get him to show his hand. Do vampires get drunk?"

"Search me," Pendragon replied. "Now, we've got to set this up carefully. If anything happened to one of you, those women would have my guts for garters. Monday is usually a quiet night at the Pig. We'll try for then. I'll be there with someone else. We'll be backup and we'll bring the stakes."

"Who's going to be with you?" Andrew asked.

"An Other who needs to pull his weight," Pendragon replied.

"How many more are there?" Peter asked.

"None of your business, young fellow. I'm not fingering him. Getting him to come in with us will take a bit of doing but I fancy I can convince him."

Andrew reached for a glass to dry. He'd thought this a rather sleepy little village when he arrived back in June. Mistaken wasn't the word for it. He couldn't help wonder what impossible thing he'd end up believing next.

Chapter Twenty-Five

"It's not exactly the finest satin," Gran said, as they spread the billowing white fabric on the lawn. "But it will do."

It had seemed a good idea at the time. Alice had heard stories of people cutting up parachutes for the fabric. There'd even been talk of three women over in Epsom getting into a fight over one, but now she actually had one in her back garden, Alice wondered. "It's a bit mucky."

"Nothing that won't wash out." Gran handed them each a pair of scissors. "First we cut off all the straps and metal bits. We don't need them now, but we'll keep them. Who knows what might come in handy later on? Then we cut it along the seams. We can give it a good wash and get busy."

"We'll enough left over for a second dress." She gave Gloria a knowing smile. "In case someone else needs one."

"PC Jones was eying it for his wife," Alice said, "but I think Gloria comes first and I'd say Andrew's actions of Friday pretty much constituted a proposal, wouldn't you?"

Gloria rolled her eyes. Now was not the time to talk about it. Not yet. "I'm not so sure!"

"Don't be silly, Gloria, it doesn't suit you. He's head over heels in love and so are you," Gran replied. "Now, while cutting this, I need a quick word. At least they'll be busy for a while." She angled her head toward the kitchen door. "Now," she went on, "we need to put our heads together.

"Gran?" Alice asked, although she had a good guess what was coming. "This isn't just about my dress, is it?"

"Of course not, my love, and don't think for one minute that lot in there are discussing the best way to do the washing up. Howell seems to have a nonsensical idea that he has to be the big brave leader. All well and good if it makes him feel useful, but meanwhile, we have to get busy."

"You're sure about him, Gran?" Alice asked.

"Would I say so if I wasn't, dear? This creature's Other. He might make a nice loaf of bread, but I can't get over what Doris said about him."

The pause was so predictable. "Yes, Gran?"

"Aside from the man acting as if she was his serf, both times she's been there to clean, she left with a blistering headache. Doris wondered if it was the big gas oven." Gran smiled.

"He mind-probed?"

Gran smiled and started cutting a canvas strap from the edge of the parachute.

"Just a minute," Gloria said. "I'm a bit lost here. You're telling me this vampire can read minds?"

"Influence minds," Gran replied. "At least weak ones." She gave a chuckle. "He was backing the wrong horse with Doris Brewer. Not one to be easily swayed is Doris but I do worry a bit now. I heard he's using Charlie Lovat to do his cleaning. His mother was thrilled he had a job, but if ever there was a lad likely to be swayed."

"Charlie Lovat! He's simple-minded," Gloria said.

"Not the same as easily led," Alice said. "But Charlie was always one to do what he was told." Her throat tightened. "You think this Block creature might use Charlie?" She could have answered that. "He will, won't he?"

"See what I mean about moving fast?"

"We still need to be sure. I can't see staking some innocent individual."

"We know he's not with modern baking technology so he's not what he purports to be," Gloria said. "What if he's a spy and not a vampire? We've already had one of those in Brytewood."

"And she died rather mysteriously in custody," Alice said. "Body whisked away and any time I ask a question, I get told 'Official Secrets.'"

Gran gave a snort. "And that means they don't have the foggiest notion how she died. Heart attack, stroke would be easy to announce."

"So you think it was to do with the vampires?" Gloria asked.

"I do indeed. I think we have a nasty bunch of them lurking around waiting for the day when the gunboats land and a ravening horde of Germans comes swarming over the downs."

"Then we'd better be a few jumps ahead of them," Alice said, not entirely sure how three women—alright, a pair of Pixies and a Werefox—could hold back the might of the German war machine. Sounded a bit along the lines of King Canute ordering the tide to recede.

"Absolutely, my love," Gran replied, sounding unbelievably sanguine. "It's very simple. Tomorrow, Gloria and I will go into the bakery and keep him busy. While you, Alice, nip upstairs and have a good look around."

"For what?" She'd do a lot for Gran but breaking and entering was a bit much.

"Simple things, my love. An empty pantry is the first thing. Look for signs that he doesn't eat, never uses the toilet or the bathroom. Maybe there's a radio. That would be telling."

"Is he likely to leave that lying around?"

"Wasn't that how they caught Miss Waite? When they found hers after the bombing?" Gloria said.

"Even so, it's a bit far-fetched." She didn't consider herself a coward but the Medical Board might have a thing or two to say about burglary.

"Alice, my love," Gran tsk-tsked and shook her head. "Stop making difficulties. We'll be there just after he opens, when the queue is longest. We'll keep him busy. Especially once Gloria tells everyone how her ankle was just sprained not broken. We can get you a good fifteen minutes. You nip upstairs and afterwards we'll gather at the Copper Kettle and see what you discovered. Then we'll tell that lot in there." She nodded toward the house. Obviously Pendragon's mistakenly chivalrous comment had hit Gran on a sore spot.

Alice sighed. "Alright Gran, I'll have a go, but I have rounds in the morning and a surgery tomorrow afternoon. I'll be a bit pushed to include breaking and entering."

"Don't be silly, my dear. There will be no breaking and entering. You mark my words, the door will be unlocked."

Chapter Twenty-Six

Bela watched her sleeping sister. Gela was bone thin, her skin gray and haggard. Anger coiled deep in Bela's heart. She owed so many debts to those perfidious Nazis and she would pay every one and with interest: her parents, her brothers and how many others? But to do that she and Gela had to find a safe hiding place. Very safe. The Germans had snared them before, taken all of them, and they'd be setting a net everywhere for her now. She was their link with the vampires.

She almost laughed aloud. She was the link to the vampires. She knew what they were doing. Could she link strongly enough to lure them astray? Not that she was too concerned about the perfidious British who'd handed her homeland of Sudetenland over to the Germans, but it might be satisfying to wreak a little chaos and foil a few plans.

Later.

Safety was her priority. For now they were hidden in a copse near a village. She'd found food, stealing a loaf of bread and a large wurst from a woman's shopping basket and a full milk can from a kitchen window ledge, but she couldn't do that much and escape detection and besides the trees were turning and losing their leaves. In a few weeks they'd be bare and even a Fairy couldn't hide in a winter tree. She had to find deep woods, maybe a cave or a disused animal's lair to hide in while Gela recovered her strength. Food, she'd worry about once they were safe.

Where to go? She roused Gela, as she had every hour or so, and forced her to drink some milk and eat a little sausage and bread. She seemed unable to eat much at a time. It would take weeks for her to recover.

"Bela," her sister said, looking up at her with sunken eyes. "They are all dead."

"Not all," Bela replied. "We remain."

Gela forced a weak smile. "And I, sister, am dying."

"No!" Not after all this. "We will live to avenge them all. Gela, there's so much to tell you. They put me through torture but gave me a weapon to scotch their plans, or at least some of them. First, we must move. Every night, as fast as we can."

"I can not walk far."

"I am strong enough to carry you." How long that vampire's strength would last, she had no idea, but as long as she could, she would carry her sister.

"Where are we going?"

"Home. To the mountains. Deep into the mountains where no one will find us."

Chapter Twenty-Seven

Funny how men who cheerfully discussed dispatching a vampire scattered at the prospect of a roomful of ladies armed with knitting needles. Gloria scooted off too. Claimed she really ought to have a word with Mary since she'd been left alone all day.

Just as everyone got ready to leave, the phone rang.

It was Mrs. Grayson.

"Doctor, I'm sorry to bother you on a Sunday."

"It's not a bother. How are the boys?"

"They seem to be on the mend, thank heaven. It's the baby." Alice's heart clenched. He was how old—eight, nine months? "He's real poorly, coughed up his last two feeds and now he's running a temperature."

"I'll be up there right away. Try to get him to take a bottle of boiled water with a little sugar." She hung up. "Seems I'll miss the knitting evening too, Gran. I'll be back when I can but it looks as if the Grayson baby has whooping cough."

"She can't blame the evacuees. Too soon to have got it from them."

True. "I doubt she would have. She seems a decent sort but she sounded worried and I don't blame her."

After dropping the others in the village, Alice headed up the hill toward Cherry Hill Farm and the Graysons' cottage.

The baby was flushed and fretful and poor Mrs. Grayson looked exhausted. "Did he, or you, get any sleep last night?" Alice asked.

Mrs. Grayson shook her head. "Not much, doctor, every time he dropped off for a few minutes he woke up coughing. I just thank heaven that the other two are mending. Jim has been a proper brick." Jim, sitting by the kitchen fire in pajamas and dressing gown, looked a trifle bashful. "Made me cups of tea he has, and took toast and porridge up to Wilf."

"Let's have a look at Thomas."

Poor little Thomas Grayson was well enough to complain loudly at the indignity of temperature taking and chest sounding. That was a good sign. The state of his throat wasn't, and one look below the nappy showed the torture of temperature taking wasn't really necessary.

Jim, who'd watched with anxious eyes as Thomas wailed and fussed, asked. "Should I get his bottle?"

"It might help soothe him. Is it milk or sugar water?"

"I gave him the sugar water, Doctor. But shouldn't he have milk?"

"Yes, but if he can't keep it down, it won't do any good. Try sugar water again, and if that stays down try milk later." She reached into her bag. "Here's a tin of glucose. Try that in the boiled water, easier to digest than sugar and won't eat into your ration."

Jim took the bottle from a pan of hot water sitting on the top of the fireplace stove. Mrs. Grayson had been right, the boy was a gem. "How about you get up to bed, Jim, and I'll be up in a minute to take a look at you and Wilf."

"He's doing better, I see," Alice said as Jim went upstairs.

"They both are, thank the Lord. Not sure what I'd do if they were still coughing their hearts up too." She looked down at the flushed baby, who was slowly sucking the teat. "I'm worried about Thomas, Doctor. He's so tiny."

"Little ones can be tough too. Keep his temperature down with aspirin and keep them all warm. Pneumonia is always a worry. Can you spare a fire for the boys' room now they're sitting up? I've an electric one I can lend you . . ."

"Thank you, Doctor. It's good of you to offer but I've no electric points upstairs, just the lights. I took up a paraffin stove. Smells like the dickens but the room's warm."

"Better warn them to be careful." Those stoves put out heat as well as smell. She'd burned her hand on the bathroom one when she was a child.

"I put it to one side and set the clothes horse around it to warn them. They're good boys. They listen. But still no word from their mother. It's not like her. I can't help worry something happened to her."

"I'll talk to Sergeant Jones. He can get on to the Civil Defense and have them make more inquiries." Didn't sound as though they'd get good news though. "I'll nip up to see them and either Nurse Prewitt or I will be in tomorrow."

"I thought the nurse was laid up. I heard she'd broke her leg."

Right. Here goes. "That's what we thought. Turns out it was just a sprain." Might as well get used to saying it.

"That were a lucky break!" She gave a little laugh. "Bet that's a relief."

All around as it happened. Getting used to Gloria's being furry was another matter entirely. "She was pleased. I think doctors and nurses make the worst patients."

Small boys came a close second. Jim was sitting on the edge of the bed. Wilf was sitting up, spreading out cigarette cards on a wooden tray balanced on his knees.

"Hey, Wilf," Jim said. "It's the doctor, like I said."

"Wotcher, Doctor," Wilf said by way of greeting. "Is baby Thomas sick?"

"Yes," she replied, sitting on the edge of the bed next to Jim. "He's got what you have."

"We gave it to him, right?" Jim asked.

"I don't think so. Most likely he picked it up when you did but it took longer to incubate. Don't blame yourself."

She wasn't sure they'd obey on that one. "He's so tiny, Doctor," Wilf said. "What if . . ."

"Mrs. Grayson is a good nurse and will take good care of him, just as she did you. I'll come and see him every day, or send the nurse." Wasn't much else she could say. Wilf was right. Thomas was very young to contract whooping cough. "How about you two? Let me listen to your chests and take your temperatures." The latter were down but Wilf's wasn't quite normal. And they'd be coughing awhile yet. But the room was warm. "I see you have a stove up here now?"

"Yeah, Mrs. Grayson brought it up for us from the bathroom."

"You know to be careful around it, right?"

"Of course we do, doctor," Wilf sounded affronted at the implication. "We'll be careful. Honest we will."

"So, you collect cigarette cards." She looked at the cards spread out in neat rows.

"I used to," Wilf said. "So did Jim but old Hitler put paid to that. You know, doctor, they don't put them in anymore to save the paper. It's all old Adolf's fault. He ruined my set of British Navy craft."

"And I was collecting railway equipment and uniforms of the Territorial Army," Jim added. "Got a few flowers too but don't go much for them. We've got most of Air Raid Precautions, except our dog chewed up a couple."

"You had a dog at home?"

"Yeah, but Mum said we had to have him put to sleep when the war started. Said it would be hard to get food for him and she didn't want to let him starve."

"Know when Mum's getting back?" Wilf asked.

"She'll let us know." Assuming she was still alive. "Things

are pretty difficult in London, even pillar boxes have been destroyed in the bombing. Letters get lost." Someone had to check on her and the grandmother she'd gone back to help out.

"Anything else, boys, before I go back home?" The brothers exchanged glances. "Something the matter?"

"Maybe," Jim said. "It's just . . . Well . . . doctor, do you think real people can fly?"

"Without an airplane you mean?"

Jim nodded.

"You're not thinking about the pilot who landed up near the farm earlier today?"

"Not him. We saw him though," Jim said.

"Yeah, Mrs. Grayson let us watch from her bedroom window. That parachute was big. Wish the Jerry had copped it," Wilf added.

Now was not the time to mention that the Jerry was an old friend. "Bit of excitement, wasn't it?"

"Yeah," they both agreed.

They both went quiet. "So, you didn't mean the pilot?"

"No, doctor. This was during the night and different. Flying without anything, just getting in the air and flying."

"A person?"

"Looked like it. It were bright with the moon and there were this man. He flew right across the fields, went into the trees. Honest, doctor, I'm not making it up."

How to answer this, without saying he was darn right, or pooh poohing it? And they'd better not talk about it. If the vampire heard he'd been seen . . . "Could be a trick of the moonlight or maybe, well, they're doing all sorts of secret stuff over on the heath."

"Like a secret weapon?" Wilf asked.

"Best keep it a secret between you. Wouldn't do to chatter and get the word out. 'Careless talk costs lives,' remember?" They both went wide-eyed and nodded,

"We won't tell. Promise," Jim said. "Will we, Wilf?"

"Cross my heart and hope to die. Wild horse won't drag it from us."

"I doubt it will come to that. Just keep it under your hat. And Jim, can you show me where he was flying?"

Simple enough. Jim pointed out the copse to the east. "He went that way. Then I never saw him again."

"Might be best if you don't look out anymore at night. You know, secrets and all that."

"Alright, doctor, just in daylight, right?"

Right.

She wanted to race back and share this with everyone but she couldn't refuse the cup of tea Mrs. Grayson offered and besides Gran had the knitting circle in the house. Might as well drop by Sergeant Pendragon's cottage on the way home and have a word with him and Peter.

Chapter Twenty-Eight

Mary was out. Good. Not that Gloria wished her anywhere else, but with so much to think about, a bit of time alone was more than welcome. Mind you, she couldn't help the twinge of guilt that Mary had been tossed onto her own resources but doubtless she was off somewhere now, having a ripe old time, while Gloria was deciding whether to clean the bathroom or strip her bed.

Mary had left the bathroom spotless, so with a silent thanks to her new lodger, Gloria stripped her bed and washed her sheets, throwing in any spare washing she could find. Might as well catch up properly. She was hanging them out, in the falling dusk, when Mary walked in the gate.

"Hello," Gloria said, stepping between the sheets. "Had a good weekend?"

Mary stopped in her tracks. "Gloria? Your leg?"

"I know. A bit of a story. Nip in and put the kettle on and once I get the last of these hung up, I'll explain."

That won her a few minutes to rehearse. Trouble was, no matter how she phrased it, it sounded barmy in the extreme. But she might as well start now. She'd have to repeat it to half the village in the morning. Or maybe only a third; the local hedgerow telegraph would no doubt take care of the rest.

She hung out the last few items, gathered up her laundry basket and peg bag and headed indoors.

"What happened?' Mary asked.

"Well. It was bothering me a bit, the cast I mean, and I mentioned it to Alice. She offered to do an X-ray." All true so far. "The X-ray found it had never been broken." Big whopper that, but anyone looking at the X-ray would draw that conclusion. "Seems there must have been a bit of confusion in the hospital that night. There was an air raid just after I got there and things were busy." That much was true, "So. I'm wearing a crepe bandage to take care of the sprain, but I can walk on it if I'm careful."

And her discarded, uncut cast was still lying behind the back door. Gloria dumped the laundry basket in front of it. She'd have to hide the damn thing. After Mary went to bed.

"That was a lucky break!" Mary said. "That just came out, sorry."

"Don't worry, I'm sure I'll be used to it by this time tomorrow. I'm tempted to spend the day hiding out in the clinic up at the plant, well away from the village."

"Better company up there, I hear."

"Much better." Darn, Mary had been in the village barely three days and already knew the inner details of Gloria's private life. Like everyone else for a ten-mile radius. "I promised Peter I'd help with the health checks for the new evacuees. It goes three times as fast with two of you doing it. Less time missed from class and not so much time for them to get anxious and shy."

"The poor little blighters have gone through so much. Leaving home. Half of them were sick on the boat and I swear it was from nerves. The trip up to Sheffield was a nightmare. People there, on the whole, were good, but only a couple of the children had ever left Guernsey before, much less seen a manufacturing city. Then, after we all got settled, the school was bombed. It was a blessing in disguise in the end. They're happier here. They're country children by mainland standards, even the ones who lived in Town."

"This is a good village. Gossip and character assassination are part of the daily round, but they pull together and, on the whole, have taken to the newcomers. You had a good time last night? Did you go to the flicks?'

Mary gave a brusque nod and turned to look at the kettle.

Had something gone wrong? She'd come in late. Not that Gloria had been taking note, and besides she'd been rather wrapped up in her own worries.

"Anything else besides tea I can get you?" Mary asked.

The Gallop tended to sustain you for the rest of the day but when had Mary eaten? "Want to make cheese on toast? I bought some on Friday." A day she was never likely to forget.

"How about I make us Welsh rarebit?"

"Smashing. Are you going out this evening?"

Mary shook her head. "No, I've got work to do before tomorrow morning."

She went quiet. Just as well. Gloria wasn't feeling exactly chatty. She plonked herself down in a chair and watched as Mary made toast and grated cheese. She should get up and help. Make the tea at least, but after the events of the past few hours, she was drained and weary. And seemed she was going to stir herself to help Alice dispose of the vampire/baker in their midst.

"Here you are." Mary put two plates on the table and poured tea.

Gloria pulled up her chair. She hadn't expected to be hungry but the sight and aroma of bubbling cheese did the trick. "Many thanks," she said. "We need to work out some sort of rota for meals. Split the work."

"Suits me."

Gloria poured the tea and they both ate in silence. Why did she get the feeling Mary wanted to say something but held back? "See a good film last night?"

Mary nodded and took a sip of tea. "It was nice to get out," she said. "I heard there's a dance in the church hall next weekend."

Interesting change of subject. "I don't keep up with things as much as I should. I bet there is. The parish committee organizes quite a lot: whist drives, mother's mornings, dances, and if you knit, Mrs. Burrows, Alice's grandmother, organizes Sunday evenings knitting comforts for the troops."

"A lot going on for a village."

Mary had no idea how much went on in this village.

They were on their second cups of tea, when Mary suddenly asked, "Gloria, if I tell you something that is utterly impossible will you promise not to laugh at me?"

Who was she to deem things possible or impossible? "Go ahead."

She took a deep breath. "Last night was such a beautiful clear night with a full moon. I decided to go for a walk," she paused and took a sip of tea. "I wanted to be out in the middle of the country after all those months in Sheffield. You can't believe how much I missed being in the country."

"I can, I felt cramped and suffocated the years I spent in London."

Mary smiled. "Yes, suffocated is the word. I went walking, went for miles, took the footpath by the church that someone told me led up to Hammer Pond, then came back by the road."

Some walk, had to have taken hours. "Go on."

"I was walking back, feeling renewed when I sensed someone else was out in the night."

Cripes, had Mary been near her? Sensed her? Anyway, all she'd have noticed was a bushy-tailed fox. "You met someone?" Gloria's throat went dry as she realized who—or what—Mary might have encountered.

"Not exactly met. But I saw this man. At a distance. It could have been a woman in slacks but it looked like a man and he was flying." She looked Gloria in the eye as if daring her to scorn or dismiss it as nonsense.

"Flying? I'm assuming you mean under his own steam?"

Mary nodded, and drained her teacup.

"Flying like a giant bird. Landing and taking off again?"

Mary's teacup hit the saucer with a clink. "You saw him too? Who was it?"

"I saw him last night." Might as well admit that much, the second question was a lot more difficult.

"It's someone in the village?"

Now she was pinned to a figurative wall. She could hardly say, "Yes, it's the new baker, we suspect he's a vampire and a German spy." Even if Mary did enjoy rambles in the moonlight, something the villagers would avoid like the plague as lots of them still believed moonlight caused insanity, Gloria didn't think Mary was up to coping with reality. She wasn't sure she was.

She sipped her cooling tea, just to gain a few seconds. "Must be someone from the hush-hush place on the heath. Who knows what the government is doing up there?"

"If they can get people to fly like birds, they've definitely hit on something new." Did sound utterly implausible but the truth was even less believable. "You think there's an army of them?"

"I have no idea and there's no point in asking Andrew. He's not supposed to talk about what they do up there."

Mary appeared to mull that over. Finally she stood up. "Still sounds downright peculiar. And I'm astonished you believe me. I hardly do."

Should she have told the truth? Lord, no! "I'll do the washing up. You cooked."

"Fair enough. If your ankle doesn't bother you. Mind if I bring my work down here and go over it in the warm?"

"Of course not. I'll clear one end of the table for you. I've got some paperwork too." And needed to work out exactly what to expect tomorrow with their burglary project.

* * *

Alice headed home. Not too thrilled at the prospect of an evening knitting comforts for the troops but she should do her bit. She ought to work on gloves or socks and send them to Simon. Assuming they would arrive. Seeing Hans had very vividly reminded her that Simon was languishing in his stalag, God alone knew where, in Germany. Pity they couldn't just change places but that would make too much sense. She smiled remembering her father's tale about the first Christmas truce of the last war when a bunch of soldiers from both sides engaged in an impromptu football game.

It was different this time. Nowadays they sent vampires instead.

Damn!

She was just passing the darkened baker's when she slowed and backed up. Why wait for tomorrow? She could just as easily be nosy this evening. There was no smoke from the chimney, which implied the place was empty. He was no doubt down at the Pig like everyone else. She'd knock on the door. If he opened it, she'd make up some story about visiting a newcomer and explaining her surgery hours. And if he was out, she'd have a quick sneak around and be long gone before the pub closed. Easy as pie.

She reversed a little more and parked in front of the building. Grabbing her torch, she walked up to the door on the side and looked for a doorbell. No bell. No knocker either. She rapped on the door. Not a sound within. He was out. Good. Just to be sure, she bent down, pushed the letterbox open and called, "Mr. Block, hello. It's Dr. Doyle. Anyone home?"

Apparently not.

Now she did get cold feet. Thinking and actually doing were two different things. She rapped on the door even louder. It was only half-past seven. He couldn't be in bed yet could he? Even a baker who got up before dawn didn't turn in this early. And there was no sound of a wireless. She called again, almost yelling into the house this time, and taking her courage and the doorknob, in both hands, tried the door.

As she pretty much expected, it was unlocked. She pushed it open. The place was in complete darkness. She put her head around the door and called out again as her torchlight beam played over the entry way and up the flight of stairs. Uncarpeted, she noticed. She waited for a reply. None came so she nipped inside and closed the door behind her. No point in bringing a zealous air raid warden down on her.

She went up the stairs as carefully as she could, her footsteps echoing on the bare wood. She went slowly, wondering what on earth she'd say if someone was upstairs but there wasn't a sound in the house and not a single light apart from the shaky beam of her torch.

The place was undoubtedly empty.

Emboldened she went up to the top of the stairs and looked around, keeping her torch beam low. Last thing she wanted was showing a light if the blackout curtains weren't drawn.

Moonlight shone through an open doorway. There were five doors—two closed, one open on an unfurnished room, the others a cold and dingy bathroom, and a narrow kitchen with a tap dripping into the sink. She disturbed a mouse nibbling on a loaf that sat on the wooden draining board. Perhaps he did eat but the loaf was hard and stale. Hardly edible. A quick peek into the only cabinet and the drawer in the enamel-topped table showed no food and not even a knife or fork. Seemed he didn't eat after all.

It appeared Gran was definitely on to something. At least this meant she didn't have to nose around tomorrow.

A cold shiver snaked down Alice's spine. Goosebumps rose along the back of her neck.

She wasn't alone.

She couldn't hear a sound, not movement nor a rustle of cloth but she felt the power, and the remembered evil was over her like a cloying fog. But she'd faced one before. Repelled one and then slaughtered him. She might not have Mother Longhurst's knife, but she had the power of the Pixies within her.

Alice turned and saw the dark shape filling the narrow doorway.

"*Komm in mein Heim, sagte die Spinne zu der Fliege.*" His voice oozed malevolence. A miasma of dread washed over her like a tide. Damn him! Luring her into his web was he? He didn't know she understood German and she was not playing the fly to his spider. She was Pixie!

"Begone!" she said, drawing herself up and summoning all her strength of will and magic. "Leave me! Leave my village and trouble us no more!" She threw the words at him in a surge of magic.

He laughed and leapt forward, grabbing her by her shoulders and lifting her off her feet. She made the mistake of looking into his eyes—couldn't help herself from doing so, and saw her own terror reflected back at her.

With a shudder, she drew from the very depths of her soul, raking up her last vestiges of power. "Go!" she repeated. "Leave us and do no more . . ."

The words dried up in her throat. "I have the power here. Whatever you are," he said, with a laugh that had to come from the pit of hell itself. "You came into my web, little thing. You're mine."

She went slack in his hands, her strength leeching out until the torch fell out of her limp grasp and holding up her head took all she had.

"Magic User, are you?" he asked. "Another of those wretched Fairies, I suppose. And I thought you were just some measly mortal. Do these simple villagers know their doctor is a Magic User?" He gave a most unreassuring chuckle. "Fairy blood tastes so sweet." And dug his fangs into her neck.

Pain cut though her like a razor dipped in acid. She screamed, but no sound came, just an endless sear of agony lacing through her until she went giddy, the room swam, and total darkness and oblivion took over.

Wilhelm Bloch looked down at the unconscious woman lying on the floor. Interesting. Perhaps the world was peopled with Fairies and he'd missed something all these centuries. This one tasted strange. Not quite human but her blood had a varied tang from the little Fairy who'd fought him back in their masters' headquarters. Had to be the dull climate affected the blood. What a silly little fool, thinking she could stop him. In his own territory to boot.

He pushed her limp body aside with his foot.

And a thought occurred to him.

She had believed she had power to repel him. That had been obvious. Deluded, yes, but she'd believed. Interesting. Now what would lead a country doctor to think she could repel a vampire?

Unless . . .

Unless she had been the one to annihilate Eiche. Was it possible? A Fairy—or whatever she was? She must die. That would make Weiss happy. He'd be a right misery all afternoon. Wanting reports, results and news. This would gladden the bastard's heart.

On the other hand. For a creature who dispatched his blood brother to final oblivion, something more was required. This puny thing could not have acted alone, best to send a public warning to her accomplices.

How?

He sat in the dark some minutes, thinking as he licked his fangs. Better than slow death was the death of her reputation: shaming her in front of the entire community and leaving her to live with the aftermath was a delicious prospect.

Pity he couldn't drain her. She was more enticing than that simple-minded lad he'd coerced into cleaning the shop, but death would ruin his plans for her.

She'd driven here. He'd heard her park and kill the engine. Use her own vehicle to ruin her. Delightful.

Leaving her lying on the worn lino, he ran down the stairs and toward the Pig and Whistle.

It was crowded, the air redolent with scents of human blood, cigarettes and beer.

"Evening, sir," the landlord greeted him. "What can I do for you?"

"I need a bottle of strong spirits—brandy, whiskey."

"A whole bottle, sir? We just sell by the glass. Shortages you know."

Was he going to have to compel him in front of witnesses? Bloch stepped close to the bar and slipped a bundle of pound notes into the man's hand. How could he refuse more than he made in a night? "I need a bottle of whiskey. You have one over there."

"I do but don't rightly know when I can replace it." He looked at the bundle of money, then back at the bottle. "It's not a full bottle. It's Irish and most customers go for Scotch. Alright, sir." He slipped the money into his trouser pocket and handed over the bottle.

Bloch didn't even bother to thank him, just took it and left, running up the lane and through the village back to the bakery.

The blackout aided his plans and the gathering clouds blocking the moon served even better. On a chill night like this who would venture far from their miserable hearths? And the drinkers were safe inside the pub until closing time.

Where best to stage this? Not too close to the village, but not so far that she wouldn't be found. If he'd only mastered driving one of the infernal car contraptions, he could take it out to the hill above town, but even with vampire strength pushing it that far would be taxing. In the lane behind the bakery was a small chapel and graveyard beside the river. He walked there and looked around. It was downhill, with a nicely convenient ditch, perfect.

In minutes he ran back and returned with Alice's inert body over his shoulder. He propped her in the driver's seat, released the brake, and with one hand on the steering wheel, maneuvered the car around the corner and down the lane. At what he deemed as the right point he stopped, tried to force the whiskey down her throat and, giving up, poured the entire contents over her face and clothes. Stepping back, he gave the car one last shove. It set off down the incline, gathering speed before leaving the road and lodging nose down in the ditch.

Perfect.

She would be found. Presumed drunk, and would those village gossips have a heyday over this one.

He walked back, a cheerful spring in his step. Delighted at the success of his scheme.

Morning in the bakery was going to be interesting.

Chapter Twenty-Nine

Bloch's scheme would have succeeded admirably but for two circumstances beyond his control: an hour or two before dawn, the gathering clouds broke and a downpour of twenty minutes or so soaked Gloria's newly hung-out laundry and drenched Alice through the open car window, diluting the whiskey he'd poured over her head and clothes. Cycling to work about six thirty, Samuel Whorleigh took a shortcut along the footpath that emerged just below the Congregational Chapel.

He recognized the doctor's wrecked shooting brake at once and slowed alongside. As he walked up to the car, something triggered his Other instincts. This was wrong, out of kelter with what should be, and not just having her vehicle nose first in the ditch.

Seeing the unconscious Dr. Doyle, slumped sideways, half in the passenger seat, with a nasty gash in her forehead, stopped him in his tracks a moment or two. He wrenched open the driver's door. She was alive, although what she was doing with her car in a ditch in this part of the village beat him. The lane dead-ended a few yards further on. She couldn't have been on her way to a call. What the hell was she doing here and out for the count?

It wasn't just her being unconscious and the car half in the ditch. The whole scenario smelled of wrongness. The empty whiskey bottle on the car floor convinced him. The few times she'd seen the doctor in the Pig, she'd been sipping sherry. Swigging whiskey by the bottleful just didn't fit.

He reached over and took the bottle, tucking it in his raincoat pocket. One never knew what might come handy.

The doctor opened her eyes and muttered as he lifted her out of the car, but then shut them again and lolled against him. Bloody hell! He had a shop to open and it looked as though the clouds were about to dump more rain any minute. He couldn't take her far on his bicycle so he carried her to the chapel and settled her on one the the the benches in the narrow porch, propping up her legs and, after a moment's hesitation, covering her with his raincoat.

She might not be dead yet, but she looked halfway there, her hair hanging in wet rats' tails around her ashen face.

Now what?

He should report this to Sergeant Jones, but it wouldn't hurt to have the doctor and meddling Mrs. Burrows owing a favor or two, and besides, there was more to this than a car in a ditch. Much more.

He got back on his bicycle and pedaled the long haul up the hill to The Gallop.

Took a while to rouse the old lady, and the sight of her in curlers and plaid dressing gown was one he could have done without.

"Good grief, Sam Whorleigh, what's happened to bring you hammering on the door this early? Come on in and I'll rouse Alice."

He stepped into the hall as she held the door open. "No, Mrs. Burrows, it's about the doctor I came."

"Yes. Let me get her. Someone had an accident?"

He stopped her with a hand on her arm. "Listen." She was old. Far older than he was. "Best have a seat first." He led her over to a carved monk's bench.

"Come on, man! What is it?"

"Sit down and I'll tell you."

"Something happened to Alice? I didn't hear her go out."

"I found her car in a ditch, down by the Congregational Chapel. She was knocked out. Doesn't seem otherwise hurt but I got her out of the cold and came right up here."

She shut her eyes and took a deep breath. "I see. How did you get up here?"

"On my bike."

"I see. We'll need a car. Maybe an ambulance. She's hurt, you said?"

"Don't rightly know how much, more like stunned I think. She had a cut on her head but nothing else I could see. But something's not right. Best see for yourself before you call an ambulance."

"Right. Go and wait in the kitchen, the stove's banked up for the night but it's got to be warmer than out here. Let me get dressed and make a couple of calls. I'd offer you tea but . . ."

He waved the offer away. "Forget it. Right now we need to get her out of the cold."

"Yes, of course. Phone calls first."

Initial shock over, she was back to her old managing self. Might as well wait in the warm. He could hear even with the door shut. Interesting. First call to Andrew Barrow. Why him? Right! He had transport: a lorry he'd commandeered from the plant after his own car got roasted. Alright for some people. Then she called Pendragon. Made sense. Peter Watson, the doctor's intended, was billeted there. And Nurse Prewitt? Damn! They'd have half the village there at this rate. Had the old woman no sense? Of course she didn't know about the whiskey bottle.

Oh well. It wasn't his funeral.

And the old biddy dressed fast, he'd hand her that. "Alright," she said, as she pulled on her gloves. "I'll get my bicycle and be with you in a jiffy."

Twenty minutes after he'd left for The Gallop, they were back. Mrs. Burrows ran to the porch, at a speed that belied her years, and knelt beside Alice, who barely stirred. "What happened?" she asked.

"Beats me. I found her like that slumped in the car. Thought it best to get her into a bit of shelter."

"Yes," she looked up at him and smiled though her worry. "Many thanks, Sam Whorleigh."

"Something's up, isn't it?"

She seemed halfway ready to agree, when a covered lorry pulled up. Young Watson was out of the back almost before it stopped. Nurse Prewitt leapt out of the cab along with old busy-body Pendragon and Barron, who'd driven the thing. So much for trying to keep this hush-hush, it would be over the village by breakfast.

"She's here!" Mrs. Burrows called, and Watson and the nurse rushed ahead.

"My God! What happened?" Watson said, or rather gasped. Nasty shock for him, most likely. "She doesn't have a temperature."

"She will, if we don't get her into the warm. She's soaked to the skin," Nurse Prewitt said.

"Let's get her home." Watson gathered the doctor up in his arms.

She opened her eyes. "Peter?"

"I've got you, Alice. You're safe."

She let out a terrified whine and shuddered against him as he carried her into the lorry.

"You found her?" Barron asked Whorleigh. "What happened."

Whorleigh repeated what he'd told Mrs. Burrows. Then, just for the heck of it produced the empty bottle. "I did find this in the car with her."

Barron stared. Mrs. Burrows gasped. "She was drunk?"

Nurse Prewitt snatched the bottle. "Stuff and nonsense. Alice seldom drinks and when she does, it's not cheap Irish whiskey. Someone put this in the car." Her glare suggested he had.

"I thought the same, that's why I took it. No point in having nasty gossip. Any idea who'd do that?"

She knew. He read it in her eyes. "I'm finding out. There's only one place in the village that could have come from. I need a bicycle."

She wasn't getting his. He had a shop to open.

"Take Mrs. Burrows's," Barron said. "I'll drive her back. Want someone to come with you?"

"No. You get Alice back home and warm. I'll meet you up at Alice's as soon as I can."

She was on the bicycle and ready to leave, the bottle perched in the basket up front, when she turned. "Thank you, Mr. Whorleigh, you're a brick!"

He wondered if she'd remember that the next time she sent the coppers to investigate his sideline.

"Yes," Barron added. "Thank you. We need to get to the bottom of this. I take it we can count on your discretion."

It was nice to see them grateful, and a little anxious. "Of course, That's why I went to Mrs. Burrows instead of Sergeant Jones."

"Right," he paused. "Might be a good idea to give us a head start, then stop by the police house. "Let him know you noticed the doctor's car in the ditch. Must have been stolen and dumped."

"It must indeed, sir," he added, for the sake of good will. "I'll do that but you'll let me know how the doctor does."

"Certainly."

He watched them drive off. Something was going on and he had a toe in the door to find out what. Meanwhile, he had a shop to take care of and the local constabulary to tell half truths to. Rum do by all accounts. Add this to the strange new baker, who was no more mortal man than Sam Whorleigh was, and who knew what would happen next?

* * *

Knocking on the back door of the pub at—Gloria glanced at her watch—seven thirty was less than considerate, but she was going to find out if Fred Wise sold that bottle, and to whom, or burst.

She must have woken him. He took ages to answer the door, and was wearing a long tweed coat over his pajamas.

"Nurse? Something wrong? Come in."

"I'm sorry to bother you this early, but I need to ask you did you sell this to anyone recently?" She held up the empty bottle.

His eyes narrowed. "Come indoors. It's too damn cold to stand out here." He shut the door behind her and frowned at the bottle. "Something happened, eh? I knew he was up to no good."

Bingo! "Nothing bad happened." A lie that but necessary if this wasn't to be the talk of the village for the next twenty years. "But someone tried. Who bought it?"

"I knew there was something havey cavey going on. I mean to say, who pays eight pounds for a bottle of whiskey?"

"Who did?" If he didn't spit it out she'd shake it out of him.

"The new baker. That Block chap. Came in a couple of hours before closing. Didn't want to sell it but honestly, nurse, who can say no to that sort of money?"

Someone with common sense? She kept that to herself. "Thank you, and I'm so sorry to disturb you but it was rather urgent."

"Sure no one was hurt?"

"Not badly." That was more than she should have said. "Keep this to yourself, please. I don't want him to know I found out about this."

"Right you are, nurse, now if you don't mind, I'd like to get a few more minutes kip before I have to get going for the day."

"I know, sorry again for disturbing you but thank you so much." She was tempted to hug him but decided against it.

She thanked him again and went back to her bicycle propped against the wall.

Having dropped everyone at The Gallop, Andrew headed for the village and parked across from the Pig and Whistle. He killed the engine and waited.

Not for long.

Gloria came out, wheeled the bicycle into the lane and dropped it on the grass as she saw him, running up to the lorry with a smile on her tired face.

"Andrew!" That greeting was enough to make him a very happy man. Pity he had to go to work.

"Find out anything?"

"I did indeed." She had the driver's door open and he reached down and pulled her up. It was a bit cramped with both of them tucked behind the steering wheel but she didn't seem to mind.

"Well?"

She wasted a good minute kissing him. Well, not really wasted but . . . "It was Block. He came in last night and offered Mr. Wise eight pounds to sell him a bottle of spirits, took the bottle and rushed out."

"Bastard. We need to cook his goose good and proper."

"Yes."

"Listen, Gloria, by 'we' I mean Pendragon, Watson and myself. It's too dangerous."

She kissed him. "Put a sock in it, Andrew. I'm a Were, not some fading violet sort. He went for my friend. I'm in and you can't keep me out. So put that in your pipe and smoke it!"

"I smoke cigarettes, dear. Never used a pipe."

The jab in the ribs was pretty ineffectual given the close quarters. "Alice took care of the last one. Don't forget that."

"Yes, but this one got her. She was still out for the count when they took her into the house."

"I've got to get up there. I shouldn't be here spooning with you." She ran her hand over his face, "You need to get home and shave. You look like a bandit." She ran her hand over his stubble. "Makes kisses interesting."

"Time for another then." God! She was wonderful, her mouth opened under his and she let out a little sexy sigh as her tongue touched his. She was all sweetness and warmth, turned furry under the full moon and healed her own broken bones, and he wanted to keep her safe from all harm and hurt, and her breast was soft and warm under his hand.

If he didn't stop soon he'd get them both arrested.

He broke the kiss.

"I love you," she said.

"Me too," he replied. "Sure you don't want a double wedding with Alice? Mrs. Burrows said there was enough in that parachute for two."

She went serious. "First, we're going to make sure she is well enough to get married." She placed the flat of her hand on his chest and pushed away. At least as far as the steering wheel let her. "I'm going up right now to see if we need to call in a doctor, although how we'll explain things heaven alone knows. You go into work. I'll go down to the school later with Peter and give the new evacuees the once-over. I'll come up to the camp this afternoon. Then we can work out what to do."

"Don't be late, or I'll worry that bastard got you too."

"I'll be there as soon as I can. Promise."

He wanted her right here and now but he had land mines to fuse and bullets to fill. Or rather his workers did. "Off to shave, dear. Ride carefully and stay away from bakers."

"You too," she said. "If he could do that to Alice, God only knows what he'd do to a human. We need to really plan the next step very carefully."

She kissed him again and jumped down, got on her bicycle and rode away.

He was worried stiff.

Chapter Thirty

Peter carried Alice into the house. "She needs a hot bath. We have to get her warm."

"I'll stoke up the boiler," Mrs. Burrows said. "There might be some warm water from last night. If not, we'll have some soon. Howell, please fetch me some more coke. I'll get her a warm drink. There's an electric fire in her bedroom and a paraffin stove in the bathroom. Put them all on."

Getting her wet clothes off was priority. Holding Alice close, Peter stripped her, looking for marks and hurts. There was a gash on her head and what promised to be a wacking great bump. And a livid bruise on her neck.

She shivered and clung to him, opening her eyes briefly. "Peter?" she asked, her voice shaky and confused. "Where am I?"

"You're home. In your bedroom. You had an accident. We're going to get you warm."

"I was in . . ." she frowned. "I was in the kitchen and he came . . ." She started shaking.

"Hush, love. You're safe now." He wrapped her in her dressing gown and tucked her under the covers. "I'm going to plug in the fire, and start your bath."

"Don't leave me!"

"I won't. I'm just going to get your bath going." He set the fire on high and crossed to the bathroom. Mrs. Burrows had been right, there was hot water left over. He turned on both taps before returning to Alice's room.

Mrs. Burrows came up with a steaming mug. "Horlicks," she said. "Good and warm and nourishing. She can't have eaten since dinner yesterday."

Neither, come to that, had any of them. They could wait but Alice . . . If he thought too much he'd bawl like a baby. He'd seen her demolish a vampire and now she was too weak to stand.

Alice sipped the Horlicks but needed help to sit up. By the time she drained the mug, the bath was ready and he carried her over. In the warm water, she seemed to revive a bit. With Mrs. Burrows's help, he washed her hair, and together they dried her and got her into a clean nightgown. She was as weak as a baby and still groggy.

"Can you tell us what happened, my love?" Mrs. Burrows asked, as she dried Alice's hair with a warmed towel.

"It was dark. He came in and called me a fly. He spoke German. He said he was the spider and . . ." She shuddered. "Pain after pain and it was dark everywhere and I woke and thought I saw Sam Whorleigh. Like a dream."

"He found you, Alice, and told your grandmother."

"Oh! He did? I'm so tired."

"You hit your head, my love. Best rest," Mrs. Burrows said.

Once she had Alice's hair dry to her satisfaction, Peter carried Alice back to her bedroom and tucked her into bed, along with two hot water bottles Pendragon brought up.

"She's warm and safe. Best let her rest," Mrs. Burrows said. Peter didn't want to leave her.

"We need to talk, lad," Pendragon said. "You and me. Things need to be taken care of."

* * *

Gloria was waiting in the kitchen when they came downstairs. "How is she?"

"Still in shock. No temperature but I'm worried she'll develop pneumonia," Mrs. Burrows replied.

"She's not well?"

Peter shook his head. "She's as weak as a kitten and confused. Keeps talking about a dark kitchen and pain."

Might as well share her news. "Block bought that bottle of whiskey from the Pig."

That pretty much dried up the conversation.

Mrs. Burrows was the first to respond. "I knew it! I knew it in my bones!"

"Bloody bastard," Peter said. "And trust Alice! She went barging in on her own. When she recovers I'm going to spiflicate her!"

"She's said nothing about what happened?"

"Not much," Peter said. "Gloria, you'd better look at the bump in her forehead."

"Let me wash up and have a look."

"We'll have a cup of tea for you when you're done, my love. And I bet you haven't had breakfast, have you?"

Had anyone?

"I'll give you a hand, Helen," Sergeant Pendragon said.

Peter followed Gloria upstairs. "I'm worried sick," he whispered. "Something is really wrong. She acts as if she's dazed or has a concussion but her pupils are normal. And she has a wacking great bruise at the base of her neck."

"What are you thinking?"

"That that excrement did something to her. If I had my hands on him . . ."

"It's going to take more than hands. Alice repelled, then destroyed the last one. This one overpowered her. Seems as though they sent a tougher one this time." Didn't bear thinking about, but they were going to have to.

Alice looked marginally better than the last time she'd seen her. She was at least warm and had a little color in her face, but Peter had been right about groggy. Was almost as if she'd been drugged. Did she dare take a blood sample and send it to be tested? No. That would most likely produce more questions than answers.

"What do you think about the cut?" Peter asked.

It was no longer bleeding and not deep. "I think we can leave it. There's a bruise coloring up already but it should heal." Whether Alice would recover was another matter entirely.

Gloria gave her shoulder a little shake. "Alice." Her eyes opened slowly and met Gloria's. Peter was right: No dilation. So why the grogginess? "Can you remember what happened?"

"It was dark. Empty. Not a sound. I thought no one was there and then he was." A shudder wracked her and she shut her eyes again and lapsed back into sleep.

"What do you think?" Peter asked, as they stepped outside.

She had no idea what to think. Westminster Hospital's training excluded treatment for a vampire attack. "I'm as confused as you are. I just know we have to do something and fast."

"And we're supposed to be checking the evacuees today."

"We'll see to them later. First we have to work out what to do."

They followed the scent of frying that wafted up the stairs. Mrs. Burrows handed them plates of fried bread and Marmite and fried eggs.

"Tuck in," she said. "You too, Howell. We all need it and I've plenty of eggs. Doris and I have been taking care of Mother Longhurst's chickens. They seem to have gone on an unseasonable laying binge."

"Any news of her?" Peter asked. "We could use her expertise right now."

Mrs. Burrows shook her head. "Not a trace. It's as if she disappeared into thin air."

"When we sort this problem, we're going to find out what happened," Gloria said.

No one contradicted but no one exactly agreed.

"I don't think we have long," Sergeant Pendragon said. "This attack on the doctor is a declaration of war. He knows we're on to him and will do something more drastic before long."

"But does he have any idea what you all are?" Peter asked. "He might just think he's dealing with people. Not a bunch of super Others."

"I don't feel like a 'super' anything. I feel helpless." Gloria said.

"That you're not!" Sergeant Pendragon spoke sharply, as if reprimanding a recalcitrant recruit. "None of that nonsense, nurse. You're a Werefox. Be proud of it. You can go undetected and see what mortals might miss and, don't forget, girl, you can summon all the foxes in the woods to your call. You did it that night on the heath. You can do it again if you need to.

"And as for Helen here, we all know there's far more to her than meets the eye. And if push comes to shove, darn it all, I'll shift and incinerate the pest in his own bakery. We'll nobble him right enough, so I want to hear no more of that helpless talk!"

She had to smile. "Alright, I won't but the task is daunting."

"So's taking on the Hun. We took care of him in the last one. We'll do the same again, even if he does have a few nasty tricks, like vampires, up his sleeve." he paused. "Got a refill of tea, Helen?"

She had more tea, and plenty of toast and a jar of marmalade she fetched from the pantry. "I made this batch last winter, bought the sugar just before it went on the ration. I was saving it for Christmas but I think we need a treat right now."

As if extra eggs weren't? But she was right, they all needed a pick-me-up. Peter looked positively green. She didn't blame him. If the same thing had happened to Andrew, she'd be falling to pieces. "What are we going to do?"

"It's alright for you," Peter said, looking from one to the other. "You're Other. You can do what the rest of us can't. I feel hamstrung. Not helpless," he added, with a wry smile in Pendragon's direction, "but definitely at a disadvantage."

"Don't say that," Mrs. Burrows replied. "You love Alice. There's no stronger power than love in the entire universe."

"Don't forget courage," Pendragon added. "You've got enough of that in you to make up for not being Other, Peter. We've all got weaknesses. We just need to pool our strengths."

"I do think," Gloria said, "that we need to be very, very careful not to give any indication that we've twigged him. We should act as if we don't suspect him."

"He already knows we do. Alice broke into his place," Peter said

"No," Gloria replied. "He knows Alice suspected him. He doesn't know about the rest of us."

"Now you're thinking, nurse. Good point," Pendragon said.

"But," Mrs. Burrows said, "he'll know something is off. Alice was supposed to be found, presumed drunk, in her wrecked car. She hasn't been. And," she added, "thinking I ought to act before someone else saw the car, I called Sergeant Jones and reported the car stolen. Said it wasn't in the drive when I got up this morning."

"So," Gloria said, "they'll find it and assume some local yob nicked it and drove it into that ditch." At least it would divert a gossip from her miraculously healed leg. "But he'll know, won't he? Block, I mean. And how do we explain Alice being ill? She can't do rounds or hold her surgeries in her condition."

"What if we say the car was stolen so she walked home and that's how she got sick?" Peter suggested. "She got drenched in the downpour and got chilled."

Pendragon shook his head. "Too many lies. We'll never keep up with them. Best stick to Helen's idea: someone hot-wired the car and stole it from the front drive. If Jones actually finds a culprit, then we'll have to tell the truth, but by then we'll have taken care of this creature."

"We're back there again, aren't we?" Peter said. "What next?"

"I think . . ." Mrs. Burrows began, but never finished. An awful scream came from upstairs.

In a flash, they all raced upstairs, Peter taking the lead.

By the time Gloria and the other reached Alice, Peter was holding her in his arms. She was shaking her head. "No!" she shouted. "I will not! No!"

"Alice," Peter said, "It's me. Peter. You're safe. You're home. Open your eyes and look at me."

She froze a moment or two, then shook herself in his arms. Peter just held her tighter, whispering in her ear. Then she opened her eyes and gave a great shudder. "Peter! Gran! Oh, my God!" She shook all over, clinging to Peter. "I had such a nightmare. Did I wake you?" She looked around the room. "Gloria? Sergeant? What are you doing here? What happened?"

Peter told her—or a least as much as they knew.

She added the missing bits.

"I went into the bakery on my way back from seeing the Grayson baby. The place seemed deserted. I was having a poke around, when . . ." she paused and shuddered. "Someone came in, had to be Block, I assume. He grabbed me and . . ." She gave a grimace . . . "I don't remember much but pain and waking up. It was raining and cold."

"You were in your car. We got you out," Peter told her. "and brought you up here. I'd like to know what the flaming hell you thought you were doing, breaking and entering like that? But I'm so glad you're safe." He gave her a tight hug. "Don't ever give me a shock like that again."

She gave a weak smile. "I can assure you, I'm in no hurry to repeat the experience."

"What happened just now, my love? You were screaming and looked as if you were fighting someone." Mrs. Burrows asked.

Alice exhaled. "I was remembering." Peter relaxed his hold and she settled back on the pillows. "I feel lousy, as if I've got a temperature, my head aches and . . ." she touched the bump and the bandage. "What happened?"

"You cut your head. Most likely on the dashboard or the steering wheel. Gloria and I looked at it. It isn't deep, no stitches needed."

"I need to get up."

Time to step in. "You're not going anywhere. You're staying in bed until we're sure you're not developing pneumonia. You were soaked to the skin when we found you. Peter and I can cover for you, and if we need a doctor, we'll call in a locum."

It was a mark of Alice's exhaustion that she just nodded. "Give me a day. I'll be fine. My mind is so foggy. There was something I needed to tell you, Gloria, but I can't, for the life of me, remember what it was."

"You will."

"What can I get you, my love?" Mrs. Burrows asked, coming closer to the bed and taking Alice's hand. "A cup of tea? Something to eat? A nice boiled egg?"

She went off to make tea and a soft boiled egg. Pendragon followed her, and Gloria decided she really ought to put in an appearance at the school. "Look, Peter, why not stay here with Alice? Keep an eye on her. I'll go by the school, give those poor evacuees the fastest check-up of their lives and get back here. If no one turns up people will start talking."

"Good idea. You're just going by the school, right? No heroics."

"And who are you to tell me what to do, Peter Watson?" Not that she had any intention of seeking to share Alice's horrendous experience.

"I'm your friend, Gloria, and I'd hate to see Andrew go through what I just did."

Good point. "I think what's most important is no one realizes what has happened. And the best way to do that is carry on as usual. I'll make up some story to cover you. Say you were called up to the camp or something."

"Won't work, someone will see his bicycle up here," Alice said. "Say he's busy."

"They'll think we're having a slap and tickle on government time," Peter said.

"Better they talk about us than about vampires," Alice said. "I'll make it sound plausible, don't worry."

"You're a brick, Gloria."

"Stay in bed and rest. We're going to need your strength soon, I'm afraid. I'll best be off."

Gloria had the doorknob in her hand, when Alice said, "Hang on. Just a minute."

Gloria stopped and turned. Alice was clearly concentrating, her brow furrowed and her eyes intent.

"What is . . ." Peter began but Alice hushed him with a quick wave.

They waited in silence. Alice looked fine, just very intent. She seemed to be listening, as if trying to concentrate on faint voices or a fading echo. After a few rather long minutes, she relaxed. "Well, I never," she said.

"Well, what?" Peter asked, sounding concerned again.

"You might find this hard to believe," Alice replied, "but I know what Block is doing."

"What?" they spoke almost simultaneously.

Alice gave a smile. "I know what he's doing. He just took a delivery of flour."

"You know everything he's doing?" Gloria asked.

"No, just when it's quiet and I concentrate."

"This," Peter said, "could be our much needed boost of good luck."

"I'm telling the others," Gloria said and all but raced downstairs. She made herself slow down. She wasn't up to healing a second broken leg.

As she reached the hall, the front doorbell rang. "Should I get it?" she called toward the kitchen.

"Yes, Gloria, there's a love. It's probably the paperboy wanting his money."

It wasn't.

Gloria opened the front door to a tall, fair-haired, heavy-set man. Not that heavy really but he gave the impression of strength. "Good morning."

"Good morning," he said. "Is this the right house for Mrs. Burrows?"

"Yes, it is. Can I help you? I'm Nurse Prewitt."

He took off his hat. "My name is Clarendon. Jude Clarendon. Would you please tell Mrs. Burrows I'm here to see her?"

Chapter Thirty-One

"Mrs. Burrows? Yes, she's in. Let me tell her. Did you want something in particular?" Maybe they could get rid of him fast. He didn't have the look of a door-to-door salesman but these days one never knew.

"Who is it, Gloria?" Mrs. Burrows called.

"Mrs. Burrows? It's Jude Clarendon. I came to see if all is well."

"Stone the crows!" There was a dull clunk as metal hit metal and Mrs. Burrows came out, untying her apron. "Mr. Clarendon! Indeed you're welcome. Come in. Please do."

He inclined his head with a smile and stepped over the threshold. Gloria wasn't sure whether to leave—she did have to check weight and eyesight and nits—or stay and find out who this mysterious stranger was.

"Shut the door, Gloria. There's a dear, you're letting the cold in."

That settled it. She closed the door. Nits weren't likely to go anywhere.

Whoever he was, he was obviously very welcome. There was something a bit odd about him, though. Gloria couldn't quite put her finger on it.

"Goodness gracious," Mrs. Burrows said, taking both his

hands. "You don't know how welcome you are. But tell me, did all go well?"

"Mostly," he replied. "I'm back and thought to see how things worked out for you." He gave Gloria a cautious glance. "Your difficulty was taken care of?"

"Oh yes! That one was but unfortunately we have another. Don't worry about Gloria, she's with us, and besides, she's Other." Smashing! Announce it to every stranger that comes in the front door. "Don't look so worried, Gloria. Mr. Clarendon is on our side. Come into the kitchen. I suppose I can't offer you anything to eat?"

He gave an amused smile. "Thank you, but no."

"A cup of tea? You do drink?"

"Please."

"Now have a seat. Please excuse the kitchen but it's warm in here. That makes a big difference to us. Now . . ." She poured a cup while he took a chair. "Let me introduce everyone. You met Nurse Prewitt, our district nurse and this is Howell Pendragon."

Handshakes all around. His hands were cold. Must be chillier out than she thought.

"They're both Other, as no doubt you sensed," Mrs. Burrows went on. "We took care of the last worry. Or rather my granddaughter, Alice, did, but now we have another to deal with and I must say your timely arrival is a gift from the gods. We really need your help."

"If your granddaughter has strength and magic enough to dispatch a vampire, why need me?"

"Because she's in a bad way. The second vampire attacked Alice last night. Attacked her and tried to make out she crashed her car driving drunk!"

"Hang on here, Helen . . ." Pendragon began.

"Mrs. Burrows, do you really think you should be . . ." Gloria said. Honestly, whoever this man was, why was she telling him all this?

She hushed both with a wave. "Yes, I do. Stop fussing, you two. Mr. Clarendon is on our side."

"He is, if you say so, Helen," Pendragon said. "But I'd like to know what he is and why we should trust him?"

"Perfectly reasonable," Mr. Clarendon said. "Our introductions were too brief. I know you are both Other, but can not tell what you are. I will trust you with what I am, if you will do the same."

"Of course they will," Mrs. Burrows said, giving them both a look that dared them to refuse.

"I'm a shifter," Gloria said. "A Were. I turn into a fox."

He inclined his head. "A useful ally, you can move unnoticed in the night." He turned to Pendragon.

The sergeant sat up tall. "My ancestors came from the Welsh mountains. When I shift I am the Pendragon."

Amazing how foxes got courtesy but Dragons deep respect. Mr. Clarendon's eyes widened, only momentarily but they widened. "Indeed. I have heard talk of the Dragons but never thought to meet one. Formidable is not the word for your abilities."

"I use what I have when it's called for," Pendragon replied. A bit stiffly, Gloria thought.

"You have trusted me with your natures, I will share mine. I am a revenant. I am Vampire."

"What!" Gloria stood, looking around for a weapon, teaspoon, toasting fork, wooden spoon. Whatever she could grab first.

"Settle down, Gloria. Didn't I tell you, he's on our side?" Mrs. Burrows said. "Very much on our side, I might add." She looked at Clarendon. "You've told them that much. Tell them where you've been the past few weeks."

"I have been in France," he said, with a little smile. "The Germans are not the only ones to appreciate the usefulness of our kind."

Made sense. Sort of. "They've certainly given us enough trouble."

"Then perhaps I can help."

Fight fire with fire? That was the sergeant, wasn't it?

"If you can. It will be welcome," Pendragon said. "Seems no sooner we get rid of one and another arrives."

"Just a minute! Alice's egg!" Mrs. Burrows turned to the stove, and fished out the egg simmering in the saucepan. She put it in the egg cup on the tray, and added a slice of toast cut into fingers and a cup of tea. "Gloria, be a dear and take this up to Alice. We'll fill Mr. Clarendon in. Best not mention anything to Alice, might upset her, after what happened."

She could hardly refuse without being churlish, but she rather wanted to be in on this. And she needed to get to work. Damn! Things were getting really interesting.

She took the tray. Mr. Clarendon—a vampire, she reminded herself—held the door for her and she headed for Alice's room.

Alice was back asleep. Better than having nightmares. "I brought breakfast. Might do her good if you can get her to eat it."

"Was that the doorbell?"

Peter didn't miss much. "Yes, an old friend of Mrs. Burrows stopped by. I'm going to show my face at the school or they'll be sending out search parties. Promise to give me a ring at school if anything happens."

"I will, but something tells me she's going to be like this for days."

"God. I hope not. That monster! I'd like to fix his wagon for him. Good and proper."

He shook Alice's shoulder gently and she opened her eyes. "Your gran cooked you a boiled egg. Fancy a mouthful or two?"

"Yes." She gave a weak smile. "Hadn't you two better get to work?"

"I'm on my way. Just came up to give you this. Peter's staying with you. To make sure you rest up."

"I will. Feel too washed out to do much else, but, Gloria, there's something I remembered and meant to tell you. Remember the 'flying' man you saw?"

As if she'd forget. "Of course."

"Jim Clegg, the little evacuee up at the Graysons', saw him too."

"So did Mary."

"Mary? The new teacher? When did she see him?"

"Saturday night when she was taking a moonlit stroll. She asked me if I thought it was something to do up at the plant on the heath."

"What was she doing wandering around the countryside in the middle of the night?" Peter asked.

She'd wondered that too and had an inkling. "She said she wanted to enjoy the country air after all the weeks in Sheffield."

"Odd that three of you saw him." Peter said.

"Proves we didn't imagine it." She shrugged. "I must get going."

Gloria stopped by the kitchen to say she was off.

She was a bit put out that no one begged her to stay, but that was getting silly.

"Take care, nurse," the vampire Clarendon said. "These are dangerous times and this creature's action last night shows he is desperate."

"I can guarantee I'm not going to search his flat. But there are a couple of things I want to check. Aside from twenty-seven evacuees."

She almost wished the ride were longer. She really did need time to think, but first she had to run home and wash and put on her uniform.

She had to see Andrew. Maybe she'd nip up there at lunchtime. And she had to talk to Mary. There was more to her than a mild-mannered schoolteacher.

She'd seen the "flyer" in the open land between Fletcher's woods and the heath. What was Mary doing that far from the village? It was a darn long way for a country stroll. In the middle of the night no less.

Chapter Thirty-Two

Gloria had no doubt she set some sort of speed record. By recruiting two of the older children to list names, birthdays and hosts and man the eye chart, she got the lot weighed, measured, and their hearing tested by eleven, when they happily joined the rest of the school for morning break.

She was about to skip off and make a beeline for the heath when Mary came up to her.

"Is everything alright? I heard the phone right before you went out early. Was it an emergency?"

No, just a vampire attack. Gloria bit her tongue. Think fast and pick words carefully. "Mrs. Burrows, the doctor's grandmother called. Alice is ill. A bad flu, it seems." No point in making too much of a song and dance about it. "After she called me, she discovered someone had stolen Alice's car."

"Terrible! You don't expect things like that in a village like this."

Mary had no idea what went on in a village like this. "These things happen."

Mary nodded, a little crease forming between her eyebrows. "There's something wrong, isn't there? Can I do something to help?"

What came next issued out of Gloria's lips of its own volition.

"Tell me what you really were doing Saturday night." Seeing Mary pale meant she'd asked the right—or maybe totally wrong—question.

"What do you mean?"

The nervous snappiness proved she'd hit something. She made a point of lowering her voice to a whisper. "Mary, no one in their right mind walks all that way in the middle of the night in strange countryside. You had a reason to be out and about that late. Why?" Was it any business of hers? Yes, given what was going on.

Mary swallowed, panic in her eyes as they darted from side to side. Scared someone was close enough to hear perhaps? "I had a good reason. I did no harm to anyone, I promise you. On my word of honor." She crossed her heart the way school children did.

Gloria believed her. "Please tell me."

"Not now, not here."

Fair enough. "After school?"

Mary looked her straight in the face. "What right do you have to ask me?"

None, actually. "There's a war on, Mary, and Brytewood is bang in the middle of it." Not a nice thing to say, given her situation at home. "Maybe you have skills that can help. Abilities that might aid us."

"Us?"

Gloria nodded. "If I trust you with my secret, maybe you will trust me with yours. This afternoon, I'll explain how I healed a broken ankle."

For exits, it was a good one. For common sense and caution, it was in the gutter. As Gloria pedaled up the long climb toward the heath, she wondered what the blazes had taken possession of her tongue. Either she was right, and Mary possessed some Other nature that could add to their collective abilities, or sleep deprivation and worry were eating holes in her brain.

Of course it could be a bit of both. But the big worry that

gnawed at her was what was the baker planning and when? Had to be something to do with Andrew's plant. Must be. The last try had failed, thanks in no small part to her intervention. Seemed they were having another go.

That meant they were out to get at Andrew and that was not going to happen. Not while she lived and breathed. If she had to shift in the middle of the village street in broad daylight and attack the creature herself. So be it.

Nothing and no one was going to hurt Andrew.

That conviction kept her pedaling up the entire incline at a speed that would have left a mere human on the point of collapse. She slowed as the first set of gates came into view. No point in drawing attention to herself.

Peter looked at Alice and wondered what the hell he should do. She appeared to be asleep. Not restful exactly, but her eyes had closed a few minutes ago and he couldn't decide if he should indulge himself and stay with her, or act like a responsible adult in the middle of a war, and get to work. Gloria might be covering him at the school but he was expected at the plant clinic.

But wasn't the war—or the results of it—lying in the bed in front of him? That was an act of aggression if ever there was one and damn, he was going to finish that creature if he had to do it himself. At the very least he could gather a supply of stakes and prepare the mistletoe. Without that magic knife, it was the best they had.

He'd actually stood up and turned toward the door when Alice opened her eyes. "Peter," she said, her voice still shaky. "Do you think I could be going insane?"

Maybe they all were. "What makes you think that?

"If I concentrate, I know what he's doing. He's in the shop, selling a loaf of bread to Reverend Roundtree. I can know what he's doing but it leaves me tired."

"Best not do it then, Alice, at least for a little while. You need to get your strength back."

"I think he has it."

"No!" Christ, he'd shouted, but no! He was back on the bed, holding both her hands. "Alice, we need your strength. Don't give it to him."

"He's not taking it now. It's as if we're linked. I know what he's doing. We can track him. Follow him."

It would be helpful, and if it kept her in bed rather than haring across the countryside it might be a darn good idea. "Are you sure about this? Could you just be remembering?"

She shook her head. "No, I feel a hook into his mind. I can tell you what he's doing right this minute."

She shut her eyes again, just as before. Her eyes stayed closed, her lashes dark against her pale face, and she tensed as if it took all her strength and effort. Probably did.

Her eyes flashed open. "Peter," she said, struggling to sit up and put her feet on the floor. "I need to talk to Gran. Something's up."

"Hang on a mo, Alice, what's happened?"

"Remember I said he'd taken in a shipment of flour?"

"Yes."

"He went back to look at it, and inside the bag was a packet."

"Of what?"

"I don't know. He just was very, very pleased and excited, put it in a cupboard and went back into the shop as someone came in."

Could just be an innocent bit of black market—if that wasn't an oxymoron—but given the circumstances, innocent activity was highly unlikely. "I'll tell your grandmother and the sergeant."

"I need to tell them. This could be just the break we need."

She ought to know by now nothing was that simple.

* * *

"Gracious, Alice. What are you doing up?" Gran stood and hurried over to her. "You need to be in bed."

"I'm going back, promise." Just walking downstairs, leaning on the banister and Peter's arm took all her strength but she was going to last a bit longer. "But there's something I have to tell you but . . ." She looked at the stranger who'd risen with the sergeant so the two men stood side by side. One dark and grizzled, the other blond and very young. Apart from the old eyes.

"Alice," Gran said, "first you sit right down, then I'll introduce our visitor, who's come to help."

She wouldn't argue about sitting. Her legs felt like cotton wool but the visitor? She was none too sure about him. Although Gran and Sergeant Pendragon seemed well disposed toward him. He had cold hands too, when he shook hands. She was being petty but . . . "How can you help us, Mr. Clarendon?"

He inclined his head, ignoring the rudeness she hadn't really meant. "Mrs. Burrows made an incomplete introduction. She omitted the mention that I am a vampire."

Darn good thing she was in a chair or she'd be on the kitchen floor. "A vampire, Mr. Clarendon?" She sounded a lot more composed than she felt. Gran and Sergeant Pendragon wouldn't be sitting here so complacently if the vampire meant them harm. Or would they if they'd been compelled? Blowed if she knew.

He inclined his head in the same odd formal bow. "I am, Dr. Doyle, but hasten to add, I am on your side."

"What side would that be?"

"For King and Empire. We will win." He smiled. If you could call a slight curling of the corners of his mouth a smile. "Our side has more vampires than theirs."

"You're sure of that?"

"I returned from France two nights ago. I am sure. And, I understand, thanks to you they now have one less."

"With a bit of luck, two less very soon."

Now he really smiled. Downright vicious it was. "Never consider it luck. Skill, opportunity, swift action but never luck. Luck is too fickle to be relied upon in a venture as serious and decisive as this."

She wasn't about to argue. Not with a vampire but darn, there had been an element of luck last time. This time? Who could tell?

"Are you going to help us kill this one?" Peter asked. Nothing like asking outright.

"Help, yes. This is war. Aside from the larger issues, he has attacked you. Unprovoked."

"Not entirely unprovoked." She had to admit that and told him all she remembered.

"You are daring, madam. Few would venture into a vampire's lair."

"I'm not sure I'd try it again. But it seemed a good idea at the time. However, that's not the most important thing." She told them about her mind link.

Gran looked horrified. "My love, what are we going to do?"

"Use it. If I know what he's doing, surely it'll help us corner him."

"I don't like the idea of you being in that creature's head," Gran replied.

"Neither do I," Peter added.

"Seems a risky undertaking," the sergeant replied.

"Risky!" Mr. Clarendon echoed. "It could be disastrous."

"What exactly do you mean?"

"Doctor Doyle, you do not understand? If you can enter his mind, don't you think he might be able to enter yours?"

The egg she'd eaten curdled and roiled in her stomach. She swallowed hard to keep it down. "No," she replied in a tight whisper. "That never occurred to me."

"It may not be so. But it's a distinct possibility."

When the slow shudder eased, she took a deep breath. "I'm not really happy at that idea."

"Happy!" Peter almost spat it out. "It's preposterous! First that abominable thing attacks Alice and tries to make it look as if she'd been driving drunk, now he can invade her mind!"

The vampire raised both hands, palms out in a gesture of appeasement. "Young man, I said it is a possibility, not a certainty. Most likely he can not. When I tried to invade Mrs. Burrow's mind and influence her, I failed utterly." He gave a little shrug. "Given Dr. Doyle has similar powers, she may be untouchable too."

"He certainly managed to touch me last night."

Peter muttered something under his breath that sounded like "bastard."

"Yes," the vampire went on, "he did. Are you still weak?"

"As a newborn kitten. Coming downstairs took all I had, but I wanted Gran and Sergeant Pendragon to know."

"So," Pendragon said, "we now know he had a shipment of something hidden in a flour sack. Unlikely to be counterfeit ration books."

"More explosives?" Peter asked. "Don't want to give up, do they?"

"They will never give up," Mr. Clarendon said. "Not until they take Europe, maybe the entire known world, or are defeated." He shook his head. "In France now, they have this ridiculous division: Occupied France ruled by the Reich and Vichy France ruled by the French. Who are they fooling? Does that fool Petain really think the Germans have no interest in controlling the Mediterranean? The Italians are already in North Africa, only a matter of time before Hitler decides to join them."

"I bet he'd like to get those colonies back too," Gran said. "And right now, that Adolf is looking our way. Let's just hope those vampires are all he sends over."

"You'll join us then, Mr. Clarendon?" Might as well ask.

He gave a little smile. "Until I have to return to France, my skills and knowledge are yours."

"I suppose we'd best sharpen a few more stakes," Peter said. "Were any left over from last time?"

"Sorry, Peter," Gran said, "I used them for kindling."

"Plenty more where they came from," Pendragon said. "Peter and I can gather a stock. Coming, lad?"

Peter hesitated, worrying about her, she bet. "Go ahead, Peter, as your direct supervisor, I've reassigned you." That got a startled look from Mr. Clarendon and a chuckle from Peter.

"Yes, boss. Any other orders?"

"Take care."

"Only if you promise to as well."

"I think," the vampire said, standing with the others, "that you must keep out of this venture, Dr. Doyle. You are too vulnerable right now. Stay here, rest and avoid entering his mind. The knowledge you might gain is not worth the risk of the power he might wield."

A lousy idea. "I hate to sit back while you're all working."

"What you achieved last time was above and beyond. Superhuman in fact."

"Of course it was!" Gran nearly snapped. "She's Pixie!"

"Apologies." He inclined his head. A funny old-fashioned gesture but who knew how old he was? "A slip of the tongue. No slight or insult intended. You gentleman gather your stakes, I will reconnoiter the village. How many can we count on? You mentioned more Others."

"Gloria, the Werefox. She's with us," Gran said. "There's also Sam Whorleigh, the grocer. He helped out after finding Alice, but he's not one to bestir himself usually."

"He might be glad to see the end of the competition," Pendragon said. "He lost business to the baker," he explained to Mr. Clarendon.

"So, four, maybe five, Others."

"Don't forget Peter," Alice said, "and Andrew. They are as committed as we are."

"But human."

"Humans have their strengths too. I'd never have taken care of Oak without Peter's help."

Clarendon shook his head. "I seem destined to lay insults all around me. Forgive me. I'm not used to working with Others or humans."

That piqued her curiosity. "But in France?" Alright, it was secret and all that but, "Don't you . . .?"

He shook his head. "Seldom. I work mostly with other vampires."

That really did get her intrigued but best not ask any more. He wouldn't tell anyway. She ought to get back to bed. She felt as lively as a wrung-out dishrag.

"You need to get back to bed, my love," Gran said, "and stay there. I think Mr. Clarendon is right. It's too risky having you caught up in all this."

She was too worn out to argue, but . . . Of course. "There's one more thing. Maybe insignificant but who knows." She mentioned the three sightings.

"Different people different places?" Mr. Clarendon asked.

"Jim was in his bedroom, in a cottage up near Cherry Hill Farm. Gloria was not far from the heath, a good two or three miles away, and I'm not sure where Mary was. It just seems odd. He must have been covering a lot of ground."

"Getting to know the territory," Peter suggested.

"It would seem like it. Let us talk about it later."

Not in front of her, that meant. Much as it irked, he could be right and she had no intention of letting that monster know what they planned for him.

She went upstairs to try to sleep and pray with all her might that Peter come back safe and sound. This was as bad as seeing her brothers go off to war. And here was her Peter, a CO, taking on the fiercest enemy of all.

Chapter Thirty-Three

Gloria passed though both sets of gates with a nod and a wave. Perhaps she should mention to Andrew his security was getting lax. The army types who'd been buzzing around the place after the trouble last month had mostly moved on. To rougher and more dangerous parts, no doubt, although Brytewood wasn't exactly a holiday camp these days.

Deciding the clinic could wait, she headed for Andrew's office, parked her bicycle against the wooden hut and nipped up the rickety steps.

And hesitated, her hand almost touching the doorknob.

She'd dropped by here umpteen times, especially before Peter took over the job, to talk to the administrator, or check with his secretary about supplies, but this time was different. Other times, she hadn't seen the administrator naked. Never felt his body on hers—or deep in hers for that matter—and never ever known the ecstasy of his touch and the blazing heat of his kisses.

How in heaven's name was she going to handle this?

Perfectly well. With a bit of luck.

She turned the knob, opened the door and went in.

Barry Wallsall, Andrew's gray-haired secretary, looked up

from his hunt and peck efforts on the typewriter and smiled. "Morning, nurse, come to see the guvner, have you?"

"If he's not busy."

"Nah! Just paperwork. He'll be glad of the distraction." Far more glad than Mr. Wallsall would ever guess. She hoped! "Just knock and go on in."

Actually, she knocked and popped her head around the door at Andrew's "Come in." Just seeing the light of recognition in his eyes and that wondrously sexy smile as his lovely mouth turned up was worth pedaling up the north downs a dozen times.

"Gloria, come on in."

By the time she'd closed the door behind her, he was out of his chair, around the side of his desk, and had crossed the length of his office to wrap his arms around her. All but pinning her to the wall as he plastered his mouth on hers.

There was nothing to do but kiss him back with the same enthusiasm. She opened her lips, found his tongue and was caught in a wild spin of sheer and utter pleasure as desire burst into a wild need. She pulled him close, pressed her body into his and gave a little whimper of need as she felt his erection against her belly.

She was left in no doubt about her welcome.

"Gloria," he said, lifting his mouth off hers. "I've been thinking about you all morning. Couldn't concentrate on a thing."

"I doubt I'm helping by coming up here."

"Damn work, you're much more interesting." Somehow her raincoat had come open and his hand caressed her breast. Alright, it was over her uniform but she felt every fingertip all the same.

"I came to talk about what happened to Alice."

Definitely a passion freezer if ever there was one, but darn it, the walls here were thin.

"I'm darn glad you did. I've had this fear you'd take up where Alice left off and go after the blighter single-handed."

"No." Not as a human anyway, and she was still trying to work out how a fox could down a vampire. "I wanted to see you."

"Good." He pulled back a little. "Have a seat."

"I should stop by the clinic, at least for a couple of hours. I doubt Peter is going to venture far from Alice's bedside today."

"She's alright though? Or going to be?"

"As far as I can tell. I called up before I left the school, and spoke to Mrs. Burrows. She sounded worried but said Peter and Sergeant Pendragon were preparing stakes."

He gave her a very confused stare. "You know, love, if any other creature in the world had told me that, I'd have said they were losing their mind. As it is . . ." He shook his head. "I feel as though the entire planet shifted on its axis this weekend and jolted me into another dimension."

And he still didn't know about their vampire ally. "Same world. Same dimension. You just know a few things you didn't before."

"You make it sound so straightforward and simple."

She had to chuckle at that. "Simple? Straightforward? Andrew, right now I feel I'm getting sucked into a whirlpool. In the next few days, something horrible is going to happen unless we stop it and the trouble is we can only guess at what it is."

"But you all think it's going to try another attack here?"

"Where else?" A cold stab cut at her. "I'm worried for you. And everyone else up here. Last time it was just the two guards attacked but what if this one goes for more people?"

He didn't disagree. Nor did she. Why couldn't this horrid war just go away? Why didn't the sun rise in the west? Besides, she was being very selfish. She was safe. Or as safe as anyone was. What about Mary, evacuated and her home invaded? Or Mr. Clarendon venturing into France to help. Thinking about him, "Andrew, something happened after you left. We've got an ally."

"What do you mean?"

She told him. At least as much as she knew.

"A vampire? Sure he's on our side and not another spy?"

"Not according to Mrs. Burrows. Seems she knows him. From before the war I gathered."

"And he's helping destroy another vampire?"

"He's on our side."

Andrew didn't seem too sure. She might not be, if she hadn't met Mr. Clarendon and sensed his commitment.

There was a knock and at Andrew's reply, Barry Wallsall put his head around the door. "Thought I'd go and get lunch a few minutes early. If that's alright, sir?"

"Want to get first dibs on the toad in the hole before the first shift breaks for lunch, Wallsall?"

The man grinned back. "The thought had entered my mind, sir."

"Go ahead."

As the door closed, Gloria smiled at Andrew. "Does that door have a lock?" That was forward and rather shocking and they had all sorts of worrisome things to talk about but right now she wanted to forget about the future of the world and just think of Andrew.

Judging by the grin on his face, he was of much the same mind. "No locks I'm afraid," he said, "but . . ." he picked up a chair and wedged it under the doorknob. "That should do."

Oh, yes.

His eyes gleamed with pretty much the same hopes she was entertaining. He wrapped his arms around her and spun her around, backing her up against the wall. She looked up at him, smiled and tilted her head. "Maybe we should go and taste that toad in the hole."

"Lousy idea." He didn't give her a chance to agree or disagree. Just fastened his mouth on hers, pressing her lips open as she dug her fingers into his hair and pulled him closer. As their tongues touched, a wild, seemingly insatiable desire took hold, blocking out the day, the place, the concerns of a minute ago. All was pushed aside in a tide of need and wanting and she whimpered with sheer joy.

His hands eased over her breasts as he fumbled for the buttons of her shirt. Not for long. He was inside her blouse, her bra was unhooked and his hands closed on her breasts. She leaned back against the wall, eyes shut and glorious sensation crashing though her body and flooding her mind.

The thought that this was lunacy flitted across a tiny sane corner of her consciousness but the idea blinked out as his mouth left her lips and closed over her right nipple. A groan of utter happiness came from deep inside her as his mouth played one nipple and his fingers the other. Her entire mind was lost in the wonder of his touch as glorious sensation washed over her.

His lips still caressed her breast but now he was under her skirt, stroking her thigh, teasing the flesh above the top of her stocking. He was inside her knickers, stroking, touching. She was wet, soaking and needed so much more. As if he knew, his fingers opened her and pressed deep. She was gasping, whimpering, and then his thumb touched her clit.

The scream was muffled by his kiss as she came in a wild and sudden torrent of pleasure that left her limp, sagging against the wall, and clinging to him for support. Her legs weren't much use any longer and her entire body was pulsing with pleasure.

"Andrew!" she managed to mutter between gasps.

He chuckled. "Happy?"

"I think," it took an effort to get the words out, "we just rewrote the definition of happiness."

"You are so incredible, Gloria."

"What about you?" Now her pulse was slowing slightly she realized the pleasure had all been hers. "Isn't it your turn?"

"We're getting to that," he replied and whisked her up in his arms and crossed the room, brushing aside papers and books to lay her in his desk.

"You know, we could both lose our jobs over this," she said as he spread her legs and stood between them.

"Yes," he agreed and unbuttoned his flies. "Would be terrible wouldn't it?"

She smiled. Sanity would resume later.

He caught his trousers as they fell to the floor. Reaching into the back pocket, he took out a little paper envelope.

"Always prepared are you?" she asked. Very, very happy that he was.

"I was a Boy Scout. 'Be Prepared' was drilled into us."

"Really? I thought it was all fire lighting and knots." Mind you, he was pretty good at the first bit as far as she was concerned. A fire was still raging inside her.

"Lots more than that," he said, stroking the flesh just above her left stocking. "Lots, lots more." His hands eased up to her hips, holding her steady. "We must talk about it sometime." He was in her. Deep. And she didn't give a flying fig for Boy Scouts, or anything except his lovely cock deep and the rhythm of his hips back and forth, until she came again. Sensation flooded her mind. As her climax eased, he gave a cry, "I love you, Gloria!" and orgasmed.

He collapsed over her, holding himself up by his arms. He kissed her: a soft, gentle kiss that even so sent ripples of pleasure deep inside.

She must have closed her eyes. She opened them and gave a little cry as he eased out of her. She wanted more. She wanted to make love to him forever.

Not a good idea right now. She inched her way across the desk so her feet touched the floor.

"Hang on," he said, and gave her a hand up. "That was totally insane. You make me insane, Gloria."

"Speaking as a medical professional, a little insanity now and again is good for you." As long as you didn't get caught and you hid all the evidence.

Her knickers were all the way across the room. She retrieved them while Andrew took care of himself. She also picked up her hat. Hardly surprising that it had come off, but she looked around, wondering what else she'd shed. Andrew removed the chair from under the doorknob and straightened his desk.

With a bit of luck their delightful insanity would never be detected.

Jobs were safe.

Good thing too.

Now all they had to worry about was the flipping vampire.

Chapter Thirty-Four

Not quite what he'd anticipated, but an interesting morning nonetheless, Wilhelm Bloch decided, as he wrapped the fat woman's bloomer loaf in a sheet of newspaper. He'd gleaned a few useful snippets from the morning gossip.

Biggest bit of news was the theft of the doctor's car. Theft indeed! If they wanted to believe that, let the peasants delude themselves. The local version of the truth was spread by the flat-footed fool of a police sergeant—who would be one of the first to expire after victory. Not only had some unnamed miscreant driven the doctor's vehicle into a ditch but the doctor was abed with fever, chills, influenza or pneumonia, depending on the informant. The woman's condition had steadily deteriorated throughout the morning and at this rate, she'd be dead by teatime and good riddance!

The other burning topic, at least as far as the peasants were concerned, was the discovery of a dead woman in an overgrown ditch some miles outside the village. The thought of a fresh dead human going to rot rather offended his vampire's soul, but one villager more or less was of scant concern to him. The inhabitants of Brytewood appeared to differ. Seemed this old biddy would be missed. As if one old woman mattered an iota in the scheme of things.

There was interesting chatter about the imminent engagement or marriage (opinions seemed divided) between the administrator of the supposedly secret munitions plant and the district nurse, and comment about a fresh row of concrete defenses—the silly peasants called them dragon's teeth—across someone or other's land.

Not enough information to reinforce victory but maybe worth mentioning the next time Weiss summoned him.

Which might be soon.

An early delivery brought the promised flares. He had Weiss's map and to be sure he'd cover the ground again tonight. There would be no mistakes. He was, however curious about what to do if it rained.

Might be worth a phone call to Weiss, just to irk him and set him blethering on about caution and security.

"Mr. Block? Good morning."

It was the old woman from up the hill: the doctor's grandmother. "Good morning, madam. What can I do for you this morning?" Besides wishing her troublesome granddaughter the other side of Hades.

"Just came in to check on my order for bridge rolls. Remember? I need them for the whist drive on Wednesday night. I thought I'd pick them up just after lunch, if that suits."

As good a time as any. Since he planned to leave as soon as the attack concluded. "I'll have them ready for you, madam."

"Lovely. Today I'll have a large loaf, please."

"Sorry to hear about the doctor's car," he said, as he handed her the loaf.

"What's a car?" she replied, tilting her chin and giving him a most peculiar look. "It's the person who hurt my Alice who will get their just deserts sooner or later!"

Fool! He'd scoured the doctor's mind of her memories. There was no way in Hades she could remember what happened. And if this old bat thought for one minute . . . He stared at her as she met his eyes, lifting her gray eyebrows and squaring her ancient shoulders.

For a wild second he fancied she could see into his head.

Utter nonsense. She might be one of these pesky odd creatures that inhabited the village but what could an old woman do against him? Other than irritate. "Your change, madam."

She put the coins in her purse and clicked it shut. "I'll be back Wednesday, Mr. Block." she said, and the bell over the door jingled as she went out.

Silly cow!

Helen Burrows considered herself a civilized woman. She was Pixie, a cut or two above your average human female, but oh, right now she'd be divinely happy to act the brawling fishwife. To look at the creature, knowing what he'd done, and tried to do, to Alice was enough to try the patience of a saint, and Helen Burrows had never held expectations of canonization. She wanted that creature to suffer, to expire, to dissolve into murky ashes like Oak had. He meant no good, was here to do harm, more harm than he had already, and was nothing but a potential disaster.

He had to be taken care of.

Unfortunately, Alice could barely stand, much less summon all her powers, and without the magic knife, would stakes be enough?

Their only hope lay with Mr. Jude Clarendon. He and Howell were planning strategy. Helen didn't think strategy was going to be enough. To beat this specimen, they'd need magic, strength, subterfuge and a lot of luck.

But beat and destroy him they must. They really had no other alternative.

The queue outside the butcher's was too long to even contemplate. She'd try Whorleigh's for sausages. Looked as though she'd be feeding a houseful again tonight. Good thing

Mr. Clarendon didn't eat. Not that she wanted to inquire too closely into what he preferred for dinner.

Joey was sitting in his push chair outside the grocer's. Good! That meant Doris was inside and Helen really wanted a word with her. "Hello, Joey," she said.

He looked up from playing with the beads on the front of his push chair and gave her a lovely, toothy smile.

Helen pushed open the door and joined the queue of four women waiting. Doris was last in line. Even better.

"Morning, Mrs. Burrows," she said, turning at the sound of the doorbell. "How is Alice?"

"Morning, Doris. Thank you for asking. Just a nasty bout of flu, I think. I'm so glad I ran into you. Can you give me a little extra time this week? I've some parachute silk I plan to use for Alice's wedding dress. I have the pattern she wants but I need some help."

"Oh, I'd love to help," Doris replied. "I can get up there tomorrow. Is the doctor alright? I heard about her car being stolen. Terrible it is, honestly who'd have thought it could happen in Brytewood?"

If Doris knew the truth of what happened in Brytewood . . .

"Alice is going to be stuck in bed a few days so this is a perfect chance for a bit of secret sewing."

"I'm game, Mrs. Burrows. All for it! If fact I could come this afternoon, after Joey has his nap."

Not with a vampire hunt in the planning stages. Doris was a good soul and could keep her mouth shut when needed but she didn't need to know what was going on up at The Gallop right now. "What about Wednesday? Come early, if you can." They would surely have the vampire taken care of by then. "Bring Joey, of course."

"I'll be there. I'll have to stop by and see to Mother Longhurst's chickens first. Though what's going to happen to them I dunno. I'd keep them, if no one wants them, I'd be glad of the eggs for Joey. Wasn't it awful news? Being found in a ditch like that and they're saying she was stark naked."

"I think, Doris, village gossip added that little detail." At least she hoped so. Either way it was terrible.

"You think there's a connection? It's odd her getting killed and then the doctor's car getting stolen."

Wasn't impossible, but best not get distracted. "I don't think so. Mother Longhurst went missing last week." Which, come to think of it, was about the time this so-called baker arrived and set up shop. Now that did bear considering.

"Yeah, she did, and I've been taking care of those chickens ever since. Want me to bring up some eggs tomorrow? I'm preserving them for the winter but we can only eat so many."

"Thank you, Doris, that would be wonderful."

"Can I help you, madam?"

While they'd talked the queue had gone but good heavens, the man did sound testy! Didn't bode well for what Helen Burrows had in mind. Too bad. After a bit of debate and arguing, Doris bought a quarter pound of sliced brawn, some porridge oats and her weekly butter ration and left, repeating her promise to be up at The Gallop just as soon as she could on Wednesday.

By some wonderful quirk of fate, no one else was in the shop, apart from the assistant unpacking tins of baked beans.

"What can I get for you, Mrs. Burrows?" Whorleigh asked.

"Pork sausages," she replied. "A pound and a half, please."

"Can't let you have that much, Mrs. Burrows."

"I think you can, Mr. Whorleigh. Especially since you're coming for supper tonight. Seven thirty." That got his attention. She wondered if he'd ever been invited out for a meal before. He wasn't the most liked member of the village.

"I beg your pardon, Mrs. Burrows."

"You heard me, Mr. Whorleigh. Come."

"And why would I do that?"

"Let's say it's my mark of appreciation for the favor you paid me recently."

"To come to dinner and eat my own sausages?"

Dear me, the man was prickly. Distrust had to be mutual, but she was getting desperate and whatever he was, she could surely add his talents. "Mr. Whorleigh, do you care for the future of this island and the outcome of this war?"

"Of course I do!"

"Good! A pound and half please." He weighed them out and rolled them in greaseproof paper but when he put them on the counter, he kept hold of them. "This morning proved we have trouble. Mr. Whorleigh, your particular gifts will be invaluable." Whatever they were.

He stared, eyes wide, plump cheeks flushed. "What are you saying?" He looked up as the bell over the door signaled another customer.

She whisked the package from his grasp and put it in the basket over her arm. "Thank you, Mr. Whorleigh. Seven thirty. Don't be late." And left. He'd put it on their account, and no doubt charge them double but it would be worth it, if he joined them.

She had no idea what he could offer, but he was Other and it was high time he joined the fray.

Wild sex before lunch, endless injuries afterwards. Or so it seemed to Gloria. Most were minor, apart from one poor woman who'd lost the end of two fingers when the bullet she was sealing exploded on her. After summoning the ambulance and dispatching her to hospital, Gloria was back to handing out aspirin and condoms, and bottles of eye drops for what seemed to be a budding epidemic of pink eye. Seemed the government had issued protective eye shields, but not enough, and they were shared between shifts.

She asked the shift manager to make sure all masks were

wiped with diluted carbolic between wearings and to pass that request on to the other managers. He groused about it but let up when she pointed out that having a widespread epidemic that decimated the workforce wasn't the way to aid the war effort.

She was writing out a requisition for extra carbolic and hoping Peter would take his job back tomorrow, when Andrew put his head around the door.

Luckily he caught sight of the two women waiting on folding metal chairs, before he spoke. Not that he needed to speak, she picked up his meaning from his eyes.

"Nurse Prewitt, could I have a quick word? After you finish with your patients of course." He nodded to the waiting women.

"Of course. I'll drop by your office on my way home." She wasn't sure she was up to a repeat performance but a few tender embraces to send her on her way wouldn't be unwelcome.

She handed a small vial of oil of cloves to the toothache sufferer, and suggested she go to the dentist in Dorking on her next day off, or sooner if the pain got worse, and handed a tin of medicated talc to the other girl, who had a bad case of athlete's foot.

She made a couple of notes for Peter about stocks that were looking low, locked up and walked along the concrete paths that crisscrossed the area, until she reached Andrew's office, where she'd left her bicycle propped against the side of the hut.

Her trusty old black Hercules wasn't there. Had someone nicked it? She ran up the steps and pushed the door open.

"Is Mr. Barron—" she began, then realized he was standing, coat on, waiting for her.

"He is," he replied, with a grin. "I popped your cycle on the back of my lorry. I'll give you a ride back."

Only he turned right at the gate, not left.

"Going back to the village, are we?"

"Eventually, but we have about half an hour before it starts getting dark, I thought it might be an idea to sharpen a few stakes."

So, they were back to fighting vampires, or at least contemplating the prospect. "If we're going in that direction, let's detour toward Cherry Hill. I really should visit Mrs. Grayson's. I know Alice planned to go back today and check on the baby."

"Fair enough. Stakes first, whooping cough second. Perhaps we could swing around to Leatherhead and dinner at that little place down near the bridge that Alice mentioned?"

Why not? "Think we should tell Mrs. Burrows? Wasn't she expecting us back?"

"We can stop off there on our way home."

She understood then, or thought she did: they were running away, stealing a few short hours together but preparing for the looming terror.

Without any idea how they were going to survive.

Sharpening stakes with pocket knives as they perched on a five-barred gate seemed the sort of activity Girl Guides might do on a weekend camp. Except Girl Guides didn't rub the pointed ends with squashed mistletoe berries.

"Are you sure this helps?"

Andrew shrugged. "Peter told me it was what they did, as per Mother Longhurst."

Couldn't hurt.

Chapter Thirty-Five

He'd had enough of this inane gossip and the constant reminders that somehow his efforts to disgrace and disable the meddling doctor had been foiled. If he knew the culprit, he'd suck him dry without compunction and damn Weiss's caution. Trouble was, this wretched village seemed buzzing with interference. The intrusion by the doctor was just a beginning, he suspected. And he wasn't about to ignore the fact that someone in this accursed village, most likely the aforementioned doctor, had dispatched Eiche to his final end.

Shouldn't Weiss know about that?

With that thought in mind, Bloch closed up early, with a smiling lie about running out of bread, and set off for Weiss's.

And was greeted with a snarl.

"Haven't you been instructed to only come when summoned?"

He had. "I could not risk this to the telephone, those stupid girls might listen in and blow everything. This is important. Vital." A bit of an overstatement, but it got him admittance.

"Well?" They were standing in the narrow hall of Weiss's billet. No invitation to sit down this time. Made Bloch wonder if there wasn't another person in the house. A woman? Someone Weiss used for sustenance?

With a nod, Bloch explained all was not exactly "well" in Brytewood.

"So, you have been exposed."

Smashing! Now it was all his fault. "I don't believe so. There are creatures in that village that are not human. I've sensed them. Seen them. This doctor is one of them."

"So, you disposed of her, without thought that it might endanger our mission?"

Damn Weiss! "Leaving her free to wander and intrude was potentially a bigger threat to our mission."

"You left incriminating evidence in your quarters?"

Did Weiss think he was a total fool? "I had nothing there. That, perhaps, was the problem. No food, no drink. No toilet paper even. Given someone in the village destroyed Eiche, they must know what we are."

That gave Weiss pause. "But she is disposed of."

"Not completely." He described the inexplicable outcome of his actions.

Weiss was not pleased. "Fool! You can't even kill properly!"

"My intention was to follow your orders and not kill. She should have been publicly disgraced."

"Should have been! Instead she is free to meddle and disrupt."

"Not entirely. She is reported to be ailing."

Weiss went very quiet for several moment. "So, what am I supposed to do about it?"

"About the fool of a doctor? Nothing. But two laying flares would help."

"No! Schmidt can not come. He has other duties." Obviously Wiess didn't sully his hands with field work. "Do I have to report that you can not complete your assignment?"

"No. It will be done. The flares arrived this morning and I will scout out the positions this evening."

"Don't fail."

That, Bloch chose to ignore. He opened the door and stepped out into the gray afternoon.

He had time. Plenty of it. Might be amusing to seek Schmidt out. Or look for sustenance. The pimply adolescent he'd suborned to him was no longer amusing. And after Weiss's snide comments, Bloch felt little compunction to spare a human life.

He strolled down to the lower part of the town. In a side street, he found a narrow shop, a cobbler's, manned by a man of fighting age. He should have been out on the front lines, waiting to stop a German bullet.

Bloch smiled. "Could you help me?"

"What can I do for you?

"My shoe. I seem to have worn a hole in the sole and it's my only pair."

"Hand it over, sir. I'll see what I can do for you."

Bloch slipped the door lock and switched the sign on the door to "Closed."

"Hey! What do you think . . ."

The fool never finished the question but he got his reply. Fast as only a vampire could move, Bloch was over the counter and had the man in a deadly embrace. Fangs pierced his neck, cutting off his voice, and in no time at all, he stopped struggling as Bloch drained him to his death. When he dropped the body to the floor and kicked it aside, Bloch understood why the man wasn't in uniform. He had an artificial leg.

Curious, but hardly interesting.

Wiping his mouth on a rather greasy cloth he picked up near the industrial sewing machine, Bloch unlocked the door and walked out.

Then he began to run.

"Do you think a dozen's enough?" Gloria asked, looking at the heap of sharpened stakes lying on the grass.

"Since it's unlikely our vampire baker will stand around waiting to be jabbed. I think it's ample," Andrew replied. "One or two would probably do the trick. Or not do it."

She looked up at him, his face in the shadows from the setting sun. "Have you any idea how we're going to manage this?"

"None," he replied, "but Mrs. Burrows seems to have it all under control. And you know, love, once I accepted you'd turn furry and grow a brush when the moon is full, everything else was comparatively easy."

Gloria wrapped her arms around him. "I've sorry you got dragged into all this."

"I'm not. Gloria, with you I'd go to hell and back."

"I'm afraid we might."

"We're together. Alice and Peter survived it. Besides, there's a whole team of us now."

"Think we should go back now?"

"You're turning down my invitation to dinner?"

"Sort of. We really ought to see what's going on and I'm still worried about Alice."

"Let's go back, then."

Good idea only . . . "Drat! We have to stop by the Graysons'. Won't take long but Alice was worried about the baby. He's only eight months or so and the older boys are no doubt chafing at the bit at being quarantined. I must stop. Won't be long."

"I'm with you, Gloria, all the way."

That she did not doubt.

Back in the lorry, the pile of stakes on the seat between them, Gloria looked at the man she loved: The love of her life, who, against all human logic, accepted her Other nature with no apparent qualms and wanted to spend the rest of his life with her.

How could she say no?

"When do you want to get married?"

He looked at her, eyes wide, and the lorry swerved across

the lane. "Damn," he muttered as he wrenched the steering wheel and pulled the lorry to the verge by the side of the lane.

"Is that a yes to my proposal?"

She grinned. "It is." She flung her arms around him, scattering stakes with a clatter, fastened her mouth on his and tasted heat. Sheer molten longing flared between them. He pulled her close and kissed back, opening her mouth with his lips, or maybe she opened his. Really was irrelevant. Their tongues touched. She wrapped her leg over his thigh and the damn gear lever got in her way but at this point it didn't matter. All that mattered was his lips on hers, his touch and his hand fumbling under her raincoat to cup her breast. Then he was inside her clothes, skin on skin, and she let out a sigh of sheer happiness as she caressed his tongue.

She wanted him. Now. Here and forever.

He lifted his lips, just enough so they both gasped for breath. "Gloria, we keep this up we'll get arrested."

He was right, if Sergeant Jones bothered to pedal his bicycle up here. They sat up and shifted apart and as she reluctantly rebuttoned, something passed them, like a flash of dark in the growing twilight.

"What the hell was that?" Andrew asked as he looked out of the windshield.

There was nothing there.

"A trick of the light?" she suggested.

"Beats me. Not that I care. Who would after the woman of their dreams at long, long, last agrees to marry them?"

"You only asked me yesterday."

"Feels like twenty years."

She gave him a gentle shove and rested her head on his chest. "I love you, Andrew Barron."

"I love you too, Nurse Prewitt, soon to be Mrs. Andrew Barron."

She lifted her face and looked into his lovely dark eyes. "Yes, please."

The next few minutes didn't need much in the way of conversation. War, vampires, trouble were all obliterated as they kissed and held each other.

"Let's get married soon," Andrew said. "I don't believe in giving you time to change your mind."

"I won't change it, that's a promise."

"When then? Soon?"

"Yes, but let's do it quietly. I'd hate to steal Alice's thunder, the whole village is looking forward to it."

"We could wait a month or so and get married just before Christmas."

"We could," she agreed, "but honestly, Andrew, the long white dress and veil and bridesmaids bit has never appealed. Let's nip over to the Registry office in Epsom and do it quietly."

"Suits me. When?"

"After Alice and Peter get back from their honeymoon. I want her there. She's been my best friend here in Brytewood."

"They're having a honeymoon?"

"Sort of. Peter booked them for two nights at The Angel in Guildford."

"Wish I could do better than that, but once this war's over we will. I'll take you to France, where my grandparents have a house. Assuming it's still there of course. It's not far from a rather wild part of the Auvergne. We can drive up into the woods. You can shift and run through to your heart's content and I'll come with you."

"Sure you can keep up with me?" she asked with a grin.

"Let's see."

It was a wonderful thought. To run free in wild countryside, then shift under the canopy of the stars and make love.

One day.

When peace came.

"Right now, I'd better see to the Grayson baby."

Chapter Thirty-Six

"He's no better, nurse, but no worse either, thank God!" Mrs. Grayson said as Gloria picked up the fretful baby.

"How is he eating?"

"He was bringing most of it back up, but seems he keeps the glucose water down. Most of the time, anyway."

"His temperature isn't going higher and he's keeping glucose water down. Good signs. You keep him here all day?" She had the pram in a corner by the fireplace.

"Yes. At night I put him in bed with me. Keeps him warm and if he has a whooping fit, I'm right there."

"Wilf and Jim seem to be mending nicely." They were both seated at the kitchen table, sweaters over their pajamas, playing cards.

"Thank heaven," Mrs. Grayson whispered. "In fact, Jim has been a treasure. Don't know what I'd have done without him. Fixing cups of tea and making sandwiches. He can even do a nice cheese on toast."

"Good for you, Jim," Gloria said. "Maybe you'll grow up to be a chef."

He shook his head, a serious light in his eyes. "Nah, nurse. I'm having a stall in Leather Lane, like my uncle."

"I'm not," Wilf said, looking up. "I'm going to be a farmer

and keep pigs. So as I can have all the pork pies I ever want."
He smiled, showing his missing front tooth. "And bacon too.
Lots and lots of lovely bacon."

"Meanwhile, best get well and work hard at school. You'll
need to be good at sums for both those jobs."

"Will you stop for a cup of tea, nurse?" Mrs. Grayson asked.

Jim slipped from his perch and crossed to the hearth for the
kettle. "I'll make it."

Watching him stand on tiptoe to fill the kettle at the deep
white sink, she hadn't the heart to refuse but . . . "I'd love to,
but Mr. Barron from the plant is waiting outside. He's giving
me a lift down to the village. My ankle is still a bit wonky."

"I heard you'd had an accident and broken it." Gloria bet
she'd also heard who else was involved with that accident and
that news of their little Friday exhibition had also made its
way up here.

"Seems they made a mistake. It's just a sprain."

"Good thing too, especially now with the doctor laid up.
Don't know what the world's coming to. Stealing her car like
that and driving it into a ditch. Never mind." She pulled herself back to immediate concerns of tea. "You tell Mr. Barron
he's welcome to have a cup too. If he'd care to that is."

"Are you sure?" Andrew asked, when she came up to the
lorry. "Didn't you want to get down and see how Alice is?"

"I did and I do, but it's just a quick cup. If we don't, she'll
be offended and apart from that, I think she's desperate for
adult company, cooped up here with those two boys and a
sick baby. You have had whooping cough, I hope?"

It was a legitimate excuse, since she sensed his reluctance.

He nodded. "Back when I was a boy. We had an epidemic
at school. I'll come on in."

There was a crack of light from the door standing ajar.
They nipped in and closed the door behind them, shutting out
the gathering dark.

She should have expected more than a cup. In the time it
had taken her to slip out and fetch Andrew, the kettle was set

to boil on the black stove and Jim was making toast by the open door of the firebox, while Mrs. Grayson laid the table and Wilf cleared away the cards.

Half an hour later, the night had fallen outside, and they'd finished off second cups of tea and numerous slices of toast and dripping when Mrs. Grayson produced a plate of jam tarts. How she found time to bake astounded Gloria, but she knew better than to refuse one.

"Gooseberry jam," Andrew said, as he bit into one. "My favorite."

"Have another, sir," Mrs. Grayson insisted.

"Thank you." He reached for one and smiled at Wilf, who sat on his right. "They feed you well up here, don't they?"

Wilf nodded. "I miss Mum though. She should be back soon."

Gloria met Mrs. Grayson's eyes. Their mother had been missing almost two weeks now. "Not to worry," Mrs. Grayson said. "We'll be hearing something soon."

And it would most likely be bad news.

"What have you boys been doing? Apart from being wonderful helpers to Mrs. Grayson?" Gloria asked.

"I sort my cigarette cards," Wilf said. "Wish the war would be over so I could get some new ones. It's all Hitler's fault we don't get them any more."

"I wish the war would be over so we can go home," Jim said, then looked at Mrs. Grayson and half smiled. "I like it here, but I do miss London."

"I know, love," she replied, reaching over to give him a pat on the shoulder. "But until then, I'd really glad you're here."

"I bet you help in the garden too," Andrew said. "I saw those rows of cabbages as I came in."

Jim nodded. "Yeah, almost as big as those you get in the market they are. We got carrots too and had tomatoes until it got too cold for them."

"You work at the secret place, sir, don't you?" Wilf asked.

Andrew smiled. "It's not as secret as all that if you lot know about it."

"Everyone knows about it," Jim said, then after a pause asked, "I know you can't tell, but is it you can make the man fly?"

"Oh, Jim, you know that was something you dreamt," Mrs. Grayson said.

"The doctor believed me," he replied, his mouth showing a stubborn pout.

"If I did, I couldn't say, could I?" Andrew said. He'd caught on right away.

"How's he flying?" Gloria asked, aware of Mrs. Grayson's silent disapproval.

"Across the fields behind us," Jim replied. "He kept looking at the dragon's teeth then flew right away. It's a big secret weapon, I bet."

"Then," Andrew said, his voice was steady but Gloria couldn't miss the excitement underneath, "best keep it a secret. Never tell another living soul."

Jim's eyes lit up and he grinned. "My lips are sealed, so are Wilf's. Right, Wilf? Cross my heart and hope to die. You too, Wilf."

Wilf crossed his heart and hoped to die, and Mrs. Grayson asked if anyone wanted another cup.

Gloria's mind whirled. Both she and Mary had seen the same man and now there was a third witness. She wanted to tell Jim he hadn't imagined it, whatever sensible, practical Mrs. Grayson wanted him to believe. Had to be the vampire examining the defenses. Thank heaven Jim had been safe in the house.

It took all she had not to rush out, dragging Andrew with her, but she finished her tea, gave a last check on the sleeping baby, accepted a gift of a fat cabbage, and finally they pulled on their coats and got back into the lorry.

"Well?" Andrew asked, as he turned the key in the ignition.

He was asking her to make a decision and she was still trying to get her brain around what Jim had told them. "I saw him too," she said, as the car pulled away and headed downhill.

"The flying man, I mean. So did Mary. He was crossing the fields up on Ranmore when I saw him. Mary's been a bit vague. Said she went walking and saw him coming back from the Hammer Pond." She was going to get to the bottom of that too. "And now Jim saw him hopscotching over the fortifications. If his target is the plant, just like the first vampire, why look around? Everyone knows where it is. All he had to do was ask. It might be disguised from the air, but at ground level you'd have to be blind to miss all that barbed wire."

"He wasn't looking for the plant," Andrew said and went quiet.

So did Gloria. Think. Why was he up this way, if his target was the munitions plant? Unless . . . "Do you have a torch, Andrew?"

"Of course, but why? We don't want to show a light."

"You have a map?"

"Yes."

"Grab the map and the torch and we can get under the lorry and look at it there. That will block the light."

A human might have missed the look of surprise on his face. Men were incredible, never quite expected women to have original ideas. Perhaps that wasn't entirely fair but it was close. This time at least.

"Alright." He took the torch from the ledge under the dashboard and rummaged in a pocket in his door for the map. "Let's hop out and get under."

It was very close quarters but the smell of petrol and engine oil rather killed any possible romantic ambiance. He spread the map on the ground between them and, shading the torch with his hand, turned it on.

"What are you thinking?" he asked.

It was a standard four inches to the mile Ordnance Survey map. Wasn't hard to pick out Brytewood, the open part of the heath where the plant stood, the Hammer Pond, the Longhursts' Cherry Hill Farm and even the row of cottages where Mrs. Grayson lived. "We're about here," she said, pointing to a spot on the map. "The plant's here." It was a bare spot on the map. About a mile or so away as the crow flew.

"What's our johnny doing out this way if his target is the plant?"

"Maybe he's not hitting it but someone else is," Gloria suggested.

"You mean bombs?" He sounded half surprised again.

"Why not? A lot more efficient and no risk of getting disturbed by a prowling vixen." She grinned at him. This had to be it. "They're going to bomb the plant and he's finding a way to signal the target."

She could feel Andrew tense beside her. He was thinking of all the workers who'd die in an attack. "How the bloody hell do we know when? Could be any time. God damn! Sorry, love," he said,

"Don't apologize. It's enough to swear over." She scowled at the map as if it could give up the date and time they needed. "Just a minute. Jim said he was flying over the defenses. Where would they be if they were on the map?"

"The line crosses the road, just ahead of us, about here,"

"Yes," she agreed. "Then it crosses the meadow and curves around the contour of the hill."

"But look," Andrew said. "The line isn't a neat curve, it goes along the edge of the drainage ditch for about eight yards, then follows the incline."

She looked at the map, where his fingernail marked an imaginary line. "And just ahead a mile or less, in a pretty much straight line, is the plant."

"They'd make great markers wouldn't they?"

Her throat clenched and the dripping toast in her stomach did a polka. It was wildly far-fetched but so were Vampires and Werefoxes and Pixies, to say nothing of Dragons. "What do we do now?" she asked.

"We might try getting off this hard road and back into the lorry."

"I rather like being this close to you. Could we use the map as a ground sheet d'you think?"

"Not big enough. I've got a nice double bed in my house. Much nicer than here."

"Kiss me first. Then we need to get a move on."

That was pretty much indisputable. "We ought to stop by The Gallop first, tell the others what we've worked out. Come on then."

He folded the map, switched off the torch and took her hand. They'd wriggled out and were about to stand when Gloria's vulpine sight caught a movement, like a dark wind, emerge from the woods in the distance and head their way. As it drew close, it looked like a man. Her Other sense knew it wasn't.

"That's it," she hissed at Andrew. "The stakes!"

As luck would have it, he'd left the driver's door open. He grabbed a handful but as he turned, the vampire raced toward them like a storm gust across the meadow.

If she'd doubted his identity a moment earlier, this confirmed it. He came at them, Andrew raced forward, stake in hand and as the creature closed on him, jabbed the stake into his chest.

The force of the impact threw Andrew to the ground. The vampire, now close enough to be recognized as Block, reeled back, but the stake hadn't penetrated deep enough and he yanked it out, throwing it into the air with such force that it struck and penetrated the roof of the lorry and shattered, the stub still embedded in the metal, like a short feather decorating a dowager's turban.

And Andrew! The vampire had him by the throat!

She'd never changed so fast in all her shifting existence, but anger, fury and sheer terror for the man she loved effected instant change. She leapt out of her clothes and shot forward.

The vampire was so intent on meeting Andrew's eyes, set on terrorizing before killing, that he never noticed the streak of red fur that flew at him, teeth snapping on his wrist. The vampire let go of Andrew, or rather tossed him down and tried to shake her off.

He succeeded but only for an instant. He met her eyes. His gaze might mesmerize a human but she was a crazed beast. She leapt again, knocking him off his feet, and then dug her claws into his face. His arms came up and grasped her under her forefeet, his grip like a vise, but as he lifted her, trying to throw her off, he rolled with the incline of the hill and stumbled. As he tried to regain his balance, her jaws closed over his neck. Summoning every shred of strength, she tore the flesh, severing his windpipe.

She leapt away as he stood, blood pouring from his ripped throat.

He didn't speak. Probably unable to but what would have killed a human wasn't enough to stop a vampire. He gurgled at her, fury lighting his eyes bright red.

She'd scotched the snake, not killed it. Now was not the time to quote Macbeth!

The vampire stood, looking from her to Andrew now struggling to his feet. She didn't even think, just ran snarling toward the vampire, snapping at his ankle, ripping flesh and pulling him to the ground.

She longed to throw back her head and howl, as she had weeks earlier defending the camp from Oak, but she didn't dare stop. She leapt up at the creature again, slashing his face with her teeth. Then he gripped her head in his hands. As he tightened his hold, she latched her jaws deeper in his bloody face, the scent of blood in her nostrils driving her to bite deeper and harder, but he kept his grip until he let out a great yowl that resounded in her ears, and his hold loosened.

She leapt back ready to reattack, but saw there was no more fight in the creature. Andrew stood over him, driving a stake though the vampire's chest, pinning him to the ground.

The vampire was weakening but still lived. If lived was the right word. She looked up at Andrew, her head ringing and her eyes still blurry from the vampire's grasp.

The creature stirred. As he raised a hand toward the stake,

she rushed forward and bit again, driving her teeth through the bones.

"Need another!" Andrew said, and raced away. While he ran back, she jumped over the supine creature and destroyed its other hand. His flesh and blood took on a sour tang. He was decaying.

As Andrew returned with the second stake, smoke, thin and acrid was rising from the wound in Block's chest. The flesh around the stake softened. Gloria backed away, blocking Andrew's approach. Who knew what might happen? Did vampires explode? Give off noxious gases? Fly into little pieces? Alice had been vague on that point.

None of those happened. As they watched, the thing dissolved into a heap of black ashy goo that soaked into the earth.

"What the hell?" Andrew said.

Damn! A fox couldn't speak. She shifted back and had to cling to him as her legs wobbled. Two fast shifts one right after the other was too damn much.

"He's gone," she said. "Done for. We need to work out what he was doing."

"We need to put clothes on you! Much as I relish having you naked, Gloria, this is not the place."

Nor the time, come to that. "But what was he doing? Setting signals?"

"That can wait. If he was setting flares, he's not here to light them. We're heading back to Alice's. Now."

She was too weary to argue. Andrew put his raincoat around her shoulders, helped her into the lorry, and gathered her scattered clothes. Or what was left of them, and headed downhill.

Block was dead, but was it over?

Chapter Thirty-Seven

Bela felt the surge of power. There was no doubt! She laughed at the realization that another of the filthy vampires was dead. Whoever or whatever they were fighting, they had met their match. Maybe the English were more than perfidious, weak betrayers of her homeland.

Did she care? Not one iota!

As darkness fell and she was ready to rouse Gela from their hiding place in the wood, her body flooded with power. "Gela," she said, shaking her sister by the shoulder, "wake up."

"Bela?" her sister said. Looking up at her with dark rimmed eyes almost sunk into their sockets. "I'm worn out. Leave me here." An emaciated hand grasped Bela's arm. "I can't walk any longer."

"You don't need to."

She scooped Gela up in her arms, and placed her over her shoulder, like a sack of coal. "It won't be comfortable, sister, but I will run us to safety in the mountains."

She'd judged the first hills to be a two or three days' walk, but now she'd run them with the strength of a vampire. She closed her hands over her sister's legs and began to run.

Exhilarated with her new and fleeting strength, she raced across stubble fields, roads and farm gardens and skirted villages. Legs aching, she ran on, carrying her sister's frail weight. On she went, until she reached more woods, and the ground sloped uphill. Pines appeared among the almost bare trees. Better cover, if she cared. No one could catch her as she ran with vampire speed. She'd run until dawn paled the sky, then find them shelter and food. She could have stopped on the way in one of the villages but she'd been driven by the need to cover distance while her new strength lasted.

As she paused in a small clearing, two dark figures stepped in her path, moonlight glinting on their guns.

Bullets she could not outrun.

She wanted to scream! Not to come this far to be recaptured. It wasn't possible,

"Who are you?" a voice asked,

"Who asks?" They couldn't be soldiers or SS. They would shoot before asking.

"I do."

This voice came from behind. She spun around. Two more stood behind her. They were all armed, wore dark clothes and needed a good wash. These were not soldiers? Partisans? In Germany? Was it possible? She certainly hadn't crossed any frontier.

"My name is Bela Mestan. This is my sister, Gela. We're unarmed."

"Honest Germans don't run through the woods at night."

"Nor do they carry guns like yours."

"I never claimed to be an honest German," he replied. "Do you?"

"I just rescued my sister from hell," she replied. "We've been hiding for days."

"What hell?"

"Flossenburgh."

"How did you get her out? It's impossible!"

"Not impossible. Just very difficult."

The man laughed. "Yes. Very difficult but if you know how

to succeed, we can use you." She caught a faint trace of accent in the voice.

"My sister needs food. She's been starved. I stole a little as we passed but she needs more."

"If we take you in and feed you, you can never leave. You must join us."

"If you fight those who run the hell my sister was held in, I will join you with pleasure."

"Come on then. We'll have to blindfold you. Peter, take the unconscious one."

They put a scarf around her eyes and took Gela. She hated to give her up but finding her own way blindfolded was going to be hard enough. Someone took her hand and they walked for almost an hour, over the soft pine needles of the forest floor and later over rocks. All the time climbing, until the path leveled off. She was helped to sit down and the blindfold removed. She blinked in the light as she looked around a large cave.

"Welcome to Adlerroost," the earlier voice said and her heart froze with horror.

"No! Not possible!" To come all this way and end up back there was worse than a nightmare.

"It's alright," a woman's voice said, as a pair of hands held Bela's shoulder. "You're safe."

Yes, there was more than one eagle's nest in Germany and this was here to attack the first.

"You're partisans?"

"We're loyal Germans who oppose the Third Reich. I'm Rolf," the first one, presumably their leader replied. "Loyal Germans, some Jews in hiding and we get a little help from our friends across the Channel. What can you do to help us?"

"They killed all my family and tried to kill Gela. I'll join you." And one day tell them they now had two Fairies in their company. "Gela needs food and rest."

"If you want food, you have to earn it," Rolf told her.

"I will gladly work to earn enough for both of us."

"Fair enough," he replied. Bela wished she could place his accent but gave up. She was weary, hungry, and then Gela stirred.

"Sister!" she cried, looking around her with terror in her eyes. "We're taken!"

"No, we're safe," Bela replied.

"I'll get you some food," the woman said. "I'm Rachel by the way."

A few moments later, she handed Bela a steaming bowl. The aroma of meat and onions set her mouth watering. She was famished, but Gela needed it more. She turned to feed Gela, but Rachel stopped her.

"You eat. I'll feed her if she'll let me."

"Don't give her too much," Rolf said. "If she's been starved for weeks, months, her system won't take it."

"I just feed her small bites," Bela said, "and she has difficulty chewing."

Rachel fed Gela a few spoonfuls as Bela watched, then the aroma was too much to resist. She wolfed down the lot, tipping the bowl to drain the last of it and gladly finished off a second bowl and a hunk of dark bread.

"Food's a bit iffy," Rolf said. "We don't eat every day but we manage as best we can. And we hinder the Third Reich at every opportunity."

"Good!"

Chapter Thirty-Eight

"I wonder if we shouldn't have waited for Andrew and Gloria," Helen Burrows said, looking around the table at empty plates and satisfied faces. At least Howell and Peter looked very satisfied, Alice had eaten half what she normally did, but that was twice what she'd eaten at lunch and the color was returning to her face.

"No," Alice said. "We needed to get the meal out of the way before Mr. Clarendon gets back."

He'd promised to return with another vampire, maybe two. The prospect was anxiety-making, but fight fire with fire, as the saying went, and she didn't want Alice facing this nasty thing again. Killing the other one had been a matter of luck, skill and magic. Mr. Clarendon favored an all-out assault with their combined strengths. Given this one's strength, seemed a good idea. And with two vampires on their side, how could they fail?

Alice was still pale but improving by the hour. Had to be her Pixie blood that foiled the nasty thing. And to think there was a time the girl had scoffed at Magic. She'd learned.

"You surpassed yourself again, Helen," Howell said, pushing his plate away. "Sam Whorleigh missed a fine dinner."

"Wish he'd come," Helen replied. "I'm afraid I might have

been a bit too sharp with him, but honestly, the man is Other and uses his skills to cheat the law."

"And rescue Alice," Peter pointed out.

"I hadn't forgotten that, but we could have used him in this battle."

"We'll have two vampires on our side, if Mr. Clarendon keeps his word," Alice said.

"He'll be back." Uneasy as she still was around him, she trusted him. He was under no compunction to come over this morning, but he'd promised to come when he returned from France, and there he was. He said he'd return with another of his colony and she trusted him.

"Hadn't we better clear away?" Alice said.

"You stay put," Peter said, "I'll help."

He and Howell pitched in. Everything was washed, dried and put away, leftovers covered and sitting in a warm oven just in case Andrew and Gloria came in hungry, and they were settling down to a nice cup of tea when the front doorbell rang.

Helen Burrows knew darn well she was not the only one who went still. If it was Mr. Clarendon, they were about to meet more vampires. Benign ones. Ones who were engaged in war work apparently but vampires nonetheless.

"Want me to get it?" Howell asked.

"I will," Alice said, rising.

"No, you will not, my love. Sit back down. I'll get it," Helen said, untying her apron. "I was the one brought him into this, I'll answer the door."

It was Mr. Clarendon but it was the two with him that had her staring. One was a woman: short, dark-haired, but something about her put Helen Burrows in mind of the old Queen Mary. The other one was tall, broad shoulders, and the blackest man she'd ever seen.

"Mrs. Burrows," Mr. Clarendon said, "I bring reinforcements."

"Yes," she said, and stood aside. "Come on in." They'd

have the air raid wardens down on them in a minute, if she kept the door open

The two men waited until the woman entered. Nice gentlemanly manners or was it because she was in charge?

The woman smiled. "I am Gwyltha. Jude says you have an intruder in your midst."

That was one way of putting it. "Welcome, Gwyltha. I'm Helen Burrows."

"And this," Gwyltha said, indicating the black man, "is Toby Wise, who frequently lives up to his name."

"Madam," Mr. Wise said, in a cultured voice that had Helen thinking of Oxbridge or royalty.

"Thank you," Helen said, "for involving yourselves in our trouble."

"It's our trouble too," Gwyltha replied. "This war is everyone's trouble."

Pity that Sam Whorleigh wasn't around to hear that. "Come in. It will have to be the kitchen, I'm afraid." She should have lit a fire in the drawing room but it was too late now.

"We're honored you trust us in your house," Gwyltha replied. "Few mortals would."

Few mortals believed in vampires but it might seem rude to mention that. "We're grateful for your help."

After another round of introductions and Peter fetching a couple of extra chairs, they settled around the kitchen table.

"So," Gwyltha said, smiling at Alice, "you are the human who dispatched the previous intruder."

"With Peter's help, and a good bit of assistance from a magic user in the village, but I'm Pixie, not just human," Alice replied.

Helen's heart swelled with pride. The girl was truly accepting her heritage.

"Yes," Gwyltha said. "So I heard. I have seldom encountered a Pixie and not for centuries, and now I meet two. The village is fortunate."

That Helen wouldn't deny but seemed a bit forward to agree out loud. "We do what we can. And we have had good friends." One of whom was now dead.

Gwyltha turned to Howell, "You're not human either, are you?"

"No, madam," Howell rose and gave a rather courtly bow. "I am Pendragon. The one. The Red Dragon."

"I thought so. Don't see many of your sort either these hard and skeptical days. Are there others?"

"I have a son, madam. Fighting for his country."

"As are all of us gathered here." She looked at Peter, sitting beside Alice, his arm around her shoulders. "You are mortal, but trusted by these Others. Most unusual."

"I'm here for Alice," he replied, "and England."

"As are we all. Now, to business. You have an intruder in your village who means harm. We will dispose of him for you. We will need one of you to enter his habitation and invite us in."

"I'll do it," Peter said. "Name the time and date."

"Tonight," she replied. "He has intruded in my territory without courtesy of passage, has caused injury and clearly means more harm. This can not be permitted. Such actions might lead mortals to believe in us." She shook her head. "That could be disastrous."

"There is another matter." She looked at Alice. "You still have the Druid knife you used?"

"No," Alice replied and explained the issue, ending with Mother Longhurst's death.

"So, the knife has disappeared. Bad news," Gwyltha said.

She didn't sound too happy at the thought of that knife sitting around in someone's kitchen drawer. Unfortunate all around, especially for poor Mother Longhurst. "That can't be helped. Best concentrate on the business at hand. We will dispose of this rogue vampire for you and in return all we ask is . . ." She broke off and looked toward the blacked-out window. "A vehicle approaches."

She had better than Pixie hearing if she caught that. The other two vampires rose to their feet. Their presence expanded to fill the room.

"Who is it?" Alice asked.

If it was Sam Whorleigh his timing was lousy. Couldn't be. He didn't have a car and now they could all hear an engine coming up the drive and cutting off. A door opened and a voice called. "Someone help!"

Howell and Peter raced to the back door. "Who is it?" they called simultaneously.

"Me! Andrew! Gloria's hurt!"

The door was flung open, blackout curtain pulled aside, and in staggered Andrew with Gloria, wearing nothing but a torn and bloody raincoat, in his arms.

"Oh, my God!" Alice was on her feet. "It got her too!"

"No!" Andrew replied, in a shaky, but jubilant, voice. "She got it! My Gloria ripped its throat out."

"The rogue vampire?" Gwyltha raised her aristocratic eyebrows.

Mr. Clarendon shot across the room.

"He bit her!" Clarendon said.

Certainly looked like it. "Let me get some warm water," Helen said.

"No!" Gloria's voice was shaky. "It didn't bite me.

"But all that blood!" Peter said.

"That's his blood. He bled an awful lot," she said and fainted.

"What happened?" Clarendon asked.

"Just as I said," Andrew replied. "She did it in. It came for us. I had a go at it with a stake and missed his heart so he yanked the stake out. Made a bit of a dent in government property with it too. Dunno how I'm going to explain that. Then Gloria went for it. Started snapping at it. While I went for another stake, she ripped its throat out. That almost did it in and I helped by finishing it off with another stake."

"Incredible," Gwyltha said, "since she snapped at it, with teeth strong enough to tear out a vampire's throat, I assume that this young woman is more than human too?"

"She shifts," Pendragon said, in a voice that refused further details.

Gwyltha acknowledged with a nod. "Indeed. This is an interesting village. Seems you do not need our assistance after all."

"What if she's been bitten?" Wise asked.

"I don't think she was but she bit him repeatedly."

"She might have swallowed his blood," Mr. Clarendon said.

"If she did, time will tell what effect it has," Gwyltha replied, crossing the room to where Andrew held Gloria on a chair by the fireplace. "She may well come to no harm. What is she?" she asked Andrew.

"I'm a Werefox!" Gloria replied, opening her eyes, "and I feel as weak as a mouse."

"Most people do after slaying a vampire," Gwyltha replied. "It goes with the job. Did you swallow his blood?"

"I tried not to, It tasted like sour ashes." Gloria went pale, or rather paler. "Is that bad?"

"I truly don't know as I know nothing of this vampire, other than his belligerent intentions."

"I'll say they were belligerent," Andrew said. "He was out to destroy my plant, like the other bastard. Sorry," he added with a glance at the women in the room. "That just slipped out."

"Justified in the circumstance, I believe," Gwyltha replied. "Whatever he was planning will not come to pass. As for you"—she turned back to Gloria—"if you just swallowed blood, it should have no effect, except perhaps increased speed and strength for a while. But if you feel any unexpected changes," she paused and handed Gloria a visiting card, "I can be contacted at this number. Call me. But I think it unlikely you will need me."

"What about Andrew?" Gloria said. "I saw it bite him."

All three vamps looked in Andrew's direction. "Did he?" Mr. Wise asked.

"I believe so." Now it was Andrew's turn to go pale. "Does that mean I turn into a vampire?" He'd gone from pale to ashen at the idea.

"Cheer up, it's not that bad," Mr. Clarendon replied. "It's not that easy either, but a bite from an unknown vampire could turn nasty. We don't know how he feeds or what his personal habits were."

He looked at Mrs. Burrows. "Do you have any spirits? Whiskey, rum, gin?"

So much for keeping it for the wedding. Still this mattered more. "I'll get it."

"Come over to the sink," Wise told Andrew. He and Clarendon took off his jacket and Wise looked at his neck.

"Looks fine. Barely grazed the skin. Hang on, this won't be much fun." Andrew winced as Wise pulled the skin. Mr. Clarendon took the bottle from Helen's hand. He uncorked it and poured it over the open wound.

Andrew grimaced, groaned and let out a tight whistle.

"That should do the trick," Mr. Wise said. "Stop it getting infected."

"This is a doctor's house. I do have plenty of antiseptics: carbolic, aquaflavine, Dettol, you name it. Wouldn't they have worked?" Alice asked.

"Not as well. Pure alcohol works best, but failing that, good old spirits seem the best antidote for vampire bites."

"I'll remember that," she said. "They skipped that bit at Barts."

"I hope to heaven we never need to use that little bit of knowledge," Peter said. "Will Andrew be alright?"

"Most likely," Mr. Wise replied. "It takes more than a bite to turn a mortal vampire. If you feel anything strange, your body seems alien to you. Call the number Gwyltha gave Miss Prewitt."

Helen prayed they never had to. Ever.

"Thank you for coming to our aid," she said. "Sorry it was a wasted journey on your part."

"Wasted?" Gwyltha gave a little smile. "To meet a Dragon, Pixies and a Shifter? No, it was not wasted. But it is time we left."

Like that they were gone.

"Who were they?" Gloria asked, her voice weak and fading.

"Allies we didn't need, after all," Alice replied.

"Allies?" Gloria asked.

"Stop these questions," Helen said. "Plenty of time for questions and answers later. Gloria needs a bath. So do you, Andrew, and that raincoat needs burning. If anyone in the village sees that they'll think you've been illicitly slaughtering pigs."

"I've got a few questions," Howell began.

"So do all of us, but nothing that can't wait. Peter, you go upstairs and light the bathroom heater. I'll stoke up the boiler so we have plenty of hot water, and Howell, you carry Gloria upstairs in a few minutes. Andrew looks done in."

"I ought to get back home," Gloria said. "Mary is going to be thinking I've moved out."

"Yes, that young Mary," Helen said, "I was thinking we might have needed her. She's Other, you know."

"I know," Gloria replied, "but I don't know what."

"She'll confide in you sooner or later and we'll need her yet."

"There's plenty of war still to come. We've won this battle," Howell said. "Won't be the last but best get cleaned up. Helen's right, you look as if you've been slaughtering pigs."

"Think there's more to come?" Helen was alone with Howell. Gloria and Andrew had left, wearing borrowed clothing, and Alice and Peter were in the study, doing what engaged couples were supposed to do.

"We stopped two vampires, but there's still an army over there in France waiting to hop the Channel."

He was right. "We've stopped this one but we know of at least one other."

"One day at a time, Helen. One vampire at a time."

"Maybe I should embroider that on a chair back. That would get the knitting ladies talking."

"I'd better be going myself, or they'll be talking about us."

"You'd mind that, Howell?"

"Not for me, but for you, yes."

She kissed him. "Bye, Howell, but come back."

Chapter Thirty-Nine

"I can't believe it," Mrs. Chivers fussed at the cluster of villagers waiting outside the baker's. "Ten o'clock in the morning and he hasn't opened yet. Honestly, is that any way to run a business? Doesn't he realize there's a war on?"

Howell Pendragon smiled to himself. He'd come down out of nothing better than idle curiosity and was being treated to a proper carry-on. Amazing how nice ladies got so worked up over a loaf of bread.

"It's just not good enough," sweet-tempered Miss Boxe fussed. "He knew I needed a fresh loaf this morning. I mentioned it specially on Friday and what is he doing?"

"Playing around if you ask me," Edith Aubin, the cook from up at Wharton Lacey snapped. "We have people coming for dinner tonight and I special ordered crusty rolls. Now what am I supposed to do? Make my own? I can't stand here all day."

"Disgraceful!" Mrs. Bennet was less loquacious than Mrs. Chivers or Miss Aubin but no less put out.

"I am not waiting any longer," Mrs. Chivers announced to the world. Stepping up to the door, she hammered on it with her fist.

"He's either deaf or ignoring us," Miss Aubin announced, to anyone who'd listen.

Since overnight onset of deafness seemed unlikely, the latter possibility incensed Mrs. Chivers, who renewed her assault on the oak door.

"Now, here, ladies," Sergeant Jones said, as he slowed his bicycle at the curb. "What's going on?"

The queue, now lengthened to seven impatient women and Howell, turned at the policeman's approach. Mrs. Chivers, as the self-appointed spokeswoman, told him.

"Well I never," Jones said, shaking his head. "Looks like a rum do to me. Not like him at all. I'd best go have a look around the back. Make sure everything's as it should be. Now you ladies, you wait here," he added before anyone could move to accompany him. He caught Howell's eye. "How about you come with me, Sergeant Pendragon? We'll be back in no time at all, ladies, you just hang on."

"What do you think, sergeant?" Pendragon asked as they rounded the building and approached the back door.

"Beats me but since he's been open early like clockwork ever since he arrived, it don't sound right to me and after that business with the doctor's car, who's to say what's happened? Besides, if he has had an accident, no point in distressing the ladies."

Howell suspected their distress would be more over not getting fresh bread than concern for the baker's welfare, but he kept that to himself. Sergeant Jones rapped on the door, then tried the knob. It was opened onto a dingy hallway. "Hello, there, Mr. Block. Police! It's Sergeant Jones."

The only sounds were repeated hammering on the front door that echoed in the empty rooms. They stepped over a copy of the local newspaper and a postcard that lay on the floor, and into the cold bakery kitchen.

"Let's have a look upstairs," Jones said. Pendragon followed him, pausing on the way to pick up the newspaper and put it on a table. He pocketed the postcard. The picture of Guildford High Street intrigued him.

"He isn't one of creature comforts is he?" Jones said as they walked through the sparsely furnished, or even unfurnished rooms, the bathroom with no towels or soap to be seen, and the unstocked upstairs kitchen. "I wonder if he did a flit," Jones said, opening a narrow cupboard in the bedroom. "Except he left his clothes. Or some of them."

Two shirts and a spare pair of trousers hung on wire hangers and a couple of pairs of rolled up socks sat on a shelf. That was it.

"Don't rightly know," Jones said, shaking his head as he closed the wardrobe door. "What do you think, Sergeant Pendragon?"

"Hard to tell." Especially when you know the truth would risk getting you committed.

"You fancy he got called away maybe? Family emergency?"

"Could be."

There was another tattoo on the door downstairs. "Better break the news to the ladies, there'll be no fresh bread today."

Jones looked as if he'd rather cope with half a dozen downed German pilots than the good women of the parish deprived of fresh bread.

Howell did a cowardly thing and left him to it, nipping down to Whorleigh's to alert him to the return en masse of his bread customers.

Sam Whorleigh roared with laugher. "Coming back, are they? That was a short lived baker." Maybe very long lived, but he'd be baking no more. "Need anything, sergeant?" he asked.

"I'll take a loaf of bread, just in case you sell out later."

Whorleigh grinned. "Here you are. Cut back on my order, I did. Better up it for tomorrow by the look of things. Anything else I can get you? I've got the end of a ham bone. Seeing as it's you, I'll let you have it at a special price."

"What about adding some split peas?"

"Four ounces do you? Nothing like a nice bowl of soup in this weather."

Howell took the packages and left, just ahead of the parade of agitated ladies descending from the baker's, and headed home.

Helen had been right about Whorleigh being Other, but to have included him in their ventures? No, Howell Pendragon didn't think so. The fact he'd refused Helen's summons pretty much proved the man was only interested in his shop and his profit. But he had come up trumps over Alice and the car. One never knew.

Howell filled his largest pan with water, added a couple of onions and the ham bone. A pan of soup that big would keep them going for a couple of days. He might just invite Helen down. If he could convince young Peter to visit Alice. He rather fancied an evening alone with Helen Burrows.

That taken care of, he made a cup of tea and fished out the postcard he'd purloined.

And stared. "The first eleven arrives Monday at three. Tuesday if rain stops play."

Cricket? This time of year? Impossible. Maybe it was an old card. With Sunday's postmark? Interesting. Had to be some sort of code. Well, whatever had been planned, Gloria and Andrew had postponed play permanently.

Chapter Forty

Three weeks later

"You picked a nice day to get married on, lad," Sergeant Pendragon said, popping his head around Peter's door, a cup of tea in hand. "Thought you might like a quick cup before you nip in the bath. I've stoked up the boiler so we've plenty of hot water for the pair of us." The lad looked as if he'd been awake half the night. "Been up a while?"

"Yes," Peter replied. "I keep getting up to check I had the ring and the license and that I hadn't forgotten anything."

"At this point, if you have, you'll manage without. Want breakfast? It's a good while until you get to the reception."

"Maybe toast."

Toast? He had a good fry-up planned. The lad had a long morning ahead of him. "You get first dibs on the hot water. I'll get in after breakfast."

He went back downstairs. Nice of the lad to ask him to be best man. Seeing as how his family couldn't, or wouldn't, come up for the wedding. Mind you, his mother had sent a nice Coalport dinner service that had been her mother's. Pleased Alice no end it had. And not the sort of thing you'd find anywhere these days.

Pendragon picked up the post from the front door mat. A letter from Gryffyth. What a nice surprise. The boy didn't write often and his letters were short when he did, but it was good to hear from him, even if he had to read around the censor's black ink.

It was just one sheet. About what Gryffyth usually sent, but Howell Pendragon read it twice, the news chilling his blood. After surviving Trondheim, where so many were injured, seemed his son had a terrible accident and lost his left leg.

That was it, no details. They were, no doubt, under the thick black censor's marks, but Gryffyth was being sent home for recuperation leave in a couple of weeks and expected to be invalided out.

What awful news on a day that should have been joyous. Damn. It would be! He wasn't sharing this news with anyone today. He'd put aside his worry for a few hours. This was Peter and Alice's day and by golly, it would be perfect.

And he'd start with bacon for breakfast.

"Gran, it's truly beautiful. You and Doris worked a miracle," Alice had said the same a dozen times but looking at the dress on the hanger, she repeated herself. "You'd never know it was an old parachute." Donated, albeit unwittingly, by her old flame. Funny how life worked out.

The skirt had ruched panels, the close-fitting bodice had leg of mutton sleeves and a bunch of orange blossom at the point of the sweetheart neck. There had even been enough spare to dye turquoise and make a bridesmaid's dress for Gloria.

"It is lovely," Gloria agreed. "The lace train adds a nice touch. You'd never guess it was once curtains at the French windows."

"They were no use against the blackout anyway," Gran said. "You'll look a proper picture, my love. Now both of you, get yourselves ready. We don't have all day."

"Want to borrow it?" Alice asked as Gloria hooked her up after they'd bathed and done their hair.

"Thank you, Alice, it's a lovely thought but no. I want a quiet, fast registry office do. Suits me better I think."

Andrew had been appointed driver. He arrived in a gleaming black Bentley.

"Where did you get that?" they all asked.

"Borrowed it," he replied. "It wasn't being used so I requisitioned it with the help of a friend."

Better not ask too many details.

He took Gloria down to the church first, then returned for Alice and her grandmother.

Alice walked under the lychgate and toward the church, where Reverend Roundhill waited.

The small church was packed. People stood at the back and in the side aisles.

"So many people?" she whispered to her grandmother. "I never expected."

"All set are we?" Reverend Roundhill asked.

Peter waited at the altar. He turned and smiled.

She was ready.

The organ switched from the Trumpet Voluntary to the Wedding March. The congregation rose and turned in her direction. Gran took her arm, Gloria straightened the lace curtains—oops, train—and took her place behind, and Alice Doyle walked down the nave of St. Michael and All Angels to the man she loved.

"It's been a very nice do, but I'll be glad when they get away," Andrew whispered to Gloria. "Can't be long now, can it? We've had the speeches, the toasts and the cake."

"And an incredible spread. I think the whole village pitched in."

"Yes, very nice. How much longer do you think?"

"What's the hurry?"

"You need to ask?"

She didn't, but might as well anyway. "Getting impatient are you?"

"I was just thinking once they leave, I have to return this borrowed vehicle. Want to come with me?"

"Where to?"

"Ashtead. I thought we could drive over, stop at the Leg of Mutton and Cauliflower. Perhaps have a nice dinner and get the bus back."

"Remember what happened another time we went out for a nice dinner?"

He grinned. "We could see if the good old Leg of Mutton has rooms."

They could indeed.

Try the other books in Georgia Evans's fantasy series . . .

BLOODY GOOD

In the first of a supernatural trilogy, one Dr. Alice Doyle finds that the power to fight evil comes from places she'd never believe . . .

While the sounds of battle echo through the sky, a lady doctor has more than enough trouble to keep her busy even in a sleepy hamlet outside London. But the threat is nearer home than Alice knows. German agents have infiltrated her beloved countryside—Nazis who can fly, read minds, and live forever. They're not just fascists. *They're vampires.*

Alice has no time for fantasy, but when the corpses start appearing sucked dry, she'll have to accept help where she can get it. If that includes a lowly Conscientious Objector who says he's no coward, though he refuses to fight, and her very own grandmother, a sane, sensible woman who insists that she's a Devonshire Pixie, so be it. Indeed, whatever it takes to defend home and country from an evil both ancient and terrifyingly modern . . .

Alice Doyle was exhausted. Staying up half the night to deliver twins will do that to you. The elation and adrenaline of her first set of twins had carried her this far home, but as she turned into the lane that ran through Fletcher's Woods, weariness set in. It had been a good night's work though. She wouldn't easily forget the rejoicing in the Watson farmhouse and Melanie's happiness through her fatigue as she breast-fed her lusty sons.

"A fine brace of boys. Gives one hope for the future, doesn't it, Doctor?" Roger Watson said as he smiled at his grandsons. "If only Jim were here to see them." The Watsons' only son, Jim, was somewhere in Norfolk with the army and Alice couldn't help worry how Melanie, a Londoner born and bred, would fare with her in-laws in a farm as remote as any you could find in Surrey.

Still, Farmer Watson was right: whatever the politicians did or however many bombs fell, life went on.

The numerous cups of tea she'd consumed through the night were having their effects and she still had several miles to go over bumpy country roads. She pulled over to the verge and got out. Other traffic was unlikely out here. Few locals enjoyed the supply of petrol allocated to doctors. Even so, Alice climbed over the gate and ventured into the woods for a bit of privacy.

She was straightening her clothes back, when she realized she was not alone. Darn! A bit late to be worrying about modesty. Deeper into the woods, someone crawled toward her. Assuming injuries, Alice called, "I'm coming. I'm a doctor."

It was a stranger. One of the workers from the hush hush munitions camp up on the heath, perhaps? What in heaven's name was he doing rolling on the damp ground? As Alice bent over him, he looked up at her with glazed eyes. Drunk perhaps? But she didn't smell anything on his breath.

"What happened?" As she spoke, she saw the stains on his sleeve. Blood loss might well account for his weakness. She looked more closely at him and gasped. Part of the branch of a tree was embedded in his upper arm. How in heaven's name? Had to be drunk. If there wasn't enough to do, she had to cope with boozers who impaled themselves on trees. Seemed that was his only injury. No bleeding from the mouth or nose. Heartbeat was abnormally slow but steady, his breathing shallow and his skin cold to the touch. Shock and exposure would explain all that. Best get him out of the damp.

"Look," she said, trying her utmost to keep the fatigue out of her voice. "I need you to walk to my car. I've my bag there and I'll have a look at your arm. Then I'll take you down to my surgery in Brytewood and call an ambulance."

The odd glazed eyes seemed to focus. "Thanks," he croaked.

"What's your name?"

He had to think about that one. Definitely recovering from a wild night. "Smith." Really? Aiming for anonymity perhaps? "Paul Smith."

Alice got behind him and propped his shoulders until he was sitting. "Come along, Mr. Smith," she told him. "I'm going to give you a boost and you have to stand. I can't carry you."

They succeeded on the second go and made slow progress toward her car, Alice supporting Mr. Smith from his good side.

He was a lot lighter than anticipated as he slowly staggered toward the road. He supported himself against the hedge, as Alice opened and closed the gate, but once they emerged from the shade into the thin afternoon sun, he collapsed.

Thank heaven for her father's old shooting brake. She got her patient into the back so he was lying against the sack of potatoes the Jacksons had insisted she take with her.

"Mr. Smith, I'm going to examine your arm. I'm afraid I'll have to cut your shirt sleeve."

Taking the nod as agreement, Alice snipped off the sleeve. The shirt was good for nothing but rags anyway. Her first observation had been right: several chunks of fresh wood had penetrated the flesh of his upper arm. "How did you did this, then?" she asked as she opened her bag and reached for sterile swabs and Dettol.

He cried out as he grabbed her free hand in a viselike grip and bit her wrist.

He was more than drunk. He was insane. Alice tried to push him away but he held on, digging his teeth into her flesh. She finally grabbed his nose until he gasped for breath and released her.

"Behave yourself! I'm a doctor. I'm here to help . . ." She broke off when she saw he'd passed out.

BLOODY RIGHT

It will take all of Brytewood's Others to save their village from destruction in the climax of a Georgia Evans's supernatural trilogy . . .

Gryffyth Pendragon has done his bit for the war effort when he comes back to sleepy Brytewood from the battlefront at Trondheim. It cost him a leg, and his chance to use his Dragon's strength against the Nazis—or so he thinks. Until he finds out that his little village is facing a plague of vampire spies set on delivering it to the Third Reich. They've come up with a plan that, if they can pull it off, might break all of Britain's will to fight . . .

But there are more allies for Gryffyth in Brytewood than he'd ever imagined, and while a doctor, a nurse, a schoolteacher, and a couple of sexagenarians doesn't sound like much of a battle force to him, there's more to his cohorts than meets the eye. Against ancient and impossibly powerful agents of evil, they will need every man, woman, and Dragon-shifter they can get . . .

Once the adrenaline rush from the part change faded, Gryffyth Pendragon found himself sitting on a heap in the lane. Fumbling around, he touched broken glass. So much for a torch to help him get home. And where the hell was his stick? To say nothing of what in hades had attacked him? What now? Could he stand without his stick? He couldn't walk without it. Unless he had Mary to support him. Thinking of her brought a smile to his lips, but didn't help his current predicament. And on top of it, the sleeves of his shirt and new jacket were in tatters.

Shit! Should he hope someone would come by on their way back from the Pig? It was hours until closing time.

The narrow beam of a shaded bicycle lamp appeared in the distance.

Help, thank the heavens, but how to explain his condition? Convince them he was drunk this early?

"Hello," he called.

"Son?"

Crikey, if wasn't his father! "Dad?"

The bicycle stopped just a couple of feet away as his father leaped off, letting it fall, and crouched over him. "What the flaming hell happened to you, son? You tripped? You shouldn't be walking home in the dark."

"Dad! There's a thing loose in the village." He'd probably think he'd been drinking but . . . "It grabbed me and had fangs."

"Not another one? Damn! Let me help you up." He grabbed him by the armpits and steadied him to his feet.

"What do you mean 'not another'?"

"Let's get you home first. Remember I said I had things to talk about?" Gryffyth had imagined it meant a catch-up on village gossip. "Well, unless I'm mistaken you just encountered one of those things. Where's your stick?"

"I dropped it." What was the old man talking about?

"Hang on a tick. Here, hold onto the handlebars." His father stooped and retrieved his fallen bicycle. "That'll steady you. Now, let's see if I can find your stick." He pulled a torch from his coat pocket and shone the beam over the ground. First thing he found was the broken torch. "This yours, son?" he asked, bending down to pick it up.

"No, Mary lent it to me."

"Mary Chivers?"

"Lord, no, Dad. Mary LaPrioux. The girl I danced with on Saturday night."

"Oh." Amazing how much meaning and speculation the old man could pack into one syllable. "She lent it to you."

"Yes, Dad, she did!" And right now he was not in the mood to share the circumstances. "I'll buy her another to replace it."

"You might have a hard time finding one, Son, but never mind that right now." He'd happily change the subject, too. "Hang on, let's see if I can find your stick."

Less than a minute later, Gryffyth had his stick secure in his hand. "Right, son, let's get back home, get you cleaned up."

In the light of the kitchen, Gryff looked a proper fright—his hair on end, and his jacket and shirt ripped to the elbow.

"Haven't I always told you to roll up your sleeves before you shift your hands?"

"There wasn't time. And what the hell was it came after me? You know, don't you?"

"Yes, son. I do. I should have told you before, but I wanted you to get settled and honestly never thought it would happen like this."

"Like what, Dad? And what the bloody hell was it?"

"Don't you start swearing at me, son. You get a move on and clean yourself up and put on a new shirt. I need to call Helen Burrows and tell her I'll be a bit late and you're coming up there with me now you're home."

"Up where, Dad?" He was in no mood for a social call.

"Up to the Council of War." He avoided more questions by going out of the kitchen and picking up the phone.

Gryffyth took off his jacket and shirt and went over to the kitchen sink to wash up.

His dad reappeared minutes later carrying a clean shirt and a knitted pullover. "Here you are, son. Put them on. At least you'll look presentable. We'll see what we can do about mending your jacket in the morning. For now, let me tell you a few things."

"Alright, Dad, but first, what do you mean about 'Council of War'?"

"Just that, son. We've been under attack. And I don't just mean the Blitz or the invasions." He shook his head. "I should have told you the whole business, but things have been quiet since the last one, I wanted you to relax a bit. My mistake."

"What 'last one'?"

"There's been two of them, maybe three."

"There what?"

"Vampires, son. Vampires."

"Spare me, Dad. Vampires don't exist." Stress of the war had addled his father's wits. "They're a figment of Bram Stoker's imagination and a scary thrill for filmmakers."

"Now look here, Gryffyth. They do. You just faced one. You can't deny it. Wish you hadn't had to meet it unprepared but that's done now. And before you start on about vampires being fiction, remember there's a lot of people would say Dragons don't exist."

"But we're real, Dad."

"So's what you met in the lane a little while back. What did you see? Feel?"

What had he? Gryffyth shuddered, thinking back. "I felt menace, violence, and I saw a twisted face in the dark and . . . fangs."

"We've got another one to deal with. Make no mistake about it."